Love @ First Site

Also by Jane Moore

FOURPLAY

THE EX FILES

Jane Moore

BROADWAY BOOKS
NEW YORK

Love @ First Site

A NOVEL

LOVE @ FIRST SITE was originally published as DOT.HOMME in the United Kingdom by William Heinemann, an imprint of the Random House Group Ltd.

A hardcover edition of this book was published in 2005 by Broadway Books.

PRINTED IN THE UNITED STATES OF AMERICA

BROADWAY BOOKS and its logo, a letter B bisected on the diagonal, are trademarks of Random House, Inc.

Visit our Web site at www.broadwaybooks.com

First trade paperback edition published 2006

Book design by Jennifer Ann Daddio

The Library of Congress has cataloged the hardcover edition as:
Moore, Jane.
Love @ first site: a novel / by Jane Moore.—1st ed.
p. cm.
I. Title.

PR6113.O557L695 2005
813'.6—dc22
2004057530

ISBN-13: 978-0-7679-1691-2
ISBN-10: 0-7679-1691-3

1 3 5 7 9 10 8 6 4 2

Love @ First Site

One

Cuddly, Ferrari-driving 38-year-old, GSOH, travels extensively with job, WLTM fun-loving woman and see where life's wide open road takes us.

*I*t's 8 p.m. and a particularly gripping *EastEnders'* plotline is reaching its long, drawn-out conclusion in homes across the country.

I'd like nothing more than to be curled up on the sofa watching it, with a glass of chilled white wine in one hand, a tube of salt and vinegar Pringles in the other.

But instead, I'm on a blind date with Chewbacca.

Cuddly? The man is a walking rug, with the notable exception of the top of his head, a shining dome that gives way to an ample forehead you could show movies on. In wide screen and with subtitles.

"Shall we order?" he says, snapping his fingers in a rapid-fire motion at the waitress. With each click, my neck sinks further into my body.

"Just a main course for me, thanks," I simper. Please God, don't let him order one of those complicated dishes that takes twenty minutes to prepare.

Of course, if this was my friend Madeleine, she would have established at first sight that her date could be tried under the Trades Descriptions Act, excused herself to the loo, then slipped out of a back door never to return.

But I'm too nice to do that. And cowardly. I'm worried he might track me down through my e-mail address and start stealing underwear from my rotary washing line, shortly before putting it on and turning up seminaked at my parents' Ruby Wedding celebrations. OK, so I have an overactive imagination, but you get my drift.

Nope. Coward that I am, I'm stuck with Yeti man for at *least* the next hour.

"So!" I say brightly, desperate to resuscitate a conversation that's already flatlining, "you travel a lot?"

"Yes, I do." Chewy—otherwise known as Graham—says this with the measured gravitas of a man who's just announced he's head of a global peacekeeping crusade. He doesn't show any signs of elaborating.

"Abroad?" I persevere.

"Sometimes." Leaning across the table with a large lump of bread in his hand, he wipes it, Neanderthal style, across the top of the butter and rams it into his mouth. The things you see when you haven't got your gun, as my old grandma used to say.

"So, tell me about some of the places you've been to." Oh God, I have suddenly metamorphosed into a daytime television presenter. It can only be a matter of minutes before I'm asking him his favorite color.

"Not much to tell." He shrugs, cramming yet more bread into his mouth. A large blob impales itself on his stubbly chin. "Mostly

Germany, occasionally France, but most of the time I travel around Britain."

It's a personal rule of mine never to resort to the "what do you do?" question within half an hour of meeting someone for the first time. But on this occasion, the word *desperate* doesn't cover it.

"So what do you do?"

"I work with cars." He sits back in his chair, which creaks ominously, and I get my first glimpse of the sizable paunch he's been hiding under the table.

"Ah, hence the Ferrari! I don't know much about cars, but even *I* know that's an impressive one to own." I inwardly sigh with relief, thinking that, finally, I have dredged up something that may inflame an enthusiastic response from this world-beating dullard.

But no. In fact, he looks a little sheepish, and a vein on the side of his hairless temple starts to pulsate rather noticeably. "I don't actually own one, I just drive them occasionally."

"What, like Michael Schumacher?" I laugh. He doesn't reciprocate.

"My car company sells them." He clicks his fingers at the waitress again, indicating for her to fill up our wineglasses.

"*Your* car company," I emphasize, determined to get to the bottom of his deeply mysterious job description. "Oh, I see. You own a Ferrari garage?"

He shifts in his chair in obvious discomfort, and a bead of sweat appears above one bushy eyebrow. His right cheek twitches. "Not as such, no. The company is owned by someone else, I'm involved in the regional redistribution side of things."

I blink a few times whilst my brain computes his explanation. "You mean you're a deliveryman?" I say. "Basically, you're one of those men who takes new cars to customers, then stands on the side of the road with the temporary registration plates trying to hitch a lift and save your expenses?"

Knocking back two large glugs of his wine, he wipes his mouth with the back of his hand. "Well, there's a bit more to it than that, but if you insist on talking in sound bites, then yes, I deliver cars."

"Ferraris?"

"As I said, occasionally," he says testily, clearly annoyed by my questions.

Call me pedantic, but I always hate to feel I've been bullshitted, even by someone I don't know. "So why did you describe yourself as 'Ferrari driving' in your ad?" I plow on.

He blatantly scowls at me and sits back in his chair with an irritable sigh. "*Because*," he almost spits, "that's what you women want, don't you?"

The waitress appears brandishing two steaming plates of food, a pasta primavera for me, a Texan-sized steak and chips for him. She places them in front of us, passes over the mustard tray from a nearby table, and beats a hasty retreat.

"Sorry?" I persist. "Run that by me again? *What* are you saying *we women* want?" Dog with a bone now, that's me.

"You want men with pots of money and fast cars, you're not interested in anyone ordinary," he states, hacking into his steak and taking a large bite. "Ugh!" His face screws up in disgust. "This is repulsive."

This time, the clicking fingers are abandoned in favor of his clapping hands, loud enough for him to attract the attention of just about everyone in the restaurant except the waitress, who's taking a booking on the phone. Anxious at the disruption, the manager scuttles over. "Yes, sir?"

"This steak is totally inedible," Graham booms. "I can't believe you've had the gall to serve it to me."

"What's wrong with it, sir?" The manager keeps his voice low.

"Everything. Your chef is clearly incapable of cooking anything but the simplest dish. Just bring me one of those," he says dismissively, pointing at my plate of pasta. "That is, of course, if he can manage not to screw that up too."

Grim-faced, the manager scoops up his plate and catches my eye as he turns to walk back to the kitchens. Mortified, I smile apologetically, praying my expression encapsulates the fact that I don't really know this oaf, am here under sufferance, and will *never* . . . ahem . . . enjoy his company again after this evening.

I'm torn between castigating Graham for his atrocious manners and returning to the patronizingly sexist remark he made shortly before tasting his steak. The former seems too ingrained for change, a lost cause.

"I have to take issue with your comment that women only want men with money and fast cars," I say quietly. "That's grossly inaccurate and unfair."

"Some do," he sniffs.

"Some, maybe," I acquiesce, "but by no means all. Far from it. That's like saying all men want stupid women with large breasts."

He looks wistful for a moment at the thought. "Well, why else are *you* here?" Taking another slice of bread, he wipes it across the butter. "Go on, admit it, the bit about driving a Ferrari made you think I had money."

His expression is so self-satisfyingly smug that, just for a second, an image flashes into my mind where I leap to my feet and pronounce: "I'm out of estrogen and I have a gun" or, at the very least, press my hand down on the back of his head and grind his face into the crumb-covered butter dish. Amazing, I ponder, how such a large head can house such a small brain.

"Actually, it was the 'good sense of humor' bit that caught my eye," I say matter-of-factly. "And the fact that you looked very genial in your photograph." I resist the urge to point out that both were woefully wide of the mark. "When was that picture taken, by the way?"

"Two to three years ago."

More like twenty-three, I think mutinously. Either that, or his hair did the off with the lightning speed of Lance Armstrong.

"Anyway, never mind all that," he says rather conveniently, considering it's a tricky subject for him, "are you seriously telling me you have never . . . how shall I put this . . . *sexed up* a description of yourself to attract members of the opposite sex?"

He's absolutely right, of course. I have. Shaving a couple of years off my age is an old favorite, as is pretending to be far more extensively traveled than I am. And of course, my trusty Wonderbra is a deception in itself, presenting the illusion of ample bosoms to any admirer, only for them to miraculously disappear the minute it's unclipped. Which, if I'm honest, isn't very often these days.

"No, never," I reply piously. "I don't see the point because they'll eventually rumble your exaggerations anyway. So you may as well just tell the truth in the first place."

"Hmmm." Graham looks unconvinced by this argument. "Well, I find the Ferrari reference gets me a lot of dates."

"Maybe," I shrug. "But it doesn't keep them, does it? Or you wouldn't be here with me."

My barbed remark is somewhat lost on him as, like a condemned woman approaching the hangman's noose, the waitress homes into view with Graham's pasta. Garnished, no doubt, with extra spittle.

He sniffs disdainfully as she places it in front of him. "Let's hope this is an improvement on the last culinary fiasco," he intones.

"It's not her fault," I whisper as the poor girl slopes away. "She just serves it up."

"She's the front line to the customer, so dealing with complaints goes with the job." A strand of tagliatelle dangles from the corner of his mouth and I feel quite queasy. "I don't make the cars I deliver, but I have to deal with any fallout. Same thing."

"Except that I doubt you're on minimum wage," I counter, pushing my empty plate to one side.

We lapse into silence for a few moments, his cement mixer mouth devouring pasta, me showing fake interest in the painting behind his head that looks like an Alsatian has parked its soiled backside on the canvas and wriggled around.

Much as I know I should step away from the subject, his obvious conviction that the majority of women are mercenary is compelling me to explore further. The neuroses that people lug around with them from one relationship to another have always fascinated me, and I suspect Graham's baggage is best described as a boarding school trunkful.

"So why do you think women are only interested in money?" I ask, taking care to keep my tone casually neutral.

He shrugs. "No reason. Just a gut feeling."

"Have you ever been married?" There I go, emotional potholing, crawling right into what I'm pretty sure is the nub of the problem.

He looks slightly taken aback by my directness. "Um, yes. For about five years. It ended a year ago."

"Amicably?"

The cheek twitch is back. "No, not really. She fleeced me for most of my life savings, as well as the house I bought and lovingly renovated before I even met her. Then, when the ink was barely dry on the decree absolute, she moved her boy toy in. The only saving grace is that we didn't have children, or she'd still be fleecing me now."

Ah, a shorter tunnel than even I expected. "The high cost of leaving, eh?" I smile. "And you think all women are like her?"

"Aren't they? You tell me."

I'm suddenly overpowered by a sense of weariness at having dinner with a man who has (a) few social graces and (b) a chip the size of Mount Everest on each shoulder. Which both add up to (c) I don't find him in the slightest bit attractive.

It also strikes me that, during a torturous date that has wasted two hours of my life, he hasn't asked me one question about myself.

"Did that meet with Sir's satisfaction?" The manager has reappeared to remove our empty plates. He's looking at Graham with an expression that suggests "Don't upset me, I'm running out of places to hide the bodies."

"It was passable," says Graham, shoving the plate towards him. "But we won't be coming here again."

We? Ye Gods, I probably won't be coming here again—mainly because of the prices—but I'm damned if I want them thinking we're an item. "He's not speaking for both of us," I say chirpily. "I'll be back again, definitely. The food was lovely."

"Thank you, madam."

The manager vacates the area, leaving me faced with a glowering Graham. I'd like to say he gets more attractive with each mouthful of wine, but I'd be lying on a grand scale.

"That was rather unnecessary," he says pompously.

"So was the rude way you spoke to the waitress," I retort, throwing caution to the wind in the sure knowledge this date is in its dying throes. My left leg has now gone to sleep and the rest of my body is desperate to join it.

He lets out a long, impatient sigh that suggests he's dealing with a petulant child. "Well, this has been a complete waste of time and money, hasn't it? I think we both know we won't be seeing each other again."

I nod silently and unhook my handbag from the back of the chair, relieved this charade is over. I knew from the moment I clapped eyes on him that he wasn't my type, yet dating etiquette propelled me to sit here and see it through to the end.

You may be wondering why I came here at all . . . why I put myself through this experience when I clearly don't have the inclination, or indeed the stomach, for it.

But the fact is, it wasn't my idea. Let me explain . . .

Two

*g*ood-bye thirty-three. Hello thirty-four. I can say this quite calmly, so clearly the midlife madness isn't going to strike me down just yet. Maybe next year.

After all, it was thirty-five that did for Julia, my trusty drinking partner from college days. She literally went to bed one night, full of anticipation for our forthcoming eighteen-to-thirty holiday (OK, so we lied on the application form, but doesn't everyone?), then woke up the next morning sobbing that she was on life's giant shelf and was sick of just being taken down and dusted occasionally.

"I want some permanency in my life," she wailed, before canceling our holiday and marrying the first man who crossed her path. Literally. I went to her wedding to the pizza deliveryman, but haven't seen her since.

So here I am, on my way to my "surprise" birthday party, organized by my dear friend and fellow TV producer Tabitha. Except that I know all about it, because my sister Olivia rang to warn me. She knows that I loathe and detest surprises and would be highly likely to walk straight back out again if one is sprung on me.

Instead, I shall arrive at the pub where I'm supposed to be

meeting Tab for "a quiet drink," then put on an Oscar-winning performance of shock and delight at seeing the others there too.

As I walk in the door, I crane my neck above the crowds to seek her out. She leaps to her feet as soon as she sees me.

"Hi! Happy birthday!" She envelops me in a hug, then stands back and gives me the once-over. "You look great. Come on, I've booked a quiet table for the two of us through here."

Leading me by the hand, she guides me through to a small, oblong-shaped room with a circular table plonked in the middle of it, rather tellingly laid out for several people and decorated with lots of birthday kitsch from the 99¢ store.

At one end of the room, there's a dark plum velvet curtain, from which a jeweled mule is protruding quite obviously.

"Ta da!" Mule-owner Madeleine emerges from behind the curtain, tugging it back to reveal my other "mystery" guests, all grinning like jackanapes and chorusing "Surprise!"

"Oh my gosh!" Pulling my best Macaulay Culkin expression, I shriek loudly, then start running up and down on the spot for good measure. Seeing Olivia glaring at my pitiful overacting, I stop immediately. "Wow, you guys really fooled me! I had absolutely *no* idea."

There follows an excruciating few seconds where they all burst into a halfhearted chorus of "Happy Birthday," an imbroglio of flat notes, high-pitched wailing, and even a moment's hesitation when they clearly forget who they're singing it for.

"Thanks." I beam insincerely. "Shall we sit down?"

Now the attention has thankfully shifted from me and everyone is jostling for position and opening their napkins, I should take the opportunity to introduce you to a few of the usual suspects.

First of all, there's Madeleine, my social salvation. That's her sitting directly opposite me, fussing over who wants still and who wants sparkling. She's single too and, consequently, we see an inordinate amount of each other in our quest to find the "perfect" man we can then try to change beyond recognition. In the meantime, Madeleine happily indulges in lots of meaningless flings, not least because she's stunning and slim and a lot more successful at attracting men than I am. She thinks it's every man for herself and, as a dancer, her ability to lift her leg onto their shoulders in wine bars helps enormously. Tonight, as usual, she's wearing what I always describe as one of her "nuclear" outfits, with 50 percent fallout. But as she once told me, she never shows her underwear unintentionally.

At the table, she's flanked on either side by Richard and Lars, or Dick and Arse as I affectionately call them. Richard and I met when we were both TV researchers on *Good Morning Britain.* He worked in the showbiz department, whilst I was in "human interest." You know, those "I had one black twin and one white twin" kind of stories which are really just car crash viewing, but we have to pretend we're doing a public service by highlighting this problem and run a phone number saying "If you've had twins that are different colors and would like help, then call this number . . ." blah blah blah.

Richard has stayed in light entertainment, though he's risen to the lofty heights of a senior producer on the Saturday night game show *Till Divorce Do Us Part*—catchphrase "The bounty after the mutiny"—where warring couples win the glittering prize of an all-expenses-paid decree absolute.

His French boyfriend, Lars, a striking six-foot-three black man, is one of the dancers who high kick their way across the studio floor when the contestants win the chance to live happily ever apart. I met Madeleine through him.

Oh, hang on. Something's happening. My sister Olivia is banging the table.

"Here's to Jess. Happy thirty-fourth birthday. Cheers!" She raises her champagne glass and takes a swig, and everyone follows suit.

"Cheers," I parrot, knocking back a mouthful myself. "This really is terribly nice of you all."

Olivia is my older sister by two years and something of a heroine of mine. Unlike other siblings so close in age, she has never been a thorn in my side. For as long as I can remember, far from being a tormentor, she has always been supportive and caring. Most memorably, when I had nightmares as a child, she would sit and stroke my hair until I drifted back to sleep.

When she left home to go to Bristol University, I was distraught for at least a week, sobbing into my pillow and refusing to be consoled by our mother. Then I met a boy in sixth form and became temporarily obsessed by him instead.

The tinny sound of metal cutlery banging against glass drags me out of my nostalgic thoughts.

"Shall we do presents?" It's Kara, the friend I have known the longest but like the least. We've all got one, haven't we? Inexplicably, we stay in touch with them, like moths to a flame, even though they drive us to distraction most of the time. Men are very emotionless in such situations, unashamedly severing ties with anyone they consider surplus to requirements. But we women hang on in there, making excuses for the excesses of a ghastly friend, loyal to the bitter, drawn-out end, ever hopeful that one day they'll justify our patience.

I can't quite put my finger on what's wrong with my relationship with Kara, but there's definitely an undercurrent of jealousy on her part. It's as if she hangs around only to delight and luxuriate in the bad things that happen to me, and that any happy event in my life is a tangible disappointment.

It wasn't always like that. When we met at sixth form college, she was a formidable ally and fantastic fun. But over the years, her loyalty became questionable and her face increasingly sour. These days, the best way to sum her up is that she's always there when she needs you.

Tonight, she has dragged along her boyfriend, Dan. He's an amiable enough chap who wombles through life doing no one any harm, but for some reason he's been ensnared by Mrs. Danvers. Kara has already told me he will propose by Christmas, but I'm not sure she's told *him* that yet.

Everyone places their presents in a huge pile in front of me and, rather self-consciously, I start to unwrap them with oohs, aahs, and you-shouldn't-haves in all the right places. A beautiful fawn-colored pashmina from Olivia, a Walkman from Richard and Lars, a popcorn maker from Tab and Will, and a suede-covered photo album from Madeleine, with pictures of our various excesses glued inside . . . finally, Kara hands me an envelope.

"This is from all of us, but mostly me." She gives me a thin excuse for a smile.

Oh puh-lease, a bloody gift voucher or book token. How original, I think mutinously. But when I open the envelope, there's a folded piece of paper inside and my brow furrows with curiosity. All eyes are on me as I pull it out and, worryingly, I notice that my sister looks particularly apprehensive.

The first thing I clap eyes on is a photocopy of a rather indistinct head and shoulders photo of me, grinning vacantly like a halfwit. I remember it was taken at my birthday party last year, shortly before I vomited into the wine bar's ice bucket after drinking my own weight in sangria. Classy, huh?

To one side, there's a printed paragraph and I start to read it out loud.

"I am a thirty-four-year-old fun-loving woman interested in meeting someone similar. My friends are baffled that I'm single, so perhaps you're the one to clear up the mystery?" . . . I tail off, my blood freezing in my veins as it dawns what it is.

"Please tell me you haven't already placed this?" I look directly at Kara, who is positively glowing at my discomfort.

"Of course I have!" She smirks. "It's your birthday present!"

I scan the table for signs that this is a joke, but absolutely no one is looking me in the eye except her.

"Get it stopped." I throw the piece of paper across the table and point at her mobile. "Call them *right* now and pull it."

"Can't. It's already on the Internet." She pouts, trying to look apologetic. But I can tell she's extremely pleased with herself.

Taking a deep breath, I hold it for a few seconds. Knowing Olivia inside out, I glance at her quickly and realize that this whole ghastly business isn't a windup. It's 100 percent genuine.

"Did you know about this?" I look at her beseechingly.

"Yes." She nods slowly, wincing with discomfort. "But only when I got here this evening, so there was absolutely nothing I could do about it."

The Exorcist's Linda Blair has nothing on the head swivel I use to turn back to Kara.

"How fucking dare you!" I glare at her and it takes all my willpower not to lunge for her scrawny throat. "You had no right to do this, it's *totally* intrusive."

Even she looks taken aback by my sudden outburst. "It's only a bit of fun," she pouts.

Richard turns down the corners of his mouth and stares at the table.

"It might be a bit of fun to you, but that's *my* name on there." I jab my finger at it. "Not yours. I can't *believe* you think I'd find that funny . . . I'm going to put a stop to it first thing in the morning."

Having swallowed my meal in large, indigestible lumps of injustice, I knock back yet another glass of house white and close my eyes for a second. When I open them, Richard has sidled into the now empty chair beside me.

"Hi," he smiles sheepishly.

"Low," I reply, with my best disconsolate expression. "I'm at rock bottom and starting to dig."

"Darling, just relax," he drawls.

"Relax?" I scoff. "It's only the tension that's holding me together." The pair of us stare across the table for a few silent seconds, watching Olivia and her husband, Michael, totally engrossed in their conversation, his hand caressing the back of her neck.

"On the one hand," I say, nodding in their direction, "they give me faith. On the other, I despair I'll ever meet anyone I could love that much."

"Of course you will, darling," says Richard in the syrupy, patronizing tone my mother always used to assure me that, provided I did my best, I would pass all my exams. I took her advice but flunked most of them anyway. "But, of course, you won't meet him if you refuse to put yourself out there."

I raise my eyes heavenward. "*Dick*," I say pointedly, a tactic I always use when he's doing or saying something ludicrous, "I'm hardly the hermit woman of Balham. I do go out, you know."

"Yes, but only with me or Tabitha, and we're hardly ideal for attracting heterosexual men. I mean, bless her, but Tab easily hits the danger zone on the mooseometer."

I feel terrible laughing, but do anyway. "Don't be rotten."

"You need a more direct approach," he continues. "And by the way, you live in Tooting."

I scowl for a moment, puzzled by his remark. Not the Tooting bit, he's always ticking me off for pretending to live somewhere slightly posher than I do. No, I'm thrown by the direct approach bit. Then it clicks.

"No. Absolutely not!" I slam my hand so hard on the table that a narrow vase containing a single yellow rose topples over and spills its water. "I flatly refuse to date some anorak-wearing cyberman from the Internet."

Richard pulls a pooh-poohing face. "Why not? Everyone's doing it these days. It's the new sexual revolution, darling, but instead of Woodstock and flower power orgies, it's taking place through your fingertips." He mimics tapping a keyboard.

"Not through *my* fingertips," I whisper, inexplicably checking the ends for any signs of cyberinterference. "I prefer the old-fashioned method of meeting a man."

He places a hand over his mouth and feigns a yawn. "What, endless nights spent propping up a bar in the hope that one of the surrounding men might be single? If they've registered on the Internet, you *know* they're looking for a relationship, so it cuts out all the crap. It's the fast track to fun fun fun."

I wrinkle my nose. "It's just not *me.*"

"Yeah, yeah, I know" . . . he waves his hand dismissively. "You're unique . . . just like everyone else."

His remark may have punctured my ego somewhat, but inside I am reluctantly admitting that he has a point. My persistently single state indicates that maybe I have been going about dating in the wrong way, that maybe it *is* time for change.

Possibly suspecting a slight thaw in my chill, he warms to the theme. "There are literally thousands and thousands of them online, just waiting to be plucked. Darling, even *you* stand a chance with those odds."

"Cheers." I smile sarcastically. "I'm still not doing it."

Richard pours me more wine, presumably in the hope it will help weaken my resolve. "Take a look, at least. That won't do any harm. You can log on and scroll through the potential dates. Just think—your very own hunk superstore, and they won't even know you're there."

"Hmmm. The best I can offer is that I'll think about it." Put like that, I don't know what else to say.

Madeleine hones into view, her eyes crossed with frustration. "God, how do you put up with *her.*"

"Ah, Kara," I smile, following her glance. "Yes, she's quite a girl, isn't she? Who's she been spitting bile about now?"

Madeleine casts a furtive eye over her shoulder. "I was talking about dancing, and she said, 'Bit old for that, aren't you?' Fucking cheek! She barely knows me."

"Oh that never stops her. Everyone is entitled to her opinion." I steal a crafty puff of Richard's cigarette while my censorious sister is looking the other way. "The only thing that cheats Kara out of the last word is an echo."

"And she's got such an innocent, harmless look about her," continues Madeleine. "As if butter wouldn't melt."

"Yes, the face of a saint." Richard nods. "Trouble is, it's a bloody Saint Bernard. I just feel sorry for that poor sod of a boyfriend. Talk about under the thumb."

"Nah. Dan's easygoing, but he's no pushover," I say. "I'm sure he stands up to her, he's just too polite to do it in public."

"Anyway." Madeleine looks at Richard but jerks her head towards me. "Have you persuaded her yet?"

"Persuaded me to do what?" Then it sinks in and I let out a low groan. "Oh God, you're not on about that wretched Internet thing again?"

"Go *on*, it'll be a laugh if nothing else," says Madeleine. "What have you got to lose?"

"My dignity?" I retort. Then a thought strikes me. "I tell you what, I'll do it if you do."

Of course, as a woman who makes Mae West look positively virginal, Madeleine is quite simply the worst person I could have thrown out this challenge to.

She shrugs. "Absolutely fine by me. But I'm not the one looking for a serious relationship. I'm happy with the occasional fling with whoever life throws at me."

"She's so discerning." Richard smiles sarcastically. "Anyway, she says she'll do it too, so that's it now, you *have* to go ahead with it."

My heart doesn't just sink, it's got concrete boots on. "OK, three dates, no more," I say resignedly. "But if none of them turn out to be Mr. Right, then it's back to the old method of trawling wine bars and late-night bus stops."

"Fantastic!" Richard slaps his thigh D'Artagnan style. "All for fun, and fun for all!"

Three

O h God. I have just logged onto my computer, and I have thirty-seven e-mails from total and utter strangers. The jaw-dropping, knuckle-scraping, head-hanging shame of it.

But also, deep down, I have to admit to feeling a slight thrill too. I don't know them, they don't know me, and best of all, they have absolutely no way of making contact other than through e-mail. Much better than standing by the bar, fending off the approaches of Mr. Never-in-a-Thousand-Years. Unless, of course, I reply and grant them the honor of knowing my phone number.

Yet I can call up their dating ad, along with thousands of others, and pore over their photographs and personal details. Even more astonishingly, I can read the answers to the kind of gallingly intrusive questions it would usually take at *least* two or three traditional dates to even dare broach. Such as "How much do you earn, and do you want to have children?"

There's something rather addictive about cutting through the crap so comprehensively and finding out if you're singing from the same song sheet before the band even strikes the first chord.

It's 8:3o a.m. and I have deliberately come into the office early, leaving myself free to browse through the sex supermarket without fear of being ridiculed by any nosy work colleagues. I decide to leave the thirty-seven replies to my ad until later, and take a cyberstroll through the general site first.

A form pops up asking my requirements, as if I were simply buying a car. I can tap in my preferred requirements, such as hair color, height, and religion, and up comes a list of all the men who fit my specifications. How very Third Reich.

I decide to hedge my bets and keep it vague, asking for someone between the ages of thirty and forty-five who lives within twenty-five miles of London. The machine makes a faint grinding noise as it searches.

"Shit!" I exclaim out loud as it tells me I have 3,456 matches. Each has a passport-sized photograph they have provided, alongside their brief description of themselves. It instructs you to click on their picture to get further information.

"Bob764," catches my eye and I double click right on the bridge of his nose. The photograph enlarges and, although slightly blurred, I can see he has rather striking blue eyes and an attractive grin.

I lean forwards slightly, scrutinizing him. Could he be the one? Could I really, in all seriousness, meet the man I might spend the rest of my life with by way of a computer? And even if I did, what would we say when someone asked how we met? I'd rather say our eyes met over the condom counter at the drugstore than fess up to the truth.

Another, "Crespo," is very handsome but rather off-puttingly suggests he's a man who could fulfill a girl's greatest fantasy. I toy with the idea of asking him to fix my roof for nothing.

"Hmmm, he's tasty."

I jump out of my skin, rapidly hit the "close" button and swivel round in my chair. "Oh, thank fuck, it's you!" I press the palm of my hand against my chest, waiting for my raging pulse to subside. "What on earth are you doing in so early? Is the end of the world nigh?"

"I was going to ask you the same," says Tabitha. "But now I know why. I have to call Australia to research that piece on Lizard Island, and I'm buggered if I'm using my home phone to do it."

She plonks her handbag on the desk next to me and sits down. She nods towards my computer. "I hope you're going to put him on your list of potential dates. He looks just your type."

"What do you mean, *my type*?" I scowl, mortally wounded by the thought that I might be predictable in some way.

"Oh, you know. The romantic, penniless-poet type. The one who could be the next Dylan Thomas . . . if only someone would recognize his potential."

She's absolutely spot on, of course, and my laughable relationship history backs this up. There have been a succession of short-lived poetic ne'er-do-wells in my life and one giant, musical one to whom I gave the best years of my thighs.

After five years of giving him endless emotional and financial support whilst he tried, unsuccessfully I might add, to get a recording deal, he left me just over a year ago for a twenty-something Trustafarian with a small brain and a large fortune.

Nathan, he was called, or Satan as Richard refers to him. Even now, I can only just bring myself to say his name. But Tab's right. Unfortunately, being kicked in the teeth by Mr. Futon Potato hasn't dulled my appetite for airy-fairy "creative" types.

"Sod Australia. I'll get them out of bed later," says Tab, pulling her chair closer to my screen. "Let's have a look at some more."

We spend the next half an hour engrossed in what unfolds before us on the flickering screen, oohing and aahing in equal mea-

sures at some of the seemingly high-caliber men offering themselves up, laughing like drains at the low-caliber barrel-scrapers.
All human life is here, from seventeen-year-old spotty youths
right up to a couple of octogenarians.

"Look at this one!" I shriek, double clicking on "Alf, 74." His
ad reads: "I'm 5' 5" but used to be 5' 7". I can remember Mondays
to Thursdays, so if you can remember Fridays to Sundays, then
let's put our heads together for some action."

"Well at least he's got a sense of humor," laughs Tab. "I might
even give him a go myself."

I pull a suck-a-lemon face. "What does 'action' mean? Do you
think he's referring to sex? Look at him, poor love, he'd have to
bring along an eighteen-year-old and a set of jumper cables."

A door creaks open in the distance and footsteps come towards us. Seeing it's Janice, our executive producer, I hastily click
the "sign out" option on the screen.

"Bloody hell, are you two on a sponsored work-in for charity?"
Sarcasm is just one of the services she offers. She looks at
the clock. "I don't normally see either of you for at least another hour."

"I've been making calls to Oz on the Lizard Island piece," lies
Tab with consummate ease. "Jess stayed at mine last night, so
came in early with me."

I simply smile in mute agreement, not trusting myself to say
anything. Janice has always intimidated me.

"Good." She smiles thinly, her eyes narrowed in suspicion.
"Feel free to come in early to the office any time you like."

"This isn't an office. It's hell with fluorescent lighting," mutters Tab to her retreating back.

Once Janice has disappeared into her walnut-clad corner lair,
I wait a few moments, then retrieve the notebook I'd hastily
stuffed into the top drawer of my desk as she loomed.

"That's a good morning's work there," smiles Tab, tapping the cover with a plum-colored talon. "I have a strong feeling the future Mr. Monroe may be among them."

*I*t's 6 p.m. and I'm sprinting, well, more lolloping really, towards the station, my overstuffed handbag on one arm, an overnight bag on the other.

It's Olivia and Michael's seventh wedding anniversary today and he's booked the honeymoon suite at the Dorchester for them. Rather than fork out for a babysitter overnight and have all the worry of the children possibly waking up and being upset by the presence of an almost stranger, I said I'd happily stay over.

It's absolutely no bother for me; in fact, I really relish my own little slice of what I see as an idyllic family life from time to time. I can fantasize that one day I, too, will be living in domestic bliss with a man I adore and our two beautiful children.

It baffles me that women who choose to do that are often regarded as inferior to those who slave away in an office for fourteen hours a day before going back to their empty "home" and heating up a quick microwave meal for one, before falling exhausted into bed and starting the whole soulless process again the next day. I'm all for people doing what they want, but not when they sit in judgment on other people's choices in life, as if they are somehow selling out by opting to concentrate on a successful relationship and parenthood.

To my mind, if you're prepared to study and work hard, and have the gift of the gab, then you can succeed at pretty much any career in life. But achieving a well-balanced, happy home life that takes the concerns of others into account? Well, that's never guaranteed for anyone, however rich, clever, or hardworking you are. Achieving *that* takes maturity, wise choices, and more compromise and emotional plate-spinning than even the best magician could ever aspire to.

My sister Olivia has the perfect life, the one I would give my right arm for but don't even know where to begin to achieve. She and Michael met in Bristol, where he was studying medicine and she was doing a three-year physiotherapy course. She says that as soon as she clapped eyes on him in her local pub, she knew he was "the one."

Our mother always told us we'd know when *he* came along. She'd spin us magical tales about when she first saw Dad, and how it felt as if she'd been struck by a thunderbolt. She often chose to omit the less flowery fact that, at the time, he'd been selling her a two-seater sofa in orange tweed.

As an adult, I now realize the circumstances and their alleged exchange of dialogue would change a little with each telling, as she reinvented history in her starry-eyed pursuit of romance. But as children, Olivia and I had unquestioningly absorbed every word and carried the ideal through to adulthood; a giant expectation we would either fulfill or fail dismally at.

Olivia had hit the jackpot with Michael, but my giant expectation had become a millstone round my neck, weighing me down with the assumption that, unless I feel like I have been struck by no less than Zeus himself, the man I'm dating isn't "the one."

The "experts," as they like to call themselves, always say those from broken homes are disadvantaged when it comes to finding lasting love, because they have no blueprint to work from. But what if you have a blueprint of near-perfection, as drummed into me through my formative years by my mother? What then? Believe me, it can be just as inhibiting.

Olivia and Michael live in a large Victorian house at the end of a long, leafy street in Dulwich village, the place where those who previously occupied Clapham's "Nappy Valley" move to once they have acquired a bit more money. Their main reason for choosing the area was so six-year-old Matthew would be well placed to attend the prestigious Dulwich Elementary, with its spacious playing fields so rare in London.

I open the black metal gate with the "Beware of the Dog" sign left by the previous owners, and rush up to the highly glossed front door in British racing green. Externally, everything about the house is conventional. Olivia's only nod to eccentricity is the tinny electronic doorbell that plays Anita Baker's "Ring My Bell." A mortified Michael disconnects it every time they have a dinner party.

As a computerized Anita warbles on, I peer in through the front window to see Matthew and four-year-old Emily glued to the television and completely ignoring the fact that I am hopping from one foot to another outside. Ah, the bliss of those selfish, guilt-free years. It's such a shame we don't appreciate them at the time.

"Hi!" Michael opens the door, smiling broadly. He looks smart in a black cashmere sweater and black trousers.

"Bloody hell, it's the Milk Tray man!" I tease.

"And this lady loves him." Olivia appears behind him and places her arms round his waist, squeezing tightly. Michael turns and kisses the end of her nose.

"Yeuch." I wrinkle my nose. "Book a room, will you?"

"We have." Michael looks at his watch. "Which reminds me, let's get going so we can make use of it before dinner." He disappears from view into the sitting room, leaving Olivia and me standing in the narrow hall whose walls are covered with family photographs.

"Right!" says Olivia in her best take-charge voice. "The kids are fed. So all that's left is bath, cocoa, and story."

"And what about them?" I quip. I know their routine inside out. "Leave it to me. You go and enjoy yourselves."

"Believe me, we will." Olivia's eyes were shining. "Just think, uninhibited sex without fear of interruption or being overheard by the rugrats," she says, using her pet term for Matthew and Emily.

"*Any* sex would be nice," I say ruefully.

"You'll meet someone soon, pumpkin." She ruffles my hair. "You'll see. It'll happen when you least expect it."

I look doubtful. "Maybe I should take up jogging. At least I'll get to hear heavy breathing again."

Olivia laughs. "An easier option would be to go out on dates. You never bloody do."

"Actually, I've already had thirty-seven e-mails answering that ad the dreaded Kara put on the Internet."

Her eyebrows shoot up. "Really? Blimey, talk about instant gratification. In the old days, you had to wait for a bundle to be forwarded on from your PO box number."

I shoot her a cynical look. "As if."

"Yes, I *know* I've been lucky. But luck doesn't keep a marriage going. You have to work at it, particularly once you have kids." She bends down to scoop up one of Emily's headbands discarded on the floor. "It just depends on whether you both rise to the challenge. If it's too one-sided, that's when it doesn't work."

"Maybe one of the thirty-seven will rise to the challenge." I'm trying to sound positive. I follow Olivia through to the kitchen at the back of the house.

"Any of them look promising?" She looks at me questioningly.

"I haven't looked at them yet. It's a bit difficult at work. I've just looked at some of the ads placed by men on the general Web site. They're quite a mixed bag."

"Well, once you've got the kids to bed, don't forget Michael's computer is upstairs. You can peruse your thirty-seven potential soul mates without fear of being rumbled."

I smile appreciatively. "I might well do that."

"Ready?" Michael reappears, clutching a large black-leather overnight bag, his jacket slung over his arm.

Five minutes later, I'm standing at the door with Matthew and Emily, waving them off. Neither of the children seems the slightest bit perturbed at seeing their parents disappearing off into the sunset, and I feel a warm flush of love for them as I realize it's because I'm here. If it had been Juanita, their cleaning lady and erstwhile babysitter, Emily would no doubt have attached herself to Olivia's leg and been dragged up the garden path screaming like a banshee.

But "Aunty Jess" is the next best thing to Mum and Dad—in fact, sometimes she's even better because she indulges them that little bit more. Tonight, the night I have my future to think of, is no exception.

"Aunty Jess, can I watch my *Spiderman* DVD?" pleads Matthew, as soon as his parents are out of earshot. He grabs hold of my forearm and squeezes it. "Pleeeeeeeaaaase!"

"Me want to see *Anstay*," says Emily, referring to the Disney cartoon *Anastasia* that she's seen at least twenty times already.

Luckily, thanks to Michael's sizable salary as a heart consultant at Great Ormond Street Hospital for Sick Children, theirs is a two-DVD-player household. So after their bath, I plonk them down with a mug of cocoa each, watching the film of their choice in separate rooms.

Once I know they're engrossed, I sneak upstairs to Michael's study and settle myself down in front of his computer.

Waiting for it to load, then make that torturous, squealy noise as it dials up AOL, I sit and gaze around the small room that would normally accommodate a single bed. The desk is old-fashioned mahogany with a red leather top and brass drop handles on the drawers.

The computer and its accessories take up most of the available space, but there's a little corner left for a framed picture of Michael and Olivia on their wedding day.

I remember it well. I was twenty-seven and maid of honor, a title that only served to hammer home that I had no proper relationship of my own to speak of.

It was pre-Nathan, and I was having a rather patchy fling with Greg, an Australian surfer dude who floated in and out on the tide of life. He was gorgeous and said very little, which I initially took to mean he was from the "less is more"school of thought. Then I realized it was simply because he had absolutely nothing to say. In fact, he was so unutterably thick that light bent round him.

I didn't invite him to my sister's wedding, mainly because I couldn't rely on him to turn up, but also because I knew he'd be way out of his depth with the other guests. And that included the four-year-old twin bridesmaids who were Michael's nieces.

So I went on my own and endured an entire day of looking a fright in tartan (Michael's Scottish) and being asked by just about every other guest if I was going to be next up the aisle. By the end of the day, I was thinking of wordlessly handing everyone a press release that read: "No, I haven't got a rewarding, fulfilling relationship like my sister Olivia. I am the emotional runt of the family, the lost cause."

"You've got mail." The computerized female voice stirs me from my trance and I stare at the screen. The thirty-seven e-mails have now mushroomed to forty-eight. I double click on the first one.

Hi, I'm Simon . . .

I magnify his picture to discover he's very handsome with dark blond hair and a tanned face. It's clearly been taken on a beach somewhere, in that dusk sunshine that's always so flattering. It's the first one, and it looks promising. Not a bad start.

"Shit!" I glance at my watch and leap up. It's 10 p.m. and I've forgotten all about Matthew and Emily watching their films.

I creep into Michael and Olivia's room and Emily is fast asleep in the middle of the bed, her empty mug still clasped in her chubby little hand. The television has clicked off DVD onto ITV, and *News at Ten* is just starting. I switch it off and pull the covers over Emily's bare legs. I'll sneak in next to her later.

Downstairs, Matthew is still watching *Spiderman*, obviously second time around.

"Come on, you. Bed." I flick off the machine and ruffle his hair. "Don't you dare tell Mum and Dad I let you stay up this late. It's our little secret."

"OK." He smiles, a mischievous glint in his dark blue eyes. "But only if you read me a bedtime story."

"Oooh, you're ruthless. You're going to go far, you are." I tuck him into bed and grab a Spiderman comic from his bookshelf. I start to read, an Oscar-winning performance even if I say so myself, with all the dramatic "Pows!" and "Bams!" in their right place. But by the end of the third page, Matthew's mouth has fallen open and he's emitting tiny, butterfly snores. Flicking off the bedside light, I sit in the half glow for a while, just listening to the steady rhythm of his breathing and studying his motionless face.

Although I didn't actually give birth to him and Emily, I can't imagine loving them any more than I do. This scenario—married life with two or three children and all the angst, hard work, and sacrifice it entails—is absolutely, 100 percent what I want.

Kara has always said she doesn't want children, which is probably a good thing rather than pass on her grumpy cow chromosome. She says she's too selfish and wants to carry on having a nice car and foreign holidays, as if they were somehow mutually exclusive from parenthood.

It always amazes me how people think a tiny seven-pound bundle is going to control your life, issuing orders from its high chair, banning vacations and insisting that only a sensible, family estate car will do. What utter silliness.

Sure, it's probably easier to holiday in Britain and drive a roomy tank, but if you want to fly off to Barbados and drive a two-seater sports car, you can. And there's not a damn thing little Junior can do about it.

Once, when Olivia was a bit squiffy from too many gin and tonics, she confided in me that, although she would never admit it to anyone else, she felt slightly superior to women who chose not to have children. She said she pitied them for not ever being able to know the strength of love between a mother and her child.

"I loved my carefree, single years," she murmured. "But if they stretched on endlessly without contrast, they would seem very empty indeed."

I knew what she meant. At thirty-four, I'm bored sick of my single, selfish life. *I* want that contrast Olivia spoke so passionately about, but the big question is, am I going to get it? And from whom?

Occasionally, a woman I work with tells me how envious she is of me and my uncomplicated existence. She has three lovely children and a solid, if unremarkable, marriage, but said she longs to do what she wants, when she wants.

"No, I envy *you*," I replied.

"Yeah, right," she said ruefully, before wandering off to the local grocery store to get her family's tea.

Some women genuinely enjoy life without the major responsibility of incumbents. But I'm not one of them. I can only liken it to craving a slice of chocolate cake when, say, family life is chocolate free. A day at a health spa with your girlfriends, swigging champagne and not worrying about getting home or having a hangover in the morning—*that's* your slice of chocolate cake.

But imagine being able to have it whenever you want. Huge, unlimited, stodgy slices of it. See? Loses its appeal, doesn't it? Well, that's the prolonged single life for me. Unappealing.

I kiss Matthew on the forehead and creep out of his bedroom, edging back down the stairs to the mezzanine level, where Michael's study is. Shutting down the computer, I fold up the piece of paper with twelve names written down—the dozen potentials chosen from forty-eight replies.

Stuffing it into my jeans pocket, I sigh as I watch the power drain from the screen. I want family life and it doesn't seem to be coming my way via the usual routes. So I'll just have to take matters into my own hands.

Tomorrow, I'll whittle the twelve names down to three and arrange my first foray into cyberdating.

Four

Hi, I'm Simon. I'm 35, of athletic build, and have a black belt in judo. I'm about to get my pilot's license, but to fund my passion for flying I have to work occasionally as an account manager for a West End advertising agency. But don't tell my mother that's what I do, she thinks I'm the doorman in a brothel! The woman of my dreams will be equally adventurous, but most of all, great fun.

J thought Saturday lunch was good place to start. Broad daylight, informal, as long or, more importantly, as short as I like.

It's a surprisingly warm, sunny day for late May, and I have arranged to meet Simon at Buona Sera, a lively Italian restaurant down a small side street in Covent Garden. I have already told him, via e-mail, that I have a hair appointment at 2:30 p.m. A complete lie, of course, but I figure that if he turns out to be loathsome, then I need a good ploy to get away. And if we hit it off, then it's a good ploy to leave him wanting more. I'm a genius.

Being a Taurus and obsessive about punctuality, I get there slightly early and settle myself outside in the sunshine. Taking the seat with the best view of the entrance, I figure I'll also get a good few seconds advance warning of what I've let myself in for. So far, only an elderly couple and a lone woman have arrived after me.

Ten minutes later, I have read the menu so many times I could sweep the category in *Jeopardy*. Glancing around in frustration, I look across the street and notice a man standing motionless, staring in my direction. It looks vaguely like the man in the photograph, but I can't be sure.

He walks across the road towards me. "Hi, are you Jess?"

Wow. Now he's come into sharp focus, I can see the Web site picture doesn't do him any justice. He looks like a young Harrison Ford, what Madeleine and I would describe as an "NGR," "no gin required."

In answer to his question, I nod mutely.

"Hi, I'm Simon." He extends his hand for me to shake, but looks utterly ill at ease. Probably because, up to now, he thinks he's about to have lunch with Helen Keller.

I flash him my best smile. "Nice to meet you."

Nope. That hasn't loosened him up. His eyes darting nervously around him, he finally directs his gaze somewhere over my right shoulder.

"Do you mind if we eat inside?"

I frown slightly. Because it's a beautifully sunny day, all the other tables outside are now taken, meaning my early arrival had nabbed us a prime piece of real estate. I feel irritated at the thought of having to give it up. "Why?"

He looks perplexed. "Sorry?"

"*Why* do you want to eat inside? It's a gorgeous day." In case he hasn't noticed the blue sky, I gesture towards it.

"I'm not very good in the heat," he says lamely. "I get hay fever and go all blotchy."

"In May? Bit early, isn't it?" I don't bother to hide my incredulity, then shrug. "OK, then. Let's go."

Once inside, he relaxes instantly, his face lighting up with a smile that makes Tom Cruise look like Lurch.

I feel the small butterflies of excitement in my stomach. It's my first date and it's with a man with movie star looks. Suddenly, the Internet I have hitherto shown little interest in is the greatest invention since the push-up bra.

As he peruses the menu on which I am already word perfect, I take the opportunity to scrutinize him closely. He has short, dark blond hair that's slightly spiky at the front and a faint tan that brings out the paler blue in his eyes. I could stare at him all day.

"You're not looking at the menu."

Oh God, he's just caught me gawping at him. I hastily try and make it seem like I was looking over his shoulder, making myself look more ridiculous in the process. "Um, I glanced at it before you got here. I've got a photographic memory," I burble.

"Me too." There's that stomach-lurching smile again. "Trouble is, the lens cap's on most of the time."

He glances back down at the menu for a few seconds, then slams it shut and places his elbows on the table. "So how come someone like you is advertising on the Internet?"

I'm rather taken aback by the directness of the question, but manage not to show it. "I could say the same to you. You're not exactly Quasimodo."

"No, but I've got a hunch we're going to get on."

We groan simultaneously.

"Seriously though," he persists. "Why did you advertise?"

"I didn't as such. My friends did it for me. They thought it would be a fun birthday present." I raise my eyes heavenward.

"Ah, I see." He nods slowly. "Well, I'm glad you decided to give it a go, or we'd never have got the chance to meet." He knocks his water glass against mine. "In the absence of wine, a toast to our first date."

Wine. First date. Pathetic, I know, but I clutch at these as positive signs. Suddenly, I'm regretting my invented hair appointment and wondering if there's a plausible explanation for missing it without him thinking I'm desperately keen.

After ordering our food and some real wine from a waiter whose reluctant demeanor suggests we're interrupting his modeling career, we settle down to learn something about each other.

He tells me he's one of three privately educated brothers, from Tunbridge Wells in Kent, son of a former bank manager and stay-at-home mother.

"When Dad retired, my parents moved to Eastbourne. Apparently, it's the law." He smiles.

I, in turn, tell him about Olivia and my parents. "It's a funny thing, isn't it, getting old?" I say. "My mother still looks great, but she's started recording daytime TV programs, a sure sign that senility is setting in. And no matter where Dad sits, there's always a draft."

"Aren't you a daytime TV producer?" he says, referring to the tantalizing description I gave him in an e-mail. His expression suggests he's rather impressed.

"Sounds glamorous, doesn't it?" I laugh nervously. "It isn't really though. I work for *Good Morning Britain*, fixing up the facial scaffolding for the makeovers."

He purses his lips, accentuating how beautifully defined and kissable they are. "Don't do yourself down. I really like that show. Many a time I end up watching that instead of coming up with an eye-catching design or slogan for the blank sheet of paper in front of me."

"So what sort of designs do you do when you're not absorbed in our flower-arranging and cookery items?"

"I work in the print ad section of GFDS. I'm supposed to come up with groundbreaking newspaper and magazine ads for clients. But eventually, I want to get into making ads for TV and film."

"Ooh, I've heard of that agency. I'm sure we did an item last year on one of its ads; the one with the half-naked supermodel practically having an orgasm because she'd just tasted a new margarine. There were loads of complaints about it."

"Yep. That was mine." He grins. "I'll have you know the orgasm was crucial to the story line. Fortunately, in my line of business, attracting lots of complaints is treated as a huge accolade rather than a sacking offense. At least it gets the product talked about."

The food arrives and he tucks into his chili con carne with a side order of garlic bread. I pick at my salade niçoise, my appetite quelled somewhat by the far more temptingly delicious sight sitting across the table from me.

"Everything all right with the food?" It's the sullen waiter again, noting my full plate.

"Fine, thanks." I pop an olive into my mouth to illustrate my satisfaction. When he's walked off, I poke my tongue out at his retreating back.

Simon laughs. "You're funny." He holds one finger in front of him. "Funny." He holds up another. "Pretty." Then a third. "And successful. Which makes me wonder why you're having to go on dates like this. You must have men crawling all over you."

I feel myself blush, and hope it's an endearing pink flush rather than my usual blotchy puce.

"Hardly," I scoff. "I haven't dated anyone for over a year."

Worried that makes me sound like a desperate saddo, I add an afterthought. "Well, not seriously anyway."

He looks thoughtful and finishes chewing a piece of bread. "So, who was your last serious relationship?"

I curl my top lip. "Nathan. Otherwise known as Satan to my friends. He was my five-year mistake."

Simon's eyebrows shoot up. "That's a long time to waste on someone who's wrong for you."

"I know. But it wasn't always bad. It just became particularly unbearable towards the end."

I look up from my virtually untouched salad, but he doesn't seem to be listening. He's staring over my shoulder at the restaurant door, something he seems to have done every time it's opened.

He blinks a few times and turns his attention back to me. "Sorry, I *was* listening. I find sitting near doors very distracting, because although I don't mean to, I always look to see who's coming in."

"I know what you mean," I say reassuringly, although I don't really. With him in front of me, I have absolutely no desire to look anywhere else. "So what about you?"

"Huh?"

"When was your last serious relationship?"

He ponders the question for a moment, rolling the rim of his wineglass along his bottom lip. "Um, it ended about six months ago. We were together for three years."

"I'm sorry to hear that." I'm not sorry at all. In fact, I'm ecstatic. Borderline hysterical even.

"Oh, don't be. It had been in its death throes for some time, then she decided to go and work in Australia."

Could he be any more perfect? Gorgeous, funny, successful, easily capable of holding down a long-term relationship, *and* with an ex-girlfriend who lives on another continent twelve thousand miles away. Thank you, God.

He glances at his watch. "It's two-fifteen. Haven't you got a hair appointment?"

Bugger bugger bugger. Why the hell did I ever say that? Just as the conversation is becoming more intimate, I have to leave for an urgent appointment with my empty flat and afternoon made-for-TV movie.

"I could always cancel," I blurt.

He looks puzzled. "Really? Won't they charge you for not turning up?"

I can hear false, tinkling laughter. It's mine. "Oh no, Mario is really laid back about all that. I've been going to him for years." Mario, what a cliché. My hairdresser is actually called Colin.

"Well, if you think he won't mind . . ." He picks up the wine list. "You make the call and I'll order us another bottle."

My insides on full spin, I dial my home number and leave a message on my own answering machine. "Hi there. It's Jessica Monroe. I have an appointment with Mario at two-thirty, but can you can tell him I can't make it? You will? Oh, thank you so much. Bye!"

I've heard more convincing performances on *Crossroads*, but it doesn't seem to have aroused his suspicion.

"Wine's on its way." He smiles. "I must say, I'm enjoying our lunch very much."

"Me too." I lean towards him a little more. "You're my first cyber date, you know."

"Really? And how lucky you were to hit the jackpot first time." His expression is mischievous and he leans forward and plants a playful kiss on the end of my nose. "Hope you don't mind."

"Not at all." At the point of impact, it felt as though a million volts had shot through me. I'm keen, some might say desperate, for him to gravitate towards my mouth.

But the waiter arrives out of the blue with the wine and fills up both our glasses. I wait until he's out of earshot.

"How many dates have you been on?" I ask with as much non-chalance as I can muster.

"Let's see." He holds up his hands and starts flicking his fingers up and down until I can no longer keep count. "Your face!" he laughs. "Just two. You're my third."

Taking a rather large glug of wine for Dutch courage, I swallow hard. "Have you seen either of them again?" Say no. Please say no.

"No. They weren't really my type, to be honest."

My body may seem outwardly still, but my inner spirit is doing handsprings followed by a full stag leap around the restaurant. "So what's your *type* then?"

"You are, actually." He extends his chest across the table and kisses me full on the mouth. He lingers there, clearly waiting for a response, and I can't help myself. Pinch me, pinch me. We are gently smooching and I think I might actually pass out with sheer pleasure. I can't remember a Saturday afternoon as satisfying as this since a teenage Kara tripped up in the precinct whilst trying to impress some bloke with her new cork wedges.

Eventually, for the sake of decorum, I gently pull away. "Yum."

Yum? *Yum?* Jesus Christ, as witty, coquettish bon mots go, that's right up there with "glad," my least favorite word of all time. Memo to self: Must practice and learn Dorothy Parker–esque repartee.

He makes a circling motion on the back of my hand with his forefinger. "As you might have guessed, I'd like to see you again."

"Fine by me." I'm grinning with unadulterated delight, but I can't help myself. Having heard and read so many dating horror stories, I can't believe my luck.

The door behind me creaks open again, but this time he

doesn't tear his gaze away from mine. "Good. I'll e-mail you to fix a date. Shall we make it dinner next time?"

"Good idea." It's Richard and Lars's anniversary dinner tonight, but if Simon suggests this evening I might just mutate into the worst friend of all time and say yes. But he doesn't. "It's funny, you know," I say, looking down at the table and smiling to myself. "I was really dreading this lunch . . ."

I'm about to fess up to the mythical hair appointment, and glance up to make sure he's hanging on my every word. He isn't.

Lowering his eyelids and tucking his chin into his chest, he mumbles: "Excuse me, I have to go to the loo." Silently pushing his chair back, he scuttles to the rear of the restaurant and disappears through the door marked "Restrooms."

Maybe the chili con carne is working its magic, I think, tittering to myself at the thought. Taking another mouthful of wine, I turn in my chair to view the rest of the room. The diners who arrived when I did have mostly left, to be replaced by the next shift of Saturday afternoon shoppers who probably ate a late breakfast. One large group has clearly just arrived, as they noisily choose who sits where and remove coats.

I turn back and stare at the empty chair in front of me, deep in thought. Who would have guessed that Kara would be doing me such a favor when she placed that ad? Certainly, that wasn't her intention. I smirk with joy at the thought of her meeting the gorgeous man she has indirectly hooked me up with.

Five minutes pass and I wonder whether I should go in there and check if he's all right. But I talk myself out of it. After all, a stomach upset is undignified at the best of times, but on a first date, it must be horribly embarrassing. I'll wait a bit longer and pretend it's been no time at all when he finally emerges.

Ten minutes now. I look at my watch just to check, then glance over at the door to the loos, willing him to walk back through it. The last thing I want is for him to get the shits and have bad memories of our first date. Perhaps we'll laugh about it another time, when we've been together a month or so.

Twelve minutes. Now I really *should* go and see how he is. Otherwise, he might think me horribly uncaring. Throwing my handbag over my shoulder, I stand up and walk to the back of the room.

Through the door, three options face me: Private: Staff Only, Dames, and Guys. Standing outside the latter, I tap on it. "Simon, are you in there?"

No answer. A bit louder now. "Simon! It's me, Jess. Are you OK?"

No answer again. Suddenly, the door from the restaurant swings open and a middle-aged man in a suit walks through. He looks at me strangely.

"Sorry." I smile weakly. "But my friend went in here a while ago and hasn't come out. Would you mind checking if he's all right for me?"

His face relaxes slightly, now confident I'm not some mad stalker with a gents loo fetish. As if. The stench is making me want to throw up what little of my salade niçoise I actually ate.

"Of course. Hang on a minute." He disappears inside.

My ear pressed to the door, I can hear him knocking on cubicles and saying "Hello?"

A few seconds later, he opens the door again and I fall forwards, clutching his shoulder to break my fall. "Sorry," I gasp.

"There's no one in there." He looks at me strangely and I realize it's pity.

"My mistake," I gush. "We must have passed each other. He's probably back at the table." Mustering as much dignity as I can, I turn and walk back through to the restaurant. My eyes closed, I murmur a small prayer, then open them.

He's not there.

My Prince Charming has seemingly vanished into thin air, with not so much as a smelly dock shoe left behind. In his place, the facially challenged waiter is standing next to the table scowling at the two empty chairs.

There *has* to be some perfectly reasonable explanation. After all, we were getting on brilliantly and *he* was doing all the chasing.

I approach the table and plonk myself dejectedly into the chair. All pretense of dignity gone, I look at the waiter with an expression of puzzlement and disappointment. A swell of nausea rises from my stomach to the back of my throat and I feel close to tears. "Have you seen the man I was having lunch with?"

"Yes." He tears the bill from his pad and places it in front of me. "He went out through the kitchen a few minutes ago. He said you'd pay."

Five

He's married. Absolutely no doubt about it." Richard's mouth sets in a firm line, suggesting that now he has delivered his verdict, that's the end of the matter.

Doubtful, I purse my lips. "He didn't seem married."

"Darling, of *course* he didn't. He was pretending to be single because he wanted to have his cake and eat it. You know, get his leg over."

It's 8:30 p.m. and I'm at Richard and Lars's flat for a party to celebrate their first anniversary. They moved in together after just one month, both impetuous types.

There are about twenty people expected, but so far it's just them, me, Tab and her boyfriend Will, and Madeleine. They have all cornered me, chomping at the bit for news on my hot date, and I have told them everything—right down to the humiliation of being abandoned and saddled with the bill.

"He's not necessarily married," says Tab, placing a reassuring hand on my forearm. "There might be a simpler explanation."

"Like what?" scoffs Richard. "He's got X-piles?"

"Eh?" Tab looks bewildered.

"Unwanted visitors on Uranus, darling. Because that's the

only other reason there could possibly be for spending so long in the bog, then disappearing into thin air."

"No," perseveres Tab. "He might have received an emergency phone call whilst he was in the loo and had to rush off."

"Through the *kitchen*?" says Richard scathingly. "Tabs, sweetie, you're lovely to try, but there's no point sugaring the pill. Jess has been taken in by the oldest con man in the book. He's married and he wanted a little extra-cunnilingular activity."

I scowl at him for such coarseness, but inside I feel horribly nauseous and overwhelmingly depressed. I just want to go home, curl up in a ball under the duvet, and never come out. Instead, I have to stay here and celebrate someone else's happy, rewarding relationship. Hip hip hoo-bloody-rah.

"But if, as you say, he was only after one thing, why would he suddenly leave when he was so close to getting it?" I flush at the thought of the wine-induced kiss. I don't know why I'm still flogging this dead horse, but there's a strange masochistic comfort in talking about it.

Even Richard has to give thought to my question. "Hmmm," he says slowly. "Let's see. What happened between the snog and him disappearing?"

"Nothing." And I meant it.

He looks incredulous. "Think. There must have been *something*. What about elsewhere in the restaurant?"

"What do you mean?"

"Well, did anyone come in?"

I think for a moment, then shrug. "People were coming in and out all the time. I had my back to them."

"Ah, so *he* could see them?" Richard narrows his eyes and rubs his chin Columbo style. "How did he react to them?"

All eyes are glued on me and I feel like the main witness in a murder trial. I can't help myself.

"Now that you mention it . . ."

Almost imperceptibly, they all lean forward a few millimeters.

". . . he *was* in the library with the lead pipe."

It takes a couple of beats for my remark to sink in, at which point they all sigh collectively and sit back in their chairs.

"Ha fucking ha." Richard hates it when the joke's on him. "Well, if you want to be a spinster for the rest of your life, you go right ahead and laugh at our efforts to try and help you," he says huffily.

"Sorry." I look suitably sheepish, then put on my best expression of concentration. "He did get a bit distracted every time the door opened, but he mentioned it himself and he wouldn't have done that if he was trying to hide something. Would he?" I look imploringly at Tab and Madeleine and, in the true spirit of the girly code, they shake their heads reassuringly, even though they probably think it's total hogwash.

"A psychological double bluff," says Richard dismissively. "And did he get distracted by the door just before he legged it?"

"Not that I saw, no. A large group came in, but he didn't seem to notice them. We were rather engrossed in each other at that point." The nausea has returned.

"And absolutely nothing else unusual about his behavior?" Richard's clearly not convinced.

I jut out my bottom lip, deep in thought. "Only that it was a beautifully sunny day but he didn't want to sit outside."

Richard slaps both his hands on his knees in a gesture of triumph. "I rest my case, your honor."

"Sorry?" I'm scowling again.

"Well, how much proof do you need?" He pulls a "duh" expression on me. "He didn't want to sit outside because he was afraid he'd be seen with you. Now why could that be?"

He has a point. The more I thought about Simon's reluctance to eat al fresco, and the way he got so easily distracted by the door, the more it all backed up Richard's theory.

"He must have seen someone he knew among the big group of people that came in," I say morosely. "That's why he went out the back way."

My misery descends like a black cloud over the gathering, the silent gloom eventually punctuated by the doorbell.

"I'll go!" Lars leaps up a little too gratefully.

"There'll be plenty of other, more suitable dates," says Tab comfortingly. "I can see you meeting someone a little bit older and really successful . . . you know, a big gun."

"As long as he's not of small caliber and immense bore," says Richard.

I feel bad about being a manic depress-o-gram on their anniversary, but I can't help myself. I kissed my Prince Charming and he turned into a frog. Things couldn't be worse.

"Hello!" a familiar voice rings out.

Yes they could. Kara has just walked in, her beady eyes scanning our dejected faces.

"Are we contacting the dead?" She raises a quizzical eyebrow.

"Almost," says Tab. "We've just been hearing about Jess's first Internet date."

"Really?" The delight in Kara's voice is not dissimilar to that little slurping noise Hannibal Lecter makes at the thought of a gently poached human liver with a glass of Chianti. *"Do tell."*

Tab opens her mouth and starts to speak, but I do the verbal equivalent of wrestling her to the ground. "Nothing to tell really," I babble. "He was quite nice, but there was no spark. I won't be seeing him again."

Kara looks dubious, her narrowed eyes assessing everyone's reaction to my little statement. Tab is staring at the floor, Will looks impassive, Lars has flushed bright red, and Richard's tongue is so deliberately and firmly wedged in his cheek that he looks deformed.

"And the *real* story?" Kara fixes me with her best steely glare.

"He did a bunk before the end of the date, and we think it's because he was married," I mumble.

"God, what a bummer." It's Dan, Kara's boyfriend. I hadn't even noticed him enter the room. "Do you know where to find him? We'll send the boys round." He looks at Richard and Lars for support, then clearly thinks better of it. "Well, me and Will anyway."

My arms suddenly break out in goose bumps, despite it being a fairly warm evening. "Christ, maybe none of it was true . . ."

"None of what?" Madeleine tops up my wineglass in a show of sisterly support.

"His name, his background, his job . . . maybe it was all a huge, fat lie." I replay it all in my head, trying to assess the viability of everything he said.

The doorbell rings again and, this time, Richard drags himself away to answer it. Craning his neck to try to see who's at the door, Lars turns back and looks directly at me. "Did you not zay you heff been e-mailing each other?"

I nod silently.

"So e-mail him and ask him vy he dunked you in ze big end."

"You mean dropped me in at the deep end." I smile. "In fact, left me in the lurch would be even better. No, even *I* have too much self-respect to chase him for an explanation." I stand up. "Right! Enough of this depressing bollocks, let's party!"

I put on a good show of being the life and soul with the rest of Richard and Lars's friends who are now arriving at the party, but inside I'm dying. Not from embarrassment that my friends had to hear my tale of abandonment, but from genuine disappointment and, if I'm honest, a little bit of hurt.

My brief taste of the heady mixture of alcohol-fueled lust and a warm spring day has reminded me just how much I miss intimacy. I had been coping well with celibacy, but now I feel like my insides are on spin cycle. A little bit of what you fancy leaves you wanting more, but sadly "more" doesn't seem to be an option.

Locking myself in the downstairs bathroom for a brief respite from party chitchat, I lean my forehead against the cool wall tiles and wonder whether my next date will be as bittersweet. After all, I've promised to have two more.

There's a team of *Till Divorce Do Us Part* dancers jumping around inside my head as I attempt to lift my face from the pillow. It flops down again almost immediately.

Basically, I drank to forget. And drank. And drank. The party had eventually whittled down to the usual suspects, and we'd all sat round the kitchen table talking bollocks and teasing Lars about his new Garth Brooks album blaring out of the CD player.

It led to Richard demanding that everyone had to come up with a spoof title for a country and western song, and Tab had kicked off with "Get your tongue outta my mouth, cos I'm kissing you good-bye."

By the time it got to Richard, who came up with "Her teeth were stained, but her heart was pure," I was in danger of wetting myself and had to sprint to the loo. The next thing I remember was Richard shaking me awake in the spare room, where I lay after apparently crashing there an hour earlier.

He said he fully intended on leaving me there until morning, but trouble was, my gaping mouth was pressed against Kara's pink suede jacket. Worse, as Richard gleefully pointed out to me, I had drooled all over it and left a stain that, rather prophetically, resembled an angry woman with her fist in the air.

Once stirred from my slumbering stupor, I became obsessed with getting home to my own bed so I could tuck up in my fleece jammies and lie in to my heart's content the following morning.

Except my hangover clearly has other ideas, and I can't fall back to sleep because of a persistent thumping between my eyes. The phone rings, the usually faint tone sounding like Big Ben going off next to my head.

"Hello?" My voice cracks with inactivity.

"Hi pumpkin. You all right?" It's Olivia. "I was just checking you haven't forgotten lunch."

I have. "Lunch?" I rub my right eye, trying to soothe the dull throbbing.

"Jess! I knew you'd forget. Don't you *dare* try and wriggle out of it."

My hand automatically slaps against my forehead, not a good idea in my current state. "Oh God, the parentals." It's our collective pet name for Mum and Dad.

"You got it. One o'clock sharp. You know how Mum hates us to be late."

I groan with a ferocity to rival a wounded warthog. "I've got such a terrible hangover I can barely form a sentence. I'll just hang out in the den with Matthew and Emily."

"No you won't." Olivia's tone is faintly apologetic. "They're not coming. Emily has a tummy bug, so Michael's gratefully staying at home with both of them. It's just you and me, I'm afraid."

Four cups of black coffee and several cold water face sluices later, and I'm on my way to Surrey, wearing the same outfit from the night before. Decision making isn't my strong point at the moment, but at least the outfit's fairly smart. You see, there's no just pitching up for Sunday lunch in comfy jeans and a sweater. Not with my mother anyway.

As children, Olivia and I were always dressed immaculately with matching frocks, highly polished patent shoes, and frilly socks. Think Minnie Mouse on acid.

Our mother was very slim and trendy, the Jackie O of Surbiton. She stood out a mile amongst the suburban crowd, quietly setting her own personal standards, oblivious to the astonished stares of those around her. "Never forget, girls," she used to intone loudly. "Life belongs to the pretty."

Consequently, at school dances, when the rest of the year was wearing the latest tight top with Hunny Monster shoulder pads and polka dot crop trousers, Olivia and I stood sullen-faced in midcalf floral dresses, our hair relentlessly brushed into a silky ponytail.

Olivia was the first to rebel, though she wasn't brave enough to let Mum in on the secret. With a hidden-under-bed stash of clothes bought from thrift stores, she would leave the house looking like Pollyanna, retrieve a carrier bag from a hedge down the road, and arrive at the disco looking like punk queen Polystyrene.

It took me another three years to pluck up courage to do the same, but neither of us ever had a hair out of place in mother's eye line. Consequently, one of our shared greatest joys in life is to slob around the house in sweats, hair unbrushed and wearing no makeup.

But I know when I show up at the parentals, Olivia will also be wearing something smart. At thirty-four and thirty-six, old habits die hard and we're still indoctrinated to be on parade.

"Darling! How very . . . black," my mother falters, scanning my outfit up and down. She leans forward and sniffs my shoulder. "Do I smell smoke?"

A dilemma. Do I let her think, incorrectly, that I have puffed my way through twenty fags on the journey down? Or do I tell her the truth, that her daughter is such a slovenly disgrace that she's still wearing last night's clothes?

As she's Chief Constable of the fashion police, it's difficult to gauge which scenario will prompt the greater disapproval.

"I wore it last night to Richard's party and ended up staying there. So it was this or his Carmen Miranda Mardi Gras outfit." The sleepover lie is inspired, I think.

But mother seems unimpressed. "Jess, you simply *cannot* sit through lunch in yesterday's clothes."

I open my mouth to protest that I had only worn them for a couple of hours the night before, but she doesn't let me speak.

"No buts. Go upstairs to the little wardrobe in the spare room. There's a clean outfit there I keep for such emergencies."

World famine, motorway pileups, droughts, monsoons—all bona fide "emergencies." In Mum's world, add faintly unkempt daughters to the list.

By the time Olivia arrives twenty minutes later, I'm sitting at the lunch table in a pale pink twinset with tiny, embroidered flowers around the neckline and a beige, A-line skirt. The "emergency" shoes were too small, so I'm still wearing my black stilettos with strict instructions from Mother to keep them firmly wedged under the table.

"Ah, the emergency outfit," smiles Olivia, once Mum is out of earshot. "What have you done to deserve that?"

"I turned up in last night's clothes." I sniff sullenly.

"Good one. I had to wear it once when Matthew spilled orange juice down my front just before Mum's lunch guests arrived."

She sits down opposite me. "So, the sleepover. Anyone nice?"

I raise my eyes heavenward. "I wish. I was at Richard and Lars's for their first anniversary party." I lower my voice even more. "I didn't actually stay. I just fell back into the same clothes this morning and they smelled of smoke . . . so, bingo!" I tug the twinset.

Mum arrives back in the room, clutching a steaming tureen of vegetables. "Where *is* your father? I sent him for some fresh strawberries about an hour ago."

On cue, Dad's highly polished old blue Bentley purrs past the window, the tires crunching on the gravel drive. It was a sound that evoked memories of my childhood, waiting for him to return home from work and feeling butterflies of excitement when he arrived.

Olivia and I walk to the door to greet him.

"My darling girls!" he exclaims, enveloping us both in a double hug. "How delightful to see you." He proffers two punnets of strawberries at Mum as she breezes past.

My father, Alan, is a tiny bit bonkers, but we love him dearly. By day, he's chairman of GBHome, one of those giant furniture companies that always has a sale on. He started at the bottom, put his motto "Don't work in a shop unless you like smiling" to good use, and worked his way up.

By night and weekends, he's an inventor. Not a very successful one, I might add, but it made for a fun childhood throughout which we tested various inventions of varying success. My favorite was a pair of slippers with mops as soles, perfect for doubling up as floor cleaners.

The highlight of my father's life had been when his car-drink-holder-cum-ashtray was accepted and featured in the Innovations catalogue. It sold only a couple of dozen, but Dad didn't care. In his mind, he'd won the jackpot.

"Remind me to show you my latest invention after lunch," he says, and Olivia and I share a secret, fond smile.

"Oooh, what is it?" I enthuse.

He goes pink with pleasure. "You'll have to wait and see."

Mum reemerges from the kitchen with a vast joint of lamb and places it in front of Dad. "There we are, Alan. Carve away." She plants a little kiss on the top of his head.

Placing an arm around the curve of her back, he pulls her towards him and gives a little squeeze. "Well done, dear. I'm sure it'll be delicious as always."

Watching them, I feel a warm swell of nostalgia for the family lunch we religiously share every Sunday, come rain or shine. It is a house rule that no one is to make any plans that would jeopardize the sacrosanct gathering, the glue of our family life. Around this table, we catch up properly on each other's week, who is doing what, who is up, who is down and, most importantly of all, who needs a bit of family TLC.

"So." Dad starts carving. "First things first. How are my gorgeous grandchildren?"

Olivia smiles. "Emily's got a tummy bug, but apart from that, they're both fine."

Dad turns his head towards me and raises his eyebrows questioningly.

I shrug. "Sorry, no grandchildren to report on. But little old me is just fine, thanks."

Mum spoons carrots onto my plate and looks at me pensively. I know what's coming.

"Any man on the horizon?" she asks casually, belying what I know is the razor-sharp intention beneath.

"Nope." I pop a new potato into my mouth with the sole purpose of disabling my jaw for further comment. I wasn't accounting for Olivia.

"But things might pick up soon, eh?" she says, giving me an encouraging smile.

Mum's eyes shoot up from her plate. "Oh?"

The potato is hotter than I thought, and I'm throwing it around my mouth, trying to make a "shut up" noise at the same time. To no avail.

"Yes," Olivia plows on. "She's joined an Internet dating service."

A deathly silence descends, as if she's just announced I'm now transsexual and changing my name to Josh.

After a few seconds, Mum glares at me direct. "Is that true?"

A large lump of gristly lamb has wedged in my throat and I swill it down with water, rapidly gathering my thoughts at the same time.

"Not strictly. Kara put an ad on the Internet without my knowledge. For my birthday . . ." I add as an afterthought.

"I see." Mum visibly relaxes a little. "So I presume you just had it removed," she says, as if my potential love life is simply a troublesome carbuncle.

At this point, I could simply lie and say yes, and that, blessedly, would be the end of the matter. But I find myself feeling faintly annoyed at her blatant disapproval.

"No. Everyone persuaded me I should at least go on a couple of dates to try it out. Including *Olivia*," I say pointedly.

"Olivia!" admonishes Mum. "Fancy encouraging your sister to resort to something so desperate."

An apologetic-looking Olivia opens her mouth to reply, but I power in first, propelled by sheer indignation.

"It's not desperate!" I say firmly. "It's entirely normal in this day and age."

Mum looks doubtful. It's clear she views the whole idea of women advertising for men immensely distasteful.

"But darling . . ." Her tone is conciliatory. "Surely the men on there are just pitiful creatures that no one else wants? The kind who live lonely lives, who could die in their little bedsits and not be found until they were eaten by maggots and a neighbor noticed the smell." She has always been one to overdramatize.

We are all momentarily stunned by this gory analogy, simply looking on silently, our noses faintly wrinkled at the thought. Dad pushes the remainder of his food to one side of the plate.

"I mean, Jess, sweetie, they could even be ax murderers," she plows on.

Enough already. I feel my back stiffen with annoyance. "Am *I* pitiful?" I demand.

"No, of course not," she replies in syrupy tones. Dad shakes his head reassuringly in support.

"Am *I* unwanted?"

"Of course not." She's tutting now for extra effect.

"An ax murderer then?" I scowl.

"Now you're just being silly."

"Well, *I'm* advertising on the Web site, so it figures there will be some nice, normal men as well."

Mum looks doubtful but says nothing, clearly knowing better than to interrupt such an impassioned protest.

"People go on the Internet because they're just too busy to socialize much," I continue. "Not because they're desperate saddos."

I stop speaking and look around the table for some moral support, but all I see are pitying expressions.

"I read an article the other day that said twenty thousand people *per month* are joining Internet dating sites. They can't all be psychos. In fact, I met a really great man on my first date." As soon as the words leave my mouth, I could kick myself.

"Really?" I can virtually see the bit clamped between my mother's teeth. "Jessie, that's wonderful news. Tell us more."

Even Olivia leans forward with an eager expression and I remember she knows absolutely nothing about this.

I shrug, biding time for a hasty backtrack. "Nothing much to tell really. He was very nice and we had a lovely time, but there wasn't a spark there so I doubt we'll be seeing each other again."

"Oh." Mum pushes out her bottom lip in disappointment. "That seems a bit of a hasty conclusion. After all, the spark might come later."

"She's right, you know." Olivia looks at me imploringly. "Michael and I didn't hit it off immediately. It took a good couple of dates before we really clicked."

I turn my shoulders slightly, so my face is obscured from the parentals, and pull a pained expression, silently urging her to shut up. She complies immediately, her mouth clamped in a firm line.

Dad rarely gets involved in our girly ding-dongs, usually preferring to sink behind a newspaper and let us all get on with it. But I can see his brow furrowing in anticipation of what he's about to say.

"Do be careful though, Jess." His face is deadly serious. "I know Mum exaggerates, but it's true that people can pretend to be anything they like behind the anonymity of a computer screen."

Yes, they can pretend to be single whilst they're probably married, I think forlornly. A depression descends again.

"Point taken, Dad. I'll be very careful, I promise. I'll meet them only in public places and they'll have no idea where I live." I smile reassuringly and stand up to start gathering the plates, hoping it will move the conversation on.

When I return from the kitchen, they all stop talking and look guilty. Clearly my unconventional social life is troubling them, but I'm not about to reopen the subject for yet more debate.

"So, Dad," I say breezily, "what's this invention you're so keen to show us?"

An hour later, after dutifully enthusing over Dad's swivel car DVD holder, Olivia and I pull out of the driveway in convoy, waving at the parentals standing cozily in their doorway.

I have barely reached the main road when my mobile trills its distinctive "Dancing Queen" ring tone. The caller ID says "BigSis."

"How can I miss you when you won't go away?" I quip.

"Very funny. I want to know all about that sparkless date. What really happened?"

"Is it that obvious?"

"Yep."

"He *was* great and lovely. But I left out the bit about him doing a disappearing act through the kitchen."

"You're kidding!"

"Sadly not."

"Why did he leave?"

"Richard thinks it's because he's married and saw someone he knew."

"No! The *bastard*."

"Precisely." I stop at some traffic lights and glance to my right to see a picture-perfect family sitting alongside me in a Mercedes estate car. There's a boy of about four or five who looks like Little Lord Fauntleroy and an angelic baby girl straight from a Pampers ad. The parents are sharing an animated conversation, both laughing heartily.

I let out a long sigh. "Still, two more dates to go. One of those might look like Brad Pitt—though knowing my luck it'll be his long lost brother Cess."

Olivia laughs, then her voice turns serious. "Maybe these

dates aren't such a good idea after all. As Dad says, they can pretend to be one thing whilst being someone completely different."

"They can do that in wine bars too," I reply. "Besides, too late now. I'm leaping straight back onto the horse after my nasty fall. I've got another date lined up for tomorrow night."

Six

Hello, I'm Larry, and I graduated with a degree in electronic engineering from Cambridge. I often work late into the night trying to unravel the mysteries of microprocessors, but I'm seeking a lovely lady to persuade me there are better ways to spend one's evenings.

Bruised by my experience over lunch with "Simon," or whoever he may be, this time I'm playing it safe and opting for just a coffee by way of introduction. That way, I can make a quick assessment of his suitability without wasting another few hours of my life.

We have arranged to meet outside Niketown on Oxford Circus, chosen by me as somewhere highly public and therefore anonymous.

But I soon realize it's a mistake as the crowds pour through the entrance area, some to shop, others taking a shortcut from the tube exit to bustling Oxford Street. My head swivels from left to right like a Wimbledon spectator, not very subtly trying to spot Larry before he sees me.

My eyes rest on a disheveled white man with short dreadlocks and a scruffy anorak, looking furtively down the street. Please God, no. He suddenly looks across at me and I rapidly glance away, wondering whether to make a run for it.

After several seconds of inaction, I sneak a look at him again and am overwhelmed with relief to see his attention has turned to his frayed shoulder bag. His hand reaches inside and he pulls out a rolled-up stack of fliers. Panic over.

A hand taps my shoulder. Panic back.

I turn round to find what I presume is Larry smiling anxiously at me. I say I presume because, although the hair is the same sandy color as in the photo he e-mailed me, the rest of his features don't ring any bells at all.

"Hi." His voice is cracked and squeaky, like a twelve-year-old boy on the change. Perhaps it's nerves, I think benevolently.

"Hi." I smile. It's a false one, but he probably doesn't know that. "I presume you're Larry?"

"You presume right. Are you Jess? It's just that you don't look anything like your photo."

I gasp audibly. "Excuse me? My photo is one hundred percent genuine, if a little out of focus. Which is more than I can say for yours."

He looks slightly taken aback. "It's definitely me. I was on holiday in Greece at the time, so I was quite brown. Maybe that's what threw you."

Yes, particularly as I'm now looking straight into the face of Casper the Unfriendly Ghost. Since the photo was taken, I doubt this man has even seen daylight, never mind sunlight. His features are so woolly he looks like someone's knitted him.

"So let's get that coffee then," I say, inwardly thanking my lucky stars I hadn't suggested lunch. I have decided on sight that I don't find him physically attractive, and I doubt his personality is going to change my opinion.

I gesture for him to walk with me down to the north end of Regent Street, and as he steps forward he shrinks by three inches before my eyes. I look down to see he's been standing on a step.

Pasty-faced, cheese-paringly critical, *and* a bloody dwarf. Great. I mentally decide to make the coffee an espresso.

Two blocks down, we find a small, independently run coffee shop with a lavish display of gooey cakes in the window, tempting save for the couple of overexcited bluebottles buzzing around them.

I sit down at a table by the open front window, pleased to have a view of passersby to dilute any tedious conversation.

"Isn't that a bit close to the traffic fumes?" he says with an expression of distaste. I don't answer and he lowers himself into the seat opposite me like a man being strapped into the electric chair.

"Now then, what type of coffee would you like?" I pick up the menu and scan the options.

He shakes his head. "None thanks. I don't drink coffee or tea because of the caffeine, and I don't drink alcohol either. I'll probably just have a glass of still water." And there it was. The seemingly innocuous little statement that sealed his doom. Apologies to all teetotalers, but I could never spend the rest of my life with a man who doesn't drink. I would feel as though I were permanently being frowned upon every time I got a bit tipsy, and to me, so many relationship truths are eased out by the lubrication of alcohol. When wine goes in, secrets come out.

Hey ho, now all I have to do is get through the next half an hour with laughing boy.

As he peruses the menu, I take the chance to study him properly. The bronzed, smiling man who beamed out from my computer screen couldn't be further from the squat, pasty-faced creature with a sweaty top lip and mid-length, greasy hair. I doubt he ever cuts it, just gives it an oil change occasionally.

On the plus side, he has kind eyes, but unlike my Nana, who married Granddad "because he had all his own teeth," methinks a little more is needed to sustain a modern relationship.

A smiling waitress approaches our table, notepad in hand. "What can I get you?"

"A glass of still water and an espresso, thanks," I say, silently willing her to bring them quickly and release me from this purgatory.

"Is that all?"

I nod, and she starts to walk away.

"Hang on," says Larry. "I want something to eat."

I contemplate writing "Help me, I'm a prisoner" on a piece of paper and smuggling it into the waitress's hand, such is my desperation. But she's looking at him intently, waiting for his order.

"Are the vegetables in batter cooked in vegetable oil?" he asks. "If so, I'll have those."

The waitress nods and leaves.

"Don't tell me," I say, closing one eye and pointing at him. "Vegetarian, right?"

"Yes. I try to follow a macrobiotic diet too, but it's not easy when you eat out."

I nod, feigning interest in his dreary eating habits whilst mentally logging that he backs up my theory that most vegetarians look like they've crawled out from under a stone. I glance down at his sneakers and note that they're plastic: He's *that* fanatical about it. I suspect he wouldn't even wear a donkey jacket on the grounds it involves an animal in the title.

"So what do you do?" There it is again. The abandon-all-hope-ye-who-enter-here question.

"I'm an engineer." He sniffs self-importantly.

"What, like a mechanic sort of thing?"

He smirks slightly at what he clearly perceives to be my misguided ignorance. "I don't think so. No, I work for British Aerospace, designing engines."

"Oh." I can't think of anything I know less about. "Do you enjoy it?"

"S'alright." He shrugs, then shifts in his chair, seeming to tire of the subject.

I mentally prepare a quick sentence to make my job sound varied and exciting when he asks. But he doesn't.

"Oh my God!" He's staring at the floor with an expression of abject horror.

"What?" I look and feel alarmed, worried that a giant snake has just slithered under my chair. But Larry is staring into my handbag.

"You smoke!" he says accusingly.

Rather thrown by his outburst, I recoil slightly in my seat. "Um, only very occasionally. That pack is a couple of weeks old now."

He looks at me as if I have just admitted to part-time membership in the Ku Klux Klan. "You didn't say that in your ad."

I shrug. "I didn't know it was relevant."

A slight sneer plays on his increasingly moist top lip. "Of *course* it's relevant, especially to someone like me. I could never have a relationship with someone who smokes."

The temptation to stuff all fifteen or so fags in my mouth at once and light them almost overwhelms me. All I can think about is escaping from this dullard.

Feeling and probably looking much like a battered vegetable

myself, I breathe an audible sigh of relief when his food homes into view. The end is nigh. Time for a change of subject.

"So what films have you been to see recently?" I ask cheerily. "I went to see the new Spielberg movie the other night . . . it was terrific."

He waves his hand dismissively, a piece of battered broccoli falling onto the table. "Commercial nonsense. I don't see any point in going to the cinema unless you're going to be educated by it."

Someone remove the butter knife before I throw myself on it. I'm about to reply that sometimes it's nice to just chill out and have fun in life, when he speaks again, his mouth full of unchewed florets.

"I still can't believe you smoke." He shakes his head to illustrate the fact. "Do you know that every time you light a cigarette you are taking several hours off your life? And quite apart from that, your smoke when passively inhaled by others is the cause of several deaths a year."

I know I shouldn't expend energy on rising to the bait. I know I should just agree with everything he says, promise to stop smoking and get this dirge-filled date the hell over with. But I can't.

"My great-grandmother smoked forty fags a day, ate copious amounts of dairy, drank a tumbler of whisky every night before bed, and lived until she was ninety-seven." I look at him defiantly.

He makes a pooh-poohing face. "A fluke. She was lucky, but just think of all those poor people she killed with her secondhand cigarette smoke."

"Bollocks." OK, so I'm not Jeremy Paxman when it comes to debating, but it's heartfelt. "I read a report the other day that said the so-called dangers of passive smoking have been blown out of all proportion."

"Saw it," he says flatly. "The report was commissioned by a collective from the tobacco industry, rendering it totally invalid."

He flicks at a small piece of unidentifiable vegetable lodged in the corner of his mouth, making me feel quite queasy.

"And all the reports saying it's killing innocent bystanders are probably commissioned by people like you, with an agenda to tell the rest of us how to live our lives," I reply indignantly.

He holds his hands in the air. "Hey, if you want to kill yourself by smoking, go right ahead. Just don't kill me in the process."

Don't tempt me, I think mutinously, fantasizing about force-feeding him the steaming, bloodied steak just being served up at the next table. What was a minor irritation on my part has now mushroomed into fist-clenching frustration at this man's infuriating sanctimony.

He's what my father would describe as a wishy-washy liberal but, like so many of them, is anything but. Rather than fight for everyone to have a choice—surely the essence of being "liberal"?—they strut around the place telling the rest of us what we should and shouldn't do with our lives.

He'll be telling me about the repression of black people next, how they're treated like second-class citizens by an "institutionally racist" society. But he won't get the irony of a white, privately educated, middle-class boy preaching to others about the lot of the poor, underprivileged blacks, as if they are somehow too downtrodden or inarticulate to speak for themselves.

To my mind, his pompous assumption that the black community would even want, let alone need, someone like him to speak up for them is racist in itself.

I'm really annoyed now, so I resort to trying to pick a cheap but satisfying argument. "So how old is the photo you posted on the Internet?"

He looks momentarily thrown. "It was taken about ten years ago."

"That explains why it looks nothing like you. Why don't you use a more recent one?"

Shrugging, he takes a tiny sip of water. "That was all I had. It was taken by my ex-girlfriend in the early stages of our relationship and she left it behind when we split up. I don't take photos myself. Don't see the point."

I raise my eyebrows in genuine surprise. "Oh, I *love* looking through old photos and remembering various happy times throughout my life."

He nods sagely, as if my statement has simply confirmed his worst fears. "A lot of people feel that way. They feel there's something missing in their lives, and memories are the glue that holds them together."

That's it. Now even *photographs* can't be pleasurable, and I can't bear this pompous bore a moment longer. I raise my hand in the direction of the waitress. "Can we have the bill, please?"

When it arrives, he picks it up first and I inwardly marvel that, at long last, he has a redeeming feature: generosity.

Pulling out what resembles a child's denim purse from his jeans pocket, he lays the bill in front of him on the table. "I'll pay for my vegetables, you get the drinks. I only had a water."

My face visibly drops. When he starts counting out coppers onto the table, it caves in completely.

"Oh, for fuck's sake. I'll get it." I grab the bill and march to the back of the café, desperate to hasten my exit from this godforsaken situation.

When I return, he's still sitting with the handful of coppers in front of him. "Thanks," he says sullenly. "But it was totally unnecessary to swear."

"Wankety wank, wank, wank, WANK!!!" I bellow, before flouncing out onto the street and breaking into a liberated sprint towards the tube station.

Seven

"Two dates so far, and I've paid the bill both times. I must have 'sucker' tattooed on my forehead. Have I?" I jab my finger into the crease above my nose.

"No," laughs Tab, "you haven't. You've just been unlucky, that's all. Maybe you've had all your bad dating karma in one go and the next date will be someone like Sean Penn," she says, choosing my unfathomable crush as a crumb of comfort.

"Or Pig Penn," I mumble through a mouthful of croissant.

We are in the *Good Morning Britain* canteen, home to various "breakfast rolls" with unidentifiable fried objects in them, pastries that could break the teeth of Jaws from the Bond films, and the salmonella poisoning of a game show contestant that was hushed up and miraculously kept out of the gossip columns.

Tab pulls a hair out of her bacon roll, stares wordlessly at it, then places it at the side of her plate and carries on munching. It's so commonplace that neither of us consider it worthy of comment.

I knock back a swig of black coffee. "Aaaaah! Let's hope the caffeine kicks in pronto. God knows I need it this morning."

smiles at Tab, and minces back towards the exit in his bright pink trainers.

"Gosh." Tab looks taken aback. "Is he always that high maintenance?" In her department of cookery and gardening items, the worst she has to deal with is the wandering hands of an overly lecherous expert on herbaceous borders who comes in from time to time.

I nod. "Most of the time. But there's never a dull moment, and I much prefer that to having to while away the hours with nondescripts."

"Maybe." She shrugs, staring into the middle distance.

"You OK?" Amid the Kevin whirlwind of the past few minutes, I noticed Tab had seemed a little distracted.

"Not really." She shuffles uncomfortably in her seat. "I got my period this morning."

I look at her blankly for a couple of beats, knowing her desperation for a child, but wondering why the arrival of this period should be any more devastating than any of the others.

She registers my incomprehension. "Which means the IVF has failed."

I instinctively clasp my hand over my mouth, horrified by my own thoughtlessness. "Tab, I'm so sorry." I feel a total, self-obsessed heel. "You poor thing. What awful, terrible luck."

It was Tab and Will's first attempt at IVF, and even before knowing the outcome, they had been to hell and back, enduring the effects of her hormone injections and the uncomfortable egg-harvesting procedure. Not to mention the $5,000 cost they could ill afford.

"Don't they say that the second attempt is usually the most successful?" I say, dredging back through my memory to some IVF slot we'd run on the show months earlier.

"I don't know." Her voice is small and there are tears in her eyes. "But I do know it'll be a while before we're able to afford it."

We lapse into silence for a few seconds, then I clear my throat. "I wish I could lend you the money, but I'm broke," I say, rather pointlessly.

She smiles weakly. "Thanks, but don't worry. Will's parents have already offered, but we want to pay for it ourselves rather than build up huge debts."

Silence again. Then she leans forward, an urgent look on her face.

"Jess, what if I can *never* have children? What will I do?"

I'm rather floored by the question, so opt for the get-out clause. "It won't come to that." I shake my head. "No way. You'll have children, I can feel it in my bones."

"Do you really think so?" She visibly cheers up at my psychic nonsense, and it suddenly strikes me how quacks and cowboys easily make so much money exploiting desperate people at such a vulnerable time of their lives. Want to get pregnant, ma'am? Just pay us several hundred dollars for this course of "miraculous" powders and potions. Women in Outer Mongolia swear by them and they're having babies all the time.

The irony is that, over the years, Tab and I have had endless discussions about contraception, worrying about the threat of unwanted pregnancy. Once, several years ago and with a previous boyfriend, Tab even thought she *was* pregnant. It turned out to be a false alarm, but not before she'd spent a week agonizing about it. Now, here she was, desperate to conceive and nothing was happening.

"When did you get your period?"

"Here, this morning." She looks pale with disappointment. "Just after the morning meeting."

"Have you told Will?"

She shakes her head. "Not yet. He's in a meeting himself until ten. I'll wait until later. He'll be so disappointed." A tear falls silently down her cheek and plops into her tea.

I lean across the table and squeeze her forearm. "Don't cry, sweetie. Everything will be fine, you'll see."

She brushes the moisture from her cheek. "If it turns out that I can't have children . . ." Her eyes are huge and inquiring. ". . . do you think Will would leave me?"

I scoff loudly. "Don't be ridiculous, of course not. He adores you."

"I know, I know." She nods. "But if I can't give him what he so desperately wants . . ."

"Tab." My stern tone surprises even me. "Stop being so negative, that won't help your mind-set at all. You've had bad luck with the first try, and even then there are a million other options after that, including egg donors or even adoption. Believe me, you *will* be a mother, so start thinking positively."

"You're right." She looks sheepish. "There are so many other people worse off than me. I should stop being so self-obsessed."

I didn't actually mean it like that, but as she's looking a bit happier, I decide to leave things the way they are.

When I first met Tab through a friend of a friend, we were both keen to break into television in some behind-the-scenes capacity. We had a lot in common in other ways too, so when my particularly loathsome South African flatmate buggered off back home—leaving me with a $600 phone bill to clear—Tab moved seamlessly into the empty room.

By day, we wrote endless amounts of application letters to TV companies, by night we either stayed in watching and eating crap, or went to the local wine bar in search of any Mr. Will-do-for-nows.

Eventually, Tab landed herself a research job with Granada

Television, working on the daytime talk show *What's Your Problem?*
It was a fantastic opportunity, with one drawback—it was based
in Norwich. That was the end of "the Dangerous Sisters," as my
father affectionately referred to us, and I was looking for a new
flatmate.

Naturally, we stayed in regular touch, more so when I landed a
research job on a local news program and we'd exchanged letters
packed with industry gossip. Four years later, Tab transferred
back to London when the all-powerful host of *What's Your Problem?*
was unearthed as having a raging affair with a Granada executive
and moved the show to London to be closer to her.

By that time, I had scraped together enough money to buy a
one-bedroom, top-floor flat in Tooting, so she crashed on my
floor for about three months, then rented a place of her own.

We resumed our wine bar crusades, but this time Tab had a
different agenda. She didn't quite hand any potential suitors a
questionnaire, but she may as well have done. During every first
date, she would throw in the question "Do you want to have children?"

Sure, she'd try to make it sound as casual and spontaneous as
possible, but of course the men would balk instantly, most visibly
paling, some even spluttering their drink.

In their minds, she had suddenly transformed from this
amiable girl they'd met in a wine bar into a wild-eyed bunny
boiler who would have them choosing kitchen units before they
could say "commitment-phobe." Needless to say, they'd never
call again.

"Maybe you should refrain from asking about children until
you've been on a few dates . . ." I suggested during a lunch we
shared the day after one date had made his excuses and left less
than ten minutes after the big procreation question.

Tab wrinkled her nose in disapproval. "I don't see why I

should waste even a few hours of my time on someone who doesn't have the same objectives in life that I do," she said firmly. "If he's not man enough to deal with such an obvious, sensible inquiry, and see it for what it is, then I'm not interested."

And then along came Will. True to form, she asked him the killer question on their first date, and he answered: "Oh yes, I want children more than anything else in the world."

And, pow, that was it. Within weeks, Tab was telling anyone who'd listen that he was "the one."

My view of Will now is exactly the same as when I first met him. He's an affable, rugby-player type whose social uniform is a Hackett shirt with the collar turned up, faded cords, and battered deck shoes—as befits him and all the other real estate agents based in Fulham.

Despite an expensive public school education, he isn't terribly bright, and I've always felt he wasn't interesting enough to be with Tab. But I've never doubted his unswerving loyalty to her and she, in turn, seems happy with him. So who the hell am I to question their relationship?

The canteen has suddenly emptied and I look up at the clock. It's 10 a.m.

"Shit!" I jump to my feet. "We're on air in an hour and I've got Gollum waiting to be transformed upstairs. I'd better go check on the progress."

Tab stays where she is. "I'm just going to sit here for a few more minutes," she says quietly. "My prerecorded item is finished anyway."

I walk across the canteen to the exit, and just before I reach the double doors, I turn back to look at her. She's staring at the table-top, deep in thought and, presumably, lost in her problems again.

What with everything she's going through, my infrequent pangs of loneliness pale into insignificance. So I wasted a few hours with a pair of ne'er-do-wells and ended up paying the bill . . . so what?

Galvanized by this, I decide to give Madeleine a call and see if she fancies a spot of old-fashioned wine-bar trawling tonight. It can be a scientific experiment into old dating tactics versus the new.

Eight

I have absolutely no idea how I got myself into this. OK, I do. Basically, I allowed Madeleine to bully me into it during one of our long, late phone chats last night, during which I filled her in on Larry—he of the macraméd vests and wicker shoes, a man who lights up a room when he leaves it.

"He probably just needs a damn good shag," was her verdict. And she's probably right, but I'm not the woman who's going to offer it. I don't date outside my species.

Anyway, the upshot of our conversation was that Madeleine thinks the way I'm meeting potential dates is far too time-consuming. Given that I have now wasted well over four hours on two men who were both totally unsuitable, she has a point.

So here I am walking into a vast bar on the Kings Road, desperately scouring the crowd for Madeleine before we venture to the private function rooms downstairs for . . . wait for it . . . a speed-dating event.

Yes, we really *have* stooped that low. I could tell you that it's vital research for an item on the show, or pretend that's it just a laugh between friends, one more hilarious anecdote in the rich comedic tapestry of life. But I'd be lying. Transparently and pathetically.

I am here because, lurking among the battery hen lines of men, I valiantly hope that someone will leap out at me. Not literally of course, but in a sparky, good chemistry kind of way.

On a more basic level, Madeleine's here because she wants someone to have regular, no-strings-attached sex with. The same Madeleine, I might add, who has so far steadfastly failed to go on the Internet dates she promised she would as part of our deal.

"Here I am!" She's waving at me from a high stool positioned at one end of the bar. She's flanked on either side by two men in suits.

"This is my friend Jess," she says as I approach. "Jess, this is Paul . . ." She curves her hand one way towards the smaller of the two men, then curls it back in the direction of the taller one . . . "and this is Dave. They're something big in the City."

"Really?" I keep my voice as flat as possible, having already made the swift decision that neither of Little and Large is my cup of tea.

"Yes. They think we should give the speed dating a miss and stay up here with them." She lets out the tinkling laugh I've heard so often when Madeleine has been on the prowl in the past.

"Really," I say again.

"Do you say anything except 'really'?" says the taller one, giving his friend a smug smile.

"Rarely."

"That's posh speak for really," says Madeleine. There's that tinkling laugh again.

"Are we going?" I deliberately turn my back on our social carbuncles and jerk my head towards the staircase in the far corner.

Madeleine has known me long enough to recognize a certain

look in my eye that says I've reached the end of my tether and won't be persuaded otherwise.

"OK, OK." She hops off the stool and smoothes down her corduroy miniskirt. "Sorry guys, gotta go." She follows me across the bar towards the stairs. "Did you have to be *quite* so rude?"

"Sorry Mads, but I'm not as good at all that small talk as you and they looked a right pair of shifty sods. Besides, I'm rather nervous about this." I nod towards a sign at the top of the stairs that reads "Private: Extreme Speed-dating Event."

"Fear not." She links her arm through mine, her two new best friends already forgotten. "I'll look after you. Come on."

As we descend the stairs, my brain computes the extra, unexpected word it read on the blackboard and I stop in my tracks. "Hang on—what's *extreme* speed dating?"

Madeleine makes a casual waving gesture with her left hand. "Oh, it's just a more concentrated form of speed dating, that's all." She starts to descend the stairs, but I stay stock still.

"Concentrated? Explain . . ." I feel a pang of uncertainty.

Grabbing my forearm, she physically tugs me down two more stairs. "Bigger and better than most," she says vaguely but firmly. "Come on, don't be a baby."

As Madeleine has organized this, I have had no insight whatsoever into what to expect. She even paid my entrance fee as a belated birthday present.

As the stairs turn a corner and lead down into a vast reception area, I see five "greeters" sitting behind a desk. Above their heads is a sign that reads "If you haven't yet paid your $75 entrance fee, we accept checks and all major credit cards."

"Seventy-five dollars!" I splutter. "They can't be serious."

Madeleine puts a finger to her lips in a shushing gesture.

"Jess, this is going to be a serious night out. There's free drink and various fun events going on. It's not cheap."

Various fun events. Words that turn my pang of uncertainty into a thumping dread.

We shuffle towards the desk behind a queue of five or six others, waiting in line to register.

"Name." The greeter doesn't even look up. Some greeting. "Jessica Monroe," I say, rather wishing I'd asked Madeleine to use a pseudonym.

"Monroe, Monroe, Monroe . . ." she says loudly, moving a red talon down the list of names in front of her. "Ah, here we are!"

Reaching down by her side, she produces a plastic identity tag with a piece of red ribbon attached. Taking a blank sticker, she scrawls "Jess Munro," presses it onto the tag, and hands it to me.

"You've spelt my name wrong," I say. "It's M-O-N-R-O-E."

She looks at me as if I'm the pettiest person ever to have walked the planet. "It really doesn't matter. It's the number in the top right-hand corner that's important."

I glance down and see the number 435. I resist the temptation to sweep my hand across the table of labels screeching "I'm a name, not a number."

"Four thirty-five. Is that how many people are here?" I whimper.

With a blatant are-you-still-here expression, she hands me a pack of calling cards and sighs. "There are just over five hundred of you actually. Have a good night."

Summarily dismissed, I move to one side and wait for Madeleine to join me. Taking a closer look at the cards, they have "Frisson"—the name of the event, as well as the company that orchestrates it—written across the top, followed by two empty boxes: one marked "First name," the other "number." There is also a special Frisson number, so anyone you like the look of can text you, quoting your special number. Across the bottom is printed "Strictly no mobile phone numbers to be handed out."

Madeleine, or number 436 on the dating menu, rushes up, her eyes shining with expectation. "Two hundred fifty blokes to choose from!" she gushes.

"Yeah, and two hundred forty-eight other women all after any decent ones," I mutter.

"God, you are so *negative*," she admonishes. "Repeat after me: We are the most attractive women here and shall conquer all."

"And then we woke up," I reply, following her through to the next room in the labyrinthine building.

Here, we are met by the saccharine smiles of various waiters and waitresses, all dressed in black T-shirts with *Frisson* emblazoned across the front in silver lettering. They are brandishing trays with a selection of red or white wine, orange juice or sparkling water. Both Madeleine and I lunge with undue haste at a glass of white.

On the far side of the room is a vast wall covered in Polaroid photographs, each with a plastic wallet attached to one side.

"Smile!" A balding man steps out of the shadows and fires a camera flash in my face, causing me to screw up my eyes in alarm.

Those few vital seconds of my discomfort are enough warning for Madeleine to compose herself and strike a supermodel pose when it's her go. Turning her best side to the camera, she gives a pout that makes Posh Spice's mouth look like a rip in a paper bag. Still scowling from shock, I turn to look at the rest of the rogue's gallery. "So what's this then?" I ask Madeleine.

"It's our Wonderwall," says a member of staff lurking nearby with a smile. "Take a look, and if you see anyone you fancy, just put one of your calling cards in the plastic wallet alongside."

"Hmmmm, suspect your wallet might be empty at the end of

the night," says Madeleine, peering at a Polaroid the photographer has just pinned on the patch of wall in front of her.

"What?" Scowling, I take a couple of steps to the side to take a look, then recoil in horror. "Oh my God, I look like the Queen Mum."

"On a bad day," says Madeleine, relentlessly grinding coarse sea salt into my wound.

"Can you take another one please?" I turn to the photographer and smile in what I hope is an endearing way.

"Sorry," he sniffs. "They cost a lot of money, and if I did it for you, everyone would want another go."

"I'll pay you the extra."

"Sorry, haven't got time," he says over his shoulder, on his way to destroy the self-esteem of some other poor, unexpecting sod.

"Your parents are brother and sister, right?" I shout at his retreating back.

"Don't worry, you might get the sympathy vote," adds Madeleine, smiling with satisfaction at the Polaroid of herself looking gorgeous. "Come on, you'll just have to wow them all in person."

She grabs hold of my arm and pulls me towards a set of double doors off to the right. Pushing them open, a wall of noise hits us as we walk through into a vast room the size of four tennis courts. At one end, there are several long, refectory-style tables with pink and blue benches alongside, but the three hundred or so people already here are standing in the empty section of the room. The room reverberates with the hum of nervous small talk, and they're all clutching a drink, wearing their badge, and smiling as if their love lives depended on it.

"Let's work that room, baby!" Madeleine squeezes my arm,

her eyes dancing with pure excitement. I simply feel terrified as I trail pathetically behind her, ever the reluctant bridesmaid.

"Hi fellas!" Bold as you like, Madeleine breezes up to two men huddled together on the edge of the crowd. Both are clutching half pints of lager.

I smile nervously at them both, and quickly establish that neither rock my boat. One—"Tom"—is too squat and shifty looking, and the other—"Gareth"—is clearly a rugby freak. My idea of hell. A rather swift conclusion considering neither of them has yet uttered anything other than their name, but hey, dating is a brutal business.

My hasty dismissal sets me thinking that maybe this speed-dating lark does have its appeal. After all, the squatness of Tom Thumb, as I am now silently referring to him, wouldn't have come across on a photo, and I may have wasted yet more of my life meeting him for lunch. Here, I can establish immediately that I don't find him in the slightest bit attractive.

Madeleine, however, has other ideas and hands him one of her calling cards.

"Pleasure meeting you!" she trills, placing a hand in the small of my back and steering me away from them. "One down, twenty-four cards to go," she shouts in my ear.

I pull a face. "Madeleine, he's so short he's in danger of scraping his chin on the floor."

"Darling, we're all the same size lying down," she replies, pushing me towards a handsome waiter with a full tray of drinks.

Grabbing two full glasses and replacing them with our empties, Madeleine hands me one and smiles seductively at the waiter. Out of the corner of my eye, I catch her hand withdrawing from his back pocket.

"What were you *doing*?" I hiss, as we walk away.

"Giving him one of my cards. He's one of the most handsome men in here," she says matter-of-factly.

"Aren't you peaking a little early?" I say testily. "The cards are supposed to last us all night."

"Oh bore bore, snore snore." She makes a little snorting noise. "You can be Little Miss Cautious if you like, but I prefer to be generous with my potential affection."

"Obviously," I reply sarcastically, but it's lost under the ear-splitting sound of a siren noise that prompts me to wince.

"Ladies and gentlemen!" A voice crackles over the loud-speaker. "Let's get ready to rumble!"

A Frisson virgin, I have absolutely no idea what that means. But there are plenty who do and a wave of pressure builds up from behind, propelling us towards the tables. The urge to make a sheep noise is overwhelming.

The room has filled up more by now, and everyone starts to sit down on the benches in a remarkably orderly fashion. Men sit along the blue benches, whilst we take our place opposite them on the pink ones. No gender stereotyping here then.

"And remember, no verbal intercourse . . ." the disembodied voice pauses to allow feeble laughter for his unutterably feeble joke ". . . until the siren sounds again."

A rather mousy young man shuffles into place opposite me and smiles. His badge says "James." We sit there for a few awkward moments, both looking anywhere but at each other, neither daring to speak a word.

"Right." It's the loudspeaker again. "For those of you who are new to this, here are the rules. This is *extreme* speed dating, so rather than three minutes you each have ninety seconds to make an impression. If you like what you see and hear, hand over a card. When the siren sounds, the men move one place to their right. The women stay where they are. Let's go!"

The siren wails into life and, immediately, the sound of animated conversation fills the room.

James and I sit there for a few moments, verbally impotent and exchanging nervous glances. "I guess it's probably your first time at this too," I say eventually.

"Yes." He smiles but doesn't elaborate.

Tick tock, tick tock. It's amazing how long ninety seconds can seem when you're not having fun. Either side of us, couples are exchanging information with Broadband speed, but James is clearly a second-class male.

"So what do you do for a living?" I lean forward slightly, feigning interest.

He shifts uncomfortably on the bench. "I'm a student."

"Of anything in particular?" God he's hard work.

"IT."

Says it all really. I'm sitting opposite a man who spends most of his day conversing with a computer. With a keyboard in front of him, he's probably got a lot to say. Without it, he's to witty banter what Simon Cowell is to diplomatic relations. The siren sounds, no longer a hideously invasive noise but sweet music to my ears.

"Nice to meet you." I smile as he shuffles along to his next unsuspecting victim.

He's rapidly replaced by a dark-haired, brown-eyed man who, whilst not conventionally handsome, is quite attractive with a warm smile. His badge reads "Carl."

There's the siren again. "Hi," he says and shakes my hand. "I'm Carl, I'm thirty-five, and I work in advertising. I like the basic things in life like long walks and Sunday lunches, and I hate pretentious foreign films. What about you?"

Taken aback by this bonsai approach, I widen my eyes slightly and take a deep breath, preparing to rise to the challenge. "I'm Jess." I tap my badge. "I'm thirty-four, work in television, hate long walks, and love foreign films. But I'm with you on the Sunday lunches." He laughs and I find myself feeling quite attracted to him. My spirits rise slightly, heartened that maybe this speed-dating business isn't going to be such a damp squib after all.

With a sudden bolt of courage I didn't know I could muster, I reach into my pocket and take out one of my calling cards. "So if you fancy sharing a roast one Sunday, here's my card." I hand it over and feel encouraged when he quickly accepts it, stuffing it into his shirt pocket.

He places his elbows on the table and leans forward, a conspiratorial look on his face. "So . . ." His voice is low. "What's your favorite sexual position?"

At first, I'm not sure if I have heard him correctly above the din. But his leering expression suggests I have.

Both appalled and angry in equal measures, with one swift flick of my hand I reach into his shirt pocket and retrieve my card. "Forget it," I snap. "You're not my kind of guy."

Seemingly unperturbed, he leans back and folds his arms, staring at me defiantly. "Look, love, sex is one of the most wonderful experiences money can buy. We're both here because we want a shag, so why not just be honest about it? All this coy Jane Austen bollocks is immensely tiresome."

Before I could answer, the siren sounded and he was gone, clearly relieved to be moving on to passions new.

Although indignant at his presumption that I was lurking in the same murky shallows as he, it set me thinking. Why *had* I come along tonight? And what message was I giving out by doing so?

I could see the advantages. People with busy lives, maybe lacking small talk skills, could come here in the full knowledge that everyone in the room was amenable to being asked out. It's open season, and no one is in a relationship or married. Not that they're admitting anyway.

But the downside is that, for me, it strips away the mystique of the sexual arena, of chatting someone up when you're unsure whether they're looking for a relationship. Here, you *know* that they are. The only mystery is whether they want it to be meaningful or meaningless.

I crane my neck to peer at Madeleine, sitting about six places up from me. She has her ever-diminishing pile of cards laid out in front of her, an expectant look on her face as her next "date" shuffles into place.

I turn back to find myself face-to-face with a leering Pee Wee Herman look-alike, a canary yellow sweater slung over his narrow shoulders. My heart sinks.

The siren sounds and, as far as one can tell in ninety seconds, he turns out to be very pleasant and really rather funny. But I can't get past the sweater and the side parting, so my cards stay firmly in my pocket.

Two hours later, wearied by disappointment and repetition, I let out a huge sigh of relief when the loudspeaker crackles into life again to announce the end of the speed-dating session.

"If you'd like to make your way through to the celebrity room, the next part of the evening will commence," it boomed.

I was by Madeleine's side in a nanosecond. "Celebrity room. What the bloody hell's that?" I'm not sure I can take any more ritual humiliation.

"We all get given an envelope with a famous name in it, and we have to walk around searching for our other half. Great fun!" says Madeleine.

"Mine's bound to say Snow White," I mutter. "I've already met every one of the seven bloody dwarves tonight, except Happy."

Madeleine pulls a face that suggests she's going to ignore my negativity. "Look!" She opens her hand to reveal three cards. "I've handed out twenty-two cards so far. What about you?"

"Three," I reply meekly. "And I'm not even convinced I want to hear from those again."

True, I'd handed two out to men I was pretty halfhearted about, but the third I had passed over in undue haste to a devastatingly handsome man called Guy. He was a trainee doctor (mother would be pleased), keen sportsman, and seemingly all-round good catch. Consequently, by the time he reached me, his top pocket was bulging with the cards of available women, including, no doubt, my dear chum Madeleine.

She links her arm through mine. "Come on, Billy No Dates, let's go see if the celebrity room yields fruit for you."

A set of stairs in the corner snakes down to yet another spacious room, only slightly smaller than the last. As we and hundreds of others file in, we're each asked to take a folded piece of white paper from either of two wire baskets positioned each side of the door.

"Only one each . . . only one each . . . only one each," a bored-looking woman drones repetitively as we shuffle past.

A few steps into the room, Madeleine unfolds hers. "Scooby Doo," she reads aloud. "Which presumably means I'm looking for Shaggy."

"How appropriate," I drawl, tentatively opening my piece of paper. "Jordan." I look baffled for a moment. "The supermodel?"

"Yes," replies Madeleine. "Though I'm rather stumped as to who the other half is. God knows, it could be anyone."

The irony of one of the most flat-chested women in the world picking out one of the most pneumatic is not lost on me, and I fully expect to be the butt of several unoriginal jokes for the rest of the evening.

"Excuse me?" I approach a perma-smile woman sitting behind a desk just inside the door and show her my piece of paper. "Can you tell me who my other half is?"

Furtively, as if guarding a state secret, she pulls out a drawer and starts running her finger down the hundreds of names printed on several sheets of paper. "Jordan, Jordan, Jordan . . ." she chants in a singsong voice. "Let's see . . . ah yes, Dwight Yorke! You're looking for Dwight Yorke."

"Thanks." I smile halfheartedly at her and return to Madeleine's side. "Apparently, I'm looking for a bloke called Dwight Yorke," I repeat, with all the enthusiasm of someone entering the dentist's surgery for root canal work.

"He's a football player in the States—halfback for the New York Giants," says Madeleine brightly. "Come on, let's start searching."

I resist her attempt to drag me off, digging my heels into the floor. "Hang on, this could take hours. There are so many people."

"Yes, but the idea is that you get to meet lots of others whilst asking them if they're your celebrity match or not. We met only about half the men here in that extreme speed-dating session, so this is the ideal chance to check out the rest."

It takes me forty-five minutes and at least 150 more unsatisfactory encounters until I locate my Dwight Yorke, otherwise known as "Neil." With delicious irony, he's white, about five foot six inches tall, with ginger hair and the physique of a pipe cleaner.

After a paltry five minutes of small talk for the sake of politeness, I use the age-old girly excuse of wanting the restroom, uttering those three words so often used for dismissal in the dating arena—"See you later"—meaning, of course, "I hope I never clap eyes on you again."

In the murky half light, it takes me at least another ten minutes to find Madeleine amongst the throng. Not least because she is partially obscured by the man pressing her against a wall and snogging her face off.

Tapping them both on the shoulder, I wait patiently whilst they extract their tongues from each other's mouth.

The man, tall, blond, and rugged looking, turns round with an expression of expectancy. "Are you the Queen?" he says.

"Sorry?"

"I'm Prince Philip. Are you the Queen?"

"No, I'm her friend," I say, pointing my finger at Madeleine, who is hastily smoothing down her hair after her passionate encounter. "I just wanted to let you know I'm leaving now."

"Really?" She looks genuinely surprised. "Didn't you find Dwight Yorke?"

"Yes, unfortunately I did. That's partly why I'm leaving."

"Oh. I didn't find Shaggy, but Prince Philip and I are getting along very nicely, aren't we?" She pouts coquettishly at him and I notice she still has her hand tucked inside his jacket.

"Yeah, well I'll call you tomorrow, OK?" I mumble, turning away from them.

As I reach the door, I look back over my shoulder to see they have resumed normal service, with Madeleine barely visible behind her bulky conquest.

A member of the Royal Family copping off with Scooby Doo. Just about sums the whole evening up really.

Nine

> Am I tall? Yes. Dark? Quite. Handsome? You decide!
> My name is David and I'm looking for someone with
> whom to enjoy lazy days, long lunches, and fine
> wines. I'm pretty easygoing, so the main agenda is
> to just have fun and see how it goes.

It's been raining for three days solid now, so I have arranged an indoor rendezvous, outside the Gap in the West One shopping center on Oxford Street. It would be so much easier to drag them to a local venue, but my paranoia is still heightened enough that I don't want them knowing where I live within a two-mile radius.

I live just off Tooting common, but when they ask I simply say Lambeth, the most overpopulated borough of London.

I reach the Gap just a couple of minutes before 1 p.m. and, as usual, I'm the first there. There's only one other person loitering around with that I'm-meeting-someone expression, but he's about 5' 6" and squat, with stack heels and the worst comb-over since Donald Trump.

This time, rather than waste precious Saturday hours on what may turn out to be yet another disastrous encounter, I have slotted it into my lunch hour before returning to the studio to finish off work on tomorrow's program. Not counting the torturous tube journey there and back, it is my very own version of speed dating.

It's nudging five past one now and there's still no sign. The man opposite smiles tentatively at me and raises his eyes heavenward. He doesn't speak, but the shared viewpoint is clearly, "Bah, latecomers!"

I decide to give it another five minutes, then bugger off back to work via a quick diversion to my favorite shop, Zara.

A minute later, I can see from the corner of my eye that Mr. Squat is looking at me intently, clearly wondering whether to make the most of our mutual abandonment and move in on me. Bollocks, he's walking over.

"Hi." He's standing right next to me, his chin virtually resting on my shoulder.

"Hi." I smile briskly, clutching my handbag closer to me, about to make my excuses and leave.

"Are you Jess?"

His question momentarily winds me. Fuck, *this* is the so-called tall, dark stranger whose handsomeness is my call? Well, ring ring, it's a nerd alert.

"Jess?" I repeat. I'm stalling for time, wondering whether to take him to task under the Trade Descriptions Act or to opt for the other plan slowly forming in my head.

"Yes, I'm waiting for someone called Jess, but I haven't met her before so I'm not completely sure what she looks like." He smiles apologetically. "It's an Internet date."

I adopt the best blank look I can muster. "Jess? Nope, sorry, my name's Olivia."

His face drops. "Oh. You really look like her photo." He narrows his eyes and scrutinizes me, close enough so I get a faint whiff of halitosis.

"I'm afraid I have one of those common faces and lots of people think they've met me before." I shake my head in mock despair, glance at my watch and sigh. "Oh well, it doesn't look like my naughty sister is going to turn up. She's *so* unreliable. Anyway, nice to have met you."

I start to walk away, but he places a hand on my forearm and pulls me back.

"Look, as fate has thrown us together in this way, why don't we make the most of it and get to know each other over a coffee?" He smiles and displays fantastic teeth . . . the *only* thing that's fantastic about him.

"No thanks." I smile sweetly. "I already have a boyfriend."

OK, so it's an inflatable one bought as a joke by Richard last Christmas, now lying punctured in the bottom of my wardrobe. But it has its uses, not least being able to rid myself of the bad breath munchkin without telling a *full* lie.

I head off to Zara for some serious retail therapy.

*Y*ou did *what*?" Olivia tries to look admonishing, but her eyes are smiling. "Jess, that's *terrible*."

It's the following day and we're sitting at her kitchen table, the rain lashing against the window.

"I know, but I couldn't face spending even one hour with someone I found so physically unattractive. I have enough friends, I don't need any more." She's about to interject, but I put my hand up to stop her. "And no, he wasn't someone who would have grown on me. He had no redeeming features whatsoever, except his teeth."

Olivia smiles, then stares out of the window watching the rain cascade down from a piece of loose guttering into a well-placed barrel below. She seems quieter than usual, distracted even.

"You OK?" I inquire as I walk over and flick the kettle on. My question drags her out of her subconscious trance.

"I'm fine," she says with a smile, though I'm still not convinced. Silently, I wonder if everything is on track with her and Michael.

"Where did you say Michael was today?" I pour water into two mugs.

"He's gone to a soccer match with a couple of friends from work." She jerks her head towards the window. "Though looking at the weather, the game could be a bit of a washout."

Placing a mug of black coffee in front of her, I look at the Bob the Builder wall clock that's been there since Matthew had his fixation. "You'd better get ready."

Olivia has asked me to babysit for a few hours because she has a half-day token for The Sanctuary, a health spa in central London, and it's about to run out. She has booked herself a facial, manicure, and pedicure, and I'm here to hold the fort until she or Michael gets back.

"I could do with just going back to bed, to be honest," she sighs. "The bloody neighbors had their stereo blaring again until about two a.m. this morning, then Emily woke up at six."

"Why didn't you bang on their door and complain? That's what I would have done."

"We've tried that before and they told us to go forth and multiply. So Michael's latest tactic is to wait until it stops, give them just enough time to drift off to sleep, then ring them to say how much he enjoyed it." She smiles.

"Genius." I grin, remembering that any official complaint about neighbors now has to be declared and can count against you when you want to sell your property.

"Right, I'll be as quick as I can," says Olivia, taking a few glugs of coffee and getting to her feet.

"Duh. Hardly the point!" I raise my eyes heavenward. "You're supposed to relax and enjoy it. Besides, I'm happy to hang out with Matthew and Emily for six weeks if I have to."

When Olivia had given birth to Matthew, I was so excited that I made virtually daily visits for the first month of his life and quickly became besotted. I marveled at this mini-human and how he fearlessly responded to the world. He grew up almost as accustomed to my face as that of his mother, and when Emily was born it was pretty much the same story.

"Thanks, Jess." Olivia's face looks serious. "You know, sometimes I wonder what I'd do without you."

I glance up at her and she swiftly ducks her head, turns on her heel and heads for the hallway. I couldn't be one hundred percent certain, but there may have been tears in her eyes.

As I watch her retreating up the hallway, I feel a mild flutter of panic. Perhaps my first instinct was right and she and Michael *are* going through a rough patch.

If so, it's simply too much to contemplate. They are my marital utopia, the untouchable, unimpeachable couple smiling beatifically down from the pedestal I have placed them on. If they split up, everything I hold dear will be spun on its axle and messed up.

Every time I even vaguely consider settling for someone just so, as I believe Tab has done, I always think about Olivia and Michael and how fantastic their marriage is. It spurs me on to keep up the eternal quest for something similar.

Having tentatively broached the subject of her welfare earlier and been met with "I'm fine" in reply, I know now is not the time to probe further. But I make a mental note that, if she still seems down the next time I'm alone with her, I'll mention it again.

We've never been a family that brushes things under the carpet or keeps things from each other, so I'm not about to start now.

Ten

It's 7:30 p.m., and I'm in the back of a cab, having raided Olivia's wardrobe and makeup bag. I'd like to tell you I'm off to see the latest Hollywood blockbuster with the man of my dreams, or heading for the airport for a relaxing holiday with my nearest and dearest chums.

But the reality is far, far more mundane than that—grim, even. It's Kara's birthday and I'm on my way to her local wine bar for a celebratory dinner. Olivia was supposed to be coming with me, but by the time she returned from The Sanctuary—curiously looking more fragile and puffy-eyed than before she went—she didn't feel up to turfing out again.

She apologized profusely, and I was about to tentatively broach the subject of her and Michael when I heard his key in the lock. So instead, I rang "International Rescue," in other words, Richard, to accompany me to tonight's debacle.

"Ring her now on the mobile and say you've had a terrible car crash and can't come," he says. "Then you and I can just go to that great new club that's opened up in Ramillies Place."

Richard and I are sitting in our prearranged rendezvous, a little bar just a few yards from Kara's birthday venue.

"Believe me, I'd love to," I reply, taking a rather unladylike glug of my white wine. "But I can't. She'd never let me forget it, *and* she'd demand to see the medical records."

Richard pulls a face. "Remind me again why you're friends with her?" It's a regular battle cry of his.

"Excuse me? *My* friend? I vaguely recall she was at your anniversary party the other night."

"That's because Lars likes her," he sniffs. "If it was up to me, she'd never darken our door."

"Come on, we'd better go." I grab my Anya Hindmarch handbag with a print of Matthew and Emily on the side and stand up. Adopting the reluctant teenager stance, Richard ambles out, orangutan-style, behind me.

Steph's wine bar is a low-lit temple to pickup joints. It has pink lightbulbs (great for disguising cellulite), cherry red faux suede banquettes in the shape of lips, and a smattering of disco balls across its claustrophobically low ceiling. Think Hugh Hefner's bedroom.

Richard's nose wrinkles in disgust as we scan the room for Kara, our eyes narrowed in concentration. "You just know the food is going to be dire," he says. "The only blessing is we won't be able to see what we're eating."

"Yoohoo, over here!"

I follow a voice through the fog of smoke to my right, and there's Kara, waving enthusiastically in our direction and smiling for once.

"Isn't Prozac marvelous?" murmurs Richard, waving back with all the borderline hysteria of a game show contestant.

"Remember . . ." I scowl at him and make a zipping motion across my mouth. "A closed mouth gathers no foot."

"Fantastic to see you!" Kara envelops me in a showy hug, then leans back to air kiss my cheeks—thankfully, the ones on my face.

When she pulls back, I notice a couple of people I don't recognize sitting alongside her, and realize the effusive welcome was for their benefit. She even brings herself to kiss Richard, but unlike little old people-pleaser me, he makes no secret of his surprise.

"Bloody hell, and I thought you loathed me," he says, pulling a "get her" face at the two strangers.

The sound of a misfiring machine gun fills the air. It's Kara laughing maniacally. "Oooh, he's such a card, isn't he?" She looks at the couple for a response, but there isn't one. "I told you he was a real laugh."

Glum and Glummer simply stare back at her, their faces impassive. The woman, in particular, has a face that could chop wood.

"Anyway, introductions!" Kara claps her hands together like a tour guide trying to assemble Japanese tourists. "OK, then. Jess, Richard, this is Harry and his wife, Clare. Harry, Clare, this is my oldest friend Jess and her boyfriend Richard."

Boyfriend? I'm just about to open my mouth and ask her what the hell she's on about, when she shrieks "Drinks!" and grabs both Richard and me by the elbows and steers us towards the bar.

Out of earshot, her jolliness evaporates like water on a hot plate. "You said you were bringing Olivia," she hisses, jerking her head towards Richard. "What's *he* doing here?"

"Charming!" Richard puts one hand on his hip and strikes an indignant pose.

"Olivia's feeling out of sorts and I didn't want to come on my own. I sent you a text to tell you," I lie.

"Didn't get it," she snaps. "But never mind, we need to work quickly here. Harry is my boss and, to put it mildly, he doesn't like gays." She stares pointedly at Richard. "So I'd be grateful if, just for tonight, you'd pretend to be a couple."

Richard and I stare at her for a couple of beats, both clearly expecting her to punch us in the chest any second and shriek "Only kidding!" Then I remember it's Kara and she's deadly serious. With the emphasis on deadly.

"Kara, shame on you," I admonish. "This is 2004. You're not seriously expecting us to play Romeo and Juliet in front of your bigoted boss . . . are you?"

Her mouth is set in a thin, resolute line and the look in her eyes tells me that, yes, that's *exactly* what she's expecting. I glance at Richard for moral support, but he looks surprisingly calm and places a reassuring hand on my arm.

"Don't worry, Jess, I totally understand where Kara is coming from. This is her birthday and it's her boss, and she wants to impress him. Fair enough." He links his arm through mine. "Let's play ball."

Mute with astonishment, I can only gape at the both of them as Kara takes delivery of a bottle of white wine, her sickly smile firmly bolted back on her face.

"Great!" she enthuses. "Now let's go party!"

As she walks back to the table and Richard moves to follow, I sharply tug his arm to hold him back. "You're not seriously going to go along with this homophobic bullshit, are you?"

"Am I fuck," he says firmly. "Quite the opposite in fact. I'm about to make Carson Kressley look like Bob Dole."

Placing a hand on his right hip, he minces away from me with such rolling exaggeration he looks like he's dislocated a leg. Kara is already sitting back down, her back to us as we approach the table.

"Now then, who's the naughtieth boy here," lisps Richard, placing a finger on his chin in mock thought. "Oooh, you know what? I think it's Harry, I really do!" With that he backs his rear end into the small space between Harry and Clare, maneuvering himself into position and forcing them apart.

I hover nervously at the end of the table, eventually daring to glance in Kara's direction. It's not a pretty sight. If looks could kill, then she's brandishing a Kalashnikov in each hand.

"Sorry!" I whimper. "But as you know, he's a law unto himself." I look back to Richard, who now has an arm linked through both of them. He leans towards Harry and places his head in the crook of his neck.

A faint smile playing on his lips, Kara's boss seems to be taking it all in good humor, but his wife is patently livid, her already ungenerous mouth shriveling to cat's arse proportions.

"So I take it you two aren't an item then?" drawls Harry, patting the chair next to him as a gesture for me to sit down. I find myself warming to him.

"No." I smile. "It was Kara's little joke on us. She knew full well we'd never be able to carry it off." There I am again, being a people-pleaser and making sure Kara's boss doesn't think badly of her when, in fact, she deserves to be exposed as the uptight dishrag she truly is.

"I see." He looks unconvinced. "Wine?" He waves a bottle of Sancerre at me.

I smile and nod, pushing my glass towards him. "So, you're a bigwig at Lincolns?" I ask, referring to the book publishers where Kara has been an editor for the past five years.

He laughs. "I suppose so. I'm chairman."

"Oh, you're *the* bigwig then." I should have known Kara would go straight to the top with her birthday invite. No mid-management or worker bees for her.

I'm about to question him further on the company, when I see Kara's brother Jason hone into view, closely followed by her boyfriend Dan.

"Where have you two been?" She scowls. "You said you were just having a quick drink down the road. Now half of my birthday night has gone already." She pouts as she says it and I notice a faint expression of irritation flicker across Dan's face.

"Well, we're here now," he says in clipped tones. He plonks himself down between Kara and me, whilst Jason occupies the empty chair on the other side of his sister and next to Clare.

Seven people. That's all Kara can muster for her birthday, and two of them she barely knows. Then there's her lover, brother, and Richard, who wasn't even supposed to be here. Which just leaves me, her one and only close girlfriend, and even I'm there under people-pleasing sufferance.

She's always had some inexplicable hold over me, probably because in some thirteen-year-old way, I've always been anxious to be liked and she represents the perpetual challenge. A psycho-analyst would probably say we are locked in a victim/abuser relationship, and no prizes for guessing which one's me. The more Kara behaves awkwardly or just downright unpleasantly towards me, the more I dance around her, hoping that, one day, she'll make all the angst worthwhile by turning round and telling me how much she appreciates my friendship. But it's been twenty-three years now and, ho hum, I'm still waiting.

Food and extra wine ordered, we all settle down into the inexorably polite small talk that throttles any dinner party gathering until alcohol loosens the inhibitions. Harry is asking me about *Good Morning Britain*, but I keep losing the thread of what I'm saying because I'm half earwigging Richard's conversation with Clare, who seems to have thawed slightly. Oh God, he's talking about his unruly pubic hair.

"Richard!" I interject, smiling weakly at Harry and his wife. "I'm sure Clare doesn't want to hear about your bodily foibles."

"Au contraire." He pokes his tongue out at me. "Clare is a beautician who specializes in Brazilians. And I'm not talking about Ronaldo."

Harry laughs. "I've got one."

Suddenly, Kara's seemingly staid boss and his wife have metamorphosed in my mind's eye into major swingers, the kind of couples who send naked pictures of each other to porn mags and advertise for threesomes. The alcohol must already be working its magic.

"Got one what?" It's Kara, smiling engagingly at Harry.

"A naked nob, dear, that's what," chips in Richard. "Your boss here . . ." He jerks his head towards Harry. ". . . has had his bits shaved by Sweeney Todd here." He jerks it towards Clare, who's grinning as broadly as her weeny mouth will let her.

Kara's face is a Kodak moment. Bug-eyed, her brain is clearly computing Richard's words, followed swiftly no doubt by the imagined image of her boss's hairless genitalia. "I see," is all she can muster, before lowering her eyes and fixating on the plate of food in front of her.

The evening I was dreading is suddenly turning out to be tremendous fun, and I take an extra-large glug of wine in celebration. After so many torturous times where it's been me flailing around in the social sea while Kara menacingly circles me, it's deliciously satisfying to see her verbally harpooned for a change.

But, silly me, I should have known the feeling would be short lived. She regroups swiftly and her revenge arrives around the same time as the pudding.

"So, Jess, seen any more married men lately?" Her remark is loud and aggressive enough to stop everyone else's conversation in its tracks.

Clare, who has hitherto been throwing me the occasional warm smile, suddenly looks at me as if I were the anti-Christ in stilettos, intent on stealing her husband. I could be mistaken, but Harry appears to edge a bit closer in my direction.

"Actually, I've been on a couple more dates since then." I scowl. "And they were both very nice and very single." I'm inwardly praying that Richard, who knows the disappointing truth, doesn't drop me in it. For once, he keeps his powder puff dry.

Kara sniffs and looks unconvinced. "Jess has joined an Internet dating site," she tells Harry. "But the first man turned out to be married."

I can feel my face flush scarlet. "Correction, Kara. *You* signed me up to the site and the first one *may* have been married."

"Whatever." She waves her hand dismissively.

Harry has definitely edged closer, and his leg is now pressed firmly against mine. Almost imperceptibly, he's now rubbing it backwards and forwards. Help.

"I can't imagine a girl as pretty as Jess would need to trawl the net for dates," he says. "There must be hundreds of men out there who'd love to . . ."

Love to what, he doesn't say. For which I should probably be thankful, particularly as Clare is now giving me a psychotic stare that makes Glenn Close's character in *Fatal Attraction* look like Miss Congeniality.

"Hear hear." It's Dan, grinning broadly at me. "I'd give it a go."

Now it's Kara's turn to glare at me, her eyes darting back and forth between Dan and I, every little glance in my direction a small knife embedding itself in the banquette behind my head. Oh what fun I'm having.

I look at my watch. "Blimey, is that the time?" I lean forwards in front of Harry and tap Richard on the leg. "I'm going to the loo, but when I get back we should make tracks. Don't forget you've got that early start in the morning." Total fiction, but again he didn't let me down by pooh-poohing my attempts to leave. A sure sign he had tired of his little game and was fed up with Kara's disingenuous banter.

Washing my hands in the bathroom a few minutes later, I stare into the mirrors in front of me and silently curse, for the umpteenth time, the "designer" that decided to use overhead lighting. I look knackered, with dark circles under my eyes and a nose shadow that makes it look like I'm sporting a small Hitleresque moustache. Like those small portable fans people hold in front of their faces during blisteringly hot summers, I'm thinking of pioneering a small, handheld face flashlight for women to use when frequenting public restrooms. Forget wrinkle cream, a direct light straight into the face takes years off you.

A woman walks in and stands right next to me. We exchange a polite smile and I note ruefully that her eyes are bagless, despite the dodgy lighting.

"That's a lovely necklace." She nods towards the tiny silver pendant hanging round my neck.

"Thanks." I smile warmly. "It was a twenty-first birthday present from my parents."

She raises an eyebrow. "Really? And it's still so shiny after all these years!"

With that, she saunters into a cubicle and closes the door, leaving me speechless and feeling 125 years old.

Walking out into the corridor, I'm mentally planning the patent for my face flashlight when I turn the corner and crash straight into someone's chest.

"Ah, here you are." It's Harry.

"Um, yes," I falter, slightly unnerved by his sudden appearance. "I went to the bathroom."

"Yes, yes," he says dismissively, looking nervously back over his shoulder. "We haven't got much time. Clare gets very jealous, you know."

"I'm sorry?" I ask him, baffled as to why time is running out for two virtual strangers simply passing each other in a toilet corridor.

"Look." His tone is urgent and he grasps the tops of my arms. "There's a spark between you and I. I can feel it here." He thumps the center of his chest. "I *have* to see you again. When are you free?"

I stare at him unblinkingly for a few seconds, studying his careworn face. He's about fifty, with small blue eyes, a large nose, and graying hair shaped by gel into a tussled boy-band cut that screams midlife crisis. He's wearing a Nehru shirt, faded jeans and—Oh God why didn't I notice them before?—white sneakers with red laces.

"Never, Harry. That's when I'm free," I say firmly.

He looks genuinely surprised by this rebuttal. "Never?" he parrots.

"Never. You're a married man."

Relaxing his grip on my arms, he takes a step back and studies me up and down. "Don't worry about it, we have an open marriage."

"Really?" I drawl, gobsmacked by the arrogance of the man. "Does your wife know that?"

He shrugs. "She has to, or she'd lose me."

"And what a huge loss you'd be." I step round him, shaking my head in disbelief. "Bye, Harry."

As I walk away, I hear him turn round to face my retreating back. "At your age, married men is all you'll get," he shouts.

Without bothering to turn round, I twist my head so he can hear my retort. "In that case, I'll stay single."

I leave the loathsome reptile with my dignity intact, but I won't pretend I wasn't hurt by his remark, as well as slightly panicked.

Maybe he's right. Maybe I *will* shrivel into old age with only the occasional morsel from another woman's marital plate to sustain me. Could that really be the case?

Only time will tell.

Eleven

I'm 35, tall, dark, and lonesome after the demise
of a long-term relationship. WLTM someone who
fancies taking it softly softly, having a bit of fun,
and seeing where life takes us.

O K, so it's not the wittiest, most innovative dating ad in the
world, but if truth be known he could have written
"rhubarb rhubarb" and I'd have fixed a meeting on the
basis of his photograph alone. Shallow, I know, but hey, what's a girl
to do when her calendar's empty but her inbox is full of eligible men?

His picture shows him bare-chested, standing on what looks
like a Spanish beach, judging by the "All the Sangria you can drink
for 20 Euros" sign on a bar in the background.

He's slim, with very dark brown hair and the kind of chiseled
jaw that usually graces the pages of *GQ* magazine. He's not smiling,
but I can imagine he has pearly white, perfectly even teeth.
Though knowing my luck of late, they'll probably look like Stone-
henge in a storm.

It's 1 p.m. and we've arranged to meet outside the door to the Hippodrome nightclub in Leicester Square, no doubt peppered with vomit and urine from last night's revelry. This time, though, I'm taking no chances at being the first to arrive and finding myself faced with some gremlin look-alike.

Instead, I position myself in a doorway across the road, easily hidden by the endless stream of office workers marching purposefully from one place to another, or tourists wandering aimlessly, baffled by the grubby, litter-strewn square in front of them that looks nothing like the pristine image in their city guide. As usual, there's one appallingly bad street musician, and several arty-farty, theatrical types pretending to be statues.

There's only one man currently occupying the doorway of the Hippodrome, and as he's lying down on a dirty blanket and clutching a can of Special Brew, I can only pray he's always there and isn't my mystery date.

A woman walks past him and ignores his extended hand. "Bitch!" he shouts, dribbles of lager foaming at the corners of his mouth. Oh dear. Maybe this wasn't such a wise choice of location after all.

A few more minutes pass and several more insults are bellowed. I wonder whether my date has already clocked the unsavory scene and decided to keep walking. Then, good news, he appears. Better news, he's every bit as gorgeous as his photograph.

He stands a few feet to one side of the doorway's inebriated occupant who, thankfully, seems to have drifted off into a drink-induced state of unconsciousness.

Smoothing down my coat and the back of my hair, I resist the urge to apply yet another layer of lip gloss for fear of sticking to him if there's a small kiss by way of greeting. Taking a deep breath,

I start walking through the throng of people, my heart in my throat. I haven't felt this nervous before, and I wonder whether it's because he's *so* stunning. Good looks do funny things to the beholder, and to those blessed with them it can be the barrier to developing a really attractive personality. After all, if everyone's going to approach you anyway and laugh raucously at everything you say, why bother brushing up on witty or interesting anecdotes?

Now I'm just a couple of feet away from him, but he's facing the other way. Tapping him on the shoulder, I adopt what I hope to be a smoldering gaze and sexy half-smile, and wait for him to turn round. When he does, he has the most piercingly blue eyes I've ever seen, and my stomach does a somersault.

"Jack?" I ask, having learned his name when he e-mailed me to arrange the time and place.

He takes a small step back and, almost imperceptibly, looks me up and down. His face remains impassive. "Jack? No, sorry, you must have made a mistake."

I'm momentarily baffled. The man standing in front of me is an exact replica of the man in the photograph, right down to the little kiss curl of fringe above his right eye.

"You're not called Jack?" I try again, my eyes darting suspiciously from his face to the ground and back again.

"Nope, sorry." He looks faintly defiant, ramming his hands into his jeans pockets and moving shiftily from foot to foot.

Slowly, realization dawns on me. This *is* him, but having seen me in the flesh he's clearly deeply disappointed and doesn't want to take it any further. Here I am, getting a large dose of the same medicine I dished out to some hapless man the other day, but as I'm now on the receiving end, I can feel my nerve ends bristling with the indignity of it.

"You must think I came down the Clyde on a banana boat," I scoff, staring defiantly at him.

"Sorry?" He's trying to look perplexed by the sight of this strange madwoman accosting him in the street, but his cheeks have flushed bright red and he's blinking rapidly. You don't have to be a detective to know he's guilty as charged.

"You *are* Jack," I persist. "Either that, or your identical twin is advertising on the Internet and, by a sheer trillion-to-one coincidence, he has failed to turn up and you're here to meet someone else purely by chance." I'm not sure if what I've said has even made sense, but I stand my ground in front of him, glaring.

He blinks uneasily for a few seconds, clearly mulling over what to do or say next. "Well, you look absolutely nothing like *your* photo," he says indignantly. "I was expecting someone much prettier and slimmer."

My mouth is now wedged open with shock at the injustice of what he's just said. OK, so I'm not Kate Moss, but I'm not exactly chopped liver either. And *slimmer*? What does he want, a pipe cleaner?

"So what are you saying?" Great. As if his insult wasn't bad enough the first time round, I now seem to be asking him to repeat it.

He sighs. "I'm saying that what I saw is not what I've got standing in front of me. Your photograph is deceptive."

"No it isn't. My friends say it looks just like me."

"They're being kind," he says dismissively, looking at his watch. "Look, no offense, but I just don't fancy you. So what's the point of going for a coffee, or whatever, if I already know that?"

"I see. So, such is the depth of your personality, that you judge people purely on looks alone?" I demand, pushing aside the hypocritical recollection of how I'd felt when I first clapped eyes on his photo.

He shrugs. "Not just looks, no. More chemistry really. A spark."

He was making perfect sense, of course, but the lingering sting of rejection wouldn't let me admit it. *I* was allowed to say things like that, but he was supposed to be blown away by the mere sight of me. "A spark can always come later," I retort.

"No." He shakes his head. "The fire comes later. The spark that makes the fire has to be there from the outset and it's just not there for me . . . sorry," he adds as an afterthought.

"Yes, yes, so you keep saying." I frown, momentarily distracted by the sound of Mr. Special Brew stirring to my right.

"Look . . ." Jack's expression and tone have softened. "It's nothing personal, honest. I'm just very focused on what I want, and you're not it. But I'm happy to go for a quick coffee if you like, just to show there are no hard feelings."

Oh God, he's pitying me now, offering me a consolation prize. That's worse than being told, in so many words, that I'm an unattractive heffalump not fit to sully his eye line.

I can feel my irritation ebbing into depression now. I have to get away.

"No point," I say wearily. "I think I've wasted enough time here already. I'd better get back to work."

"OK, nice to meet you." He flashes me a movie star smile. "And sorry again."

"Not as sorry as I am." The drunk behind me has now leaned forward and is tapping my ankle asking for money. "But thanks anyway, it's been really . . . er . . . forgettable."

I turn away from him and fumble in my coat pocket. Finding a pound coin, I stoop down and place it in the grubby, open palm of the dosser.

His bloodshot eyes look down and focus on it, his mouth clearly curling into a sneer under the mass of unkempt beard.

"Tight bitch!" he bellows at my retreating back.

Thank you, God. What a humdinging, bells ringing, bunting-waving arsewipe of a day.

Little did I know that things were about to get much, much worse.

Twelve

True to form, next door's dog starts yapping at precisely
8 a.m., the time his elderly owner gets up to make his
first cup of tea. I know this, because he has an ancient
water tank that cranks noisily every time he turns on a tap. Ah, the
joys of cheek-by-jowl London living. As the old joke goes, the
walls are so thin that every time I have sex (rare), my neighbors
have a postcoital cigarette.

Lifting my head slightly, I prize out my pillow and flop it over
my face, hoping to block out the noise. It dulls it slightly, and I
manage to drift off into one of those shallow, hallucinogenic
morning dozes where all manner of strange things happen to
you—on this occasion, being chased by Regis Philbin, who's brandishing a Frisbee in one hand and a bottle of baby oil in the other.
As "experts" say all dreams are about sex, the mind boggles.

He's just caught up with me and grabbed my faux fur collar
when I'm dragged back to consciousness by the sound of the
phone. It's 9:15 a.m.

"Hello?" I wearily prop myself up on one elbow.

"Hi, sis."

"Hi, Liv. Boy, am I glad to hear from you. You just saved me from the oily clutches of Regis Philbin."

"Right . . ." She sounds distracted. "Look, sorry if I've disturbed you, but what are you up to later this morning?"

As her voice seems subdued, I decide to ignore the fact that she considers my bizarre remark as unworthy of comment. "Oh, now let me see . . . Colin Farrell is picking me up on his motorbike at one, then we're speeding off for lunch at The Ivy, before retiring to our luxury hotel room for an afternoon of steamy sex."

She says nothing for a few seconds, then coughs a little. "Michael is taking the children ice skating this morning, followed by lunch at Pizza Express. So I thought I might come over and see you."

It's enough to immediately arouse my suspicion. After all, even in the unlikely event that she didn't want to join the family outing herself, under normal circumstances she would certainly have savored having the house to herself for a few hours.

The fact that she wants to come over here makes me even more convinced there's something wrong between her and Michael, and she wants to talk about it.

She arrives shortly past eleven, giving me just enough time for a hasty tidy-up, lobbing the contents of cluttered surfaces into cupboards and quickly whipping a Swiffer liberally around the place. Not that Olivia would even notice, but the layer of dust that's built up is enough to shame even slovenly old me.

I greet her with our usual hug, but her shoulders feel more rigid than usual. Her face is undoubtedly pale and looks slightly waxy, and I notice immediately that her usually trim nails look irregular and bitten.

I suddenly feel nauseous, my mind spiraling forward to what may be about to unleash. Michael having an affair with a young, pretty nurse, Olivia falling apart, Matthew and Emily left baffled and heartbroken . . . oh God, Matthew and Emily. The thought is too horrible to even contemplate.

"Coffee?" I smile at her.

"Thanks." She attempts to smile back, but it's so weak as to be barely noticeable.

She follows me into my small kitchen with its low, raftered ceiling and tiny, murky window. A top-floor flat, I refer to it as "Anne Frank's attic" because of its propensity to feel slightly gloomy and enclosed. In winter, it's undoubtedly cozy and homey, but come the summer it can become too stifling and claustrophobic for comfort. But my bank balance, or lack of it, won't stretch to anything else.

Reaching for my prized "Aunty" mug, which Matthew and Emily bought me during a family seaside holiday, I give Olivia the dainty, bone china cup I usually reserve for Mum's infrequent visits. The last time she came, I had spent four hours frantically cleaning the place prior to her arrival and she *still* walked in the door and immediately pointed out how untidy it was.

But Olivia never notices. Or cares. I'm not sure which.

"I thought you would have jumped at the chance to have the house to yourself," I say casually, not daring to broach directly what's weighing on my mind. I'm desperate to be put out of my misery, but can't quite bring myself to ask her outright.

"Not really." She shrugs and stares up at a Simpsons calendar hanging on the noticeboard above her head. It's endless blank squares are symbolic of my uneventful life.

"Why not?" I heap a generous teaspoon of sugar into her cup.

"I know I hate my own company, but that's because I get so much of it. You never have *any* time to yourself, so I thought you'd relish it."

She looks in my direction, but remains expressionless. "I just didn't fancy it today. I wanted some company."

"Oh." I pour in the boiling water. "So why didn't you go with Michael and the children then?"

This time, my question prompts a reaction and she looks slightly concerned. "Is there a problem with me coming over?" she asks. "Do you have something else planned? I thought you said you were free."

"No, no problem at all," I reply hastily, placing the steaming cup of black coffee in front of her. Owing to my Borrowers-size kitchen, there's only room for a three-foot by two-foot table along the far wall. She's sitting at one end and I hover at the other. "Shall we adjourn to the living room? It's a bit cramped in here."

She nods silently, picks up her cup, and follows me down the hallway. We sit side by side on my bright red, two-seater Ikea sofa bed, a housewarming present from the parentals.

"So what's new? How's everything?" It's usually such a harmless question between friends or family, but on this occasion it's loaded with meaning. For a few seconds, waiting for her answer, I forget to breathe.

"Oh, same old same old," she says vaguely, staring at the ceiling as if seeking inspiration. "Um, the children are great. Matthew made the first team for school rugby, which Michael's thrilled about . . ." She stops and takes a sip of her tea. "And Emily has been chosen to play Mary in the school nativity."

"Wow!" I'm genuinely impressed and thrilled for her. "The nearest I got was being one of the Three Kings when Ian Clark went down with chicken pox at the last minute."

Olivia smiles properly for the first time since her arrival. "I remember. I also remember you were a bale of hay the year before."

I screw up my face. "It was strapped round my waist and stuffed into my tights. I didn't stop scratching for a bloody week!"

She smiles again at the memory, and we lapse into silence for a few seconds.

"And Michael?" I venture. "How's he?" It feels so peculiar asking such formal questions. Normally, our conversation would flow easily, but this time it's as if we both know something big is coming. Something unpleasant.

She nods slowly. "He's fine. Very busy at work though, so it's hard getting any time alone together at the moment."

Her remark simply compounds my feeling of unease that she hasn't chosen to accompany him to the ice-skating rink. "You could have spent time with him today," I say gently, anxious not to sound accusatory in any way.

"True." She takes another tiny sip. "But I told him I wanted to come and see you . . . on my own . . . and today was the ideal time to do it."

Told him. The words leap out at me. That means they discussed it, undoubtedly making it a much bigger deal than her simply popping in to see Little Sis on the off chance.

The more I think about it, the more my mind runs away with the theme. They have clearly been struggling to save their marriage for some time, but now they have finally reached the point of no return, and people have to be told. First me, then Mum and Dad over a Sunday lunch, then finally . . . the children. I can't stand it anymore.

"Olivia, what's going on with you and Michael?" I blurt. "Are you splitting up?" My heart is racing with anguish at the mere thought.

She stares at me blankly for a few moments, then shakes her

head slowly. "No Jess, that's not it at all. Michael and I are absolutely fine."

I flop back onto the sofa, a wave of relief washing over me. "Thank God for that!" I even laugh a little. "I was convinced you'd come here to tell me you were on the point of getting divorced."

"Whatever gave you that idea?" She looks puzzled.

"Oh, I don't know. That day when I came round to look after the kids and you went off to the health farm, you didn't seem yourself. You seemed miserable and distracted."

I stop speaking and look at her, but she doesn't respond. So I continue.

I'm smiling now, a mixture of relief and amusement at how I could have misinterpreted her behavior so badly. "And then, when you called this morning and wanted to come over whilst Michael was out with the children . . . well, I assumed the worst."

"I see." She smiles halfheartedly but still looks sad. "There are other unpleasant events in life you know, other than relationship breakups."

I wave a hand in her direction. "I know, I know. But most of them pale into insignificance by comparison."

"Not all of them." She looks deadly serious, her eyes almost brittle with pain.

My mind's off again, racing at breakneck speed towards every worse-case scenario I can possibly think of. "Has something happened to Mum or Dad?" My voice is breaking and I have turned cold.

She immediately senses my concern and reaches forward to place a reassuring hand on mine. "No, seriously, nothing like that. They're absolutely fine. Or they were when I spoke to them last night."

This time, my relief manifests itself in mild annoyance at Olivia's seeming reticence to let me in on whatever's troubling her. If it's not Michael, or the children or Mum and Dad, then what could possibly warrant such a dramatic buildup?

"Then what *is* it, Olivia?" My tone is faintly irritable. "Because you're sure as hell not being yourself."

Her chin starts to dimple, the corners of her mouth twitching with distress. She lets out a small crying noise and her eyes fill with tears. "Jess, I'm so sorry," she sobs.

"What? What is it?" My heart is thumping against my chest. "Olivia, stop it, you're scaring me."

"I've got breast cancer."

Thirteen

B reast cancer?" I parrot her words, not because I doubt
her, but more because I need to hear it for myself—to feel
the description on my tongue, to face front on this turn
of events that is about to change all our lives.

"Yes, breast cancer." Her voice is calmer now, but tears are
still flowing silently down her face.

A tight knot has formed in my throat and I want nothing more
than to break into self-pitying sobbing, scared witless at what this
might mean for the sister who means more to me than even my
own life itself. But I know that would be far too selfish.

"How bad is it?" My voice is barely audible.

She smiles weakly, a small trace of bitterness there. "Who
knows? Only time will tell, I suppose."

My mind is racing with all the questions I want to ask, but
there's only one that stands out as crucial right now. The need to
know overwhelms me. "Are you going to die?"

Her eyes are swimming with tears now, her hands shaking.
She clasps her fingers together in a bid to steady them. "The truth,
Jess? I really don't know. They seem reluctant to make any predic-

tions at this stage." She shakes her head in a gesture of hope-lessness.

It's so curious, this thing called bad news. Here, sitting oppo-site me, is the woman I have known since birth, the woman I have shared all my hopes and fears with, the woman I can't contemplate being without. Yet for some reason I feel paralyzed, totally inca-pable of leaning forward and enveloping her in the kind of hug that usually comes so easily to us.

It's as if the word "cancer" has built a huge wall between us, as if I fear she might break if I so much as touch her.

"You must have *some* idea," I say desperately. "Someone must have had something positive to say."

She shrugs, wiping her face with her sweat top sleeve. "They can say what they like, but the bottom line is that I've got breast cancer and it's going to depend totally on how I respond to treat-ment and maybe surgery."

"Surgery?" I feel a small flutter of panic in my chest.

"Yep. If it's advanced, then it will mean at least one off, maybe two." She looks down at her breasts and smiles ruefully, the pain in her eyes belying her flip tone.

This time, I instinctively lean forward without thought and throw my arms around her. "Oh, Olivia, not you. I can't bear it." A howling noise fills the small room, and I realize it's me.

"There, there, sweetie, don't cry." She strokes my hair and makes small soothing noises. "It's not the end of the world."

It's one of those phrases people always use when things seem bad, but in this context it seems particularly meaningless. Sitting here now, in my cramped living room, it feels as if the walls have closed in to within an inch of my face. Everything else—work, friends, my paucity of eligible dates—all seems utterly irrelevant. As far as I'm concerned, my world *has* ended.

At least five minutes pass of me sobbing sporadically, being comforted by her. The wrong way round, I know, but as ever Olivia indulges me, stroking my hair and reaching into her hand-bag for a pack of tissues. Just as she always did when we were children.

After a short while, I calm down sufficiently to get my thought process into some kind of order. "I want to know everything," I sniff through a soaked tissue. "How you found out, what happened next . . ."

She lets out a small sigh. "Well, you remember when Michael and I took the kids to Legoland over February break, then toured a bit?"

I nod silently. I'm still fighting to stay calm, greedy to know everything straightaway, but knowing I must give her time to run through the chain of events in her mind.

"We stayed in a family hotel, and we had this fantastic shower cubicle but no bath. You know how I like a bath . . ." She smiles at me. "Anyway, so I had to have a shower, and there's something more thorough and rigorous about the way you wash under a stream of constant running water . . . you know?"

She stops for a moment and looks at me for a response. Again, I merely nod silently, not trusting myself to speak.

"So I was washing under my arms, like this . . ." She raises her right arm in the air to demonstrate. ". . . and the soapy water seemed to make my skin seem so much more smooth and slippery. That's when I noticed the lump."

Standing up, she crosses to the mantelpiece and picks up a photograph of me with Matthew and Emily, all smiling broadly during a day out to Madame Tussaud's. There's a blurred image of Tony Blair behind us.

Olivia gazes at it and smiles, then clutches it to her chest and returns to sit next to me on the sofa.

"It was about the size of a pea." She uses her thumb and forefinger to show the width. "And it seemed to be moving around a little. To be honest, I thought it was probably a little piece of gristle or something, and didn't think any more about it.

"Then when we got back to London on the Sunday, Michael and I were reading the papers in bed and there was an interview with the singer Anastacia, talking about her breast cancer. It jogged my memory about the lump, but I didn't mention it to Michael because I didn't want to worry him. He had so much on at work at the time, I didn't want to add to the stress."

Again, she looks at me, presumably to see if I wish to chip in at any point. But I say nothing and nod slightly towards her, indicating for her to carry on.

"I was convinced it was harmless, but thought I had better get it checked out, just to be sure. So I went to my regular doctor, who said it was probably just a hormonal thing, and that I should wait six weeks to see if it changed in size at all."

The benefit of hindsight, I know, but instantly I wanted to rush round and berate this doctor for his carefree, laid-back approach. Six weeks of crucial delay, six weeks more of a time bomb ticking away in there, growing larger and more deadly.

She sighs again. "In the daily melee of making lunchboxes, school runs, and getting myself to work, I forgot all about it again, particularly as the doctor had seemed so unconcerned. When I did check it, it was hard to tell if it had grown at all, and it was about eight weeks before I got round to going back for a follow-up visit. He thought it had grown slightly, so he referred me to a specialist."

"Did you tell Michael at this point?" My voice sounds cracked from the strain of crying.

She shakes her head. "No. Again, I was so convinced it would turn out to be nothing, that I didn't want to involve him." She rubs her face with her hands. "To be honest, because he works in a hospital and deals with dying people all the time, I felt my little lump was rather insignificant. It was totally my fault that I felt like that, he's never made me feel I can't mention any illness at home. After all, I always involve him in any cough, cold, or scrape to do with the children."

That off her chest, I steer her back to her own predicament. "Go on," I say softly.

"Well, they did a couple of tests, then I was led into this overpoweringly cheerful room, with walls painted in bright yellow and children's drawings everywhere. I just knew it was going to be bad news, then a female doctor came in with one of those patronizingly reassuring smiles that just confirmed it to me." She clutches the photograph a little tighter to her chest.

"She told me the lump was malignant, but that I may have caught it in the early stages. To find out, they will remove it, then perform a biopsy to see if the cancer has spread."

She's relaying all this so matter-of-factly that it sounds like she's reading out a menu. Presumably, this is because she has gone through it so many times in her mind that it has almost become routine. However, for me, it's a struggle to keep up with the medical jargon, and her emotionless recital makes it difficult to establish the dramatic facts from the commonplace.

My brow is deeply furrowed. "She must have said a bit more than that."

"Not really." She shrugs. "They're always very cagey at that stage, because they don't want to paint too gloomy a picture, but on the other hand they don't want to give you false hope. It's very frustrating when you have so many questions, but I can understand why they remain vague."

"So what stage are you at now?"

She purses her lips. "That's it, so far. I'm having the lumpectomy next week. To put it in simple terms, if the cancer is contained within the lump, then it's a good sign that I may be clear elsewhere. If it isn't and the cancer cells reach the edge, then I may need surgery, and radiation or chemotherapy."

Dear God, I think. I know I haven't been the most faithful, consistent of worshippers, and I know I pray only when I want something . . . but this time I *really* want something from you. *Need* something, actually. I will happily attend church every Sunday without fail, and even join a voluntary group that helps the elderly do their shopping. Whatever it takes, as long as my sister Olivia's cancer hasn't spread. Amen.

"And you've told Michael now?"

She nods. "Yes. This all happened the Friday before you came round to babysit for me on the Saturday."

"When you went to The Sanctuary?"

"Yes. Except that I didn't." She rests the photograph facedown on her lap and stretches her arms out in front of her. "I told Michael when he came home from work on the Friday night, once the children were in bed. He was utterly horrified that I hadn't told him and we had the most monumental row." Her eyes start to moisten at the memory.

I squeeze her arm. "Oh, Liv, I'm sorry."

"Don't be. He was absolutely right, I should have told him. We've always shared everything in life and he was so hurt that I had excluded him from something so important . . . something that might have a devastating impact on both our lives, not to mention the children . . ." Her voice trails off and she starts to cry again.

"And of course, he was as frightened as I was about it all. So his fright and anger all came out and he shouted at me in a way he never has before. It was truly horrible."

"But understandable," I say gently. "He totally adores you, Liv. I should think even the *thought* that you might be seriously ill would be enough to send him into a blind panic."

She wipes her nose with a tissue and nods. "Yes, I know. Anyway, it all calmed down eventually and we went to bed friends again, just holding each other with an urgency we haven't shared since the early days of our relationship . . . although for entirely different reasons, of course." She smiles ruefully.

"The next morning, he went into practical mode and started making calls to his colleagues for a second opinion. When you thought I was at The Sanctuary, I was actually visiting a specialist friend of his at home."

I sit up a little to straighten my aching back. "And what did he or she say?"

"He. Well, we talked it all through, and I told him what had happened so far and who'd I'd seen at the hospital. He said the woman consultant I'd seen had a very good reputation and that it sounded like I was in capable hands."

"Is that it?"

"Pretty much. Although, being a friend of a friend of Michael's, he was a little more forthcoming about the prognosis options. He seemed rather doubtful that the lump would simply be removed and that everything would be fine. He thought it more likely that I would need surgery followed by several courses of chemo. But he did say that he thought it highly unlikely I would die."

My hand shoots up to my chest, the palm slapping against it. "Thank God!" I've never met this man, but I love him already.

She smiles at me, but her brow is still slightly furrowed. "It's going to be tough though, Jess," she says quietly. "That's why I had to tell you, because you of all people will notice if I'm distracted or under the weather."

I grab hold of her hand. "As I said, I noticed it last Saturday, but I just thought you and Michael were having problems."

I must confess that right now, I feel the same emotions as Michael first felt, angry and hurt that Olivia didn't share her problems or concerns with me from the moment she first discovered the lump. But I know that now is not the time to bring it up, if ever.

What she needs is objective, practical support from someone close to her, not bitter recriminations.

"Are you going to tell Mum and Dad?" I ask, silently wondering how they'd cope with it. Mum, I suspect, would fall to pieces, whilst Dad would outwardly remain calm, but be panicking internally.

Olivia shakes her head. "No. I really don't see the point of worrying them at this stage. If, after the lumpectomy, things look really grim, I'll tell them then."

"And what about Matthew and Emily?" Just when I have managed to compose myself, the mere *thought* of the repercussions all this may have on their life sets me off again, although thankfully less noisily this time. I wipe my eyes with the back of my sleeve.

Again, she shakes her head firmly, her expression determined. "Absolutely not. The day I'm told I have six months to live is the day I will say something to start preparing them for life without me. Until then, they'll know absolutely nothing. You only get one childhood; it shouldn't be weighed down with the pressures of what *might* be."

"But, darling," I say gently. "If you have to have surgery or chemotherapy . . ." I have to stop a moment as the tight knot in my throat is constricting my voice ". . . then they're bound to notice something."

"True, but I've thought of that already. If they ask, I'm just going to say that Mummy has an arm problem that needs sorting out, but that it's absolutely nothing to worry about." She gives a little laugh. "Emily gets very anxious when I'm ill. I had a cold recently and she said 'You're not going to die, are you, Mummy?'"

That's it. I'm off again, the dull ache in my chest rising to a crescendo and bursting from my mouth in a strangled sob.

"Don't cry, Jess." Olivia shuffles towards me on the sofa and wraps me in a tight hug. Her body feels soft and warm against mine, immensely comforting. "I need you to be strong for me."

"I know," I wail, kicking myself for being so pathetically weak and self-centered. "I'm so sorry. It's just such a shock, that's all."

"It is. But we'll beat it together," she murmurs.

We will. The alternative is just too hideous to even contemplate.

Fourteen

It's the mother of all Monday mornings. Granted, not a great day at the best of times, but this one is particularly grim.

As usual, I wake up and enjoy that blissful two-second hiatus where my brain hasn't quite kicked in and, with touching naïveté, I think there's lots to look forward to in life. Then a gloom descends as I realize it's the dawn of yet another week toiling away at the shit face of *Good Morning Britain*.

But then even that pales into insignificance when Olivia suddenly pops into my head and I almost retch at the memory of our conversation.

Yesterday, I'd had a humdinger of a day lined up, the kind I love. A bit of a lie-in, then a wander down to my local Starbucks for a cafe latte and pore over the Sunday papers in splendid isolation, give or take a few hungover souls scattered around me.

After that, it was to be lunch on the Kings Road with Richard and Lars, then a little putter around the shops before retiring home for an afternoon nap and a Marks and Spencer meal for one in front of *Coronation Street*. Utter bliss.

But after my emotionally draining Saturday with Olivia, I ended up canceling the lot and just slopped around the house, alternating between bouts of sobbing and drifting off into uneasy catnaps after a virtually sleepless night.

Now it was Monday, and it was tempting to use the food-poisoning excuse I gave Richard and Lars to sneak a day off from work. But having spent the previous day feeling so miserable, I knew the feeling was increased threefold by having so much time on my hands, so going to work was probably the best thing to do under the circumstances. Now, sitting at my desk a couple of hours later, I'm wondering whether I have made the right decision. Sure, I'm here in body, but my spirit is crushed and I'm unable to concentrate on the task in hand for more than a few seconds at a time.

"Jess!!!!"

"Huh?" I feel a sharp tap on my shoulder, stirring me from my deep, dark thoughts. It's Tab.

"I have asked you the same question three times now and you've ignored me every time," she says crossly. "What planet are you on?"

"Sorry." I blink rapidly a few times, feeling myself close to tears. "I don't feel terribly well."

Her expression changes immediately from one of irritation to concern. "Oh you poor thing." She places a reassuring hand on my back. "Come to think of it, you *do* look rather peaked. What's wrong?"

I'm desperate to pour my heart out and tell her everything, particularly as I know she's 100 percent trustworthy and wouldn't tell a soul. But I promised Olivia I wouldn't say anything to anyone, and it's her secret, not mine.

Trouble is, whilst Olivia now has me as an outlet for her hopes and fears, I don't feel I can burden her with mine. I feel I have to be strong and unerringly positive at all times, which is why it would be nice to be able to tell Tab and have someone I could occasionally fall apart in front of.

"I ate a dodgy prawn on Saturday and I spent all day yesterday retching," I lie. "I have stopped being sick now, but I'm still very shaky and totally exhausted."

She rubs my back. "Why on earth did you come in to work, you idiot?" she chastises. "Come on, get your coat and go home. I'll tell Janice, so don't worry about her."

I smile weakly. "Thanks, but I'll be fine, honest. Besides, there's a disabled single mum of three coming for a makeover today, and if she can struggle through each day without whining, I'm damn sure I can."

In the event, the woman—Sandra was her name—was the best person I could have met that day. Just forty-one years old, she had been a normal, happily married mother of three small children when she was hit by an out-of-control car ten years ago.

She had been pushing her youngest in a buggy at the time and, seeing the car hurtling towards them across the pavement, had managed to shove the child out of harm's way whilst taking the full brunt of the impact herself.

She never walked again.

Soon after, her husband said he "couldn't cope" (*he* couldn't cope?) and left her to bring up their three children alone—popping in sporadically when his guilt got the better of him. Eventually, the visits died away to nothing, and she discovered through mutual friends that he'd remarried and was expecting another child.

As she was telling me all this off air, the tears started to course down my cheeks, a mixture of sadness for her and shame that I was being so self-pitying over Olivia. If this woman can get on with life without falling to pieces, I'm damn sure I can.

"Please don't cry," she says soothingly. "I stopped weeping about it all years ago. You have to get on with life, don't you?"

"You do indeed." I smile, silently vowing to think of Sandra whenever I lapse back into gloominess.

Consequently, when Tab says she's meeting Will for a drink at 7 p.m. and invites me along, Sandra's smiling face pops into my mind and I find myself saying yes.

Besides, a couple of glasses of wine and an hour or so of mindless chitchat will be a lot better for me than sloping off home for a solitary mope in Anne Frank's attic.

The Mulberry Bush is a busy, modern pub frequented by the post-work overspill from nearby offices and our television studios. As Tab and I walk in, the wall of noise and smoke makes us both reel backwards.

Will is sitting in the far corner, with a persistently beeping jukebox on his left and a persistently bleating woman to his right who is clearly giving her male companion a hard time about some misdemeanor. His glazed expression suggests he gave up listening long ago.

"I'm glad you're here," says Will, casting a sideways glance to the woman at the next table. "I need a break from this, so I'll get the drinks in while you guard the seats."

When he returns about ten minutes later, he's accompanied by a man who looks to be in his mid-twenties, clutching a glass of white wine in each hand. His face is slightly chubby, but he has an endearingly friendly smile he's exercising to great effect right now.

"This is Ben Thomas," says Will. "We play rugby together at weekends. I found him lurking at the bar on his own."

"Just call me Billy No Mates," grins Ben, extending his hand first to Tab, then to me. "Will invited me to join you. I hope you don't mind?" He looks inquiringly at us.

Tab and I both shake our heads in unison, and she shifts along the bench to make room for him.

"Do you work round here?" she says. Unimaginative, but what else do you say to someone you have no clue about?

"No," he splutters, through a mouthful of lager. "I've just had a meeting over at Carlton." He jerks his head towards the TV studios opposite.

"Oh?" It's my turn to do the polite social chitchat now. "Do you work in television?"

"Oh, good God, no!" he says, shaking his head emphatically. "I work for a charity and I was having a meeting with the local news program about the logistics of them coming to film a forthcoming fund-raising event we're having."

"And what's wrong with working in television?" I say, rather more snappily than intended.

"Sorry?" He looks perplexed.

"All that 'good God, no' business, as if working in TV is second only to shoveling pigshit for a living." I glare, inwardly amazed at my defensiveness and wondering what's brought it on.

His expression has transformed from geniality into one of genuine concern. "I didn't mean it like that at all," he says. "What I actually meant was good God, no, I don't do anything as glamorous as that."

"Oh." I sniff slightly, now embarrassed by my overreaction. Particularly as both Tab and Will are looking at me as if I've lost my marbles. "Sorry, it's just that I get sick of people being scathing about the world of television."

Tab makes a small choking noise into her wineglass. "Jess!" she laughs. "You're normally the first to say how shallow and meaningless it all is."

I'm desperately trying to think of a convincing reply, but Ben beats me to it.

"It's OK. It's human nature that *we* can all say what we like about our jobs or relationships, but when a complete stranger says something we think is out of turn, we immediately become a little defensive." He smiles at me reassuringly.

I smile back, though halfheartedly, slightly annoyed by this holier-than-thou man who does some worthwhile, do-gooder job *and* benevolently bales out someone who has just been incredibly rude to him.

"More drinks?" He stands up and gathers our glasses.

"Christ, what's with Father Teresa?" I say grouchily at his retreating back. "Where did you find him—Saints R Us?"

"Yes, he's a nice bloke, isn't he?" says Will, my sarcasm whooshing over the top of his head.

Tab is a little quicker off the mark. "Now, now," she admonishes. "You just got off on the wrong foot with him, that's all." She looks across the table to Will. "She's not feeling very well."

"I'm fine," I say testily. "But I'm going to go home after the next drink if you don't mind. I *am* very tired."

They exchange the kind of knowing glance usually shared between the parents of a misbehaving, overwrought child, but I ignore them.

A few seconds later, Ben returns and places a glass of white wine in front of me.

"Thanks," I mutter, pretending to search for something in my handbag so I don't have to look at him.

"So!" Tab enthuses, clearly slipping into overcompensation mode. "Which charity do you work for?"

"It's called Sunshine House," replies Ben, smiling warmly at her. "It's a hospice for terminally ill children and their families."

That's it. Floor open and swallow me up. Right now, please.

I arrange makeovers for a lightweight, daytime TV show. He shares the precious, final days between parents and their children. The contrast seems all the more unbearable in light of my sister's sudden plight. It's official, I am a Grade A, 24 karat, unbeatably self-obsessed prat. Even though deep down I know it's completely irrational, it's hard not to feel that Olivia's illness is somehow the universe's way of punishing me for all my griping about what was in fact a perfectly good life—soulmate or no.

Unable to take any more, I knock back my wine with indecent haste and get to my feet.

"Sorry guys, gotta go." I smile quickly at Tab and Will. "Thanks for inviting me along and sorry I haven't been great company." I notice neither of them rush to disagree with me.

"And Ben . . ." I extend my hand towards his and shake it. "Lovely to meet you. Sorry about earlier, I don't know what came over me. I'm now going home to lie down in a darkened room."

He laughs a little. "Forget it. It was just a misunderstanding, that's all. Nice to meet you, too."

Outside, I walk a few yards along the darkening street until I know I'm out of sight, then I place my back flat against a brick wall and take in several deep breaths of cold air in swift succession.

My heart is fluttering like a trapped bird against my rib cage, and I feel sweaty and breathless. It's not a feeling I recognize from personal experience, but the symptoms are synonymous with something we once featured on the program. My skin shivers at the thought, but there's no getting away from it.

I'm having a panic attack.

Fifteen

*I*t's 9 p.m., the electric blanket is on full, and I'm curled up in a tight ball under my duvet. I don't ever want to come out.

It was all I could do to hail a cab and stumble through the front door, gratefully falling onto the bottom stair and staying there for a good ten minutes trying to compose myself.

I was trapped in a vicious cycle, panicking about my panic attack, scared witless by my complete lack of control over my emotions.

I can only liken it to the one and only time I ever took an Ecstasy tablet. It was two years ago, during a party at the house Madeleine shared with four other girls, and almost immediately I started to go cold and get the shakes.

I found a quiet corner to sit in, and huddled there viewing the rest of the room as if through the bottom of a bottle. When I made a conscious effort, I could force my brain to take in what was going on around me, but most of the time I was lost in my own world.

Initially, it was a somewhat pleasurable feeling, but then a man I didn't know sat next to me and tried to strike up a conversation. I felt myself go brittle with discomfort, inwardly panicking at this intrusion into my own private reverie.

When I mustered up the strength to search for her, Madeleine, by contrast, was flying high, telling anyone who'd listen how much she loved them. Her pupils were the size of dinner plates, and she was grinning broadly from ear to ear, gabbing endlessly about nothing in particular.

"Isn't this fan-fucking-tastic, Jess!!" she'd shrieked above the music, spinning me around until I felt utterly sick. "I can't believe we've never taken this stuff before."

"Actually, I don't feel too great," I'd replied, before persuading her to give me the key to her bedroom upstairs.

Gratefully, I had switched her electric blanket on full, clambered into bed, and lain there quietly, waiting for my feelings of paranoia to pass. Once I was cocooned in my locked, impenetrable shell, safe from the loud intrusions of downstairs, the panic dissipated rapidly and I passed a pleasurable couple of hours with the fond memories of my life playing through my mind with movie camera clarity.

Now here I am, cocooned under the duvet once again, but this time the thoughts in my head aren't so reassuring.

Day in day out, I have to deal with other people's misfortunes on *Good Morning Britain*. Women like the indomitable Sandra dealing with her children all alone, women who have been beaten by their husbands, men who have been thrown on the job scrapheap in their forties. The bad-luck stories stay the same, only the faces change.

But the face attached to this particular piece of bad news is one I know and love dearly—my wonderful, vibrant sister Olivia. Wife to Michael, mother to Matthew and Emily, daughter to my parents and friend to countless others.

An hour passes, I think, because I can hear the faint strains of the ten o'clock news through my neighbor's wall. Or maybe it's nearly two hours. I'm not exactly sure what time I struggled back here from the pub, but I have been drifting in and out of an uneasy sleep ever since.

Now I have a raging thirst. I know I'm going to have to muster the energy to walk through to the kitchen, but my head flops back onto the pillow for a few more moments.

For the first time in years, I find myself yearning to be at home, with my mother fussing and clucking around me. Seeing me so out of sorts, she would be making me her cure-all potion of lemon, honey, and brandy and practically force-feeding me with smooth, milky porridge to "line the stomach."

Sighing deeply, I sit up and try to practice some of the positive thinking we have preached so often on the program. There's absolutely nothing wrong with me physically, it's just that I feel so wretchedly down in the dumps and can't seem to snap out of it.

Is it purely because of Olivia's crisis? Or was that simply what tipped me over the edge of my own life? I cruise along in my job, but could never say that I love it. In fact, for some time now, I have been feeling dissatisfied with the endless diet of recipes, gardening advice and makeovers, wanting to get my teeth into something a little more newsy or worthwhile.

Then there's my love life, or lack of it. Most of the time, I tell myself that I don't mind, that I'm happy to trundle along on my own, doing what I want when I want. And sometimes this is true. But deep down, it does bother me. I love my friends and would never give them up for anyone, but they're not enough. There's no substitute for a fundamentally good romantic relationship, complemented by great friendships. Saturdays usually pass in a blur of lie-in, lunch with a friend, shopping, and a party or pub crawl in the evening. But Sundays are more difficult, and I often mope around tormenting myself with thoughts of other people's lives. Richard and Lars, Tab and Will, Michael and Olivia, and yes, even Kara and Dan. All probably lounging around together, conversation interspersed with quiet moments of reading the papers or watching the television. Just knowing there's someone else around is reassuring, someone who cares about you, someone to share life with.

The phone rings and stirs me from my self-pitying thoughts.

"Hi, sweetie, it's me." It's Olivia, and to my eternal shame, she sounds a lot more cheerful than I feel.

"Hi!" I force myself to sound lively. "How are things?"

"Oh, not bad. I'm having a good day today. But then I'm having the lumpectomy tomorrow, so after that, who knows?"

She's having the lumpectomy. Not me, the piteously self-obsessed blob sitting here feeling sorry for myself because I'm not that keen on my job and don't want to be single anymore.

Irritation at myself propels me into an upright position. "Is Michael going with you?"

"Yes. He's told his boss at work about the situation, so he has quiet carte blanche to take whatever time he needs, although I'll be in and out in a day."

"What about Matthew and Emily? Who's looking after them?" My mind is already whirring with the possibility of taking tomorrow off work so I can help out.

"They're both at school until three-thirty, then we've farmed them both out for tea at friends' houses, which naturally they're thrilled about," she says. "Michael will pick them up after tea."

"Oh." I'm mildly disappointed that I won't be needed. "Well, if you get stuck, then just give me a call and I'll collect them."

"Thanks." She sounds astonishingly calm, as if we're merely discussing a run-of-the-mill day in family life.

Silence descends for a few moments.

"So, once you've had the lumpectomy, how long before you know the results?"

"Not long, I think, could be immediately, could be a couple of days. And of course, Michael's part of the medical grapevine so hopefully that will speed things up a bit."

"Well, I'll keep my fingers and everything else crossed for you," I say lightly, belying the thumping sense of dread I feel inside.

"Good. I'm sure everything will be fine anyway," she replies breezily. "Now let's talk about something else. I need a diversion."

"Um . . ." My usual aptitude for small talk seems to have deserted me. "Work is pretty dreary at the moment, although I did have this amazing woman in the other day . . ."

"Not work . . ." She cuts across me. "Tell me about your dates; that's much more interesting."

Dates. Dates. I have to dredge back through my memory to remember. It all seems so trivial now.

"The last two have been pretty disastrous, even more than the one who was probably married. At least he actually went through with the date."

"What do you mean?"

I groan and tell her all about pretending to be someone else when I didn't like the look of the man outside the Gap, then, warming to the theme and embellishing my story with sound effects of horror and indignation, I fill her in on the gorgeous man outside the Hippodrome who rejected me because, according to him, I didn't look like my photograph. I finish it off with the anecdote about the tramp calling me a tight bitch.

"I mean, the fucking cheek of it!" I shriek down the phone. "Can you imagine *anything* more humiliating?"

Olivia is laughing uncontrollably on the other end and it's a wonderful sound. "Stop!" she pleads. "My stomach is hurting."

Galvanized by the sound of my sister's joy, I swing my legs out of bed and onto the floor. Grinning from ear to ear, I take the cordless down the hall with me towards the kitchen.

"So I think that's it for me on the Internet dating front," I conclude. "I can't take any more." Ducking into the fridge, I pour myself a long grapefruit juice and take several large glugs.

"Nonsense, I won't hear of it!" admonishes Olivia. "What on earth will I have to laugh about in life if you don't keep regaling me with your stories."

"I'll tell you what." I sit down at the kitchen table. "I won't go on the dates. Instead, I'll just make up stories to tell you. That would be far less time-consuming."

"It won't be the same," she replies petulantly. "Besides, Jess, I really want to see you meet someone special."

Her voice has turned serious again and I know she's thinking of the future, both mine and hers. It's unspoken, but she's alluding to the fact that if she doesn't make it, she'd like to know that I'm on route to being settled and happy in life.

"I might meet someone through the usual means, like work," I say halfheartedly.

"What, the gay hairdresser?" she scoffs. "Or maybe one of the older men featured in an item about prostate problems? Jess, get real. You've got to get out there and seize life with both hands."

She doesn't actually say "or one day life might slip away from you," but we both know that's what she means.

"OK, OK," I sigh. "I'll go on a few more dates . . . just for you."

"No, not for me," she says. "Do it for yourself."

Spontaneously, we both break out into a chorus of *Sisters Are Doing It for Themselves*, the song we used to sing as teenagers before we went out for the night.

I have never loved her more than I love her right now.

Sixteen

My name is Tom, I'm 48, and very solvent, with homes in France, an apartment in London, and a 15th century listed home in the country. I'm marketing director for a major PLC and describe work as "playtime." I don't have any hang-ups, quirks, or kinks, I'm just a well-traveled, well-brought-up man of the world who never "goes Dutch." I have a GSOH and listen well, even on my pocket phone. I like a lady to be educated and independent.

OK, Olivia, this one's for you.

Consequently, I have chosen someone who talks of "pocket phones" and "ladies" and sounds more mature than the piece of cheese that fell down the back of my fridge three weeks ago. Memo to self: *must* retrieve.

This is a concerted attempt by me to move away from the potential, roguish flibbertigibbets, as my father might refer to them, and steer myself towards someone more obviously straightforward and a better long-term prospect.

During our subsequent, brief e-mail exchange, Tom suggested sharing a bottle of champagne at the Ritz. And as he was so emphatic about never going Dutch, how could a girl refuse?

"It could also mean he expects the *woman* to pay for everything in these enlightened times," teased Madeleine, when I spoke to her on the phone earlier today.

"In which case, I'll be washing dishes at the Ritz for the foreseeable future," I replied.. "He's forty-eight and calls women 'ladies.' He'll definitely pay."

"Oooh, old and grateful," said Madeleine. "Perfect!"

Forty-eight? Hardly old, but for a woman with a penchant for "young stud muffins," as she calls them, I suppose it's positively ancient. Madeleine always says the reason she avoids older men is that, when it comes to sex, they just don't have the stamina for the sex marathons she adores but most ordinary women find unappealing in the extreme.

Having agreed to partake in a bottle of champagne, I have made the date for a Saturday lunchtime rather than midweek, when I'd run the risk of returning to the office slightly worse for wear.

And as it's the Ritz, I have plucked what can only be described as one of mother's emergency outfits from the back of my wardrobe. Last worn to Emily's christening, it's a beige linen skirt suit, teamed with a cream, short-sleeved cashmere top underneath. I look like I'm going to a job interview.

In the photo Tom jpeg'd to me, he seems to be on holiday. Sitting on a plastic garden chair with the backdrop of a swimming pool, it looks like one of those generic Spanish apartment blocks you see on the news when there's been an outbreak of Legionnaires' disease or listeria. Wearing just a pair of pale yellow drawstring swimming shorts, he looks in pretty good nick for his age, with thick dark hair just starting to go gray at the sides.

I can see him now, occupying a corner table in the Ritz tearoom and, surprise, surprise, he looks just like his photograph, although slightly paler.

"Jess?" He smiles and stands up, his hand extended towards me. His cheeks have the mottled pink hue of someone who likes a drink.

"Hi." I shake his hand and stand to one side as he wrestles with a chair, trying to pull it out from the under the table.

"There we are!" he declares triumphantly. "Do sit down."

The bottle of champagne is already on ice, in a freestanding bucket to one side of our table. I notice his glass is empty.

He raises his hand towards a waitress. "Would you be so kind as to pour the champagne now?" he asks.

Nice manners with the waitstaff, I note. That's a tick in the "good" box. "I hope you haven't been waiting long?" I say, in my best heroine-from-1940s-film voice.

"No, not at all. I come here a lot on my own anyway, so it wouldn't have mattered."

To me, people dining alone is such a sad sight. Whenever I see it, I silently imagine how they have come to this. Perhaps their wife has recently run off with another man, leaving them bereft and devastated, hating their own company. Or maybe she has died and their children have all grown up and lead their own, active lives, with little time for their lonely, old dad.

"I stay here on business a lot." Tom's voice interrupts my thoughts. "So rather than sit in my room, which I find rather claustrophobic, I bring a book or some paperwork and eat down here."

Ah. Never thought of that option.

I raise my glass of champagne. "Well, it's lovely to meet you, and thanks for this." I notice it's Krug and must have cost him a fortune.

"My pleasure." He smiles warmly. "Would you like something to eat as well? They do a fantastic kedgeree with smoked salmon, if you like that sort of thing."

"Sounds great," I enthuse.

"Shall I order for you?" He looks at me questioningly.

I nod. "Yes, please do."

"What *don't* you like?"

"Um . . ." I think for a moment. "Broad beans. That's about it."

He reaches to his side and picks up the suit jacket carefully laid there. As he rummages through the inside pocket, I notice the label is Armani, without an "Emporio" in sight.

I could get used to this, I silently muse. Chilled, top-of-the-range champagne at the Ritz, and a well-dressed, well-mannered man who takes control *and* pays for everything. I'm starting to understand why some women prefer the company of older men.

He takes out a small case and opens it to reveal a pair of rimless glasses. Putting them on, he takes a cursory glance at the menu, then gestures to the maître d', who is hovering a couple of tables away. While he orders, I take the opportunity to study the roomful of privileged travelers who enjoy a way of life with which I have little or no experience.

The next table to ours is occupied by "ladies who lunch." Dripping in diamonds and the latest Chanel outfits, three of them have identical Hermès Birkin bags in red, costing a few grand each. The fourth is sporting a classic Chanel bag, but with a chrome strap rather than gold, proving it's the very latest. All four, without exception, have hair that looks like it's been injection molded on a conveyor belt. Highlighted blonde bob, side parting, sprayed to such rigidity that when they turn their heads, not a hair moves.

Their nails are all perfectly uniform, hands unsullied by the housework of the common woman.

Tuning in to their conversation for just a few seconds is compellingly dreadful. One is berating her son's boarding school for refusing to keep him there over a long weekend, lamenting that she and her husband will have to forgo their planned skiing trip, whilst another is complaining about the Filipino nanny who looks after her toddler daughter.

"I came home from the hairdresser's on Thursday afternoon, and Araminta greeted me with the words 'Herro, Mammy,'" she says, mimicking a Filipino accent. "I mean, can you *imagine*? The nanny will have to go."

Or better still the mother, I think mutinously, astonished that this woman could relay such a damning story against herself without the slightest trace of irony.

"All done. It'll be here in a few minutes." The waitress has disappeared, and Tom has removed his glasses again and is now following my eye line to the next table. "Hideous, aren't they?" he whispers. "I see them in here a lot. It's *Sex and the City* with the whiff of formaldehyde."

I laugh and take another sip of champagne. "Sometimes I think I'd like a life like that," I muse. "You know, swanning around shopping all the time, meeting my friends for lunch . . . but I know I'd get bored."

"Worse, *you'd* be bor*ing*," interjects Tom. "They have absolutely nothing to say that's of any interest, and believe me, I have overheard plenty of similar conversations whilst I've been eating alone."

"What do they talk about?"

"Hair, nails . . ." He holds up a finger for each subject. ". . . clothes, their kids—when they can remember their names— and lastly, their husbands."

I take a furtive look sideways again. "I wonder what their husbands do?"

Tom purses his lips. "They'll be company directors, something big in the City . . . that kind of thing. They will also spend a lot of time away from home under the pretext of work, but find plenty of time to cold call on their warm mistress installed in an all-expenses-paid little pied-à-terre somewhere."

Initially, I grin at what I assume to be his little exaggeration, then swiftly realize he's deadly serious. "Really? How do you know?"

He shrugs. "I don't know about *them* as such." He jerks his head towards the next table. "But I know an awful lot about women like them. I was married to one myself."

"Really?" I really . . . whoops, there it is again . . . must think of a new word to utter in such circumstances.

"Yep." He nods sagely. "We didn't even have any kids, so all my wife did all day was drink coffee with her equally idle friends, go shopping and play tennis. On the rare occasions I came home in time, dinner would be something heated up in the microwave whilst our relationship just went cold. So I had a mistress, too. You have to do something to relieve the monotony, don't you?"

My mouth drops open. Attractive, I know, but I can't help it in the face of such top-notch, revelatory gossip from a man I've only just met. "Blimey," I splutter. Well, at least it's not "really."

In true soap opera cliffhanger style, two steaming plates of kedgeree arrive as our very own ad break.

"Tuck in," he says breezily, "this is my favorite thing on the menu, so I hope you like it too."

He shows absolutely no sign of returning to the fascinating subject of his checkered past . . . well, I *assume* it's in the past . . . so I take the conversational rudder and steer it back.

"You were saying about your mistress . . ." I say casually, as if asking him to finish a story about his car breaking down.

He stops eating for a moment, fork poised in midair. "Oh, that was all a long time ago. I'm a good boy now, though more through lack of opportunity than choice." He smiles, presumably to show it's a joke.

"So, no mistress and no wife either?"

"Some would say you can't have the former without the latter," he replies, arching an eyebrow. "But no, I don't have either. The wife found out about the mistress and ran off with her tennis instructor. And once the subterfuge had gone, I found myself tiring of the mistress very swiftly, particularly when, knowing my wife was no longer on the scene, she started nagging me to make a commitment."

I loathe and detest the word "nagging," mainly because it's never used in referring to men, but I decide to let it pass on this occasion. The conversation is too good to get sidetracked.

"So you ended up with nobody?"

"Indeed." He smiles ruefully. "But I'm at an age when I'd rather be on my own than with the wrong person."

"But you're still shopping around on the Internet, I see."

He nods. "I'm hopeless at hanging round wine bars, not least because I hate that loud, ubiquitous rap music that sounds like Pam Ayres on steroids. And I tried a couple of traditional dating agencies, but after parting with a small fortune and being introduced to one nymphomaniac and a couple of bunny boilers, I felt it was better to trust my own judgment and use the Internet."

"Nymphomaniac? Sounds like every man's dream date." I laugh.

"Sorry, I forgot to mention she looked like Marlon Brando in a dress." He winces at the memory.

"What about the bunny boilers?" Enjoying myself immensely, I take another swig of champagne.

He narrows his eyes in thought. "One was just plain bonkers and carried a small rodent-like dog everywhere with her in a basket. She never left the house unless her daily horoscope was a positive one, and said the only reason she'd met with me was because she'd got my date of birth from the agency and our star charts were compatible."

I chuckle encouragingly and shake my head in disbelief.

"The second one," he continues, " was really attractive, and we had a lovely time on our first date. I remember thinking, 'Wow, I've hit the jackpot here.' " He stops briefly to finish off the last of his kedgeree.

"At some point during the evening, I must have mentioned I liked doughnuts, because the next day a basket of them was delivered to my office with a note that read: 'Thanks for a lovely evening. Here are a few of your favorite things.' "

I raise my eyebrows slightly, curious to know how that makes her a bunny boiler. Because from where I'm sitting, it's an impressively stylish and original gesture. He notes my skepticism. "Which, of course, was a nice touch," he adds, "and I rang immediately to thank her . . ."

He pauses for dramatic effect, gesturing for the waitress to remove our plates and taking a couple of mouthfuls of champagne. "Then a basket arrived the next day . . . and the day after that . . . and the one after that. In fact, *every* day for the next two weeks." He shakes his head. "And all the while, she's bombarding my office with calls, issuing instructions to my PA about making sure I get a doughnut with my morning coffee as that's what I like best." He makes a circling motion around his temple with a forefinger.

"So how did you get rid of her?"

"I wrote 'return to sender' on all the doughnut deliveries and refused to take her calls. She finally got the message," he says wearily. "But not before she turned up at reception and started sobbing loudly when I refused to go down and see her. She had to be gently removed by security."

I splutter with laughter, and a small amount of champagne tries to escape down my nose, causing my eyes to water. "Bloody hell," I choke. "You really *have* been unlucky."

Grinning, he passes me a fresh napkin. "I know. But enough of my dating disasters, I want to hear all about *you.*"

We pass the next hour very pleasantly indeed, sharing a hefty slice of black currant cheesecake whilst he asks me all about my background, my family and my job. He proves to be a great listener, interrupting with questions only when he wants to know more about something I have merely skipped over. I don't tell him about Olivia's health, preferring instead to talk of our happier days.

Over coffee, he senses my disillusionment with the world of daytime television and makes some suggestions for facilitating a change in a more serious direction. He even offers to link me up with an old friend of his who makes documentaries.

By the time we reach a post-coffee lull in the conversation, it's 4 p.m. and even the ladies who lunch have gone home, presumably to refresh their hairdos for some swanky dinner. As they are all stick thin, one presumes they spend a lot of time vomiting.

"So do you like being a marketing director?" Come on, give me a break. It's taken three hours for me to resort to such a question. Not bad going really.

His eyes light up. "I love it, because I have such freedom. Being *creative* . . . ," he emphasizes the word, ". . . means you can be where you want, when you want, as long as you have your pocket phone." He points to his matchbox-size mobile—the only thing men boast about having the smallest of.

"What do you market?"

"All sorts of products. My company makes everything to do with the fast-food life, from sugar sticks and drink sweeteners to malt vinegar and ketchup packets. I travel all over the world re-searching new ways of doing things."

Three slightly more elderly women shuffle into the empty table next to us and settle themselves down.

"They've had their afternoon nap and come out for high tea," whispers Tom. "They'll all be married to old majors or high court judges." He stands up. "Excuse me, nature calls."

Watching him cross the room, I notice he moves well. He has the self-assured walk of a man who's comfortable with himself, borne out of a fulfilling career and finally knowing what he wants from life.

Glowing from a surfeit of champagne, excellent food, and his highly entertaining company, I know I have an important decision to make before he returns to the table.

Without wishing to sound boastful, I'm pretty sure he would like to see me again. But is the feeling reciprocal?

Pros: attractive in an elder statesman kind of way, successful, wealthy, warm, funny, generous, a good raconteur, and seemingly emotionally uncomplicated.

Cons: I don't fancy him.

The question is, are all those plus points canceled out by the one minus? *Could* I ever fancy him? And if not, does it matter?

Men often say we're sexually and emotionally fickle, and of course we always flatly deny it. But just think about it. We *say* we want men to be x, y, and z on the Mr. Perfect tick list, but when it comes down to it, sexual attraction overrides everything else.

Consequently, a man can be jobless, feckless, and reckless with our feelings, but if we fancy him, that's all right then. For a time, anyway.

No, we must rise above such shallowness and I'm going to start the trend now by agreeing to meet Tom for a second date. He's my most eligible date yet and, who knows, he might have me panting with lust before you can say "Viagra."

"Would you like anything else?" He has reappeared at the table, and I notice he has combed his hair, drawing attention to his meticulously neat, old-fashioned side parting.

"No thanks, I'd better be going." I smile. "But thanks again for a wonderful lunch. I'll send you some doughnuts on Monday as a thank-you."

He laughs uproariously. "You're funny. Would you like to do this again? I always say you can't beat a chilled glass of champers and the company of a delightful young lady."

Just as I'm about to run with the baton of mature womanhood and agree to a second date, his last remark sends me metaphorically crashing to the floor, baton flying haphazardly through the air.

Instantaneously, with his talk of "champers" and "delightful young lady," his face has now morphed into that of my dad. The age difference may only be fourteen years, but he's an old forty-eight, and I'm a young thirty-four, so it suddenly feels like a gaping generational chasm.

My heart sinks to irretrievable, *Titanic* depths. "Tom, I've had a really lovely time, and I mean *really* lovely. But . . ."

"But you don't want to see me again." He smiles ruefully.

"No, I *do*," I bluster, feeling like the biggest heel since Vivienne Westwood's platforms era. "But only as a friend."

"Ah, I see," he says defeatedly, handing his credit card to a passing waiter. "Look, Jess, I've really enjoyed your company, but

I already have enough friends in my life, ones I probably don't see enough of as it is. Frankly, I'm looking for something a little more than that."

We are both standing now, facing each other over the table, the previously warm and jolly atmosphere now as cold and unpalatable as our leftover coffee.

"I'm sorry, Tom. I can't be that woman."

He mirrors the gesture. "Can't be, won't be, whatever. I appreciate your honesty though." He extends his hand, just as he did at the start of our date, and lets out a small sigh. "Anyway, it was lovely to meet you. I have really enjoyed our couple of hours together, regardless."

"Me too." I smile. "And I really hope you meet someone soon." God, that sounds patronizing, though I didn't mean it that way.

"I'm sure we both will."

Somehow I doubt it. Walking away from the table and towards the exit, I mull over the expectations of two strangers united in their desire to meet a special someone.

A forty-eight-year-old man clearly seeking a much younger woman who's slim, attractive, and possibly able to provide him with a family. Not for him a woman of his own age, perhaps past her physical prime but with many other plus points. And a thirty-four-year-old woman, slim, some might say attractive, endlessly looking for someone she fancies; turned on by unsuitable types who, invariably, are disastrous long-term prospects.

Each stuck in their dating rut. And subsequently, each facing disappointment time and time again.

But, albeit separately, our search will go on. I mean, let's face it, what else can you do?

Seventeen

*a*unty Jess!" Emily opens the door and flings her arms around my neck, squeezing tightly and lifting her feet off the floor so her body weight almost strangles me.

"What a welcome!" I splutter, tucking my hands under her bottom to take some of the strain. "I shall most definitely come here again."

As I step into the hallway and place her down, the most delicious smell of roasting meat assails my nostrils and, just for a moment, everything seems reassuringly normal.

Then Olivia walks into the hallway, wiping her hands on a tea towel. She's smiling, but looks pale and tired.

It's long been the routine that I would be invited over to join their family Sunday lunch about once a month, and I know she's keen to keep everything ticking along as usual. But underneath the cheery greetings and smiles exchanged in front of the children, I know we are both feeling weary and apprehensive.

The night of her lumpectomy, I called her at home, anxious to know the result. She told me it had been inconclusive, but that as soon as she knew she would call me. Since then, our only conversation had been to arrange this lunch.

"Hi, Jess, come on through."

I follow her into their welcoming kitchen, made larger by an extension onto the side of the house. Down one side is a long wooden table where Michael is sitting reading the papers.

He looks up. "Hi, little'un." He often calls me that, and Olivia is "big un," a rather ambiguous description she's not too fond of.

I am instantly struck by how drawn he looks. His eyes seem black with sadness and a small muscle in the side of his cheek twitches constantly. Admittedly, I haven't really studied his nails before, but now they are noticeably bitten to the quick, with visibly inflamed red patches.

Taking the glass of white wine Olivia offers me, I sit down at the table with Michael and start to flick through the stack of Sunday supplements, marveling that anyone finds the time to read them all.

Idly turning the pages, it strikes me how many stories there are relating to various types of cancer: how to spot it, how to beat it, miracle cures, and, horror of horrors, deaths. They have probably always been there, but of course now they leap out at me.

I become absorbed in an article by a television presenter who discovered she had colon cancer and now campaigns to raise awareness. As I take a sip of wine, I raise my eyes slightly and see Michael staring down at the page in front of me. We exchange a swift, knowing glance before he stands up and walks across to Olivia.

"Shall I lay the table?" he says briskly, opening the cutlery drawer.

She smiles and nods silently.

During this little exchange, there is no physical contact between them, and it strikes me as odd. Not that Michael and Olivia are ever pawing each other in public, just that they have always shared those discreet, tender little moments: like his fleeting hand on her waist, or her gentle touch on his forearm. Maybe I'm just imagining things.

"Aunty Jess, look!" Matthew careers into the kitchen, sliding across the wooden floor in his socked feet. "Mum bought me this." He waves a PlayStation game in my face which, judging by his excitement, is obviously the very latest release.

Olivia stands behind him, smiling benevolently, whilst Michael adopts a slightly mock expression of disapproval.

"I thought you loathed and detested computer games, that they are 'the scourge of modern childhood'?" I ask her, once Matthew has rushed out of the room again.

"I do," she replies. "But it's nice to treat them once in a while." She looks momentarily wistful. "Emily has the latest Barbie."

"Which, judging by my watch . . . ," Michael lifts his wrist and stares at it, ". . . should be old hat in about five minutes' time."

Right on cue, Emily walks into the kitchen carrying her trusted old teddy Roger. Barbie is conspicuous by her absence.

"Told you." Michael goes back to reading the papers.

"Hi, darling." Olivia grabs hold of Emily and clasps her in a swift hug. "Go get Matthew for me, will you? It's time for lunch."

As ever, Olivia has rustled up the most amazing Sunday roast with all the trimmings. She's always been a fantastic cook, whilst I struggle to even heat a microwave meal to the correct temperature. It's one of the few major differences between us.

Half an hour later, stuffed to the gills with garlic lamb and perfectly roasted, crispy potatoes, I sit back in my chair and let out a long sigh of satisfaction. "Thanks, Liv, that was stupendous."

Matthew is wriggling in his chair with excitable agitation. "Mummy, can I get down now, please?" His new PlayStation game beckons.

Normally, insistent that Sunday lunch is the most important event in the family calendar, Olivia would force the children to sit with us a little longer. But today she is more lenient.

"Go on then. But don't get square eyes," she says, repeating one of the old phrases our mother was always fond of.

"Actually, the telly's rectangular," says Matthew. He's in that very literal stage at the moment, where you could say it's five past three, and he'll point out that actually, it's only four and a half minutes past.

"Me too?" says Emily hopefully.

"You too, darling." Olivia smiles warmly and ruffles her daughter's hair. "Off you pop."

They rush off towards the living room, a breathless whirl of tangled hair, odd socks, and excited shrieks, leaving a distinctly gloomier kitchen table behind them.

"So how is everything?" I venture, looking at Olivia but shooting a quick sideways glance at Michael to gauge his reaction. As I haven't seen or spoken to him since Olivia told me the news, I'm unsure how to broach the subject.

"So, so." Olivia flattens out her hand and tilts it from side to side. I notice she too casts an apprehensive, almost wary look in Michael's direction.

He doesn't notice it, but clears his throat nervously and scrapes back his chair. Gathering up the pile of newspapers at his side, he stands up. "I'm going upstairs to do some work," he says, giving me a quick smile and kissing the top of Olivia's head as he passes. "See you both later."

Twisting her body to watch him walk along the hallway and up the stairs, Olivia turns back to me. "Work, my arse," she mutters.

"He'll sit on the loo for about half an hour reading the papers, then go into his study and fall asleep watching golf."

"Is everything all right between you?" I ask, worried by her uncharacteristic criticism of him, albeit mild.

"Vaguely." She turns down the corners of her mouth. "I mean, there's nothing wrong with our *marriage* as such, if that's what you mean. But this whole cancer business has thrown a bit of a hand grenade into our ordered existence. It's had a peculiar effect on him."

"In what way?" I keep my voice low, in the faint chance that Michael might be listening at the top of the stairs.

Olivia didn't seem to be worried about it, her voice almost booming. "Oh, he's gone into matter-of-fact mode, as if I'm just one of the many sick patients he sees every week. I know it's his way of coping, but I'm finding it very difficult." Her eyes look sad.

"He just won't sit down and talk about it. Every time I try to start a serious conversation, he becomes all shifty and suddenly finds something of utmost importance that he simply *has* to do. As you've just seen . . ." She gestures towards the door.

"Men have always had trouble dealing with emotions." I grin, trying to lighten proceedings. "He's obviously just gone into cave mode for a while. He'll soon be back out, beating his chest and dragging you round by the hair again. Probably, with any luck, when you get the all clear."

Olivia says nothing for a few seconds, staring at the table. Then she takes a deep breath. "I've had the results already."

I straighten my back and look intently at her, unable to read her expressionless face. "And?"

"And it's definitely cancerous. It also looks like it may have spread."

"*Looks* like? Don't they know for sure?" The word "cancerous" is enough for me to grasp that, far from being in the clear, Olivia's troubles are only just starting.

"They can't confirm it completely until I have more tests," she sighs. "The most effective way to find out is to have an MRI scan, so Michael's setting it up."

"Then what?" I can't bear it. I want to fast-forward through the next few weeks or months, to a time when we know everything will be all right.

"Then, if it has spread, I'll probably have to have this one removed," she says softly, cupping a hand over her right breast. "But they would do reconstructive surgery at the same time. So I'll have one fantastic Pamela Anderson breast and my own droopy one."

She attempts a little laugh, but it doesn't quite reach her eyes. I don't respond, my face stricken with worry and panic. There are a million other questions I want to ask, but again, a sense of injury rises to the surface and I have to know.

"Olivia, first you didn't tell me about the lump, and now you haven't told me this until now. I want you . . . *need* you to tell me about these things as soon as they happen. I want to be there for you."

She smiles sadly and strokes the side of my face. "Darling, I'm not hiding things from you. It's just that I want to tell you face-to-face, not in some distant phone call. That wouldn't be fair."

I leap to my feet, frustrated and needing to move. "Not fair on whom?"

"On you."

"You see? You see?" I jab my finger several times in her direction. "It's about *you* protecting *me*, shielding me from bad news until such a time as you're there to deal with any fallout. Olivia, I know you're slightly older than me, but you have to snap out of big sister mode and lean on me for a change." I don't mean it to, but my voice has become harsh and shrill.

Striding over to the kitchen window, I stand and stare out of it for a few moments, my hands resting on the edge of the sink. It's a calm, late-summer day, belying the whirling chaos going on inside my head.

When I turn back to face Olivia, she's staring at the floor, tears pouring silently down her face. Hastily, she tries to brush them away with the back of her sleeve.

"Oh, Liv, I'm so sorry, I didn't mean to be horrible." I rush across the room and kneel down on the floor in front of her, wrapping my arms around her hunched shoulders.

"It's not you," she says through muffled sobs. "It's just that everything is backing up on me and I haven't been able to deal with it. I'm either at work, where they don't know anything, or with the children, who mustn't be told anything until it's absolutely necessary." She casts a worried look at the doorway, then blows her nose. "They mustn't see me like this."

I stand up and sit back in the chair adjacent to her. "Surely you can fall apart a little in front of Michael when the children have gone to bed?"

She shakes her head. "Not really. You get to a point where everything seems so miserable that, when you have a couple of precious hours together, the last thing you want to do is spoil them by talking about problems."

I lean forward and squeeze her knee. "I understand, but it's really bad to bottle things up. You need to talk about it, particularly at this early stage, when it's all still such a shock."

"Well, when I want to fall apart in future, I know I can do so in front of you," she says with a weak smile. "Are you sure you're up to it?"

"Absolutely." My tone and expression are firm, but inside my rib cage it feels like an entire aviary of hummingbirds is trying to escape.

"Can we talk about something else now?" She wipes away the last vestiges of moisture from her face and smoothes down her hair. "As I said, it's not the time to fall apart with the children running around."

"Of course," I murmur. "But I just want to know one more thing . . . when are you having the scan?" It's only one of a hundred questions I want to ask, but it's the most pressing.

"As soon as possible, really. Michael and I were discussing it last night, and we thought one day next week would be good. Apparently, they will pay particular attention to my bones, as that's often a secondary site for cancer when the primary site is in the breast."

I feel overwhelmingly sick. "So you might have it elsewhere too?"

She shakes her head. "Very doubtful. They just have to check, that's all."

"Right." I smile, but I'm acutely aware it doesn't reach my eyes.

"Then, *if* I have to have the mastectomy and reconstructive surgery, we thought the October half term would be a good time. We'll send the children to stay with his parents in Bournemouth. They love it there."

"Love it where?" Matthew has appeared in the doorway, one sock missing and a splash of grape juice down the front of his shirt.

"At Grandma Baxter's, darling." Olivia gestures to him to come to her for a hug. "Daddy and I thought you and Emily might like to go there for half term."

"Yes!" He punches a small fist into the air, his wiry little body squirming with excitement. "Can we get fish and chips on the pier?"

"I expect so." Olivia beams, pulling him closer to her and

tucking in his shirt. "And if you're really good, perhaps an ice cream too."

"I'm a good girl." Emily saunters in, attracted by Matthew's noisy jubilation.

"Em, we're going to Grandma and Grandpa Baxter's to have fish and chips and ice cream!" he enthuses.

"Yeeeeeeehhhh!" Emily starts jumping up and down and they join hands in the middle of the room, swinging each other round in a cyclone of unbridled excitement.

I turn to look at Olivia. She's watching them with a smile of maternal pride, but her eyes are dark pools of sadness, and not for the first time, I wonder how she's going to cope if things get worse.

Watching the children whooping and dancing in front of me, I suddenly yearn for it to be Olivia and I, young again and free of the responsibilities and disappointments of adult life.

Eighteen

Monday morning again. I have barely slept from worrying about Olivia, and now I face yet another week of trivial faux jollity at *Good Morning Britain* whilst having to hide the angst I'm feeling underneath. Not for the first time in recent days, I feel there *has* to be more to life.

I arrive at the office, wave across at Tab, who's on the phone, and plonk myself down in front of my computer with all the enthusiasm of a teetotaler at the Munich beer festival. The mood I'm in, I can't even be bothered to check my hotmail account for any potential dates. Instead, I log on to my work e-mail to deal with any problems lurking there first.

The e-mail address Ben@sunshinehouse.com leaps out at me as one I don't recognize, so I double click on it straightaway.

Hi Jess,

Remember me?

Er, no actually, if the truth be known.

We met through Tab and Will the other night and you thought I was having a go at you because you worked in the big, bad world of television.

Ah yes, I remember now. The Archangel Gabriel in human form.

Anyway, I hope you don't mind, but I asked Tab for your e-mail address because, after you'd gone, she was telling me about the makeovers you oversee for the program. And basically, I was wondering whether I could nominate someone?

She's named Anne and she has worked at Sunshine House for the past five years, helping out with the children. They absolutely adore her and, believe it or not, she does it for virtually nothing, just a few expenses.

Her only child, Sarah, died of leukemia seven years ago, and I suppose it's her way of coping. But she's a completely selfless woman and I would love to see her pampered for a day.

A tear plops onto my keyboard and I hastily wipe my face before anyone in the office notices. All my Olivia emotions come flooding to the surface.

Anyway, I don't want to put you in an awkward position, and I understand completely if you can't help, so just let me know. But to be honest, I have been emotionally scarred since your outburst in the pub, and this might just mollify me enough not to sue.

I smile at the screen. Not such a Goody Two-Shoes total bore after all.

Anyway, it was nice to meet you.

Regards,
Ben Thomas

PS: If you fancy doing a general piece on the charity, the boy band Phit is coming to visit us soon. I could ask their people if they would mind being filmed there. To be honest, we could do with the publicity to get donations up a bit.

Without hesitation, I click on reply.

Dear Ben,

Nice to hear from you, and of course I remember you! I would like to comment on your claim about emotional scarring, but my lawyers have advised me to say nothing at this point.

That aside, Anne sounds like a worthy contender for a makeover. We have a forward planning meeting this morning, so I'll suggest it and come back to you with an answer as soon as possible.

I hope you're well.

Regards,
Jess Monroe

A number of my colleagues have already started trailing into Janice's office like the walking dead, fever pitch with excitement at the thought of yet another Monday morning planning meeting where all our ideas are knocked down like dominoes. I bring up the rear, clutching my ideas, well spaced on a sheet of paper and in particularly large type.

Janice is the executive producer of the program, which basically means she takes all the credit for everyone else's hard work. When things go wrong, however, she bats off blame in the direction of some hapless minion. Quite often me.

When you have a good woman boss, it can't be beaten. But a bad one makes any ill-tempered male employer seem like a walk in the park. Sadly, Janice is in the latter category. Unmarried with no children, she believes in what I call "presenteeism." That is, being in the office for the sake of it when there's absolutely no earthly point in being there. Like at 8 p.m. at night, for example, when any normal, well-balanced human being has gone home to live some kind of life.

Of course, Janice can justify the black void that is her home and social life by pretending it's because she dedicates so much time to her job. Whereas anyone who has met her will know it's simply because she's deeply unpleasant, petty, and socially inept. And those are just her good points. Small, with a seventies Roger Daltry haircut and brown eyes, Kevin calls her the cocker spaniel, though not to her face, of course. "She needs a good shag," he spits, whenever her name is mentioned. Though I notice none of my male colleagues ever rushes forward to volunteer.

"Ah, Jess, so glad you could make it. Sorry we had to start without you," she says sarcastically as I scuttle into her office. She uses the same, deeply unoriginal line each week to whichever unfortunate is the last to arrive.

"Right!" Her beady eyes rest on me. "Let's hope that in your case, being last means being the best. Fire away."

Normally, I would waltz through my list with the artificial brightness of someone who really believes that the ideas they're suggesting are both fascinating and original, when the truth, of course, is that it's usually a load of recycled old bollocks.

But today my heart isn't in it, and I flatly recite my ideas as if reading a shopping list.

"No, no, no, no, and no," intones Janice with relish, firing her poisonous darts as if my ideas were little funfair ducks filing past her desk.

The last one on my list is the proposed makeover of Anne, the wholly deserving woman who selflessly gives her time free of charge to help terminally ill children.

Janice wrinkles her pug nose. "Bit worthy, isn't it? Charity workers like her are ten a penny. It doesn't really grab me. Haven't you got someone a little more dramatic, you know, who's been beaten up by her husband for years and a makeover might just give her the confidence boost she needs to finally leave him."

"Er, I don't think a domestic violence issue can be solved with a bit of lip gloss and some curlers. It's a bit more complex than that." I shift uneasily in my seat. "It would also be a bit of a legal minefield to name and shame the man if they're still together and presenting an outwardly happy picture to the world."

There's a pregnant pause as we go into a stare standoff across the hushed room, she clearly willing me to defy her further, me mentally fantasizing about impaling her on the stupid cactus she keeps on her desk: according to Kevin, "the only prick she can get."

"The boy band Phit is visiting the house soon, so maybe if we do the makeover, we can persuade them to give us the exclusive on that," I offer, desperate to deflect some of the stinging criticism.

Janice's heavily penciled eyebrows shoot up. "Well, why didn't you say so earlier? Honestly, Jess, I seriously worry about your sense of priorities sometimes. Phit as an afterthought?" she says witheringly. "Fine, let's do it."

Two seconds later, she has swiveled her head *Exorcist* style to annihilate the ideas of some other quivering producer. I just sit there, their voices washing over me, wondering how on earth I found myself working for a television program so trite, shallow, and celebrity obsessed it makes the reality show *Big Brother* look like PBS.

*A*fter a gallingly wearing day of dealing with Phit's "people," I feel I have climbed Mount Kilimanjaro in a pair of flip-flops, only to slide halfway back down again just before reaching the summit.

Ben, bless him, works in a straightforward world with decent people who have no agenda other than to help others and have absolutely no delusions of grandeur. What you see is what you get. Clearly, he thought filming Phit would simply involve one phone call to their representative. The reality, as anyone who works even on the periphery of "showbiz" will tell you, is a soul-destroying merry-go-round of unreturned phone calls, numerous faxes falling into a black hole, and endless conditions and promises made to try and secure even the most benign, banal piece of footage lasting about two minutes.

It's always the same old story. Unknown, relatively untalented, glorified karaoke band wants to be famous and their publicity people bombard you with calls and increasingly desperate "ideas" to get them written about or filmed. Once you bite and contribute towards making them household names, they eventually become precious and start complaining about "press intrusion." Only the genuinely talented or those who know how to play the press game ever achieve longevity in the music business. But Phit is having its fifteen minutes of fame and, right now, I have to play along if I want to get Anne that makeover.

The main problem arises from the fact that one of the band

members—Ned Pearson—has recently been found in flagrante with a lap dancer. Not unusual for a single, heterosexual pop star, you might think, but for a supposedly squeaky clean boy band that sells itself to girls as young as ten, it's nothing short of catastrophic.

So, one of the conditions imposed is that absolutely no mention be made of this incident, either to Ned himself or in any subsequent narration on the item.

Just after I'd spent half an hour trying to convince Janice to agree to the terms, and suffering all the ritual humiliation that went with it, I returned to my desk to find a message saying Phit's record company bosses didn't think it was a good idea for them to be filmed during such "sensitive" times. All together now, aaaaaarrrrrggghh!

Incensed by such puerile self-obsession in the face of such a worthy cause, I rang the office of the chairman of the record company and ranted at his PA for a good five minutes about unreliable, talentless pop stars letting down sick little children who had hoped their big moment was going to be filmed for posterity. "It would have been a wonderful keepsake for their poor, emotionally drained parents," I added for good measure.

"Leave it with me," she said. So I had and, shortly afterwards, struggled home where I now sit, with a piping hot Marks and Spencer meal for one in my left hand and a glass of chilled chardonnay in my right. Better still, it's cold and wet outside, I'm warm and dry inside, and *Law and Order* is about to start. Ding dong. The doorbell. Ignore it and hopefully the unannounced visitor will eventually go away.

Ding dong. Bugger.

Ding dong. Ding dong. Ding dong.

If this isn't someone telling me we all have only four minutes left to live, I won't be responsible for my actions. I angrily fling open the door and scowl out into the darkness.

"He's dumped meeeeeeeee!" a voice wails from the murky gloom.

It's Kara. Before I can respond, she shoves her way past me into the hallway, her soaked umbrella showering my slippers with raindrops.

Following her through to the sitting room, I sigh heavily and switch off the TV just as the thumping beat of *Law and Order* starts. My meal for one is already developing a film on top.

"Fucking bastard. How dare he!" spits Kara, removing her coat and lobbing it onto the wooden chair in the corner. She has yet to even say hello to me.

"Sit down," I say wearily, gesturing to the comfy armchair I was blissfully nestled in just moments ago. "Cup of tea?"

"Something stronger," she barks, "wine if you have it."

Yes, your ladyship. I shuffle through to the kitchen and pour her a glass of the chardonnay. When I return, she's slumped back in the chair, staring at the ceiling.

Placing the glass of wine by her side, I sit down on the adjacent sofa. "So tell me what's happened," I say gently.

Her features momentarily harden, then almost as quickly crumple with distress. "Dan came home from work today and told me he doesn't want to be with me anymore . . ." Her voice peters away as she struggles not to sob. She shrugs, as if to indicate that's all there is to say.

"Did he say why?"

"Oh, the usual bollocks about loving me but not being *in* love with me. It must have taken him all of five minutes to come up with *that* one," she says bitterly, regaining her composure slightly.

I frown. "Has there been anything about his behavior recently to suggest this was coming?"

"No." She shakes her head. "In fact, I thought he was going to propose soon." She starts sniffling again at the thought.

Passing her a tissue from the same box I used for Olivia, I struggle to find something reassuring to say. "He'll be back, you'll see. He's probably just going through a bad patch at work and taking it out on you."

"Work?" She spits the word out as if it were a piece of phlegm. "Gigging around pubs and clubs at night, then sleeping most of the day. Hardly *work*, is it?"

Previously, Kara has always informed me that Dan is permanently teetering on the edge of the big time, so I am rather taken aback by her sudden change of heart.

Having been to a couple of his gigs myself, I can report he is the lead guitarist in a band called Tint, best described as the love child of Coldplay and REM. Several record company A&R's have been to see them, but as yet the lucrative deal remains elusive.

"You've always been very supportive of what he does," I point out, more due to a lack of anything else to say.

"Well, you have to be, don't you?" She sneers slightly. "God forbid I don't look like the supportive little girlfriend, fawning from the sidelines."

Oh dear, I've been here before. Whenever she's single, Kara is a raging feminist, finding sexism in every little male utterance. But as soon as she's dating, her sisterly principles do a runner and she's ready to play the Mrs. in a heartbeat.

"You seem quite upset," I venture bravely. "Perhaps you should try to talk to him about this, tell him how you feel."

"What, and have whatever shred of self-respect I have thrown back in my face?" She glares at me challengingly. " No thanks."

"Maybe he feels that *you* don't care enough about him, and he's doing this as a kind of challenge, to see how you react." I wince slightly, waiting for the onslaught of a feminist diatribe on how women should never prostrate themselves on the altar of men's mind games. Or something like that.

"Do you think so?" she says meekly, grasping pathetically at my emotional straw.

"Yes," I say effusively, warming to the theme. "Men are just like babies really. They do things solely to get your attention." I don't know when I became such an expert on the male psyche, but my comment seems to have the desired effect.

Kara straightens her back and visibly brightens. "I've got an even better idea."

"What?" I smile encouragingly.

"*You* talk to him on my behalf and find out. That way, I don't have to face the humiliation of being rejected again."

My smile evaporates. "Me? He's not going to tell *me* what's going on inside his head, is he?"

She shrugs. "He might. Sometimes it's easier to talk to someone fairly objective, although of course you're on *my* side."

I nod in assent, but inside I'm thinking that if I was Dan, I'd have dumped her long ago.

"Yes, that's it." She's positively cheerful now. "Take him out for a drink and tell him that I'm the best thing that's ever happened to him. See what he says."

I could probably write the script now, I think, and the words "happy ending" don't spring to mind. But I stay quiet, instead picking up her empty wineglass and returning to the kitchen to fill it.

"You know, I'm so glad I came round to see you," she shouts through the open doorway. "At first I thought, nah, what's the point of getting advice from the terminally single Jess . . . what can she possibly know about the ups and downs of a serious relationship? But it's been a real tonic, it really has."

Would Ex-Lax show up in a glass of wine? I muse. Sadly, it probably would.

Nineteen

ell, well, well, it seems my little tantrum to the chairman's PA has paid off. I really must learn to throw a wobbly more often. As my old grandma—a career complainer—used to say: "The squeaky wheel gets the grease."

I came into work this morning to find a message on voice mail saying that Saffron Records has had a change of heart and *will* now allow Phit to be filmed at Sunshine House this afternoon.

Which means I have precisely one hour to organize myself and a crew, and get down there in time. Short notice, short shrift, I'm afraid, and I just know the only available camera crew will be the two unaffectionately known as Stinky and Perky.

One and a half hours later, I'm crammed into an ancient Volvo that reeks of dogs and the BO of Stinky the soundman in whose armpit my face is practically buried. The cameraman, aka Perky, is renowned for his long-winded, tedious monologues about the state of the country and he's in the middle of one right now. Asylum seekers . . . drone drone . . . should go back where they belong . . . drone drone . . . come over here and take our money and women . . . drone drone.

Surrounded by camera equipment, my feet jammed under the seat in front, it's possibly the most uncomfortable journey of my life. Not for the first time, I mull over other career options.

"Turn left here," I mumble, trying desperately not to gag. As the car sweeps onto the driveway of Sunshine House, I have to restrain myself not to leap out and kiss the tarmac.

Ben is waiting just inside the front entrance, a pleasantly warm, welcoming, and nicely fragrant area after the traumatic, stench-filled journey. The building is modern and purpose-built from charity funds, with a small reception desk to one side and a vast, busy notice board peppered with photographs of smiling children.

There's a small clutter of chairs scattered around a low coffee table and I wonder how many anxious parents have sat there, waiting to be checked into an establishment that offers so much comfort but where you'd do anything not to have to be there.

"Hi there." He smiles, extending his hand for me to shake. "Good journey?"

"Fine thanks." I force a smile back. Now isn't the time to complain, particularly as the crew are ambling through the door.

"Great." Ben claps his hands together, then looks at his watch. "Well, we're expecting Phit to pitch up in about half an hour, so I expect you'll want to get set up. Follow me."

He leads us down the hall into a well-heated lounge area with a large television in one corner and several sofas and beanbags scattered around. In the other corner, there's a large collection of toys and a stack of well-used board games like Monopoly, Junior Scrabble, and Clue.

"This is the communal lounge area where families can get together if they wish," says Ben. "If they don't feel up to socializing, they each have their own little unit with beds and a small sitting room. But this is where Phit will meet the children."

Leaving the crew to set up the camera and lights, I follow Ben down the corridor for a guided tour of the center. He shows me an empty unit, waiting for a new family to arrive that afternoon, then leads me into an annex at the back that houses the small kitchen cum canteen. It's empty.

"We've got three families staying with us at the moment, and they're all in their units right now. Coffee?" He points at an instant coffee machine.

"That would be lovely, thanks." I wander over to a small notice board at the back of the room and study the photographs. Again, it's a selection of shots of children and their parents, just like those found in any family home. Except, of course, for the stark difference that these children have a death sentence hanging over their young, innocent heads.

Ben appears at my side brandishing a cup of coffee and two sugar packets. He points to the picture of an angelic-looking blond boy, aged about seven, grinning widely and standing slap bang in the middle of a puddle. "That's Billy. He was such a great character."

"Was?"

"Yes, he died about six months ago," says Ben matter-of-factly. "He needed a bone marrow transplant to save his life, but they just couldn't find a match for him. His whole family had the tests, and so did everyone here at the center. But I'm afraid nothing even came close. It happens that way sometimes."

Staring at the smiling face of the little boy robbed of his life before it's barely begun, I feel overwhelmed by sadness. "Did he die here?"

Ben smiles warmly. "Yes, he did. That's the whole point of this place. When parents know their child hasn't got much longer to live, they can come here and be surrounded by a support network. We have doctors, nurses, and counselors on hand if need be, as well as general staff just to help out with cooking, cleaning, or even a bit of babysitting if the parents want a break."

I walk over to a table and sit down. "So where do you fit in?"

"Me?" He sits opposite me and runs a hand through his hair. "Well, I sort of run the place, but I'm also trained in grief counseling."

We sit in silence for a few moments, him staring down into his coffee cup, me studying the top of his head whilst deep in thought.

"Doesn't it ever get you down?" I say eventually. "You know, getting to know the children, losing them, and then having to deal with their parents' grief as well as your own?"

"Sometimes." He shrugs. "But it's not about *me*, is it? It's about the children and the families they leave behind. I would feel horribly self-indulgent if I allowed my grief to overwhelm me when it's so much more valuable to hold it together and help the parents to cope. After all, their distress is always going to be much worse than mine."

"Put like that, it makes perfect sense," I reply. "But I'm still not so sure I could deal with it. I'm probably too selfish."

He makes a scoffing noise. "Nonsense. You'd be surprised what you can cope with when you have to."

Despite promising her I wouldn't discuss it with anyone, I suddenly feel compelled to tell him about Olivia. At this precise point, he doesn't even know of her existence, and that anonymity proves too tempting. After all, what harm can it do to share the burden with a virtual stranger?

"It's funny you should say that," I say with a half-smile. "My sister has just been diagnosed with breast cancer and is relying on me to hold it together." It feels odd but liberating to have finally told someone.

"And *are* you holding it together?" He looks at me intently, as if searching for clues.

"Kind of." I shrug, none too sure myself. "I'm being strong in front of her, but I must confess I have lost it a couple of times when I've been on my own."

"That's entirely normal." He smiles reassuringly. "You'd be unusual if you didn't."

"I suppose it's a form of panic really. I can't bear the thought that her children might lose their mummy."

"And that you might lose your sister . . ."

I nod. "Yes, that too." Before I know it, tears are pricking the corners of my eyes and I start to blink furiously, determined not to cry in front of someone I barely know.

Ben, seemingly nonplussed, stands up and walks behind the kitchen counter. Seconds later, he returns with a box of tissues and quietly places it in front of me.

"How bad is it?" he asks.

I dab my eyes. "I'm not really sure, as everyone involved in the diagnosis is being rather noncommittal at the moment. She's about to have an MRI scan to see whether it has spread, and if so, then probably a mastectomy."

Ben considers what I've said for a few moments. "Well, I'm certainly no expert on breast cancer, but if, as it sounds, they've caught it in the early stages, then there's still plenty of hope."

"I sincerely hope so. But it's the waiting I can't stand." I blow my nose, feeling pathetic to be disintegrating in a building full of young children that hope abandoned long ago.

"Yes, the parents here say that, too. But unlike your situation, there's no chance of a happy ending for them."

Reaching into my handbag for my notebook, I place it on the table in front of me. "Do you mind if I ask you some questions for the report? I want to make sure I get it absolutely right."

"No problem."

"Do the children know they're dying?"

He nods. "Yes. That's part of what we do here . . . help the parents to tell them and keep reinforcing the message. But children are a lot more accepting of death than adults."

"In what way?" I'm jotting it all down.

Pursing his lips in thought, he stares into the middle distance for a few seconds. "They don't get as sentimental about it, if you like. The parents think of all the future missed birthdays, the missed wedding, the missed birth of their grandchildren, but the child doesn't. They don't really have an awareness of all that, so they don't think about it."

"So how *do* they react?"

He gives a little sigh. "Um, it depends really. They pick up an awful lot from their parents, so if Mum and Dad can pretend to be quite matter-of-fact about it, then the child will cope better. But if they fall apart, the child will react to that and become very upset too."

"Are you able to tell me more about Billy?" I jerk my head back towards the notice board and the photographs.

"Yep. His parents have given us media clearance to talk about him. Some parents retreat into a shell and block out the world, but Billy's mum and dad want to help the center whichever way they can, and they also take comfort from seeing him written or spoken about."

I scrawl "Billy" on the page and underline it. "So when did he first come here?"

Ben screws up his face, trying to think straight. "It was last summer, about August, I think. He was from Kendal, in the Lake District, and he'd been under the care of a specialist unit in Bristol whilst waiting for a bone marrow match."

Seeing me scribbling to keep up, he pauses for a moment, watching and waiting for me to get it all down.

"He got weaker and weaker, until it was pretty obvious he was going to lose the battle. So his parents brought him here." He smiles at the memory. "He was such a fantastic little boy, so full of life considering what he was going through. He used to call me Big Ben . . . he thought that was hilarious." He tails off, a sad look on his face.

I put my pen down. "This isn't for the report, but I'm fascinated to know, so I hope you don't mind me asking . . . do you *know* when someone is about to die?" I can't remember the last time I asked such a weighty, significant question within the context of something work related.

He turns down the corners of his mouth, pondering the question. "Everyone's different. Some simply pass away in their sleep, which is the nicest way to go for them, but horrible for the parents because they feel deprived of the chance to have said a final, final good-bye. But Billy was quite something. He *knew* when he was going to die."

He takes a sip of his lukewarm coffee and glances over at the notice board to Billy's picture.

"Billy was a huge Manchester United fan, and his bedroom here was covered in posters and memorabilia. Even his quilt cover was Man U. His dad used to take him to quite a few matches, but that became an impossibility after he got ill, so we arranged for Ryan Giggs to pay him a visit here.

"I'll never forget his little face when Ryan walked up to his bed. It was magical." He pauses for a moment, clearly savoring the memory, then lets out a deep sigh. "Anyway, after Ryan had gone, Billy asked to watch his favorite TV show, *Byker Grove*—he *loved* that—and his mum and dad sat either side of his bed and watched it with him. When it had finished, he lay back on his pillows and said 'I'm ready to die now.' A few minutes later, he drifted off to sleep . . . and that was it."

Tears are unashamedly pouring down my face. Tears for Olivia, tears for Matthew and Emily, and tears for a little boy called Billy who I never even met but, to my mind, represents everything that is unfair and unjust about this world we live in. A world where good, innocent people get struck down in the prime of their life, whilst others with shameful existences frequently live long into old age.

Ben looks concerned and passes me another tissue. "Sorry, I didn't mean to upset you."

"Please don't apologize," I mumble through the tissue. "Bizarrely, that story makes me feel lucky, because I know that Olivia still has a long way to go before things get that bad. *If* they get that bad." I cross my fingers.

"That's the spirit." He smiles, glancing at his watch again. "Look, Phit should be here at any moment. Shall we go and find Anne so I can introduce you? She's so excited about coming up to London for her makeover next week."

I nod and stand up. It will be good to leave the sadness behind for the moment and focus on putting something happy and positive out into the world.

Twenty

It's 8 a.m. and, believe it or not, I'm sitting at my desk clattering away at my keyboard. For the simple reason that I want to make sure the report on Phit's visit to Sunshine House is as accurate and thought-provoking as it can possibly be on a television program that usually prides itself on sound bite vacuity.

Sunshine House and its special occupants deserve better, and I'm determined to give it to them—even if I have to lock antlers with Janice in the middle of the office.

After our chat in the kitchen, Ben had taken me back through to the communal lounge, where Stinky and Perky were all set up and chatting to a pleasant-looking woman in her early forties with short brown hair and the clear blue eyes of a young girl.

It was Anne, and we spent the next ten minutes huddled in a corner, talking about her work with the charity and the death of her daughter Sarah, also from leukemia.

Sarah was just six when she was diagnosed, and died in her mother's arms less than two years later. Anne told me that Sunshine House had stopped her from falling apart, and that she wanted to give something back by helping others like her. She came off as genuine and caring, with a wonderfully dry wit, and after watching her interacting with the children, cajoling them into being more confident around Phit after they'd performed and cuddling them with delight afterwards, I wanted to be her friend.

"I told you she was incredible," Ben whispered, seeing me standing to one side and watching Anne tickling a little girl named Jane as her parents looked on.

I nodded. "She is. Has she never tried to have any more children?"

He nodded. "Yes. Sarah died seven years ago, and Anne left it a couple of years before trying for another baby, but sadly nothing happened. I think she and her husband, Ralph, are now resigned to the fact that it probably won't."

"She's only forty-two," I replied, having established her age during our chat. "Surely she could go for IVF or something?"

"They haven't got the money. The NHS says she's too old for treatment, so she'd have to go private and it's an expensive business."

Especially when she works mostly voluntarily, I thought, feeling anger rising inside me at the injustice of it. "What does Ralph do for a living?"

"He's a security guard down at the local supermarket. He's very supportive and they seem to have a good marriage." Ben smiled. "They now pour all their energy and attention into their two West Highland terriers."

I had left Sunshine House determined not to let any of them down, both with the film on Phit and with Anne's makeover scheduled for next week. I know it's strange, but somehow helping out Sunshine House makes me feel as though I'm helping out Olivia as well. Just the sense of taking action is one I relish. This morning, I have already e-mailed Kevin, Trudi, and Camilla to ensure they make an extra-special effort with her hair, makeup, and clothes.

"She's a really special friend of mine," I write. A lie of course, but it feels good to say it.

An hour later, I check over the script for the Phit film and slump back in my chair, finally satisfied with it.

"Bloody hell, alert the media. Jess Monroe at her desk before lunch." It's the ever-sarcastic Janice, peering over my shoulder. "To what do we owe the pleasure?"

"I'm just finishing off the script for the Phit film," I reply with as much geniality as I can muster. "It went really well. It's going to make a great item."

"I'll be the judge of that," she says ominously, heading towards her lair.

Thankfully, despite being the bitch queen from hell, Janice knows a good item when she sees one and has just given the go-ahead for the Phit film to run tomorrow. If she hadn't, I seriously would have contemplated resigning over it, such is my devotion to the cause at this point. Now all I have to do is pray that some major news event doesn't knock it off the schedule and conserve my energy for making sure Anne's makeover still goes ahead next week.

I can just see it now. Janice will say "But we've already done Phit visiting Sunshine House. That's quite enough publicity for the charity" and I will reply "Yes, but this is about rewarding a woman who selflessly gives her time free of charge to help sick children."

Then Janice will hit back: "Admirable, I'm sure, but this is a ratings-driven TV show, not some charitable rewards scheme for do-gooders." And I will fly across the office and punch her teeth out. OK, so I made that last bit up.

After grabbing a quick sandwich with Tab in the canteen, I return to my computer to put the finishing touches to the script for tomorrow's makeover, a trucker called Barry whose wife is threatening to leave him if he doesn't shave off an unruly beard and wave good-bye to his greasy ponytail.

Wrinkling my nose, I stare at the photograph of him in his grease-smeared lumberjack shirt and black . . . at least, I *think* they're black . . . jeans, and wonder whether a damn good scrub in the bath might do the trick. I shudder to think what Kevin's reaction is going to be when he claps eyes on him.

The script is fine, littered with the usual job-related clichés such as "Barry doesn't have any truck with fancy clothes, but his wife Jill is steering him towards a new image." Pulitzer Prize—winning stuff.

A new e-mail suddenly pops into my in-box and I glance at it for a couple of seconds, vaguely familiar with the address but unable to remember who it is. Double clicking on it, my eyes scroll quickly to the bottom for a name, and I freeze with shock.

It's from Simon, the man I last saw as he hightailed it out through the kitchens, leaving me the bill and a heavily dented ego.

Hi there,

Bloody cheek. Blasé as you like.

I'd like to think you'd remember me for my wit and personality, but I suspect it will be because I abandoned you halfway through our first date. I can only apologize profusely and hope you forgive me.

I thought about e-mailing you the next day to try to explain, but

it's a complicated story and I felt the impersonal nature of computers wouldn't be appropriate. So I stalled, then days became weeks,
and after that I felt I had left it too late and that you'd probably
moved on anyway.

Anyway, my complicated story has now become a little less so
and I was wondering whether you would give me the chance to give
you an explanation face-to-face? It's just that I really enjoyed your
company, although I know my strange behavior didn't back this up!

So, any chance of us meeting up again? I fully understand if
the answer is no, but as I said earlier, all I can do is apologize for
what happened and promise to give you a full explanation if you feel
like hearing it.

If you say yes, I promise to stay put for the entire date and buy
copious amounts of champagne to make up for my ungentlemanly
behavior!

Yours hopefully,
Simon

"Well, fuck me sideways," I mutter aloud.

"I beg your pardon?" Tab is giving me a stunned look from
across the desk.

"Guess who I've just had an e-mail from?"

"Orlando Bloom?"

I shake my head and pull an "I wish" face. "No, you'll never
guess."

"Well, why bloody ask me then?" Tab raises her eyes
heavenward.

"Simon."

"Simon?" She looks puzzled.

"The bloke who did a runner through the kitchens, remember?"

She widens her eyes. "*Really?* Cheeky sod, what did he want?"

I stare at his e-mail again and scroll up and down, just to make sure. Dating on the Internet certainly presents some interesting twists. "He wants to meet me to explain why he left in such a hurry."

Tab makes a loud scoffing noise. "Well, I hope you're going to press delete and not even bother replying. Can you believe the sheer nerve of it?"

I purse my lips for a few moments, deep in thought. "It might be worth going along, just for the hell of it."

"Hell is the right word," mutters Tab down the side of her computer screen. "Have you completely lost your mind?"

"I really fancied him though." I pout. "And I don't feel that way about many people."

"You said Donald Rumsfeld had sexy eyes the other day. Are you going to go on a date with him, too?" she hisses. "If you want my advice, don't touch this Simon bloke with a bargepole. He sounds bad news to me."

We leave it at that, and Tab returns to making work-related phone calls, while I alternate between daydreaming about Simon and tinkering with my ideas list for the next forward-planning meeting. Every time Tab ventures away from her desk, I make a furtive call to one of the gang to gauge their reaction to the unexploded hand grenade sitting in my in-box. Defuse or detonate? That is the question.

"Ooooh, definitely detonate," opines Richard. "Mount his cannon, rattle his balls, and fire, baby, fire! Then leave him empty and impotent to rust in a corner." He loves a theme, does Richard.

"Vot is thees detoooonate?" says Lars.

"Set off . . . activate," I explain. "Basically, Lars, I'm asking whether you think I should ignore the e-mail or go and meet him."

"Ah. In that case, you must leave vell enough alone."

It takes me several attempts to reach Madeleine on her mobile, and when I do she's panting loudly.

"Oh God, what have I interrupted?" I wince, fearing the worst.

She laughs. "I'd like to tell you I'm halfway through the shag of my life, but sadly it's nothing more than a particularly arduous dance routine." After a few seconds, her breathing starts to sound more controlled. "So, what's happening?"

"Remember my first Internet date . . . the one who legged it without even saying good-bye? Well, he's e-mailed me and wants to meet up to explain."

"Isn't he the one you really fancied?"

"Yep."

"Then go for it," she says matter-of-factly. "Sod the explanation. Just have a laugh and sleep with him, or you'll die wondering."

So there we have it. A straw poll of my friends has come up with two "shag hims" and two "leave well enough alones."

Which leaves me with the deciding vote. What *is* a girl to do?

Twenty One

One minute I'm queuing in isolated splendor in Star-bucks, the next I'm hemmed in by buggies of every color, size, and designer name, each housing a cooing baby extending its hand towards the cake counter.

"Blimey, where did they all come from?" I say to the assistant as she hands me a cafe latte.

"It's the same every morning," she says wearily. "They drop their older kids at school, then all come here with the preschool ones to meet up for a gabfest."

On the one hand, I want to run screaming from the endless chatter about little Tommy's sleep patterns, eating habits, and bowel movements. On the other, in many ways, it's the ideal, in-nocuous environment for my meeting with Simon.

Yes, yes, I *know* I probably shouldn't have responded to his e-mail. If I had an ounce of pride, I should have simply ignored it and got on with my life. But I succumbed.

If it makes you judge me any less harshly, I *did* leave him to stew for several days before replying though.

I suppose curiosity got the better of me, and I wanted to know exactly why he'd done a bunk all those months ago and never been in touch since.

"So just ask him that via e-mail," replied Tab tersely, when I tried to explain why I was going to meet up with him.

She's absolutely right, of course. I could easily have done that and avoided the effort and potential humiliation of meeting with him. A notable advantage of Internet romance. But to be honest, there's another, more fundamental reason why I wanted to clap eyes on him again.

"I want to see if I still fancy him as much," I confessed sheepishly.

Tab made a loud scoffing noise. "That's the big difference between you and me," she said. "I could never fancy someone who had done that to me."

And I could never fancy Will, I thought, but decided against saying so.

So here I am, in the heart of Nappy Valley, South West London, waiting for the only man out of several dates to have rung my bell, so to speak. My feelings are a weird mix of anticipation—the memory of that delicious kiss still lingers in the back of my mind—and fury, that he played me for the fool and now thinks he can worm his way back into my good graces.

"Hello, Jess."

It's him, looking every bit as attractive as the last time I saw him, if not more so. My insides lurch slightly, though I'm not sure whether it's lust, nerves, or the slightly indigestible blueberry muffin I have just scoffed with indecent haste.

He's wearing a blue pinstripe suit, with crisp white shirt and salmon pink tie, and his hair is slightly longer than I remember.

"Can I get you another?" He points to my half-empty mug and I shake my head, fighting the urge to shift into normal pleasantness. I'm not prepared to give him an inch until I've heard his explanation.

Returning a couple of minutes later with a mug of tea, he squeezes himself into the seat opposite me, hindered by a double buggy parked behind. I notice several of the mothers are glancing coquettishly in his direction, but he seems oblivious.

"So, how have you been?" he says, as if we're long-term mutual acquaintances at some polite social gathering.

"Um, I've been absolutely fine, thanks. How have *you* been?"

He frowns slightly, as if taken aback by my slight frostiness. "Busy. I've been abroad quite a lot since I last saw you."

"Ah, I see." Silence again.

"Talking of which . . ." He looks uncomfortable and glances behind him at the buggy pressed against his chair. "The last time I saw you . . ."

"You mean when you ran out through the kitchens and left me with the bill?" I've found my tongue again.

"Yes, sorry about that." He looks sheepish.

"I'm afraid that's not going to do it," I say briskly, taking a mouthful of coffee.

"I can explain."

"OK, then, let's hear it." I fold my arms defensively and lean back against my chair.

"Well, it's like this . . ." He falters.

"You're married," I say, unable to resist butting in.

He looks surprised. "You know?"

So there it is. An immediate admission to what I had suspected all along. I suppose I had been harboring some small hope that there might be another feasible explanation, but now I know for certain that's not the case I'm not entirely sure what to do. So he was a cad after all, pure and simple.

"Doesn't take a genius to work it out, does it?" I say bitterly.

"No, I suppose not," he mumbles. "But I'm not married, *married*, if you know what I mean."

I roll my eyes. "Don't tell me. It was one of those Mick Jagger–style ceremonies with sacrificial chickens, a dodgy vicar, and lost documentation."

He smiles slightly. "No, I mean I'm officially separated, as I *was* when I had lunch with you."

"Really." I deliberately keep my voice flat. "So why the hasty exit then?"

"Someone came into the restaurant who's a close friend of my wife, and if she saw us, I knew she'd tell her."

I look him straight in the eye. "Why would it matter if, as you say, you were separated?"

He shrugs apologetically. "Because even though we're divorcing, I didn't want to rub her nose in the fact that I was dating again so soon. I don't hate her, I just don't want to be married to her anymore."

We stop talking for a few moments, an oasis of uneasy silence in the midst of chattering mothers and shrieking children. My head is spinning. True, what he did was appallingly rude, but at the same time . . .

"The decree nisi came through this week," he says eventually, as if it was an item of garden furniture he'd ordered from the Internet. "So in another six weeks, we'll be officially divorced."

"Congratulations." I glance around the café, feigning disinterest.

"I can show you the documentation if you like?" He gestures towards his briefcase on an adjacent chair.

"No thanks." I sniff and look at my watch. It's 9:15 a.m.

Perhaps assuming I'm about to up and leave, he cuts to the chase. "Look, I understand that you must be really pissed off with me . . ." He pauses, as if waiting for me to object, but I say nothing. "But I was wondering if you would consider letting me take you out for lunch . . . properly this time."

I raise my eyebrows. "You're joking, right?" But inside, I'm secretly thrilled that the ball has landed back in my court.

"No, I'm serious. I really liked your company, and it was just unfortunate that someone I knew came in and ruined it all. It was just bad timing then, that's all. It wouldn't matter now."

"Wouldn't matter to *you*, you mean," I say. "I, however, take exception to dating people who have lied to me." Though after all, who's to say that if I was in his situation, I wouldn't have done the same thing?

He studies my face a few moments, as if assessing whether I'm half-joking or not, then realizes I'm not. "Oh come *on*," he scoffs, "everyone tells lies in the early stages of dating. And don't tell me you haven't done it, because I won't believe you."

"Yes," I admit, "but there are the little white lies that everyone tells, like pretending to be a natural blonde or saying you earn more than you do, and then there are whopping great porkers, like pretending to be single when in fact you're *married*."

He's about to answer, but at this precise, awkward point, a little boy smeared in chocolate comes and stands at our table, poking his discolored tongue out at us. He's really rather unattractive, with a dribble of yellow mucus falling from one nostril and a chocolate-covered hand lurking dangerously close to my cream Puffa jacket, but we both feel compelled to smile indulgently in his direction. Particularly as his mother is looking straight at us.

"Come along, Tybalt, leave those nice people alone," she says brightly.

As he wanders off, we both raise our eyebrows and snigger discreetly.

"Fucking hell, with a name like that, he's either going to be prime minister or a serial killer. There's no middle ground on that one," mutters Simon with a grin.

I smile back and, not for the first time in our short meeting, realize that I do still find him attractive. The problem is, can I trust him?

Trust him? Who cares? It's Madeleine, dressed in red Lycra and horns and whispering into my right ear. *Just shag him and worry about all the other crap later. You only live once, so go for it.*

Trust him? Of course not! It's Tab, in angelic white, whispering on my left shoulder. *If he deceived you once, believe me, he'll do it again. You only live once, so protect yourself from hurt.*

"Anyway . . ." Simon's voice breaks into my meanderings. "Where were we?"

I rally my thoughts and focus on the question, though admittedly I feel notably less hostile towards him than prior to Tybalt coming out of the blue.

"You were married," I reply matter-of-factly, "and soon you won't be."

"Ah yes." He leans forward almost imperceptibly, but I notice every millimeter. "So on that basis, how do you feel about starting again with another date, and pretending the first one didn't happen?"

I dip a teaspoon in my cappuccino, scoop up a large blob of foam, then shamelessly and ponderously lick it off just inches from his face. "I'll have to think about it."

He waits a few seconds, his eyes never leaving my mouth. The memory of our drunken lunchtime kiss pops into my head again, and I feel my neck flushing with desire.

But this time, he eventually leans away from me and glances at his watch. "Time's up," he grins. "So how about it?"

I smile slowly. "Ha, ha, ha. I mean I need *proper* time to think about it. Like a few days."

He looks surprised. "What's to think about? We either find each other attractive, or we don't. And I find you very, very attractive indeed." His eyes are undressing me and my insides switch from pre-rinse to spin cycle.

Madeleine. Tab. Madeleine. Tab. Madeleine. Madeleine. Madeleine. Bugger, I have all the willpower of Rosie O'Donnell in a cake shop.

"OK then. But just *one* date and we'll see how it goes." I rummage in my handbag for my electronic organizer. I have only just learned how to switch it on, let alone store my painfully vacant social calendar. But he doesn't know that.

Tap tap tap. "I could do lunch next Tuesday," I say officiously, not wishing to look too available.

"Can't do lunches at all," he replies with lightning speed. "Remember Gordon Gekko and 'Lunch is for wimps'? Well, the advertising industry embraced it in the eighties and still haven't let go. It'll have to be dinner, I'm afraid."

Dinner. Otherwise known as the danger zone, an alcohol-fueled, open-ended arrangement that always ends in leers or tears. Or both.

"What about Saturday or Sunday lunch?" I say optimistically, not wishing to look too much of a pushover.

He shakes his head. "Sorry, no can do. Tied up this weekend, and next I'm off to New York for a seminar." He runs his forefinger along the top of my hand, prompting my nerve endings to explode. "And I'd like to see you as soon as is humanly possible."

"Understandable. I *am* irresistible." I laugh.

"Oh, and by the way, this time everything is on me."

I raise an eyebrow. "I trust you implicitly, of course, but if you go to the loo, can you leave the cash up front?"

He gives me a fantastic, heart-stopping grin. Oh, fuck it. See that wind outside? My caution has just hitched a ride on it. "OK, how about this Friday night then?"

"Great." He claps his hands, then rubs them together. "Let's do it!"

As I find him so bloody attractive, I have a sneaking suspicion we probably will.

Twenty Two

Several hours after my meeting with Simon, I have put in a halfhearted day's work at the studio and feigned a stomach complaint to rush home early and sit by the phone. Olivia's MRI scan was due to take place at 3 p.m. today, and she said she'd call me as soon as she has the result.

It's now 5 p.m. and I have heard absolutely nothing.

For the umpteenth time in the last hour, I pick up the phone and start to dial her mobile number, then hastily put it down again. I mustn't pester, I tell myself. I must leave her to call me when she's good and ready. But just how *long* do these things take? Surely she must know by now?

The phone rings and I grab it.

"Blimey, that was quick. You must be sitting on it." It's Tab.

My heart is racing but manages to sink at the same time. "I had dozed off and the shock of being woken up must have made me subconsciously grab it," I lie.

"Oh sorry, honey," she says, concerned. "I just wanted to check whether you were feeling any better."

"Not really," I lie again, desperate to get her off the phone in case Olivia calls. "In fact, I think I may have to rush off to the bathroom again right now. Sorry, I'll call you later."

I replace the receiver and within two seconds it rings again, presumably Tab thinking we were cut off.

"Hello?" I bark irritably.

"Hi, it's Olivia." She sounds wrong footed. "Are you OK?"

"God, yes, sorry. I thought you were someone else," I explain. "How did it go?"

She lets out a long sigh. "Well, no point in sugaring the pill. It *has* spread, but the good news is that it seems to be contained within the breast."

"Which means what?"

"That one breast will have to come off, but my bones are clear and so are my lymph nodes, it seems, so I won't have to have the more invasive underarm surgery."

"Oh." A breast off. Quite how that's good news baffles me, but she sounds fairly upbeat so I have to take her word for it. "So what happens now?"

"I'll have the mastectomy during October half term, as I said I would, then start chemotherapy immediately afterwards."

I take a deep breath. "And if all that works out, does that mean you're then clear forever?"

She pauses for a moment. "Hopefully. But you can never be too complacent about it because there's a chance it could come back. I'm not sure I'll ever relax about it."

That makes two of us, I think, but wisely decide against saying so.

"So how do you feel about losing a breast?" I say quietly, having read a recent article by a mastectomy patient who said she felt robbed of her womanhood.

"If that's what it takes to save my life, then so be it," she says matter-of-factly. "I'd be happy to have both off on that basis, and don't forget they do reconstructive surgery at the same time, so it might be better to have both off so I can get a cracking pair instead.

"As it is, they will try their best to replicate the remaining one, which isn't exactly pert." She laughs.

I know she's doing her best to lighten the mood, but the stomachache I made up earlier now seems to have materialized and I feel nauseous.

"And how's Michael?" I ask, almost in a whisper. "Is he still in coping mode?"

"Actually, now that we know exactly what we're up against, he seems to be much more normal. We had a really good chat about it all in the car on the way home, and when we got back he gave me a wonderful cuddle and told me everything was going to be fine. It felt great to have that bodily contact, because he's been treating me a bit like a china doll for the past couple of weeks."

I sit up and straighten my back, aching from being slouched for so long. "That sounds promising, particularly as he's a surgeon himself. He clearly thinks it's beatable now, and it was the uncertainty that was making him act peculiarly."

"I reckon you might be right." She sighs. "Regardless, I feel much more positive about everything after today."

"Glad to hear it." I smile. And I am. I just wish I could force myself to feel the same way.

Walking towards the *Good Morning Britain* reception area the next morning, I avert my eyes to avoid the ghastly giant publicity shots of the two main presenters, Eddie and Tara, with their overrouged cheeks and saccharine smiles.

On air, you'd think they were the best of friends, sharing a cozy sofa and even cozier chats. But off air, they patently loathe each other and spend most of their time locked away in their individual dressing rooms, spitting bile about each other.

Anne is sitting on one of the two stained leather sofas that dominate the reception area. Exactly how they got stained is anyone's guess, but legend has it that one is battle scarred from a late-night encounter between Eddie and a secretary, the other covered in a glass of red wine tipped over his head by the same secretary when their affair hit the buffers a few weeks later.

"Hi, how lovely to see you!" I stoop and kiss Anne on both cheeks. A kindly faced man sitting next to her smiles at me uncertainly.

"This is my husband, Ralph."

Shaking his hand, I gesture for them to follow me along the corridor. "Are you looking forward to this?"

She nods, a look of pure joy on her face. "You bet. I was just saying to Ralph this morning, I've always wanted to be pampered . . . you know, go on one of those health farm days or something . . . but we've never been able to afford it. So this is *such* a treat for me."

Leading her into the makeup room, I introduce her to Kevin, Camilla, and Trudi, who are lined up like soldiers on parade. Unsurprising, since I have placed them all under pain of death if they don't make this one of the best makeovers they've ever done.

"Hello!" gushes Kevin, breaking rank to take Anne's coat. "It's so lovely to meet you. We've heard so much about you!"

"Oh?" Anne looks baffled that she should be the subject of *any* conversation, let alone one between what she clearly perceives to be such busy, glamorous people. "Well, that's nice to know. Thank you very much."

Within seconds, she is encased in one of Kevin's plastic cloaks and gently shoved into a dentist-style chair in front of a vast mirror encircled with bright lights.

"Right!" Kevin claps his hands together, causing his various bracelets to jangle alarmingly. "Let's have a chat about what we're going to do with your hair."

Placing one hand on Anne's shoulder, I place the other on Ralph's forearm to show I'm talking to both of them. "The item works best if Ralph is surprised by your new look, as well as the viewers," I say. "So I'm going to leave you here, but take him along to the green room, where he can read the papers and get a coffee. OK?"

They both nod their agreement, but Ralph looks terrified at the thought of being left alone to deal with these fancy London types.

"Is he OK?" It's ten minutes later and Tab is sitting opposite me in the canteen, nursing a mug of coffee.

"Yes, he's fine. I left him sitting in the big comfy armchair with a copy of *The Sun* and Dee fussing over him." Dee is the bosomy, homely woman who clucks around all guests in the green room, tending to their every need. "At the risk of sounding really corny and patronizing, it's seeing people like him and Anne enjoying themselves that occasionally makes this job worthwhile."

"Are they the ones you were telling me about, who lost the young daughter?"

I nod and load another sugar into my weak, tasteless tea. "Yes. And now she puts her all into that Sunshine House place where Ben works."

"Did you see him there when you filmed?"

"Yes." I fill her in on what happened there, enthusing about the work of the charity and how Ben and Anne, in particular, are the linchpins of the entire place.

"Blimey." Tab laughs when I have finished. "You've certainly changed your tune from that first meeting in the pub. Then, you couldn't get away from him and his good works fast enough."

"I know." I sigh. "I behaved like a complete prat. But now I've got to know him a bit, I really like him."

Tab raises an eyebrow. "Like, or *like*?"

"No, definitely just like. He's a lovely man and I really respect the work he does. In fact, I hope we'll stay friends after this." I wave across the canteen to Camilla, who is rushing back out of the door with a coffee cup in her hand. She gives me the thumbs-up sign, which I take to mean Anne's makeover is going well.

Tab leans forward slightly. "I'm glad you don't fancy him, because you may have been barking up the wrong tree," she says conspiratorially.

"Sorry?"

"Will and I were talking about him the other night, and Will says the feeling among the rugby boys is that he might be . . . you know."

"What, really a woman? A secret Debbie Gibson fan?" I say facetiously.

She tuts. "No, they call him the Beaver leaver," she whispers. "They think he might be gay."

I make a scoffing noise. "That lot of pumped-up no-brains? *They'd* think Arnold Schwarzenegger was gay."

She wags an admonishing finger in my face. "Excuse *me*? That's my husband you're talking about."

"Sorry." I grin sheepishly. "Will is the exception to the rule, of course." Not. "But honestly, Tab, what evidence is there?"

She shrugs. "Nothing concrete. But Will says that whenever the lads sit around talking about sex, Ben always goes very quiet."

I raise my eyes heavenward. "That's known as being discreet, not gay."

Shaking her head, she gulps her coffee. "No, it's more than that. They say he's just not like them, he's *different*."

Intertwining my hands in front of me, I hum the theme music from *The Twilight Zone*. "Oooooh, he's *different*," I mock.

"Very funny." She sniffs. "But he is. Apparently, he's never mentioned having a girlfriend. Ever."

I shrug. "Whatever. I don't care if the only woman he's ever entered is the Statue of Liberty. It doesn't stop him from being my friend." I look at my watch and stand up. "Gotta go. I want to make sure Kevin et al. haven't turned Anne into RuPaul in my absence."

Twenty Three

It's 6:30 p.m. and I'm trudging towards the tube station with a heavy heart. Not, I'm pleased to say, because Anne's makeover was a disaster. No, in fact it was an unqualified success, which ended with her bursting into tears of happiness on air and Ralph gazing at her with even more adoration than before. If that was possible.

No, my leaden gait is purely down to the fact that tonight's the night I'm meeting Dan to try to establish why he dumped Kara.

I have nothing against him per se, in fact, since he elbowed the witch queen I have found myself warming to him. It's just that tonight, I'd rather go home and chill out alone than schlep into town on someone else's behalf. Unfortunately, Kara's been nagging me about the rendezvous ever since she showed up at my house last week. The little people pleaser, that's me.

The venue is a noisy theme pub called Badger and Biscuit, chosen by Dan, I suspect, largely because of its large plasma television in one corner, showing *Sky Sports* ad nauseam.

As I walk in through the door, a wall of cigarette smoke and stale beer hits me. The clientele is 90 percent men, the other 10 percent being disconsolate-looking women staring into their drinks whilst being steadfastly ignored by their sports-loving companions. Hmmm, just my kind of place.

I spot Dan squashed into a tight corner, a smoke in one hand and a half-empty pint of lager on the table in front of him. As predicted, he's staring fixedly at the large screen on the other side of the room, showing a soccer match between two obscure foreign teams. Well, obscure to me anyway.

"Hello." I stand in front of him smiling.

He drags his eyes away from the screen and looks momentarily surprised to see me. "You're early."

I look at my watch. It says 7 p.m. "No, I'm spot on actually."

He shrugs and grins. "I must be used to Kara's bad timekeeping. Drink?"

It's a good five or ten minutes before he manages to battle his way to the front of the bar queue and order my gin and tonic. "There you are." He places it in front of me and sits back down. We're sandwiched together like sardines, surrounded by other punters in various states of drunkenness. "Nice to see you." He clunks his glass against mine.

"Yes," I reply. "Shame it's not under more pleasant circumstances though."

"Eh?" He looks baffled.

"You and Kara splitting up."

"Oh right, yeah." He sounds unconvinced. "So, you're here on a mission, are you?"

I smile enigmatically. "Kind of."

"So what does Kara want to know then?" He looks slightly bored and takes a long drag on his cigarette.

We both know why I'm there, so I feel it's pointless to dance around the subject and make small talk. "Um, well I suppose she wants to know where it all went wrong . . . why you suddenly decided to end it."

"And she couldn't ask me that herself?"

"You tell me." I shrug. "Maybe she thought you wouldn't be amenable to the idea."

He turns down the corners of his mouth. "She's right, I probably wouldn't. And by the way, it wasn't sudden."

"Sorry?"

"It wasn't sudden," he repeats. "I've been telling her for some time that I didn't feel it was working, but she just wasn't listening. Or didn't seem to be anyway."

I take a long glug of my virtually ginless tonic. "So what *did* go wrong? Because she seems baffled by it."

"If she told you that, then she's being disingenuous," he says matter-of-factly. "Basically, she wanted to get married and I didn't."

This news takes me by surprise, but I disguise it well out of a misguided loyalty to Kara. For months now, she's been telling me that Dan was about to propose at any moment. So I'm not quite sure what to say after his declaration. I mean, what can you say about such a fundamental difference between two people? We sit in silence for a minute or so, his gaze briefly returning to the TV screen.

Draining his pint of lager, he stands up. "I'm getting another. Would you like one?"

"Thanks. This time, I think I'll have something alcoholic." I smile ruefully, looking at my empty glass. "White wine will do."

He returns with another lager and a bottle of wine with two glasses. "I'll join you after this." He points to his pint glass.

I wait for him to sit back down before returning to my line of questioning. "So why didn't you want to get married? A tad commitment-phobic, are we?" I punch his arm playfully, as if the question is a joke. But, as any woman on a mission for her friend will tell you, it's deadly serious.

He purses his lips and thinks about it for a moment. "I've never really thought about it," he says slowly. "But as you're asking, no, I don't think I am. I just didn't want to marry Kara."

"Why not?" I kid myself that I'm asking this purely so I can report back to her in full, unexpurgated detail, but inwardly I must admit I'm rather reveling in the knowledge that behind Kara's supposedly chocolate box relationship has been lurking an unpalatably hard center.

Splaying his fingers in front of his face, he studies his nails thoughtfully. "When you're in a relationship . . . well, if you're a man anyway . . . you tend to muddle along without thinking about it too deeply. It's not until your girlfriend starts putting pressure on you for it to move to another level that you actually focus on what you feel about the person. And when it came down to it, I guess I just didn't love her."

"Enough?" I ask.

"At all."

I nod encouragingly, as if I'm empathizing with every word. The reality, of course, is that the muddling-along-for-two-years mentality is completely alien to me and just about all of my gender. We all come to it with varying speeds and degrees of success, but the bottom line is that, by the time a relationship is a year old, we regularly contemplate its long-term prospects and whether the nursery will be blue or pink. Having said that, I *did* waste several years with the noncommittal Nathan, so I can't talk.

"So," Dan continues. "I ignored it the first couple of times she brought it up, but when she kept going on . . . and on . . . and on," he says in a droning voice, raising his eyebrows heavenward, "we ended up having a couple of those tense conversations in restaurants where I would tell her I didn't want to get married, and she would storm out in tears."

Just for a moment, I find myself feeling sorry for the woman in the scenario he's describing. Then I remember it's *Kara*, who would positively squirm with delight if she was hearing the same story about me.

"It got to the point where the subject was coming up about once a week, and I couldn't feel comfortable in my own home," he adds. "Every time we turned on the TV there was someone getting married on a soap opera or on some movie, or she would leave one of those magazines that features celebrity weddings strategically placed somewhere. I'm only surprised she refrained from gluing it to my forehead in the middle of the night." He lets out a long sigh.

I pour two generous glasses of white wine and push one towards him. My head is starting to feel slightly woozy, a combination of the wine, smoke, and continual noise.

"If she hadn't talked about marriage, would you have happily carried on as you were?"

"Dunno." He shrugs. "There wasn't much chance of that anyway. She has always made it quite clear that on Planet Kara, if a man hasn't proposed two years into a relationship, he's never going to."

"But she must have thought you would," I venture, "or she wouldn't have hung around for as long as she did."

He nods. "Yeah, she must have." He lights another cigarette. "She was absolutely fucking furious when I ended it, saying she had wasted the best years of her life on me and that time was running out for her to try for children. Children!" His eyes bulge at the thought. "What a mind fuck."

It doesn't take Ann Landers to surmise that, far from wavering about his decision to end the relationship and therefore being open to renegotiation, Dan has never been so sure about anything in his life and it's pointless pursuing the matter further.

I notice it has started to tip with rain outside, and a nasty gale is making the wine shop canopy across the street billow alarmingly. I could curtail the evening and brave the storm, or stay in the cozy, albeit tobacco-filled, confines of the pub a while longer and hope the weather calms down.

"My turn to get the drinks." I point at the empty bottle of wine.

For the next hour, hemmed in as yet more desperate people pour in from the cold outside, we sit within centimeters of each other and talk animatedly about the state of the music industry and how no one invests long term in talent anymore.

For reasons of space, Dan's arm is stretched along the banquette behind my head, his body turned towards me. "It's such crap," he says animatedly. "A&R's keep coming to our gigs and they all say 'Yeah, you're great,' but then give us some old bollocks about how our kind of music just isn't what the 'trend' is at the moment." He makes a quotes mark sign with his hands. "It's soul destroying."

"You've got to keep slogging away at it though," I slur slightly, the wine and heat taking its hold. "All the best bands had to do that, some for *years* before they got the big break. But then, because they've done the slog, they get taken seriously and last the course."

I'm not really sure what I've just said, or whether it makes any sense at all, but I notice that Dan is staring at me with undisguised admiration.

"You know, you have just managed to be more supportive about my music career in that one sentence than Kara was in the entire two years we were together," he shouts above the roar as some ponytailed Neanderthal on the TV screen scores a goal.

I pull a doubtful expression. "She always spoke in glowing terms about how talented you were."

"Really?" His eyebrows shoot up. "At home it was a different story. She was always on at me to get a proper job, like banking." He makes a scoffing noise. "She wanted me to get dressed up like Mister Fucking Big every day and go work in the City. I mean, can you imagine?"

No, I couldn't. Dan was a struggling musician through and through, a type I was used to after five years of Nathan wittering on about how he was going to be the new Bob Dylan.

I suppose that's why I know all the meaningless platitudes they want to hear.

"You were a musician when she met you," I say, swigging more wine. "So it seems odd that she'd suddenly want you to change careers."

"Precisely!" he says triumphantly, wine spilling over the edge of his glass. "But nothing is ever good enough for Kara. She's a fucking cow . . . not like you."

There's that admiration again. Hang on, possibly make that lust, as his hand is now idly caressing the nape of my neck. I have to admit that it feels wonderful, so intimate, so soothing.

Through the fog of alcohol, I can't focus my mind enough to decide whether it's simply the platonic gesture of someone tactile, or whether we're veering into dangerously sexual territory. As we're surrounded by people, I rationalize that matters can't get *too* out of hand, so it's best not to overreact.

"I've always fancied you," he says in my ear, brushing my hair to one side as he does so.

Oh dear. Mayday. Mayday! I'm paralyzed by excess alcohol and uncertainty, so I just sit there, saying and doing nothing.

Clearly, he takes this as acceptance, and shuffles closer so his right leg is pressed tightly against my left. I can smell the smoke on his breath as he moves in to gently nibble my earlobe.

"You do something to me," he croons, sounding uncannily like Paul Weller, a.k.a. God of sexy song writing.

Bugger, bugger, fuck, fuck. What do I do now? On the one hand, it's immensely pleasant sitting here, having my erogenous zones tantalized in the warm whilst a storm rages outside. But on the other, I came here to try to reunite him and Kara, not plunge myself into an awkward situation that, at the very best, will simply result in a meaningless shag.

Suddenly, his full body weight is pressing against me, his left arm snaking around the back of my neck and pulling my face towards his. He kisses me, pushing his tongue into my mouth.

At first, rigid with shock, I don't respond. Then, without so much as a passing thought to the consequences, I do, and we shamelessly indulge in a long, slow necking session.

"Excuse me?" A cattle prod couldn't have prompted us to spring apart any quicker. "Is this finished with?" A barmaid is pointing at Dan's empty pint glass. He nods wordlessly and she takes it.

The intrusion is enough to bring me sharply to my senses. I grab my handbag and start to extricate my coat from under me. "I'd better go."

"Why?" His hand has moved to the back of my neck again, but this time I lurch forward out of his reach.

"Just because."

"Because of Kara?" he says wearily.

"A bit, yes," I mumble. "But also because we just shouldn't."

"Well, you seemed to be enjoying it." He removes a cigarette from the packet and sticks it in his mouth, rummaging in his trouser pocket for a lighter. "And I certainly was."

I stand up, edging along the banquette and between two tables, one of which digs into the backs of my thighs. "As I said, bad idea. But thanks for the drinks."

"Pleasure." He seems relatively untroubled by my hasty exit. "And do me a favor," he adds as an afterthought, "don't give Kara any false hope. As far as I'm concerned, it's over for good."

I nod, my lips and chin still smarting from prolonged contact with his sandpapery complexion, more ten o'clock than five o'clock shadow.

"It clearly is," I mutter, heading for the door.

Twenty Four

Jesus Christ Almighty. My friend . . . OK, so I use that term loosely . . . asks me to meet with her newly-ex boyfriend with a view to discussing their possible reconciliation, and what do I do?

Snog his face off, that's what. Have I no shame? Don't answer that, I'm feeling bad enough as it is.

It's the following morning now and I'm sitting staring at my answering machine with such intensity that the small, digital screen is starting to blur. Just as well, because it's flashing "6 messages" at me, and it's fair to assume that at least five of them will be from Kara and of the "where the fuck are you?" variety. My mobile, dead since I dropped it in the washing-up water whilst trying to do two things at once last week, is now lurking somewhere towards the bottom of the fruit bowl, along with various unidentifiable keys, an ancient orange, and several hair bands.

Taking a deep breath, I press "play" on the machine and slump against the arm of the sofa in preparation for a verbal beating. Kara doesn't disappoint.

Beep. "Hi, Jess, it's me. Just calling to say hope it goes well tonight, and thanks for helping me out. Call me when you get in."

Beep. "Hi, me again. It's nine and I thought you'd be back by now. Er, obviously not. I'll wait for you to call."

Beep. "It's nine-thirty now and your mobile isn't responding. Just give me a bloody call and put me out of my misery. Please!"

Beep. "Hi love, it's Mum." I feel my shoulders relax at the sound of a friendly voice amidst the ranting. "Just calling to see how you are. Speak soon."

Beep. "Jess, this is now *beyond* beyond. It's ten, so either you've been hit by a bus, or even more unbelievably, you have fallen into bed and forgotten to call me."

Wrong on both counts actually. Because at that precise time, I was indulging in an extremely public necking session with the man who has just dumped you.

Beep. I wince and hug my knees. "Jess, it's eleven. Where the *fuck* are you?" Bingo. I knew that succinctly worded question would be there somewhere.

"You have no more messages," says the machine reassuringly.

"Thank God for that," I reply, walking through to the kitchen to make a much-needed coffee. The clock on the wall says 7:45 a.m., usually the time I'm dressed and ready to leave for work.

Ten minutes later, I'm still in my Bart Simpson nightshirt, nursing a coffee and staring out of the side window with its spectacular overview of mine and next door's dustbins. What a painfully apt analogy for the current state of my life.

Dring, dring.

I sit frozen to the spot, paralyzed by the sound of the phone and knowing what's on the other end of it.

Do I pretend to be out, making my prolonged absence from Kara's radar even more suspicious? Or do I pretend to have left for work already, thereby delaying the inevitable, furious phone call to a time when I am unable to respond freely without it being witnessed by everyone in the office?

No, there's only one thing for it. It's my high noon come four hours early, and I must face it.

"Hello?"

"Well, fuck me. I'm not actually speaking to *the* Jess Monroe, am I?" rasps the voice on the other end. "Because I seriously thought she'd been murdered, or joined one of those convents where they take a vow of fucking *silence.*"

You probably don't need me to tell you that it *is* Kara, and she's less than pleased.

"Oh, hi there." I sit down, knowing this is going to be a long one. "I did try to call you back when I got in last night, but it was engaged. Then I fell asleep." You know those three great lies? Well, I just added one.

"No you didn't. My phone was on the hook all night and no one else rang," she counteracts immediately.

"Maybe someone else was trying to get through at the same time, and we both got the engaged tone?" I say pathetically but nonetheless hopeful that she'll swallow it. "Maybe it was Dan?" I add desperately.

Eu-bloody-reka, it seems to work.

"Dan?" Her voice is still stern but slightly calmer. "Why would he try to call? What happened?"

If I tell her the unexpurgated truth, that Dan doesn't love her and has absolutely no intention of returning, I know I may as well get a shovel and keep digging south from the giant hole I'm already in.

So I sigh deeply, playing for time but hoping it will be interpreted as me agonizing over the complex personalities of two peo-

ple who are so ideally suited to one another and yet so different.
"It's hard to say," I bluff.

"Try," she snaps in her finest Miss Piggy tone.

"Well, the main problem seems to be that he knows you want
to get married, but he's not ready to just yet. He . . ."

Her response slices through the end of my sentence. "So when
will he be ready?"

Oh fuck, what have I said? Memo to self: must begin to backtrack immediately.

"He's not sure if he ever will be, that's the main problem."

There's blessed silence for a few moments, presumably as she
tries to compute my waffle. Then she rallies again. "Look, can we
try and cut through the crap here? What's the bottom line? Does
he want us to get back together?"

Now then. Faced with such a definite question, a normal person would give a straight, cruel-to-be-kind answer. But not me,
oh no. Because as much as I know that she needs to hear it, the
truth is that I'm scared of Kara. I don't trust her not to shoot the
messenger, not to find some new and creative way to make me
miserable in order to make herself feel better. Personal ads are
just the beginning. Which also gets to the heart of why we're still
connected after all these years: making rudimentary efforts at
friendship and going through the motions are easier than attempting to disengage. Hell hath no fury like Kara scorned.

"Wouldn't it be better to ask yourself if you *want* to get back
with a man who's so uncertain about marriage?" I hedge.

"It depends. Sometimes they feel differently after a brief hiatus without you," she replies. "They miss you so much, they'd say
or do anything to get you back, including walking down the aisle."

Don't hold your breath, I think. "I'm not sure this lad is for
turning," I say, trying to make light of it.

"What makes you say that? Did you discuss it with him?"

Dear God, I would do *anything* to rescue myself from this excruciating conversation. Could you just arrange a little electrical storm to sever the telephone wires? Or how about a car spiraling out of control and ending up in Kara's front garden? No one to be hurt, you understand, just a little distraction.

"Well? Did you discuss it?"

Back to reality. "Not as such, no. He just didn't seem terribly keen on marriage as a concept, regardless of the woman involved."

"You discussed other women?" Her voice is shrill enough to break glass, her response reminding me that whilst love may be blind, jealousy sees too much.

"No, no, no. I didn't mean it like that. I meant that it's nothing against you personally, he just doesn't want to marry anyone. Ever."

Silence again. Be still my beating, panicking heart.

"So if I agree to just live with him and not mention marriage, what about children?" she says eventually, her voice measured.

"We didn't discuss children," I lie, thrown slightly because she's always said she doesn't want them. "He didn't bring the subject up and neither did I," I add pointlessly.

She lets out a long, heavy sigh. "Honestly, Jess, I have to say I really had high hopes for you on this. But you've turned out to be absolutely fucking useless. I may as well have sent my brother, for all the feminine intuition you've shown."

What's best? I wonder. Kara knowing the truth, or regarding me as a total fuckwit? As I fall into the latter category with her most of the time, it's no skin off my nose to add yet another instance.

"Sorry," I mumble apologetically, relaxing slightly as I anticipate the interrogation coming to an end.

"Not as sorry as I am that I relied on you," she says wearily. "So what time did you get in?"

Danger, danger. A metal bolt of tension shoots down my back again, forcing me to sit ramrod straight. "Um, just after eleven . . . I think." It's futile to pretend otherwise, knowing she called here around that time.

"So you met at seven and, even assuming your journey home was *particularly* troublesome and took an hour," she says slowly, "that still means you spent three hours in his company?"

"Probably. I was a bit late, so maybe slightly less," I reply lamely.

"And you're telling me that in *all* that time, the only snippet of information you managed to unearth is that he's not keen on marriage." Her voice starts to rise to a crescendo. "I knew that *before* you went. What a fucking waste of time."

Ideally, when Kara is off on one, it's wise to keep quiet. But fools rush in and here I am, doffing my jester's hat and jangling my pig's bladder on a stick. "Yes, but *I* didn't know that, did I? Because you always said he was going to propose any day now."

Obviously, I can't see Kara's expression right now. But if I were to hazard a guess, I'd say it was somewhere between the girl in *The Exorcist* and Joan Crawford in *Mommie Dearest*.

"I thought he *was*!" she spits. "Whilst he was getting regular fry-ups and blow jobs, the little wanker was more than happy to give the impression our relationship was for keeps."

Whoa, a little too much information, and yet another layer stripped away from Kara's feminist pretensions.

"It sounds just like Nathan," I say supportively, desperately scrabbling for some common ground between us. But she ignores me.

"So what *did* you talk about for three hours? Plate tectonics? Global warming?" she says sarcastically.

I'm not quite sure what plate tectonics is, but feel that now probably isn't the time to ask. "Um, we talked a bit about football, because a match was playing on the big screen, but we mostly chatted about music and how it was being destroyed by download-ing and one-hit wonders."

Kara snorts derisively. "Fucking hell, dumb and dumber on the state of the record industry. I bet that was *riveting*."

Although she's spitting bile and most of it's raining down on my head, I don't much care, as long as it stops her from asking any more awkward questions about my meeting with Dan. I want to block the kiss from my mind, not keep being dragged back to it by her persistent interrogation.

It's now nudging 8:30, and my coffee is stone cold. "Look, Kara, I have to get off to work or I'm going to be in deep shit," I say wearily. "I'm *sorry* I turned out to be such a terrible spy, and I'm *sorry* I can't be the one to tell you that Dan's desperate to marry you and live happily ever after. But it just wouldn't be true."

She sniffs, though I think it's more through high dudgeon than distress. "We'll see," she says. "I still have a trick or two up my sleeve."

Dream on, love. From what he told me last night, not even David Copperfield could magically change Dan into the marry-ing kind.

But true to people-pleasing form, I say absolutely nothing.

Twenty Five

There is absolutely no way I'm going to have sex with Simon. Absolutely not. Not under *any* circumstances whatsoever.

The only reason I'm wearing my best underwear in matching peach lace is because my mother taught me that you should always wear nice undies in case you're run over and rushed off to hospital. And where I'm meeting him, there's lots of traffic.

We're starting with dinner at a trendy new place called Bardot's, then Simon suggested we go on to somewhere like China White or Sketch for a late-night drink. But we'll see. At the moment, I'm planning to knock it on the head and leave with my dignity intact straight after dinner.

There he is, sitting on a bar stool just inside the restaurant's main door, looking utterly, scrumptiously edible. Oh dear. Well, maybe just *one* late-night drink . . .

He's wearing a tight, black cashmere top, black trousers, and black suede loafers. His hair is swept back from his face and still slightly wet from the shower.

"Where's my box of chocolates then?" I quip, perching on the bar stool next to him.

"Waiting for you on my bedside table," he shoots back with a grin. "You look great."

I bloody should, having been through at least ten changes of outfit before settling on a simple black Gucci-style shift dress with black kitten heels and . . . ahem . . . black stockings and garters. Well, you have to give those poor ambulance men *something* to cheer up their job, don't you?

"Drink?" He gestures to a bottle of champagne on the bar.

"Thanks." As he pours, I take a look around the restaurant, a dark, moody place with lots of deep red velvet booths and chill-out music playing in the background. It screams seduction.

"I thought we'd finish this here . . . ," he gestures toward the champagne bottle, "then move to our table for dinner."

"Fine," I nod. So much for pacing myself, but the combination of a deliciously chilled drink, low lighting, and the company of an undeniably gorgeous man is enough to jettison what little willpower I have into oblivion.

"The foie gras is supposed to be fantastic here," he says, tapping his champagne glass against mine. "Nice to see you."

"Nice to see you, too." I nod towards the bottle. "Champagne, foie gras . . . I hope you're not thinking of doing a bunk through the kitchens tonight. I'd have to remortgage my flat . . ."

He grins sheepishly. "No, I promise I'll be staying around tonight. That is, unless my four kids come in unexpectedly, of course . . ."

Just for one fleeting moment, I believe him and my face drops.

He bursts out laughing and nearly falls off his stool with unbridled delight at my gullibility.

"Very funny," I sniff. "But if our last meeting is anything to go by, it wouldn't surprise me."

"Now, now, don't go all grumpy on me," he chides, tweaking my cheek. "Let's have a big smile . . . come on!"

"Fuck off." I grin.

"That's better." He tops up our glasses again. "So, good week?"

I shrug. "Not bad." Realizing that this is neither the time nor the place to unburden myself about Olivia, I tell him about Kara and my meeting with Dan, conveniently omitting the bit where I snogged him.

"Well, at least he's being honest," says Simon after I've finished the story. "A lot of men find themselves walking down the aisle because it's what the woman wants, then regretting it pretty rapidly. That's exactly what happened to me."

"How long were you married to . . . ?"

"Fiona. Together for four years, married for one of them," he answers swiftly, off pat. "I would have happily carried on as we were, but she wanted the big white wedding, the page boys, the cake, the lot." He groans. "I break out in a rash just thinking about it."

"So you did love her then, you just didn't like the wedding bit?"

He takes another swig of champagne, a small trickle running down his chin. The urge to lean forward and lick it off almost overwhelms me, but I restrain myself.

"I loved her enough to muddle along, but not enough to spend the rest of my life with her. Much like your mate Dan, really."

"He's not my mate," I say, a little too emphatically. "He's my friend's boyfriend."

Simon shrugs. "Whatever. It sounds like he and I were singing off the same song sheet, except that he was sensible enough to say so *before* he found himself taking part in some theatrical extravaganza in front of relatives he hadn't clapped eyes on since Grandma died and probably will never see again."

"So now you're just looking for a series of meaningless relationships," I say, deliberately making my voice sound teasing rather than accusatory.

He shakes his head. "No, not at all. I like being in a serious relationship, but I am old enough now to realize it has to be with the right person, not just someone you muddle along with."

Right answer! And your prize is to spend the rest of your life with the extraordinarily witty, vivacious, and never boring Jessica Monroe. OK, so she's flat chested and her legs are a little short, but she's big on loyalty and long on personality.

I drain my champagne glass and note the bottle is now empty. "Shall we sit down?"

"Sure." He gestures to one of the staff, who appears almost instantaneously at our side. "We'd like to go to our table now, if that's OK."

As we pick our way through the other tables, me following behind him, I quietly marvel at how comfortable I already feel in his company. Unlike the other dates where I was constantly on edge, waiting for the next irritating mannerism or neurosis to emerge, I feel excited at the thought of a whole evening stretching ahead of me with this man. Where other dates haven't ended soon enough, I already want this one to go on forever.

We settle into a cozy booth right in the far corner of the restaurant, adjacent to each other but both with a clear view of the other diners. The lighting is flatteringly low, with just a small candle on each table for atmosphere. When the menus arrive, each has a small reading light attached to the top.

Simon orders foie gras to start, whilst I opt for a chilled tomato soup. For the main course, he encourages me to choose the lobster but, mindful of bits of flesh and shell flying across the table, I decide to leave it until we know one another better and opt for lamb chops instead.

Two hours, two bottles of wine, and too much food later, I am stuffed to the gunnels and totally, irretrievably drunk. I'm warm, comfortable, fuzzy-headed, and almost sitting in the lap of a gorgeous man who has kept me entertained throughout dinner with witty anecdotes and outrageous gossip about his colleagues. What more could a girl ask for?

A kiss, that's what.

"Kish me."

"Sorry?"

"Kish me." I point to my mouth for good measure.

"I thought you'd never ask." He leans forward and kisses me with feathery lightness on the mouth, withdrawing almost immediately but staying just centimeters from my face.

Moving forward again, he begins to rub his nose gently against mine, performing a tantalizing dance where his lips almost touch mine but not quite.

Sober, it would be erotic. But in my heavily inebriated state, I feel the frustration is going to kill me. So, apologies in advance to the two ferocious women who wrote that dating book *The Rules*, I lurch forward in a most unseemly fashion and push my tongue into his mouth.

He responds fully and pushes me backwards, my back rammed firmly against the rear of the booth, my legs intertwined with his.

After about a minute of intense kissing, he pulls away, dragging me back to the reality of our surroundings and blinking rapidly with the short, sharp shock.

"Cheesy I know, but your place or mine?" he murmurs with a heart-stopping grin.

"Yours." I may be pissed, but I still have enough wits about me to know that going to his means I can leave when I want. It also gives me a chance to see if there are any visible traces left of his wife.

For the fifteen-minute taxi journey, I throw caution to the wind on the basis that as there are thousands of cab drivers, I'm never likely to see this one again. Just as well really.

Within seconds of pulling away, we have resumed our intense kissing and Simon's hand has snaked up my dress. As his hand reaches the top of my stockings, he groans loudly.

"Fuck, you're sexy."

"Thanks, so are you" seems a little too tritely polite under the circumstances, so I say nothing, simply stepping up the pressure of our kiss and placing my right hand on his groin and rubbing slowly. It's toweringly clear he needs little stimulation.

"Here y'are. That's sixteen quid, please." The driver's voice is loud, but his face impassive.

I step out of the cab, the cold night air bringing a welcome flash of sobriety. Pulling my coat tighter, I wait for Simon to pay and gaze up at the modern apartment block in front of me. All I know is that we're in Maida Vale. Somewhere.

Simon grabs my elbow and guides me towards the front door. "The lift's broken, I'm afraid, but I live only on the second floor. Come on."

A man on a promise, he leaps like a mountain goat up the first flight of stairs, turning to find me several steps behind.

"Kitten heels aren't designed for walking," I say, as I reach him in the first-floor stairwell.

But he doesn't appear to be listening. Cupping my chin in his hand, he stares into my eyes and watches them flicker with surprise as his other hand reaches up my dress. Running a finger around the top of my stocking, he tilts his head and whispers in my ear: "I've wanted to fuck you since the first moment I saw you."

The jury's out on whether this is a compliment or not, but right now, with a powerful mixture of alcohol and adrenaline pumping round my veins, my knees almost buckle with lust.

For the next flight of stairs, we are two mountain goats together, propelled to his front door by the thought of what . . . and who . . . was to come.

Fumbling and stumbling down his hallway, we shed our coats along the way, our mouths remaining firmly pressed together. We reach a doorway and he pushes me through it, moving backwards until my legs hit what feels like the edge of a bed.

Our tongues still intertwined, his hands move from my arms down to the hem of my dress, yanking it upwards until it rests above my buttocks. Then, just as swiftly, he unzips the back of my dress, pulling it halfway down my arms to expose my bra.

Now his mouth has moved away from mine and down to my right breast, his teeth pulling the lace to one side to reveal my nipple. One of his hands is splayed against my buttock, pulling me towards him, the other is rubbing the area of lace directly between my legs.

My eyes are closed, my head thrown back in abandon. I'm doing nothing in return, simply enjoying the experience.

I feel his hand tug my pants to one side, then the unmistakable nudging sensation of his flesh against mine. My eyes snap open and I clamp my legs together. "Condom. Must use a condom."

"It's already on," he murmurs, his hands pushing my knees apart again. Either he wore it to the restaurant, or the man has a sleight of hand that makes David Blaine looks positively snail-like.

Pushing me back onto the bed, my dress hitched around my waist, he lowers himself onto me and pushes himself inside.

Sorry about that," he says a couple of minutes later, falling off me and laying to one side. "Another fifty-seven minutes and that would have been our finest hour."

I laugh and pull my dress back into place. "Well, it seemed pretty fine to me anyway. I've got no complaints."

He stands up and pulls his trousers and socks off, throwing them onto a chair in the corner. "It was the big buildup. I have spent all night wanting to do that, so when we got behind closed doors I couldn't contain myself."

"I'm only thankful you managed to restrain yourself in the restaurant." I smile, uncertain what to do now it's all over.

"Next time, I'll make sure it's one of those Sting shags . . . you know, Tantric sex that lasts for seven hours."

I pull a face. "Bloody hell, I hope that includes the cinema, dinner, and the journey home. I can't think of anything worse."

He laughs. "You see? That's why men and women will never understand each other. There we are thinking you want big knobs and marathon sex sessions, and all you want is chipolatas and quickies."

"It's true that size doesn't matter to us . . .." I reply. "Well, as long as it's not small."

He snorts with laughter. "Good one." Glancing down to his crotch, he adds: "Does this condom make me look fat?"

Walking over to the back of his bedroom door, he unhooks a dressing gown and places it across my legs. "Here you are, put this on and get into bed. I'll go make some coffee."

And there it was, as simple as that. No awkwardness, no stilted conversation or hidden meanings. Just a straightforward invitation to stay the night, the whole night, and nothing but the night. Well, so far anyway.

But, judging by his easygoing, uncomplicated attitude, I sense that Simon *will* ask to see me again and this just might be the start of something good.

Folding my dress and placing it on the chair, I peel off my stockings and bind the dressing gown tightly around my waist before clambering into the king-size bed. It dominates the room, which has fitted beech wardrobes at one end, the lone chair, and two bedside tables; a remnant from his marriage perhaps? There are no photographs on display and no feminine touches whatso ever.

Laying back on the feathery pillows, I jiggle my toes in delight as I think about the feverish sex we shared just a few minutes ago and look forward to the promised, more languorous session yet to come.

Yes, yes, I *know* I said I wasn't going to have sex with him under any circumstances whatsoever, but technically speaking, it is our second date.

Twenty Six

"We're all going on a summer holiday!" I sing at the top of my voice, as the Renault Espace weaves its way around the country lanes.

Matthew gives me a withering look. "Aunty Jess, it's October and we're actually going to Grandma and Grandpa's. What a silly song to sing."

"OK, point taken." I smile. "As it's near-ish to Christmas, how about 'Jingle Bells' then?"

An arm clasped round each of them in the backseat, I lead Matthew and Emily in a pitiful rendition of "Jingle Bells" whilst keeping a concerned eye on Olivia, who's sitting in the front passenger seat whilst Michael drives.

As far as the children are concerned, this is just a routine visit to their grandparents' house for Sunday lunch. But the adults in the car know better, hence the rather gloomy atmosphere I am trying desperately to lighten in case the children pick up on it.

Olivia is booked in for her mastectomy and reconstructive surgery tomorrow, and our parents still don't know she's even got cancer. This trip is specifically so she can tell them.

I offered to look after Matthew and Emily in London, so she and Michael could face it alone. But Olivia wanted the rest of the day to feel as normal as possible, and felt the presence of the children might stop Mum, in particular, from becoming too hysterical.

"We'll have lunch, then when I give you the nod, I want you to take the children out for a long walk," she said earlier when we were packing up the car. I silently nodded my agreement.

Pulling into the parentals' gravel drive, I have to admit I'm dreading today. Usually, this is a warm blanket of a place I associate with lots of laughter, affection, good wine and food. A pleasurable haven from the often harsh realities of life.

Now we are bringing one of those harsh realities with us and plonking it right on their doorstep. But I know it can't be any other way.

"Dahling! You look so well." Mum envelops me in a hug and I want to cling onto her forever, soothed by the familiar smell of her flowery perfume combined with her favorite hairspray. But she breaks away and moves on to Olivia.

"And how's my biggest girl?" she beams, drawing Liv into her chest. "It's been too long, really it has."

Dad emerges from the front door, wiping his oily hands on an old cloth. No doubt the remnants of another ongoing invention.

"Ah, I'm glad you two have arrived," he says, rubbing the tops of Matthew and Emily's heads. "There are a couple of chocolate bars hidden somewhere in the house, and I need your help to find them."

"But they are *not* to be eaten until after lunch." Mum's voice trails after them as they run off into the house.

Greetings over, the adults troop in behind them and move into the cozy sitting room, its real log fire crackling away as the centerpiece.

"Drink?" Dad waves a whisky bottle at Michael, who holds his hand up in the air.

"No thanks, I'm the designated driver today."

"Ah, my girls have got you under the thumb, have they?" Dad chortles.

"Alan," says Mum rather sharply. "Never mind pouring yourself whisky. Have you checked on the meat recently?"

He scuttles off and Olivia, Michael, and I share a furtive, ironic smile.

"Come on through to the dining room," says Mum, hustling us in the door. "Let's find the children and get settled."

Wow, that was fantastic." I slump back in my chair, my plate now empty of the sizable portion of beef Wellington that occupied it earlier. "You really must give me the recipe for that." So it can lie untouched in a kitchen drawer whilst I carry on making baked beans on toast and Pot Noodles.

I notice that Michael has worked his way through most of his food, but that Olivia's is barely touched. She has made a valiant attempt to move it around the plate a little, but it's fooling no one.

"Aren't you hungry, dear?" Mum's expression is faintly hurt and I find myself contemplating, not for the first time during this lunch, how her cozy, ordered world is about to be turned upside down irrevocably.

Without wishing to sound overly dramatic, I know that whatever the outcome of Olivia's illness, none of us will ever be the same people again. Facing death, either your own or that of a loved one, is an experience that never leaves you and colors every life decision you make from then on.

"Sorry, Mum, bit of a dicky tummy, I'm afraid." Olivia smiles apologetically and pats her stomach.

Mum is on her feet in an instant. "I have just the thing for that . . . some nice peppermint tea. I'll pop the kettle on whilst Dad clears the plates. You three sit here, won't be a moment."

When they have both left the room, Olivia glances at the door to make sure the coast is clear, then turns back to face me. "Can you go and find the children?" she says in an urgent whisper. "Then, when Mum comes back with the mint tea, say you're taking them out for some fresh air."

"No problem." I get to my feet immediately, feeling nauseous with expectation and dread. Michael, staring rigidly at the table, looks even worse. At least I don't have to be here when they're told the terrible news, I think, thankful for small mercies.

Five minutes later, I usher Matthew and Emily back into the dining room, where Mum is pouring Olivia's tea and Dad is ensconced back in his chair at the head of the table.

"Are you going out?" Mum looks baffled.

"Yes, I thought I'd take them out for some fresh air," I say brightly, sticking to the script. "We'll probably just go across the field to the village, then back again."

Mum looks at her watch. "If you wait ten minutes, we'll all come."

"No, really," I urge. "We want to go on our own because we have a little magic show planned for everyone when we get back and we need to discuss it."

Matthew and Emily are both as surprised by this sudden announcement as I am, and make no attempts to disguise it. "What magic show?" says Emily.

"Ha, ha, *what* magic show?" I burble. "Isn't she good?" I clamp a gloved hand onto both of their backs and gently shove them towards the door. "Won't be long," I shout over my shoulder as we walk through the front door.

"What magic show?" parrots Emily again, once we're outside.

"There isn't a magic show, darling," I confess. "I just made that up because I thought it would be nice for Mummy and Daddy to spend some time on their own with Grandma and Grandpa."

"Why?" Now Matthew is on my case, too.

"Oh, I don't *know*," I reply desperately. "I just did. Come on . . ." I start to run towards the field. "First one to find a cowpat wins a prize!"

Sadly, it's me. A gigantically huge, juicy one that is now hanging in murky globules off the bottom and side of my new pale pink suede loafer. Whilst the children choose their promised candy in the village shop, I lurk outside trying to scrape off the worst of it against a milestone that reads "Pushkin, five miles."

After a few minutes, I give it up as a bad job and sit on the shop's stone step, waiting for the children to emerge.

Gazing back across the sloping field, I can just see the thatched roof of my parents' house, a small wisp of smoke snaking out of the chimney. It's a greeting card scene, belying the nightmare undoubtedly unfolding within. Just the thought makes my stomach turn over, a small amount of bile rising in the back of my throat. I try to guess the reactions of my parents, never ones to follow obvious patterns of behavior. Initially, Mum will probably disintegrate, then gather herself to rise to the challenge, going into organizing mode, making sure Olivia has everything she needs, that Michael is able to continue working, that the children are well cared for and protected from any unnecessary upset.

Dad, on the other hand, is more of a worry. He rarely reacts emotionally to anything, keeping feelings locked inside, where they either eventually dissipate or swell to such an extent that he might explode. I know he will feel intense anger that one of his daughters has been dealt this cruel blow, and that there's still no guaranteed cure for her condition when so much money is poured into other, less life-threatening issues or projects.

"Here's your change." Matthew has appeared by my side, proffering a fifty-pence piece in his gloved hand. "Thanks for the sweets." Emily is standing right behind him, munching on a licorice whip.

"Come on then, let's get back. I'll beat you at Monopoly, if you like." I wipe a smeared stickiness off the side of Emily's top lip and flick it onto the road.

On the way back across the field, we talk about everything from the Battle of Hastings to Britney Spears. I *love* talking to children, they have such a refreshing view on the world, unsullied by adult expectations and, subsequently, disappointments.

As we reach the front door, I remove my ruined loafers and stand still for a moment, inhaling long, deep tendrils of icy air into my lungs. I have absolutely no idea what I'm about to encounter, and the urge to run in the opposite direction and just keep going is almost overpowering.

Matthew and Emily are still in the front yard, kicking their way through the large piles of coppery leaves and shrieking with laughter. I click the old-fashioned front door latch and walk through into the roomy, square hallway.

Silence.

"Helloooo?" I shout tentatively.

"We're in the sitting room." It's Olivia's voice.

Walking in, the scene that unfolds before my eyes is pretty much as I predicted when sitting on the shop step.

Mum is sitting on the sofa, sobbing quietly in what is clearly the lull after the storm. Her face is a mass of bright pink blotches from crying, her eyes raw and swollen. She's wringing a soggy tissue round and round her fingers and her whole body is hunched forward, wracked with sorrow. Dad is sitting next to her, upright and stoic, his left arm placed around her shoulders. His face is chalk white, his pupils enlarged with terror, but there is no sign of tears. Every so often he whispers "Shhhhh, it's going to be all right" and rubs Mum's shoulders.

Olivia is bolt upright in one of the two armchairs adjacent to the sofa, her hands placed on her knees, her expression simply sad. She has worked through so much of her own pain in the past few weeks that clearly her only emotion right now is that of concern for her parents. Michael is sitting in the opposite armchair, looking distinctly uncomfortable.

"You've told them then," I say somewhat fruitlessly.

Olivia nods. "Where are the children?"

"They're playing with the leaves outside. They're fine."

Mum looks up at me and extends her arms. "Come and sit here," she says, patting the sofa cushion next to her.

I move across the room and sit down as she wraps her arms around my neck and starts to sob loudly. "My darling Livvy," she wails. "How could this happen to my baby girl?"

I have no idea what's happened before my arrival, but it strikes me as odd that Mum is seeking solace in my arms rather than Olivia's. Then I remember something Ben told me about how families sometimes react when told a loved one is seriously ill.

He says it's common, though by no means absolute, that initially the sick person is put on a pedestal, a fragile figure who, in the eyes of the family, has become almost untouchable in case they might break.

"The family is torn between wanting to weep all over them and feeling that would be too self-indulgent. They feel they have to be strong for them and, sometimes, it makes them go the other way and become stiff and remote," he says. "But after everyone's got used to the idea, the barriers usually come down."

His words are solace to me now as I witness the effect of Olivia's illness on our otherwise close, happy-go-lucky family.

Reaching across to the coffee table, I pull a fresh tissue from the box and use it to dab Mum's eyes. Olivia shifts uncomfortably in her seat and glances nervously at the door. "Mum, you need to try and calm down now," she says, her tone slightly stern. "The children might come in at any moment, and I don't want them to know anything's wrong."

"Yes I know, darling. Sorry." Mum blows her nose, then sits upright and uses a shaking hand to try to smooth down her hair. "Alan, put the television on to whatever channel is showing an afternoon film, will you?"

"Helen, I hardly think this is the time . . ." Dad murmurs.

Mum's voice, much calmer now, slices across his. "I didn't ask what you think. Just do it . . . *please.*"

He does, and a few seconds later a Fred Astaire and Ginger Rogers movie is flickering away in the corner, a jolly backdrop in a room shrouded in gloom. We all stare wordlessly at it, wrapped up in our own thoughts.

"Look what I've got!" Emily bursts into the sitting room, her nose and cheeks red from the cold. She's brandishing a giant ocher-colored leaf in one hand. "It's just like Mickey Mouse!"

"Let me see . . ." Olivia smiles and extends her hand towards her daughter. Taking the leaf, she holds it up for the rest of us to see. "Gosh, it *is* like Mickey, isn't it? There's the ears . . ." Her finger traces the outline, ". . . and there's the chin. Clever girl!"

Matthew has wandered in behind his sister and is openly staring at his grandma. "What's the matter?" He takes a couple of steps closer and peers at her. "You've been crying."

I feel myself go rigid, wondering what explanation Mum is going to come up with.

"Oh, nothing to worry about, darling." She takes his hand and gives it a squeeze. "Silly Grandma has been crying at this soppy film, that's all."

Matthew turns to the screen to see Fred and Ginger grinning like Cheshire cats and leaping from one chair to another in a highly energetic dance routine. If it strikes him as odd that this would cause Grandma to cry, then he doesn't show it.

"Oh," he says flatly. "Who is it?"

"Fred Astaire and Ginger Rogers," says Mum, her voice now entirely normal, having clearly switched into "cope" mode. "They did lots of films together. He was a very famous dancer who would spend hours perfecting just one dance step."

I stretch my arms above my head and stand up, pleased the atmosphere is returning to some sense of normality. "But if you think about it," I say through a yawn, "old Ginger was even more impressive, because she did everything he did . . . except she did it backwards."

Michael smiles for the first time since we arrived three hours ago. "Come on you two." He stands up and gestures to the children to follow him. "Let's see if we can find any other leaves that look like famous people. I swear I saw Pamela Anderson on the way in."

"Pamela who?" says Matthew, following him out of the door.

One hour later, with nothing more said about you-know-what and all the adults making a concerted effort to keep the afternoon as normal as possible for the children, we all pile back into the car for the journey home.

As we pull out of the drive, all waving cheerily at Mum and Dad on the front step, just for a moment I feel that everything *is* normal, that life has returned to the days when my only worries were getting to work on time and paying the phone bill before it got cut off.

Then I turn back to face the front and see Michael casting a concerned eye in Olivia's direction, the inner pain of uncertainty etched on his face.

And I know the worst has yet to come.

Twenty Seven

It's 11 a.m. and the theme tune of *Good Morning Britain* fills the studio, booming out from the monitors.

"Good Morning Britain!" says Eddie brightly, a radical change from the surly git who castigated one of the technicians just seconds earlier for not lighting him correctly.

"Boy oh boy, do we have an action-packed show for you today!"

"Yes!" says Tara, as insincere and wooden as ever. "We've got fun!" Cue clip of extremely camp travel reporter pulling a Macaulay Culkin–style face on a roller coaster. "We've got frolics!" Clip of lots of grinning hopefuls high kicking at an audition for a new West End musical. "And we've got luuurve!" Cut to clip of a couple of agency-booked wannabes—him gay, her probably frigid—clinking champagne glasses at a "romantic" restaurant.

"What a pile of old shit," I whisper to Tab, as we stand in the shadows of the studio, watching the action. "Come on, let's go back to our desks."

In precisely fifteen minutes' time, whilst Eddie and Tara are happily burbling nonsense to the nation, my sister is having her right breast removed, then reconstructed. Never has my job seemed so trite and meaningless, so downright irritating.

I wanted to take the day off and wait at the hospital, but Olivia wouldn't let me.

"I am treating this as a normal procedure, just something that has to be done," she'd said when they dropped me off at home last night. "I don't want everyone sitting around, waiting for a puff of smoke."

So I have dragged myself into work, where I'm being as much use as an ashtray on a powerboat. Waiting, wondering, worrying . . .

I sit down and switch on the computer again. Here, you never leave yourself logged on when you're away from your desk, not unless you're asking for trouble. I found out the hard way when I returned one day to find my in-box bursting under the strain of replies to "your application to join" various porn and penis enlargement Web sites.

At the top of my in-box is an e-mail from Simon. Having left his place early Saturday morning on the false pretext of having a busy day planned with my friends, I have barely thought about him since. Understandable though, given the trauma of yesterday's visit to my parents.

Hi gorgeous,

Just wanted to touch base with you after Friday night and say that I had a fantastic time. I can't stop thinking about those sexy stockings!

I glance nervously over my shoulder to check no one's lurking behind me.

I was wondering if you're free this Saturday night for a repeat performance. Maybe we could catch a movie first? Let me know,

Simon xxxx

A pen wedged firmly in the side of my mouth, I set about composing a witty but laid-back reply.

Dear Simon,

Lovely to hear from you . . .

No, far too twee.

Wotcha,

Great to hear from you . . .

Wotcha? Very cockney geezer. I hit the delete button again.

Hi there,

Yes, I really enjoyed Friday too. Saturday would be nice, but I thought you were going to New York this weekend on business?

Jess x

Much better. Chatty, positive, but not too keen. A reply comes back within thirty seconds.

Nah, I just made that up because I wanted to take you out for dinner and get you pissed, rather than a more sober, weekend lunch! So how about it? The new Colin Farrell movie looks a good bet.

S x

Just another of his effortless lies, I think, sighing gently. Though I suppose this one is flattering, rather than having the flattening qualities of the last. And at least he's very up front about wanting to see me again. I reply that, yes, Saturday night is fine and to e-mail me later in the week with details of which cinema to meet at.

My phone rings.

"Hello, Good Morning Britain. Jess Monroe speaking."

"Hi Jess, it's Ben. How's things?"

What a happy surprise. It's been several weeks since I last saw Ben, but his words of wisdom have been on my mind, especially since he remains the one person I've told about Olivia outside the family. Prophetically, he has managed to call just as Olivia is being wheeled into theater.

"You may regret asking that," I sigh, keeping my voice low. "Olivia is having her mastectomy this morning and yesterday we went for lunch at my parents' house to break the bad news."

"I don't regret asking at all," he replies softly. "Want to talk about it?"

"I'd love to, but it's bloody impossible to have a private phone conversation here without the world and his wife earwigging. It's the curse of open-plan offices . . ."

"Well, no matter, because the reason I was calling was to say I'm up in town later for a fund-raiser. So I thought you might like to meet for a drink, say early evening? We can have a chat about everything then."

"That sounds like just what I need," I say gratefully, smiling as a small feeling of temporary relief washes over me.

We meet at 6 p.m. in a small, out-of-the-way wine bar down a side street near to Tower Bridge.

Ben is already there when I arrive, tucked away in a dark corner with a copy of the *London Evening Standard* and what I assume to be two gin and tonics. He pushes one towards me.

"How'd it go?" I ask.

He wrinkles his nose. "So-so. We need money to build another unit and so far we only have half of the projected $100,000 cost. So we'll have to organize yet another event to try to find the rest."

"I could help you," I volunteer. "I have a contacts book full of numbers for various celebs we can try and persuade to come along. I'd love to do something to help out the organization."

"Thanks." He smiles. "But enough of my Sunshine House woes. It sounds like you've had a pretty grim weekend."

Whilst I fill him in on our visit to the parentals, he sits and listens intently, only interrupting occasionally with a well-placed question when I have unwittingly skipped over some crucial part of the story.

Once again, it feels liberating to unburden myself to someone who doesn't know my family, someone to whom I can talk about my emotional distress, without feeling I'm being too self-indulgent and eclipsing their own.

"Your mum was clearly being strong for Olivia's sake," he says, as I finish off with how Mum and Dad stood waving on the step. "But I suspect your father will have had to deal with some significant fallout once your car left the driveway. You'll need to keep an eye on them."

I nod. "I know. It's weird, because I have always been the little one of the family, the one everyone indulged and kept an eye on. I feel like I'm finally having to grow up and take care of all of them for a change."

"You're more than capable of dealing with it," says Ben comfortingly, placing a reassuring hand on my forearm. "You always find strength you didn't know you have in these situations. Have you spoken to Olivia since the operation?"

I shake my head. "No, but I spoke to Michael a couple of hours ago and he said it seems to have gone well. She's probably staying in the hospital for a couple of days and doesn't want to see anyone until she comes home. She just wants to sleep."

He shrugs almost imperceptibly. "An entirely normal reaction."

"The children have gone to Michael's parents for a few days, so at least they don't have to worry about them for now. But I just feel so hopeless, moping around. I want to go over there and do something, but I don't know what," I say miserably.

Ben smiles ruefully. "If it's any consolation, the relatives of someone who's seriously ill often suffer more than the patient, simply because they feel so impotent and redundant. All they can do is wait around."

"And drink!" I interject, attempting to lighten the mood slightly. "Another G&T?"

Given the place is empty except for us, I'm back at the table within a minute and keen to move the conversation on to something less gloomy. As Ben now knows my innermost fears about Olivia, I feel no shame in slicing through polite, preliminary chitchat about his life and asking outright what I want to know, what's been on my mind since my conversation with Tab.

"So, do you have a girlfriend?"

He balks slightly, clearly taken aback by a question that's a complete non sequitur to what we were talking about before I went to the bar. But I like Ben, and I want to be his friend. I also feel a strange desire to prove Will and all his other rugby thugs wrong—that just because a man isn't a beer-drinking, skirt-chasing sex machine whose idea of fine literature is limited to the sports section doesn't mean he's gay. Even Richard would back me up on this.

"No, I don't." Ben recovers well.

"Why not?" I take a sip of my drink, feeling its refreshing kick almost instantaneously.

"Probably for the same reason you don't," he shrugs. "I haven't met anyone. Anyway, it's kind of difficult when you spend most of the time out in the sticks, surrounded by sick children and grieving families."

I toy with the idea of telling him about Simon but think better of it, anxious not to steer the conversation back to me, me, me again.

"Have you ever had a serious relationship?"

He nods. "Yes, a long time ago though. We met at university and it lasted about three years before she met some dynamic City type and decided he was a better bet than dreary, badly paid old me." He feigns playing the violin to show his self-deprecation is lighthearted rather than heartfelt.

"Are you still in touch?"

"Nah. No point really. Our lives went like that . . ." He clasps his hands together, then shoots them apart in opposite directions. "No doubt she's driving one of those giant minivans now, with one Armani-clad toddler in the back and a couple of golden Labradors."

"Wearing one of those quilted car coats." I laugh, warming to the theme.

"And don't forget the Alice head band and blue and white stripey Boden top," he grins.

"So, no one else since then?"

He shakes his head. "Well, nothing serious anyway. I'm married to my job," he says dramatically, clasping his chest. "But it's shit at giving blow jobs."

"Just like a real wife then," I say with a smile, "if those marriage surveys are anything to go by. What do they say? If you put a penny in a pot for every time you have sex *before* you get married, then take a penny out for every time afterwards, you'll never empty the pot."

"Funny." He smirks. "But utter, sweeping-generalization bullshit. Oh, I'm sure some people *do* go off sex after marriage, but my parents were always at it when I was a kid. They probably still are to a certain extent." He wrinkles his nose. "Don't want to think about that too deeply."

An image of my parents having sex pops into my mind too and I shake my head to obliterate it pronto. "Yes, my parents are still very much together and happy, too." I nod. "Maybe people's expectations of what marriage should be are just too high these days. Although my sister and her husband seem to be managing very nicely."

"Sex is just *part* of a happy marriage," says Ben, picking a piece of ice out of his drink and popping it in his mouth. "If it's your be-all and end-all, then you'll hit trouble. Take the parents that come to Sunshine House . . . you think they give a shit about how much sex they're having? Of course not. In fact, I doubt they're having any at all because stress and exhaustion are the two greatest dampeners on desire. *All* they care about is their child's health, and their marriage, if it's a strong one, is their backbone, their support."

"Like Anne and Ralph?"

"Precisely!" says Ben triumphantly. "They went to hell and back when Sarah died, but in a way, their marriage emerged stronger than ever. And I doubt it's because they shag like rabbits. People need to move away from this constant obsession with sex, they really do."

I don't know what to say next. What he's said is absolutely true, even though it seems a jarring contradiction to the relationship rules that I—and everyone else I know—seem to live by. I feel myself flush slightly at the thought of my frenzied sex romp with Simon last weekend, followed by a more gentle, considered session the following morning. Two pennies in the pot already and I've known him only five minutes.

Ben looks at his watch and drains his glass. "Sorry, but I'd better get going. I'm on duty tonight, so I have to get the seventhirty train." He stands up and plants a quick kiss on my left cheek.

"Thanks for listening." I smile. "Sorry if I went on a bit."

"Stop apologizing," he chides. "I'm honored you feel comfortable enough to tell me. And it makes a pleasant change from the curmudgeon you were when we first met."

I poke my tongue out at him. "Speak soon."

"Hope so," he replies. Then he's gone.

Twenty Eight

Tab is thirty-four today, so we sneak out of the office early at 5:30 p.m. to get ready for a small, celebratory dinner party she's having at home.

Having said I'd help her prepare for it, my party outfit which, let's be honest, is barely distinguishable from any other, spent most of the day scrunched up in a Sainsbury's carrier bag hanging off the back of my chair.

It's now 7:30 p.m. and we're already quite tipsy, having swigged our way through a couple of bottles of white wine. Miraculously, however, we have managed to prepare a spectacular feast of salmon mousse to start, followed by honey roast chicken and steamed vegetables, and tiramasu. Thank God for the gourmet grocer.

Tab starts to lay the long, thin table that dominates her kitchen. First, a crisp white cotton cloth, then two matching candlesticks, followed by seven place settings.

"Wait a minute." I count them again just to make sure. "You've done one too many."

"No, that's right." She looks slightly uncomfortable.

I frown and hold up my clenched fists, unfolding a finger as I say each name. "You, me, Will, Richard, Lars, and Madeleine. That's six."

Tab winces sheepishly. "I forgot to tell you. I invited Kara."

I look at her with undisguised horror. "*Please* tell me you're joking."

"No, deadly serious. Sorry."

I slump onto a chair, knees together, ankles splayed in a gesture of hopelessness.

"Why would you do that? You don't even like her."

"True, but after you told me that she and Dan had split up, I gave her a call last week just to say I hope she was feeling OK . . ."

I scoff in horror at her hypocrisy. Although, of course, I can hardly talk.

"I know, I know," she acquiesces. "But you know me, when it comes to a sad story, I'm Little Miss Sucker."

"Isn't she a porn queen?" I can't help myself.

Tab gives me a withering look. "Anyway, since then she has called me a couple of times just for a chat, and she was really quite nice. I really do think the whole Dan business has knocked the stuffing out of her a bit. So I felt a bit sorry for her and invited her along tonight."

I throw my head back in mock despair. "I've known her since school, so it's harder for me to break from her evil clutches, but you? . . . you barely know her and you've been sucked in." I make a loud slurping noise.

"Oh don't be such a drama queen," groans Tab, flicking the side of my head with a Queen's Golden Jubilee tea towel. "Don't worry, I've made sure you're at opposite ends of the table," she says, pointing to the name cards she's placed by each setting.

"Opposite ends of the *country* would be infinitely more preferable," I mumble, pouring myself another generous glass of wine. God knows, I *really* need it now.

There's a loud knocking at the front door and Tab disappears down the corridor to answer it. Reaching across to the Welsh dresser at one end of the room, I pick up a pen and start scribbling.

"Are we unfashionably first? If so, we'll walk round the block and come back again." I hear Richard's voice, moving nearer down the corridor. "Bloody hell, it's Snow White," he says, clocking the ribbon I have tied into my hair in an attempt to spruce it up a bit.

"And which dwarf are you?" I shoot back.

"Sauced already, are we?" He jerks his head towards my sprawled legs and the empty wineglass in my hand.

"Sober as a judge."

"Darling, the best six weeks of sex I ever had was with a happily married," . . . he simulates quote marks with his fingers, ". . . high court judge, and he was like a drunken sailor most of the time." He stoops down and gives me a peck on the cheek.

Lars saunters into the room behind him, a lazy smile on his face. "Hi Jessie, you good?"

"Me very good, thanks," I reply, pouring them each a glass of wine.

Richard is already moving around the table studying the name cards. When he reaches the end setting, he looks momentarily puzzled and opens his mouth to ask Tab a question. "Who's . . ."

"It's Kara," I butt in, pulling a "shut up" face at him.

"Oh, I see." He grins wickedly. "And how is the dear creature since her dreary boyfriend dumped her? Will she be drinking, or is she driving her broom here tonight?"

"She's arriving by *cab*," says Tab. "She's coming straight from visiting her parents."

"Ooh, evening opening hours at the asylum," says Richard. "How very flexible."

I laugh loudly, suddenly looking forward to tonight's events after all, particularly with Richard in such a devilish mood.

"Stop it, you're all rotten," chides Tab. "The poor girl is devastated." She turns to glare at me. "And you should know that better than anyone, seeing as though she confided in you."

"Hardly," I scoff. "She just sent me to try and talk Dan round, because she couldn't face doing it herself in case he knocked her back again." As soon as the words leave my mouth, I regret them.

"Ooooh, really?" Richard's nostrils are flaring with the scent of gossip. "You never said."

"That's because it was *supposed* to be private," I mutter, silently vowing never to drink again. I take a swig of wine. Oops.

"There shouldn't be any secrets between friends," he says in a syrupy voice. "So do tell, what did Dan say?"

"Nothing really," I lie. "Just that they both needed a break for a while."

"Yeah, *right*," he drawls. "Oh well, I shall just have to ask Kara when she gets here."

"No, you fucking well won't!" I throw a cashew nut across the table at him.

"Hey, hey, hey!" Tab claps her hands together like a schoolteacher. "Do you two mind reeling it in a bit? It's *my* birthday and I want it to be an evening of sophistication and wit, not degenerate into mealtime with the Beverly Hillbillies."

"Sorry." We both snigger in unison.

There's the door again. This time, Lars ambles down the hallway to answer it and, seconds later, Madeleine and Will walk in, having both arrived at the same time.

Everyone equipped with a drink and seated in their respective chairs, Madeleine jerks her head towards the table. "So who are we waiting for?"

"Kara," I say flatly.

"Yes, we're all players in a new theater production of *Waiting for Godonlyknows*," quips Richard, grinding the remnant of his cigarette into the ashtray.

Tap tap tap. The wait is over.

"I'll go," says Tab quickly, clearly anxious that none of us seem capable of a cheery welcome.

She reappears with a rigid smile bolted on her face. "Look who's here everyone, it's Kara!"

She pops her head over Tab's left shoulder and gives us all a smile that doesn't quite reach her eyes. Her hair is scraped back into a ponytail, making her look more severe than usual, and she's dressed in her usual head-to-toe black. "Hello all." She bends down and rummages inside her handbag. "Before I forget, happy birthday!" She hands Tab a small, beautifully wrapped package.

"Oh, you shouldn't have!" beams our hostess, tearing at the paper to reveal a pretty silver bracelet with small fake diamonds embedded in it. Well, I *presume* they're fake.

Kara glides towards the table as if on castors, her neck ramrod straight, her expression slightly imperious as usual. "Where am I?" She hovers alarmingly by the empty space at my side, then notices that the name card reads "Tabitha."

"You're there." I point to the end of the table, where Will and Lars are already in position either side.

Picking up the name card, she reads it aloud. "Beelzebub?"

She looks for an explanation straight to Tab, who, blissfully unaware of what's going on, turns back from the sink and smiles. "Sorry?"

"It says Beelzebub on my name card." She holds it aloft.

Tab laughs. "No it doesn't, it says Kara. I wrote it myself."

I clear my throat dramatically. "Actually, *I* wrote it," I say, turning to glare at Richard, who deliberately avoids my gaze, even though the corners of his mouth twitch. "Just a little joke."

"As you can see, I'm clutching my sides," says Kara flatly, screwing up the card and lobbing it into the bin.

An uncomfortable silence descends for a few moments, with Tab busying herself by handing round the plates of salmon mousse and Will rearranging the wine bottles in the fridge.

Clearly unable to bear the conversational void any longer, Lars decides to fill it with a question. I really wish he hadn't.

"So, Jessie, did you go out wiv your married man or no?"

His words hang in the air, where I dearly hope they'll evaporate into nothing before Kara even notices they're there. No such luck.

"What married man?" She positively bristles with delight.

I sigh wearily, a lamb to the slaughter. "You remember my first Internet date . . . the one who did a bunk through the kitchens?"

Kara nods enthusiastically.

"Well, he got back in touch last week, asking if he could meet me to explain . . . I rang Lars to ask what he thought I should do."

"And me!" chimes Richard.

"And me," say Madeleine and Tab simultaneously.

"I see." Kara's tone is frosty.

"I tried calling you a couple of times, but you didn't answer," I mutter unconvincingly. "Anyway . . ." I look at Lars to show I'm talking to him. "Yes, I did go and meet him, and yes, it turned out he *was* married. With the emphasis on was. His final divorce comes through in a month's time."

"So he *says*," scoffs Kara.

"Oh sorry, Kara, I didn't realize you know him." Out of the corner of my eye, I see Richard and Madeleine exchange "oooer" glances. I know I shouldn't rise to Kara's bait, but everything about her tonight is like a maddening itch under the collar, and I'll be damned if I'm going to let her rain on my Simon parade.

"I don't," she says with a sniff, "but you have to admit it all sounds rather implausible."

"Au contraire," I retaliate. "He offered to show me his decree nisi."

Richard places a palm against his chest and rolls his eyes. "Oh, couldn't you just *die* from the romance of it all!"

I glare at him. "Don't you bloody well start."

"So what happened after that?" It's Lars, clearly making an effort to try to return things to an even keel.

I finish off the last of my salmon mousse and push my plate to one side. "I agreed to go on another date, which took place this time last week."

"And?" Richard leans forward, an intense look on his face.

"And what?"

He raises his eyes heavenward. "Oh, stop being so fucking coy. Did you have sex with him?"

"Certainly not," I fib indignantly. "What kind of girl do you think I am?"

"Darling, I *know* what kind of girl you are, that's why I ask."

Tab, who already knows the Simon story—without the meaningless, frenzied sex bit—starts to clear away our starter plates. Madeleine, who knows the Simon story *with* the meaningless, frenzied sex bit, says absolutely nothing. Bless her fishnet stockings.

"So is this going to be an ongoing thing?" asks Kara, clearly hoping I'm about to admit he did a bunk through the kitchens again.

"Yep. We're going to the cinema tomorrow night."

Thankfully, with the arrival of the main course, accompanied by the prerequisite oohs and aahs, everyone seems to tire of the subject of my love life and the conversation moves on to the show-biz gossip in that day's papers. Finally, as we're all cleaning our plates, Tabitha excuses herself to go to the loo.

"Where is it?" I hiss urgently at Richard the minute she's gone.

He stands up and scuttles off into the hallway, returning with a paper shopping bag with the words "Patisserie Valerie" on the side. "Ta dah!" He strikes a game-show-hostess pose.

"Quick, Will, large plate!" I bark, ripping off the packaging to reveal a sensational white chocolate cake with "Happy Birthday Tab" scrawled on top in spidery writing. Rummaging furiously in my handbag, I ram a gold candle in the middle and click my fingers at Richard to light it.

We fall back into our chairs just as Tab walks back through the door. "Now then, who'd like cof . . ." She stops mid-sentence as we start singing "Happy Birthday" and gesturing towards the cake. "Ohmigod!" She clamps a hand to her mouth. "That's just fabulous."

"Happy birthday, dear Scabby Taaaaart!" sings Richard at the top of his voice. "Happy birthday to yoooooou!"

Tab blows out the candle and we all applaud loudly, sinking gratefully back into our chairs.

As she starts to cut hefty slices and pass them round, the sound of metal clanging against glass cuts through the chitchat. It's Kara brandishing a spoon.

"First of all, thanks to Tab for inviting us all and I think, as an extra birthday treat, we should all wash up."

Furious that Kara is hijacking the proceedings as if she were a close friend of Tab's, I mutter mutinously to Richard: "I wish she'd *dry* up."

But no such luck.

"Now then, *I* have some news," she continues, the undeniable gleam of self-satisfaction in her eyes.

"Don't tell me, they've found the bastard who did that to your hair?" quips Richard.

"Very funny." Kara's face doesn't even crack a smile. Pausing for dramatic effect, she scans the table to make sure she has the attention of every last one of us. "No, my news is that Dan and I are back together."

My mouth falls open, a small flake of chocolate dropping out and landing on the table. I can't believe what I'm hearing.

"Kara, that's fantastic news!" enthuses Tab. "I'm *so* pleased for you both."

"Thanks. I always knew we wouldn't be apart for long." Kara directs this remark straight at me, her beady eyes gauging my reaction.

Having managed to marginally compose myself by now, I smile benignly. "Great. So when did that happen?" An image of Dan kissing me pops into my mind and I briefly close my eyes to try to blot it out.

"A few nights ago." Her eyes are shining with victory. "He rang and said he was missing me terribly and wanted to see me."

"Really?" I don't attempt to disguise my complete surprise at this sudden turnaround by the man whose final words to me were "It's over for good."

"Yes, so I kept him waiting for a couple of days . . ." She turns towards Madeleine and Tab. ". . . well, you have to, don't you? They mustn't think you're keen . . . and then I agreed to meet him just to talk things through."

"And, voilà, you just fell into each other's arms," says Richard, furtively shooting me a derisory look.

"Not quite." Kara smiles benevolently. "Obviously, I had to get a few things straight first and a guarantee that the same thing wasn't going to happen again."

"And you got that?" I ask. This just gets better and better, or is it worse and worse?

"Yep," she says triumphantly, pouring herself another generous helping of wine. "So, whilst you can never say one hundred percent, I doubt very much we'll be splitting up again." Her face takes on a dreamy look. "The making-up bit was *sensational*."

Richard pulls a "yuk" face. "Well . . ." He raises his glass. "A toast to Tab's birthday, to Jess's new relationship, and to Kara being rogered senseless again. Cheers!"

"Cheers!" we all chorus.

Toast over, the conversation moves on to other things, with Richard and Will discussing the merits of rugby player Jonny Wilkinson—though from different perspectives, I suspect. I can hear Richard telling Will that he would "never take part in a sport that has ambulances on standby."

On the other side of the table, Tab, Madeleine, Kara, and Lars are chatting about his new picturephone. So far, he reveals, the only image he's received is one of Richard's ass.

I sit facing them, my body language and expression suggesting I'm engrossed in their conversation, but really I'm in a world of my own, thinking about Olivia. And Kara. I'm still baffled by Dan's change of heart so soon after our conversation.

As for my sister, we have spoken on the phone since she returned home from her mastectomy, and she was trying hard to sound upbeat and positive. But tomorrow I will physically *see* her for the first time.

I will do my utmost to mirror her positive outlook, but inside I'm dreading it.

Twenty Nine

Michael opens the door still in his dressing gown. "Blimey!" He looks at his watch. "I don't think I've ever clapped eyes on you at this time in the morning before."

"I woke up at seven and couldn't get back to sleep," I say with a sheepish smile. "Things are on my mind."

"Yes, I know what you mean." He stands aside to let me pass. "Olivia is still in bed, so go up if you like."

I dwell in the hallway, waiting whilst he closes the front door. "How is she?" I deliberately keep my voice low.

He gestures for me to follow him through to the kitchen, minimizing the chances of her hearing us talk.

"Coffee?" He waves the kettle at me and I nod. "In answer to your question, she's as well as can be expected." He wrinkles his nose. "God, that sounds like a real doctor-ish thing to say, doesn't it?"

I smile warmly. "Yes, it does. A husband-ish answer, please."

He lets out a long sigh and I notice how gaunt his face looks, illuminated by the early morning light pouring in through the window. "She's very up and down, to be honest. When she first came back from hospital, she was quite up, hyper almost, gabbling on excitedly about how well she felt and that she was convinced everything was going to be all right. And of course she becomes extremely bright and cheerful whenever she thinks about the children coming back tomorrow. She's missing them terribly." He pauses for a moment and stares out of the window.

"Then?" I say gently.

"Then yesterday, literally just as she'd put down the phone from an upbeat chat with Matthew and Emily, she just went downhill, crying uncontrollably and saying she couldn't bear the thought of dying."

Tears well up in his eyes and he hastily brushes them away, clearly embarrassed by someone other than Olivia seeing him so vulnerable.

"Michael, it's OK." I move forward and put a reassuring arm around his shoulders. "Believe me, I have cried about it until I'm utterly exhausted. I just try to be strong around Olivia, but it's bloody hard."

"Me too." He smiles wearily. "I'm like a robot around her sometimes, because it's the only way I can stop myself from falling apart. I've taken this week off, so I haven't even got work to hold me together."

I pour boiling water into our cups and hand him one. "Michael . . ." I pause, unsure whether I should ask the question, but I *have* to know. "*Is* there still a chance she could die?"

He nods his head miserably. "Yes, I suppose there is, although I have to say that it's only a very small one. The operation went very well and once they've blasted it with chemo, well . . . we just have to keep our fingers crossed that it doesn't come back." He stops and closes his eyes for a few moments, his face wracked with pain. "I'm still trying to get a grip on all of it."

"You're doing just fine." I smile reassuringly. "Olivia's very lucky to have you around . . . you're very lucky to have each other."

"Believe me, I know." He sighs. "Sometimes, I wonder if all this is somehow our punishment for having had such a happy marriage up to now . . . you know, our payback time." He stares up at the ceiling.

"Nonsense," I chide gently. "It's just one of those things. But if anyone can beat it, Liv can." I take my coffee and turn to head upstairs. "I plan to stay here for several hours, so if you want to go out and get some fresh air or whatever, don't worry. I'll be here."

"Thanks," he says gratefully. "I might just do that."

Climbing the stairs to Olivia and Michael's bedroom, I feel the nagging thud of fear in the pit of my stomach. I'm not sure what—or who—I'll find. The door is half open, the room beyond shadowy, its curtains closed to block out the light. I tap gently.

"Come in." Her voice sounds sleepy.

"Hi, it's me," I whisper, stepping into the gloom and peering in the direction of the bed.

She's sitting upright, propped up by pillows, her head lolling back against the brown leather headboard. Her eyes are open but she looks groggy, her hair smooth one side but ruffled the other, where she's been sleeping.

"Hi!" she says brightly, making an attempt to sit up more.

"Stay as you are." I move forward and make a gesture for her to lie back again, not daring to actually touch her. "How you feeling?"

"Not bad actually, considering . . ." She smiles weakly. "Still a bit sore." She touches the area near her right breast, which, in the half light and covered by her nightdress, looks indistinguishable from before. "Look, can you open the curtains a bit? It's terribly gloomy in here, not conducive to feeling cheerful at all."

I oblige, and she screws up her eyes as a shaft of bright light streams directly onto her face.

"Too much?"

"No, I'll get used to it. Just give me a few seconds." She pats the bed. "Now come and sit down. I want to hear everything you've been up to."

The minutiae of my life seem particularly trivial today, but if Olivia wants to discuss it, I'll oblige. For the next hour, I fill her in on Tom, the older gentleman with all his talk of pretty ladies and champers, on Simon . . . yes, *with* the frenzied sex bits . . . and Kara and Dan . . . without the frenzied snog bit, which I'm too ashamed to admit to anyone. Throughout, I'm leaping up and down from the bed animatedly describing scenes, embellishing anecdotes and pulling extreme faces in a bid to make her laugh.

It works, and by the time I get to last night's denouement of Kara announcing she's back with Dan, Olivia's face is glowing with delight, wrapped up in the scandal of an outside world where others' lives are treading their usual predictable, trivial path, unsullied by life-threatening diseases.

"Oh, Jess, you are a tonic!" she declares, clapping her hands together in glee. "I *told* you I needed you to carry on dating, just so you could come round and cheer me up with your stories. And how's work been?"

"Bearable." I shrug. "The usual bollocky diet of tripe and trivia, although I *did* do a really worthwhile report recently," I add, telling her all about my visit to Sunshine House.

"Those poor, poor kids," she says, tears welling in her eyes. "At least I have managed to enjoy *some* kind of life before getting ill. Their lives have barely begun."

I nod. "I know, although strangely, they seem to deal with it far better than their parents, according to what my friend who works there says."

Olivia mulls over what I've said for a few moments. "True. For all that I'm going through at the moment, I know that it would be one hundred times worse if it was happening to one of the children instead. As a parent, you'd feel so hopeless, wanting to take the sickness away from them and bear it yourself."

I absentmindedly pick a hair from the shoulder of her nightdress. "My friend Ben says they also feel terrible guilt, because they feel that in creating the child, they have somehow created the illness too."

"So what's he like then, this Ben?" she asks, taking a sip of water from a glass on her bedside table.

"He's great." I smile. "Bit of a strange cookie though. He seems very old fashioned in many ways."

"Do you fancy him?" she grins cheekily.

I shake my head. "No. Besides, there's a chance he could be gay. Tab and Will certainly think so, and he doesn't seem to have had a girlfriend for a long time."

"Set Richard on him." Olivia laughs. "He'll find out."

"God, can you *imagine*?" I groan. "I wouldn't wish that on anyone. No, I'm sure Ben will cough up in his own good time, but meanwhile I really like his company and I admire him enormously for what he does."

We lapse into silence for a few seconds, the only sound Michael's travel alarm clock ticking away.

"Have you said anything to the children?" I ask eventually.

She nods. "Yes, a little bit. We had to really, particularly as I'll still be in bed quite a lot when they get back."

"So what do they know?"

"We didn't make a big deal of it . . . you know, building it up and making a somber announcement . . . we just told them casually that mummy has got a blood disorder that's making her a bit tired. It's *how* you relay something to children that's so important."

"So did the casual approach work?"

She purses her lips. "Seems to have done, yes. They asked a couple of basic questions, like would it make me throw up and would I still be able to cook Christmas dinner." She laughs at this point. "So I said yes, and yes. It's especially important they know that I'll be getting sick for when the chemo starts."

"Which is?"

"Middle of next week. I have to say, the thought of it terrifies me more than the surgery I've just had."

I squeeze her hand. "It'll be fine. You always deal so well with things."

She looks unsure, her face crumpling slightly. "I'm scared, Jess. *Really* scared." She clasps my hand as if she might never let it go.

"I know, sweetie, I know." I lean forward and hold her, my face embedded in her hair. "I'm always here for you; don't ever forget that."

She pulls away, visibly composing herself. "Jess," she whispers, her expression worryingly serious. "I need you to do something for me, but it must be our little secret. You mustn't tell a soul."

"Of course, of course."

She points down to the dresser drawer near my feet. "Open that and pull out the green folder that's tucked under the blanket."

Intrigued, I do as she asks and place it on the bed in front of her.

Casting a quick glance towards the doorway, she half buries the folder under the duvet. "Michael mustn't see it, he'd go mad," she whispers, opening it up.

Inside are several sheets of paper covered in Olivia's distinctive handwriting, plus dozens of photographs of Matthew and Emily at various stages in their lives.

"I'm putting together two memory boxes for the children, just in case . . . well, you know." She looks at me apologetically. "I want them to have something to remember their mummy by."

I am, by turns, both horrified and immensely touched at the thought, but I know that now is not the time to express the former. "Sweetie, you are *not* going to die, but it's a lovely idea anyway." I smile.

She looks pleased. "I was really hoping you'd say that. I can't show it to Michael because I know he'd get really cross with me for even *thinking* that I might not be around to see the children grow up."

I flick through the stack of photos on her lap. Matthew, aged about six months, his face smeared with chocolate, Emily being nursed by Olivia on the day she was born, the four of them, suntanned and smiling, sitting in a beachside café . . . all snapshots of a normal, loving family.

"And what's all the writing?" I say, pointing at the sheets of paper.

"A history of their lives so far, as I remember it," she says enthusiastically. "You know, little anecdotes like how Matthew became attached to an old dishcloth and took it everywhere with him . . . how Emily once threw up straight into our pediatrician's lap . . . when Matthew was a sheep in the school nativity and mistakenly made a mooing noise . . . and how Emily insisted on wearing a ballet tutu over her trousers for virtually the whole of last winter."

I grin from ear to ear at the memory.

"I know they're just silly little things," she adds, "but when children get older they do love to hear about their little idiosyncrasies, and if I'm not around to fill them in, I doubt Michael will know a lot of it because he's at work so much."

I nod in agreement. "And men tend to remember the big,

grand things in life. They're not very good on the small details." I smile. "So, we're agreed it's our little secret. Now what would you like me to do?"

She pushes the paper and photographs back in the folder and hands it to me to replace in the drawer. "I need you to buy me two scrapbooks, some glue, and two fancy boxes that will accommodate the books, plus some other little bits of memorabilia like Matthew's first shoes, and Emily's old blanky. Luckily, I kept a lot of those kinds of things anyway." She smiles.

"Consider it done." I press my fingers to the side of my head in a salute sign.

"Thanks, honey." She visibly relaxes, knowing that her important task is being dealt with. "And besides, if I do hang on in there, which I have *every* intention of doing, then the boxes will still be great mementos for the children, regardless."

"That's the spirit." I smile.

"Oh, and one other thing . . ." Her back straightens slightly again.

"Yep?"

"I don't know if you remember, but a couple of years ago I told you I was putting you down as one of the executors of my will?"

I frown slightly. "Vaguely, yes. Although I wasn't quite sure what it entailed."

"Well, basically, it meant . . . still does mean . . . that if I die, then you would be part of a panel, including a lawyer, Michael and Dad, to make sure that my last wishes were carried out as I requested."

I nod my understanding.

"When I first asked you, it was one of those in-the-unlikely-event-of things, but now of course I've been thinking about it a lot more . . ."

I open my mouth to contradict her, but she presses a finger against her lips.

"So now I want to ask you something else . . . something a lot more serious . . ."

"Go on . . ."

"Can I put you down as a guardian of the children? . . . along with Michael, of course. It's just that although he adores them, he could never be a *mum* to them and they'll need that if . . ." She tails off and takes a deep breath. "Anyway, you've known them since birth and they see you as a sort of surrogate mother anyway."

I listen intently, saying nothing.

"You wouldn't have to live with them or anything like that," she continues. "Just visit a lot, help Michael to make decisions, that kind of thing. And of course, make sure they get lots of mummy-style cuddles . . ." She breaks off and tries to suppress a small sob.

"There, there, don't upset yourself." I stroke her hair soothingly. "It won't come to that, you'll see. You're going to be around to give your grandchildren cuddles, mark my words." I only wish I could one hundred percent believe it myself.

Olivia blows her nose. "Anyway, I want you to think about it for a while, decide whether you're up to taking on that responsibility. If not, it's no problem at all, I can ask Mum."

"What, and subject Matthew and Emily to an adolescence of squeaky clean hair, highly polished shoes, and shirts with frilly ruffs on?" I tease. "No, I don't need any time to think about it, Liv, the answer's yes, of *course.* It would be an honor."

She lets out a long sigh of relief and sinks back onto the pillows. "Thanks, Jess, you don't know how much it means to me to hear you say that. I know I'm supposed to be thinking positive all the time, but there are just some things I need to get in place in case I *don't* get better. Then I can concentrate on fighting it."

"I know, I know," I say, stroking her hair again.

She closes her eyes. "Hmmm, that's nice. I hope you don't think I'm rude, but I feel like I need to sleep now."

I carry on stroking her hair until her breathing becomes deeper and her mouth falls open slightly. Then I sit there for a few minutes more, just staring at her beautiful, peaceful face and wondering what the future holds.

Thirty

Simon is already outside the cinema as I cross through the middle of Leicester Square, picking my through the tourists, drunks, and cuddling couples intertwined together on benches.

I can see him in the distance, huddled against the cold, his hands rammed into the pockets of his long, black overcoat. He looks at his watch, then stares into the distance across the other side of the square.

"Boo!"

He looks startled as I appear at his side. "Aha, there you are." He plants his cold lips against mine for a hasty peck. "Come on, let's get inside. It's bloody freezing."

It's one of those sit-anywhere cinemas, and five minutes before the movie starts, Simon and I are ensconced in the middle of a central row in isolated splendor, with vacant seats in front of us too.

"Looks like we're in luck," he says. "It's one of my pet peeves to be hemmed in by people in the cinema, particularly when they choose to slurp their way through a hot dog and gallon of drink throughout the film. Why don't these people eat before they come?"

Just as the lights dim and we're thirty seconds from a clean getaway, the door bursts open and Mr. and Mrs. Slob walk in. She's carrying a jumbo popcorn, he's brandishing a plate-sized burger with all the trimmings, and please God no, they start to edge their way along our row.

Just as she starts to lower herself into the chair next to Simon, he leaps to his feet. "Ah, greetings, disciples! Jesus loves you!"

I stare at him in mute astonishment, but it's nothing compared to the look on Mrs. Slob's face as she gapes open-mouthed, a fistful of popcorn poised just inches from her lips.

"He's in us all, you know!" Simon continues. "You . . . and you," He points at Mr., then Mrs. "All of us!" He spreads his arms wide to embrace the entire cinema.

"Fucking nutter," says Mrs., just as the film's rating appears on screen. "Come on . . ." She jerks her head at her companion. "Let's get away from this God-botherer."

"Works every time," Simon says with a grin, settling back into his seat as we watch them move several rows forward.

I laugh and snuggle into his arm as the film's opening scene unfolds. It involves lots of gunfire, dead bodies, and Colin Farrell cussing, but I have absolutely no idea what's going on because I have tuned out, my mind wandering back to my chat with Olivia earlier today.

After she'd fallen asleep, I'd sat downstairs for another hour, chatting with Michael about the reaction of my parents, the children, and his own thoughts on what the future holds. By the time I left, I felt emotionally drained, an empty shell who, far from stepping out to watch a vacuous Hollywood movie, simply wanted to sit at home, weep self-indulgently in front of a romantic old film, and eat comfort food. But, given Olivia's vicarious excitement at my burgeoning relationship, here I am.

Don't get me wrong. I *like* Simon and, under any other circumstances, I would have been at fever pitch all day, meticulously preparing myself for our hot date. But there's something about having a major crisis in your life that makes such things seem irrelevant in the grand scheme.

If Simon and I were a year into our relationship, he'd *know* Olivia, Michael, and the children and be experiencing firsthand the strain we're all under. He'd understand completely if I said I wanted to stay in, just the two of us, or even if I preferred to be alone. That's the beauty of familiarity: you can be miserable when you want to, you don't have to pretend.

But when it's all shiny and new, you're both constantly in buffing mode, polishing your personality for public display. To show your imperfections too early could tarnish it irrevocably.

Colin Farrell is now snogging someone and the music is reaching such a crescendo that I can only assume we have reached the end. The credits suddenly start to roll and confirm it.

"Highly entertaining," Simon pronounces, pulling on his coat. "Did you enjoy it?"

"Yes, it was great," I say vaguely, hoping he won't ask anything more in depth.

We stroll arm in arm across the square, him chatting animatedly about a particular action scene in the film, me nodding and smiling in silent agreement.

Within a few hundred yards, we arrive at the door of a new, trendy Indian restaurant with a red rope and ubiquitous, house-sized bouncer blocking the door.

"Name," he booms, looking at his clipboard. The urge to say "Julia Roberts" almost consumes me, but I doubt humor is his strong point and we'd find ourselves frequenting the nearest Mc-Donald's.

"Simon Young."

Wordlessly, the bouncer unclips the rope and stands to one side to let us pass.

It's another dark, somber joint, reminiscent of last weekend's date, with cozy tables partitioned off for privacy. I wonder if Simon is expecting a rematch of our Olympian sex session too.

"You OK? You seem a little distracted tonight," he says, passing me a menu to study.

"Sorry." I smile apologetically. "I've got a lot on my mind at the moment."

He looks at me thoughtfully for a few moments. "Well, let's get ordering out of the way; then, if you fancy unburdening some of it, I'm all ears."

So there it is, plain and simple. An open invitation for me to tell him about Olivia, to reveal the extent of the huge weight bearing down on my shoulders and see if he's up to alleviating some of it.

I have two options: tell him, or use the numbing effect of alcohol to block it out of my mind completely and have a hedonistic evening focused simply on having fun. Although Olivia would advocate the latter wholeheartedly, in my mind it would seem like a betrayal of her.

"So cough up then, what's on your mind?" says Simon, turning back to me after we've finished giving our appetizer selections to the waiter. His cheery demeanor suggests he thinks I'm about to relay a problem on a par with my car breaking down.

I wince slightly. "My sister has just been diagnosed with breast cancer. She had a mastectomy on Monday."

He says nothing for a few seconds, his face impassive. Then

a small furrow appears between his eyebrows. "God, what a bummer."

I'm not quite sure *what* response I expected to my earth-shattering news . . . well, shattering to *my* earth anyway, but I have to admit that this one wouldn't have figured highly on a list of possible options. "How terrible," yes. Or perhaps "How awful, dreadful, terrifying, or shocking" . . . *any* of those would have sufficed. But "what a bummer"? It renders me speechless for a moment or two.

"Um, yes I suppose it is," I say eventually. "It's certainly knocked our entire family for a loop."

"I'll bet." He looks uncomfortable and takes a mouthful of wine. "I had an aunt who died of cancer. I think it was liver though . . . or was it lung?"

How reassuring, I think murderously. "Well, we're hoping Olivia will fight it and go on to live a normal life," I say emphatically, trying to convince myself as much as him.

He nods and pushes my wineglass towards me, clearly hoping more alcohol might loosen me up. "So I presume that means you have to keep a close eye on yourself?"

"Sorry?"

"You know," he pats his hand against his chest. "Check for lumps. Not that I noticed any last weekend." He grins, gently nudging my shoulder with his.

I stare wordlessly out into the middle distance. This person, who clearly knows as much about cancer and its devastating effects as I do about the offside rule, has inadvertently made an off-the-cuff remark that has skewered me to my seat with deadly precision.

Amidst all the trauma of the past few weeks, the operation, my parents' devastation, the memory boxes for the children, my own emotional anguish, the *one* thing that hasn't crossed my mind is the possible physical implications for me.

Whilst there's no history of breast cancer in our family and Olivia's ill health is looking increasingly like an unavoidable bolt from the blue, who's to say the same couldn't happen to me?

"I never thought of that," I stutter. "I'll make an appointment to see my doctor next week."

"Attagirl," he says cheerily. "And don't forget, I'm more than happy to check you regularly for any lumps and bumps." He starts to nuzzle my ear.

And that was it. Not one question about Olivia's well-being, whether she was older or younger than me, did she have children, were our parents still alive and if so, how had they reacted. Nothing. He simply carried on as if my revelation had never been uttered.

"So, I thought we'd finish off here, then go back to my place," he murmurs, his hand discreetly roaming inside my jacket. "What are you wearing?"

"Clothes," I say flatly.

"Very funny, you know what I mean. Are the stockings back by popular demand?" His hand moves down to the hem of my skirt, but I clamp my thighs together and brush him away.

"Not here!" I chide. "People are looking." On the contrary, no one is taking a blind bit of notice of either of us.

"Let them look," he says. "They're probably jealous." He removes his hand from my leg and picks up his wineglass instead. "*Are* you wearing stockings?"

I shake my head. "No, it was a bit cold tonight, so it's tights, I'm afraid."

He looks fleetingly disappointed, then his face lights up and he leans forward, gazing straight into my eyes. "Then I'll just have to remove them with my teeth."

At any other time, when Olivia wasn't ill and I had consumed a few more glasses of wine, his remark would probably have whipped me into a sexually aroused frenzy. But sober and still slightly wounded from his low-key reaction to the reason for my slightly somber mood, it sounds misplaced and faintly ludicrous.

Our food arrives, a welcome distraction for me as I struggle to make a crucial decision about what happens afterwards. Do I drink to excess to numb my pain, then go back home with Simon for a night of unbridled passion? Or do I just give in to my subdued mood and put this date out of its misery until a time I feel better equipped to be windswept and interesting? *If*, of course, Simon feels inclined to hang around and wait for my return to form.

Postponing a decision until I absolutely *have* to make it, I eat my main course in virtual silence whilst he regales me with a story he'd heard that week about an elderly woman who wandered into a mobile cervical screening unit set up in a supermarket car park.

"So she walks up to one of the nurses and says 'Excuse me?' but the nurse is dealing with another patient, so tells her to go into one of the little booths and take her trousers off," he says, stuffing a piece of nan bread into his mouth and chewing rapidly.

"She does as she's told, and the nurse eventually follows her in, does the smear test, then tells her to get dressed again and register her name and address at the desk.

"Afterwards, the old duck wanders up to the receptionist and says, 'I've never had to do this to get a bus pass before!'"

He starts laughing and lolls to one side, a cue for me to laugh too. I dutifully oblige before clearing my plate of the last vestiges of chicken korma.

Simon pours the last dribbles of the wine bottle into both our glasses and waves it at me. "Fancy another here, or shall I open one when we get back to my place?"

I let out a small sigh and shift slightly in my seat. "Actually, Simon, I really hope you don't mind, but I want to go home."

"Your place then?" he says happily. "No, I don't mind at all. It'll be nice to see it."

I wince a little. "No, I mean I'd like to go home *alone.*"

His face drops almost instantaneously. "Oh, I see. Sorry, bit slow on the uptake there." He gives me a weak, sheepish grin.

"No, it's *me* who should be sorry. You've organized and paid for the cinema, brought me to this wonderful restaurant for dinner . . . ," I pause and look around, ". . . and all I've done in return is to be a total wet blanket."

He makes a tutting noise and shakes his head. "No worries. Entirely understandable considering what your sister is going through. Just as long as it's not my company that makes you miserable," he jokes, clearly not comfortable at the conversation veering towards serious matters again.

"No." I smile. "On the contrary, you've cheered me up enormously. You should have seen me *before* I came out."

He waves at the waiter and makes a scribbling motion with his hand. "I should probably get an early night anyway. I'm playing soccer with the lads tomorrow, and there'll no doubt be some ferocious drinking afterwards."

"Sounds great," I say unconvincingly. I already have my day mapped out in my head. Shopping for memory boxes and sifting through the two bin liners of old photographs stuffed in my closet, trying to find ones Olivia might like to include.

Ten minutes later, shuddering in the cold outside the restaurant, the distance between Simon and me seems even more unbridgeable.

"Well, thanks again, and sorry again," I stutter, my teeth chattering.

"Don't apologize. These things happen," he replies, as if my sister's breast cancer was simply one of life's little misunderstandings, like a lost check or a broken alarm clock.

"I'll e-mail you next week and we'll reschedule."

"That would be nice." And I do mean it, anxious that our fledgling relationship is given another chance to live up to its early promise.

"Great." He walks out into the road and flags down a passing black cab. "Here you are. You take this one, I'll find another."

"Thanks." I climb gratefully into the warm and sit down. "Head for Tooting, please," I say to the surly driver, who raises his eyes heavenward. They *hate* going that far out from the center of town.

Simon puts one foot into the cab and leans forward, planting a soft but cold kiss on my lips. "Sorry if I was a bit crap when you told me about your sister," he mumbles apologetically. "I'm not very good at that sort of thing."

"Me neither." I smile. But I'm learning, I think to myself as the cab pulls away. I'm learning the hard way.

Thirty One

When I walk into the Monday meeting—penultimately, but not last, if you must know—I hide my surprise well at seeing Eddie and Tara sitting either side of Janice's desk. A triptych of evil.

"It's the three unwise monkeys," whispers Kevin as I squeeze between him and Camilla on a two-seater sofa.

"Now then," intones Janice, indicating to Tab to close the door. "Eddie and Tara have very kindly agreed to come in on the ideas meeting because, quite frankly, they are *appalled* at the lackluster content of the program recently."

Gomez and Morticia nod in agreement, their faces set hard.

Only recently? I muse. It's been complete shit for months; some might say from the outset.

"Anyway, as from today, things are going to change around here," continues Janice.

Hoo-bloody-rah, I think. About time too.

"Number one." She holds up a red talon.

"Her counting's coming along nicely, I see," whispers Kevin to the back of my head.

"Yes, Kevin?" Janice's head swivels in his direction. "Something you and Jess would like to share with us?"

Great. Now I'm in trouble with teacher.

"I was just admiring your fantastic nails," oozes Kevin sycophantically.

"Well, don't," she snaps. "As I was saying, number one . . . no more dull and worthy items."

It takes me a couple of seconds to realize she's looking straight in my direction. And so are Eddie and Tara.

"Sorry, are you talking to me?" I place my palm flat against my chest and look perplexed.

Janice is about to answer, but Eddie holds his hand out and her mouth clamps shut like a faulty trap door.

"Two of the dreariest items we've run recently have both been yours," he says pointedly.

"Mine?" I'm struggling to think what they are, considering that 99 percent of the program could easily be described as inexorably tedious.

"Yes," chips in Tara. "They were both about that Sunshine House place."

I blink rapidly, aware that all eyes in the room are focused on me. "What, the Phit visit?"

Eddie leans forward slightly, a lion moving in for the kill. "Phit are big news," he concedes, "but by the time you'd finished with them, they were about as interesting as . . . as . . . *that* hairstyle," he says, pointing straight at some poor girl from the phone room whose crowning glory resembles a tin hat. "You didn't even ask Ned Pearson about the lap-dancing incident."

"That was the deal," I answer sulkily. "They would never have agreed to be filmed otherwise. Janice knew all about it," I add pointedly.

"Did you?" Eddie swivels to confront her.

"Don't be ridiculous," she scoffs. "I'd never agree to something like that. They need us far more than we need them."

And that was it, really. A run-of-the-mill, textbook shafting of an employee by her employer became my career Armageddon. My Thelma and Louise at the cliffside, my point of no return.

"So let's get this straight," I reply loudly, ensuring everyone present can hear. "You're saying that the country's number one boy band, with six number one singles already under their belt, two number one albums, and the likes of Jay Leno, David Letterman, and Oprah *begging* them to appear on their shows, needs the attention of a lazy, hackneyed, shitty daytime TV show presented by two of the most boring, one-dimensional people in entertainment? Don't make me *laugh*."

Kevin makes a gasping noise and clasps his hand to his mouth, whilst Tab's eyes are gleaming with pride at her friend's kamikaze actions on behalf of all the downtrodden in the room.

Eddie and Tara both sit rooted to the spot, looking pointedly and murderously at me.

"I have never been so insulted in all my life," says Tara, her prissy little mouth puckering.

"Then you should fucking well get out more." A cliché, I know, but still a damn fine one nonetheless.

"I think you'd better stop right there," says Janice icily. "You and I will talk after the meeting."

"So you can issue me with a written warning about my insubordination?" I say defiantly. "No point. Everything I have heard in this room in the past few minutes has simply confirmed to me what I've felt about this program for a long time." I stand up and move to the center of the room, facing her desk directly. "Day after day, we all churn out the same, tired old ideas masquerading behind a 'new' survey or report. The fashion always has to be *sexy*, yet the majority of our viewers wouldn't be seen dead in any of it, the cookery always has to be some poncey dish like asparagus spears or crème brûlée, when the majority are eating pie and chips with Bisto gravy granules, and the travel always has to be *as-pirational*, like Aspen and St. Bart's, when most of our viewers can barely afford to go to some cheesy resort. It's all pretentious *bol-locks*," I rant.

"And you know what? When I went to Sunshine House, I encountered *real* people, people who do a fantastic job for little or no money purely because they want to help others, peo-ple who like their lives as they are and don't want some aspi-rational message shoved down their throats by a load of patronizing TV types sitting in their minimalist, ivory towers in London.

"It was the first time in months I have done a report for this program that actually *meant* something, that had a worthwhile purpose to raise money for terminally ill kids and you . . . and you . . . and you," I point at the three of them individually, "have the fucking *cheek* to sit there and say it was dreary? Shame on you."

I glare at them for a couple of seconds, then walk back across to the sofa and pick up my handbag from the floor.

"So thanks for the offer, Janice, but no, I won't be staying for a cozy little chat. You can shove your job up your big . . . no, make that gargantuan . . . fat *arse!*" With that finely eloquent payoff, I walk out of her office and slam the door resoundingly behind me.

*O*hmigod, ohmigod, ohmigoooooooooood!!!" Tab rushes into the small backstreet pub where I'm huddled like a fugitive from justice and plants a juicy kiss on each of my cheeks. "A big congratulations to the office heroine!"

"Went down well, did it?" I smile ruefully.

"Went down *well*?" she shrieks. "They're currently erecting a statue of you in the foyer, the scales of justice in one hand, Janice's scalp in the other, and a plaque saying 'Saint Jess of the downtrodden.' God, you were *brilliant*."

"Thanks," I say flatly. "But saints do well in the next world, it's the wicked that do well in this one. Consequently, Janice is still in a job and my initial adrenaline-fueled joy has been replaced by panic about how I'm going to pay the mortgage next month."

Tab winces. "Yes, there is that. Well, let me do my bit for the unemployed by buying the drinks."

She disappears to the bar, leaving me to contemplate my jobless state. Within a few minutes of gathering my coat, grabbing a vital few bits and pieces from my desk, and leaving the building, my mobile phone had started ringing hysterically to the point that I'd flicked it over to "silent." Several had left congratulatory messages, but the only call I had returned was Tab's, agreeing to meet her for this postmortem.

"Here you go, get that down you." She places what tastes like a large gin and tonic in front of me.

"Thanks," I gasp gratefully, feeling the instantaneous kick of the alcohol. "So tell me what happened immediately after I flounced out."

She grins widely at the memory. "God, it was total magic. You should have seen Janice's face, she was puce with rage! I don't think she trusted herself to speak, she just sat there glowering."

"What about Grim and Grimmer?"

"Eddie was the first to break the silence. He said something along the lines of, 'I always told you she was a loose cannon,' then

Tara started ranting about the slur on her professionalism and how the company should issue legal proceedings on her behalf to stop you repeating it outside the building."

"As if I *ever* want to see Tara again, let alone speak about her," I say wearily.

"Then Janice found her tongue and told the rest of us that the meeting was over, but we weren't to repeat to a soul what had happened in there. She said if anyone did, they would be sacked."

"Yeah right, she'd have to prove it first."

"Precisely. The full story is already running on the *Guardian* Web site anyway, so someone's blown the whistle."

"Janice will probably think it's me." I sigh. "Not that I care what she thinks anymore."

"Anyway," continues Tab, her eyes shining with euphoria, "we all trooped out, but Eddie and Tara stayed behind and the most almighty row broke out."

"Between who?"

"Eddie and Tara. We could see them ranting at each other behind the glass, and Janice was just sitting there stern faced. It was *glorious* to behold."

"Happy to oblige." I smile weakly. "Trouble is, they will probably spread it round the business that I'm crap at my job, blah blah blah, and no other company will touch me with a bargepole."

Tab wrinkles her nose. "Nah, that pair are so universally loathed that I think you'll emerge as a bit of a maverick who couldn't take the thought of churning out any more pap on their behalf. The *Guardian* piece certainly paints you in an heroic light."

I glance at my mobile phone and see there have been another five calls. "Oh well, time will tell. I'll start looking for work tomorrow, but in the meantime, can we talk about something else? It all seems so pathetic compared to other things going on in my life."

"Like what?" Tab frowns.

It dawns on me that I haven't yet filled her in on the Olivia situation, having been sworn to secrecy initially, then not having had the opportunity since for an in-depth chat. It wasn't something I had wanted to divulge via fevered whispering down the side of our computers, or over a quick coffee in the canteen. And certainly not at her dinner party with Kara and the crew in attendance.

Now, with time on our hands and no one ear wigging, is the ideal opportunity. So, for the next ten minutes, I bring Tab up to speed on Olivia's discovery of a lump and her subsequent mastectomy.

"I went round to see her on Saturday for the first time since the operation," I conclude, "and whilst she doesn't look as bad as you might expect, I fear the worst is yet to come with the chemotherapy."

Tab's expression is one of grave concern. "God, Jess, I had no idea. You must have been under such strain these past few weeks. No wonder you finally blew your top in there this morning."

I wave my hand dismissively. "Oh, that had been a long time coming. But I suppose my anger over Olivia's cancer was what propelled me into actually speaking my mind to Janice rather than just griping behind her back all the time."

"Do you want me to talk to her in the morning and explain the pressure you've been under? She might give you your job back."

"Ye gods, no." I practically choke on my drink at the thought of it. "Say absolutely nothing. I see this as the kick up the bum I needed to get out of there."

"So . . . ," Tab winces slightly, ". . . sorry if this question seems brutal, but is Olivia going to die?"

"Don't worry." I smile. "It was the first thing I thought of and it still pops into my head dozens of times a day." I take another swig of G&T. "No, the doctors are saying she probably won't. Although in this litigious day and age, they'll never give any cast-iron guarantees. How can they?"

We sit in silence for a short while, so I take the opportunity to check the messages on my phone in case there are any urgent ones involving Olivia.

"They're all from people in the office," I say eventually, smiling apologetically for the brief interruption in our conversation.

Tab smiles halfheartedly, but I can tell her mind has moved on to more important things than that morning's showdown. "You know," she says thoughtfully, "Olivia being so ill certainly puts my problems with IVF into perspective. The next time I'm sitting around feeling sorry for myself, I shall think of her and snap out of it."

I nod. "I know what you mean, but in the past, when someone has said to me, 'Smile, there's always someone worse off than you,' I always used to think 'Yes, but there's lots who are much better off than me as well.'"

She raises her eyes heavenward. "That is *so* you."

"So many of us sit around whining about things that are totally within our control to change, like a lackluster boyfriend or a crappy job," I continue. "So now, I just think 'Well, do something about it then.' I suppose that's what this morning was all about really, because I've hated the job for ages."

"Whereas Olivia and, to a lesser extent, I *can't* control what's happening to our health," says Tab, warming to my theme.

"Precisely."

She sighs. "We're about to start another round of it, so keep your fingers crossed for us."

"Everything crossed." I wrap my legs into a knot to illustrate the point. "How's Will coping with it?"

She nods. "Fine actually. He's so desperate to be a dad that he'll go to any lengths, although of course his life continues pretty much as normal throughout the process. He still goes out drinking with the lads and plays his rugby."

"Talking of which, I have to say his chum Ben has really given me some terrific support regarding Olivia."

"Ben?" Tab looks baffled.

"Yes, I know I barely know him," I explain. "But oddly, that made it easier. When Olivia initially asked me not to say anything, I felt I *had* to tell someone, and a stranger who didn't know her seemed far enough removed not to be a betrayal of her wishes."

"I see." She nods, but still looks a little unconvinced.

"And when we went out to do the Phit segment, and I saw him in his work environment, looking after those poor children and their shell-shocked families, it just seemed like the most natural thing in the world to tell him. And I have to say, he was brilliant."

Tab smiles. "I don't know him that well, but he does seem like a great bloke." She pauses and looks at me hesitantly. "As you and he have shared such a big secret together, did he let on to you about any secrets in his own life?"

Now it's my turn to look baffled. "How do you mean?"

"Like . . . did he mention a girlfriend or anything?" She looks faintly embarrassed to be asking.

I frown slightly, casting my mind back to the conversation with Ben a few nights ago. "No, just that he'd had one serious relationship that lasted a few years before she buggered off with someone richer."

"Hmmmm." Tab looks thoughtful.

"Why?"

She lets out a little sigh. "It's just that he and Will played rugby yesterday . . . like they do every Sunday . . . and after the match

Will saw something a little untoward . . ." She stops and stares into the top of her glass, swilling the contents round and round.

"Like what?" I'm faintly irritated by her drawn-out story-telling. "An alien? Lord Lucan? What?"

She shoots me a look but ignores my sarcasm. "No, he saw Ben looking very cozy with another man."

"Very cozy? What does that mean?" I ask, resisting the urge to add "Were they sitting under a duvet drinking cocoa together?"

"They were sort of embracing . . ."

"*Sort* of?" I look incredulous.

Tab huffs. "Don't be so antagonistic. I'm just telling you what Will told me."

"Sorry." I smile ruefully. "I'm probably still locked into anni-hilate-Janice mode. It's just that you're being a bit vague."

"That's because I don't really know much more than that. Will says they had all left the changing rooms after the match . . . or so he thought . . . and he suddenly realized he'd forgotten his sweater. So he went back . . ."

I say nothing, simply nod encouragingly.

"And when he walked back into the changing rooms and round a corner, Ben was locked in an embrace with one of the other players. They sprang apart when they heard Will walk in, but not before he'd clocked what they were doing."

I purse my lips for a moment, giving the scenario some thought. "Can we just qualify what embrace means here? Were they snogging?"

Tab nods. "Will says he couldn't be one hundred percent sure because the other guy had his back to him but, yes, he thinks they were . . ."

"Oh well." I sigh gently. "I'm sure he'll get round to telling people what's what in his own good time." I drain my glass. "Fancy another drink while I've still got a few quid left in the world?"

Tab laughs. "I'll get them. You can repay the compliment once the job offers start flooding in."

"Don't hold your breath," I mutter as she wanders off to the bar. It's just one month to Christmas and I'm miserable, broke, and now jobless.

Ho ho ho.

Thirty Two

Remember when I spoke before about those blissful few seconds when you wake up in the morning? You know, the ones where your brain hasn't quite engaged and you are briefly unburdened before any major worry pops into your head and spoils it all?

Well, today life's problems are jostling for position in the race to pollute any potential happiness. Olivia's there, as she has been every day for weeks, my parents and how they're dealing with it all, and now there's the perilous state of my "career" to add to the ever-increasing pile. Worse, I can't even tell my family about it, for fear of adding to their woes.

In an ideal world, I'd hop on a plane, go trekking in Nepal, "find myself" halfway up a mountain, and return to Britain a rejuvenated woman with life's priorities reshuffled and placed in the right order. But (a) I would never leave the country in case Olivia's condition worsened, and (b) I can't bloody afford to anyway. The contents of my bank account will cover about two months of my jobless state before I have to start selling the cosmetics door-to-door.

It's now 10 a.m., approximately twenty-four hours since I told Janice to stick her job where the sun doesn't shine, and my initial euphoria has now packed its bags and deserted me. I was heroine for a day, but I know that, already, the conversation of my former work colleagues will have moved on to something else. In the fickle world of "showbiz, dahhling," I'm already old news.

Time to recharge the laptop, I think, dragging it out from the understairs cupboard where it's been lurking untouched for months. Leaving it to charge for a while, I make myself a coffee and carry it through to the lounge, where I settle myself next to the phone and punch in Olivia's number.

"Hello?" It's Michael, sounding exceptionally weary.

"Hi, it's Jess. I was just calling to see how it went yesterday." Not knowing how Olivia would react to her first bout of chemo, Michael had asked me not to call until this morning.

He sighs heavily. "Well, she had it and she's home. But she's as sick as a dog. I've already changed the bedding twice."

My heart starts thumping in panic and I feel slightly short of breath. "That sounds really bad."

"Sorry, I didn't mean to be alarmist," he says softly. "To be honest, her reaction is pretty much par for the course. She's showing all the classic signs."

Tears well in my eyes and my throat feels like someone's fist is rammed in it. I'm relieved he can't see me, as now is clearly not the time for any of us to fall apart.

"What about the children?" I ask, anxiously wondering how they're coping with the sight of their mother deteriorating so swiftly.

"Well, we told them last week that she had a blood disorder . . . to explain the tiredness . . . and this morning I said she had a tummy upset that was making her sick. They seemed to accept it, and it should pass in a couple of days, so at least they'll see her return to her old self for a bit."

"But how will you explain away the hair if she loses it?"

He pauses for a couple of beats. "Yes, that's a trickier one. I haven't come up with a good explanation yet, I'm still working on it. Anyway, do you want to speak to her?"

I take a deep breath, mentally preparing myself. "Is she up to it?"

"For a couple of minutes, yes. She specifically said she wanted to speak to you, but I've blocked all other calls, including your parents. She'll give them a call in a couple of days when she's feeling a bit chirpier. Hang on, I'll take the cordless upstairs."

A minute or so passes while I listen to Michael's short, sharp breaths as he climbs the stairs to the bedroom. Then I hear muffled voices as he passes the phone to Olivia.

"Hi there." She sounds quite bright.

"Hello, soldier." I make my voice sound upbeat. "How you feeling?"

"Oh, pretty shitty." She laughs. "But let's look at the bright side, all this vomiting is a bloody great diet."

I grimace. "Michael says you should feel a bit better in a couple of days."

"God, I hope so, it's rather knocked me down." She sighs. "And I've got another seven sessions to go after this one. If I can survive that, I can survive anything."

"You will," I reassure her. "You've always been a tough cookie."

"I'm a bit crumbly today though." She lowers her voice. "Now then, any luck with the memory boxes?"

"Yes." I'm whispering too, though I have no idea why. "I

popped out on Sunday and got a couple of really nice ones covered in a sort of red velvety material. They're each the size of about two shoeboxes."

"Excellent, thanks. I'll come and collect them when I'm feeling up to it."

"I'll drop them round if you like?"

"No, not just yet," she says hastily. "I still don't want Michael to know, as he'll see it as me being defeatist. So I'll probably bring the bits and pieces to yours and leave the finished boxes there. As I said, they'll be nice for the kids to have anyway, even if I get better."

"You mean *when* you get better," I chastise amiably.

"When. Yes, that's what I meant," she says. Her voice rises again. "Ah, my prison warder has just appeared at the door, medication in hand. He's very strict with me, you know."

I laugh, pleased to hear she's still up to teasing Michael. "OK, I'll let you go. But will you ask him to let me know when I can visit?"

"Will do. Love you," she says simply, then the phone goes dead.

I sit motionless for a few moments, staring out of the lounge window at the top of a tree swaying gently in the breeze. I'm not sure if I feel reassured or even more spooked by our brief chat. On the one hand, she sounds quite upbeat; on the other, the side effects of her treatment sound a lot more severe than I expected.

Sighing, I eventually stand up and carry my cup of cold coffee back through to the kitchen, where my laptop is still charging.

Using the main adapter for power, I switch on and sit back whilst it loads. There are thirty-two e-mails. After hitting the delete button to banish the spam, I'm left with eighteen.

The majority are from work colleagues, written just minutes after the cessation of the features meeting that will no doubt become legend. Many are guarded in their praise, written with the presumption that Big Brother might read their company e-mails; others—most notably Kevin Makepeace—less so.

> Fucking HELL!!! Go, girl! You really shafted that sour-faced old bag and I sincerely hope she gets the heave-ho. Did you see Eddie and Tara's faces? Priceless!! Would love to meet for a drink to discuss and relish the moment all over again, but in the meantime, if you need help looking for a new job, let me know. I have lots of friends in low places!

> Kevin xxxxx

Smiling to myself at his unbridled joy, I compose a swift reply.

> Hi there,

> Thanks for the supportive e-mail and glad to hear I livened up an otherwise dreary Monday morning! Once I get my act together, a drink would be nice, and in the meantime any help with finding a new company to pay my crippling mortgage would be much appreciated.

> Jess x

The next e-mail address in the list is one I don't recognize.

Hi there,

I saw your ad on the Internet dating site some time ago and toyed with the idea of getting in touch—but, as I have never re-sponded to a dating ad before, I bottled it! And now, fortified by a couple of the finest whiskies, is that time.

Maybe you have already met someone, or maybe you're still looking, but either way, perhaps we could just correspond for a while and see what happens? Who knows, we might even become friends?

I'm not sure if that appeals, so I will keep this initial approach short and wait to see if I hear back from you. Suffice to say, I'm in my thirties, live in London, and work in insurance (don't worry—I won't try and sell you a policy!). I'm wearied by the thought of trying to meet the right person on the wine bar/pub circuit, then finding out they're either a serial killer or work in insurance (I'm the only interesting one in that profession!), so I thought chatting via e-mail and establishing common ground first might be a good way forward.

I hope you feel the same.

Best wishes,
Seb Northam

Quite frankly, I need a new friend only marginally more than I need to go on yet another blind date with someone who turns out to be mad, bad, or downright dangerous to know. The mere thought is enough to make me sigh so deeply that the news-paper in front of me flaps in the breeze. But something stops me from pressing "delete." Instead, I save it to reconsider at a later date.

It's now Wednesday night and I'm still jobless. But then, in a profession where bullshit is the main currency, am I surprised? I know it's only been two days, but so far, all the promises of work from various quarters have proved empty. With one surprising exception.

Yes, Kevin Makepeace, he of the big mouth and miniscule morals, may well have come up trumps. After I returned his e-mail and said any help would be appreciated, a friend of his left a message on my mobile saying he might have some shift work for me on a new factual series for the sci-fi satellite channel Future.

OK, so what I know about sci-fi could be written on the ball of a gnat's foot with enough room left for the complete works of Shakespeare, but the series is about the far more accessible subject of psychic powers. And besides, the main bonus for me is that it's a foot in the door to the notoriously snobby, inaccessible world of factual television. Yippee.

That, combined with speaking to Olivia this morning and finding her much perkier, is enough to make me feel faintly optimistic about life for the first time in weeks.

Just as well really, as tonight is my rescheduled date with Simon after Saturday's rather awkward and gloomy debacle.

Putting Barry White's *My First, My Last, My Everything* into the CD player and cranking it up to full volume, I dance maniacally around the bedroom to force myself into "fun" mode. Happiness, they say, is a decision, not just a feeling. And I have decided to get rip-roaringly drunk and throw caution to the wind.

By the time I meet Simon at 8 p.m. in Soho's Pitcher and Piano, I have already sunk two large, homemade gin and tonics and feel distinctly squiffy.

"Hello!" I sink into the sofa next to him and give him a lingering kiss on the lips. As ever, he looks very handsome in a khaki T-shirt and faded Levi's.

"Hello you." He gives me a heart-stopping grin, clearly relieved that the gloom and doom of Saturday have been replaced by a good-time girl. "The drinks are in." He lifts the bottle of champagne from the ice bucket and pours me a glass. "Here's to a fun night ahead," he adds, raising his.

"Fun, fun, fun!" I chirrup, relishing the kick of the drink as it goes down.

By the time we've polished off that bottle and are halfway down the second, I'm feeling out of control, my head spinning with the effects of alcohol and the wall of noise we have struggled to converse across for the past couple of hours. Most of the time we haven't even bothered to try, preferring instead to snog mercilessly, oblivious to the elbow-nudging and sniggering of those nearby.

As he drains the last of the second bottle into our glasses, I know I'm rapidly reaching the point of no return and have to act quickly. "Come on," I mumble, nibbling his earlobe. "Let's go play bury the sausage."

He throws his head back and laughs. "I hope you like Cumberland."

"Very much," I slur. "Anything but chipolata."

OK, as witty banter goes, it's up there with a script from the Playboy channel. But when you've drunk as much as I have, it sounds like Oscar Wilde.

Consequently, forty-five minutes later, I'm lying back on the sofa, my skirt hitched up around my waist, one of my stockings in virtual shreds, being relentlessly shagged by Simon, who's show-ing no signs of his previous shortcomings.

Oh sorry, did I mention that it's _my_ lounge sofa we're on now, not the one in Pitcher and Piano? Better had in case you think I'm _really_ out of control.

Finally, with his head thrown back and a facial expression that suggests great pain, Simon shudders slightly and collapses on top of me panting.

"Fuck, that was good," he gasps after a few seconds.

Speak for yourself, I think, tugging my skirt into place and shifting my leg to a more comfortable position. Mind you, with the amount of alcohol I have consumed, it would take the tenacity of a marathon runner to activate even the faintest of stirrings.

He gets to his feet and hauls his trousers back on, bending over to kiss me gently. "Shall we go to bed?"

I nod silently and lead him through to next door, where my clothes from an earlier trying-on session are still strewn across the bed. Throwing them onto the armchair in the corner, I flip back the duvet. "Hop in."

Stark naked now, he duly does, and as I shed the last remnants of my clothes and climb in beside him, he extends his arm to gather me in. My head on his chest, I gaze unblinkingly towards the window, the only light from a streetlamp filtering through the linen blind.

"Goodnight." He tilts his chin downwards and plants a soft kiss on the top of my head. "By the way, I really enjoyed tonight. Nice to have you back on form."

"I really enjoyed it too," I murmur.

But did I? As his breathing becomes more labored and he drifts easily off to sleep, a pounding, post-binge headache kicks in and prevents me from doing the same. As well as the thumping pain between my eyes, my mind once again fills with thoughts of Olivia, the rest of my family, and my unemployed state.

All major crises in my life, all steadfastly swept under the carpet this evening because I didn't want to "spoil" the atmosphere by introducing them into the conversation. Instead, Simon and I had talked about his job, his family, last night's TV, and the latest movies we both wanted to see. *Anything* but drag down the mood with any mention of my harsh realities.

So I didn't mention any of it and he, in turn, hadn't asked me anything at all about the sister he knows is seriously ill. Not even to ask in passing how she is. Is that normal? Is that how a relationship should be, regardless of whether it's long term or still in its fledgling stages? I don't think so.

Suddenly feeling irritated by his presence, I slowly extricate myself from his embrace and edge my way out of bed. Grabbing my dressing gown from the back of the door, I turn and look at his sleeping form in the half-light, my hand resting on the handle.

He's successful, funny, damned sexy, and bright and personable enough to take anywhere, I muse. Surely he's every girl's dream man?

I silently shake my head at my own question. Yes, he's all of those things, but there's something vital missing, a comfort factor I now feel is crucial in a relationship. With everything I've been going through of late, my obsession with the sexual spark seems to have abated, to be replaced by a desire for something a little more meaningful, more solid. With the occasional frantic sex session thrown in, too, of course.

Jess the people-pleaser is a thing of the past. I don't ever again want to pretend I'm something I'm not, just to make life pleasant for others. If I'm sad, I want to show it; if I'm happy, I want to believe and feel it.

Light and shade are real. Constant brightness isn't.

Closing the bedroom door quietly behind me, I know this is my and Simon's epitaph.

Thirty Three

"J ess, darling, *please* don't tell me you're wearing that for Christmas lunch?" My mother holds the arm of my baggy black sweatshirt between her thumb and forefinger and wrinkles her nose. As usual, she is immaculately dressed in a pale peach cashmere top and tailored cream trousers.

I raise my eyes heavenward. "Sorry, Mum, have I missed something? Is the Queen on her way?"

She sighs indulgently. "Don't be facetious. There is such a thing as self-respect, you know."

"Yes, and I have oodles of it, thank you very much. What I *don't* need is to sit through lunch in some uncomfortable outfit just because it pleases you."

Now this little exchange may not sound like that big a deal to you, but to me, it's a major turning point that, at the grand old age of thirty-four and after a lifetime of people pleasing, I have finally found the courage to stand up to my mother's fashion fascism.

It's a start, but clearly there's still some way to go as I'm now inwardly cringing as I wait for her reaction to my rebellion.

She stares at me impassively for a couple of seconds, then says

"Suit yourself" before disappearing off into the kitchen, leaving me rooted to the spot in astonishment.

Such bravado is undoubtedly my very own symptom of Olivia's illness, a newfound set of priorities that have given me a low tolerance threshold on other people's little foibles. Similarly, or so it seems, my mother has reached the conclusion that when one daughter is battling a life-threatening disease, the ragbag appearance of the other isn't worth getting too agitated about.

Speaking of which, there's Olivia right in front of me as I saunter through to my parents' kitchen in pursuit of everyone else. She's peeling potatoes at the double drainer and chatting animatedly to Dad as he does that crisscross thing with the bottom of the sprouts.

Michael is sitting at one end of the table reading yesterday's *Daily Telegraph*, and Matthew and Emily are at the other playing a particularly noisy game of Snap refereed by Mum.

It's quite the Hallmark scene of the traditional, nuclear family celebrating Christmas Day, and I'd like to be able to tell you that there's a gloriously happy ending to it all. But the last bit is still in abeyance, as Olivia is still only halfway through her course of chemotherapy.

The bad news is that she's lost all her beautiful hair, but you know what? In a funny way, it really suits her. With my pointy chin and protruding ears, I'd look like an uglier version of the Dalai Lama, but Olivia's ears are perfectly petite and her scalp is nicely uniform and smooth.

Initially, she took to wearing a wig, or one of a vast selection of hats bought by Michael at her behest. But now she's got used to it and is bald and proud.

Emily, matter of fact as ever, had simply taken her mother's hair loss in her stride, asking just one question—where's it gone?

Once told it would eventually grow back, she had cut off all the hair from her favorite Barbie, assuming that would grow back, too. Michael had already made a hasty visit to Toys "R" Us, and a replica was hidden at the back of the wardrobe, to be swapped with the follicularly challenged Barbie the moment Olivia's hair returns to its former glory.

Matthew, by contrast, was very distressed when his mother's hair started to fall out in clumps. At first, he reacted badly and would shy away every time she tried to cuddle him, a particularly upsetting time for Olivia. Then, just as swiftly, he wouldn't let her out of his sight, hugging her as if his life depended on it and having little sobbing fits.

At the absolute low point, Michael had to visit his son's headmaster after a fight had broken out in the playground. Another boy had called Olivia "an alien" and, defending his mother's honor, Matthew had punched him.

The headmaster, an amiable man who placed absolutely no blame on Matthew's young shoulders, simply wanted Michael's permission to tell the other pupils during assembly that Olivia had cancer and it was not something to be joked about. Michael agreed, and Matthew was kept away from school for the morning so the deed could be done.

Since then, things had settled back down for him at school, and he'd stopped treating Olivia like a china doll. She even told me that one day last week, when he'd been unbelievably cheeky to her, she and Michael had punched the air with joy behind his back, thankful to see normal behavior restored.

So the loss of hair is pretty much the only bad news. The *good* news is that the doctors say she has responded extraordinarily well to the treatment and, so far, there's still no sign of any secondary site. She should finish the chemo at the beginning of

March, then will move on to a short course of far less debilitating radiotherapy.

And after *that*? Well, she'll be in remission and it will simply be a case of watch and wait, returning every three months for checkups.

I'm watching her now as she places the last of the peeled potatoes into a vast cauldron of water by her side. I'm always watching her.

"Right!" She looks straight at me. "I'm going to leave you lot to it for a while and take a little head-clearing walk across the field. Fancy coming with me, Jess?"

"Sure." I smile. "I'll just get my coat."

It's bitterly cold outside, with that eery stillness unique to Christmas Day, when everyone is hidden away inside and you feel the world is your own. Wincing in the icy air, we trudge across the field towards the village, though quite what we expect to find there is anyone's guess. It's just habit that takes us in that direction.

"So how's the new job going?" asks Olivia, kicking a stone with the toe of her Wellington boot. "Enjoying it?"

"*Loving* it!" I enthuse, without one smidgen of exaggeration.

After Kevin's friend had called to say he might have shift work, I had gone to see him for a quick coffee at Future, the sci-fi satellite channel where he worked as program editor. Doug—that's his name, by the way—had told me I came highly recommended by Kevin and he'd offered me shifts almost immediately on the channel's new series *Psychic*.

"Sadly, *I'm* not psychic and have no idea whether you're any good or not," he'd quipped, "so let's give it a month, and if you prove you're up to it I'll employ you full time as a producer."

In the event, it had taken just two weeks of me working my butt off for him to call me in and make the job official. A serious, critically acclaimed channel with a couple of prestigious TV awards under its belt, it was the breakthrough I had always needed to get into something more serious than *Good Moaning*, as I now refer to it.

Anxious not to cause them any extra worry, I avoided telling Olivia or the parentals about my walkout until after I had secured the shift work at Future. That way, I was able to make it look like a deliberate career move rather than the hot-headed, irrational risk it truly was.

Like all good friends or relatives, they had responded to *Good Morning*'s demise in my life the same way they would if a relationship broke down, muttering reassuringly: "It never suited you."

Olivia, her woolly hat pulled so far down that it nearly reaches the bridge of her nose, clambers over the stile that leads onto the main road through the village. I follow and we stand still for a few seconds to catch our breath.

"So do you think you'll stay a long time at Future?" she says eventually.

I shrug. "I hope so. But television isn't like other professions; it's far more fickle and transient. Most of the time, you get a contract that lasts only as long as the program you're working on, so I'm very lucky to have been given a full-time job." I start walking in the direction of the shop and she follows me. "I just have to hope I like the next series they assign me to as much as I'm enjoying this one."

Apart from the wisps of smoke snaking out of several chimneys, the village could have been abandoned years ago. Not an animal stirs, not a curtain twitches. The shop's shutters are down and a note on the door reads "Open again on December 27. Merry Christmas."

Olivia stands in front of it and smiles ruefully. "I know I can tell you this without getting told off, but you know what? There was a time, at the beginning of all this, when I wondered if I would actually make it to Christmas."

"Really?" Although I too had wondered many times whether Olivia would survive, it had never crossed my mind she might have died this soon. "Did you seriously think you could be *that* far gone?"

She purses her lips. "Not seriously, no. And of course I was surrounded by doctors telling me that I'd caught it early and hopefully everything would be fine." She lets out a long sigh, her breath turning white in the cold air. "It's really hard to describe, but when you're told you've got cancer everyone looks at the physical signs . . . you know, the mastectomy, the effects of the chemo . . . but for me, the hardest thing of all was, still is to a certain extent, the psychological side. It feels like there's a time bomb inside you, ticking away, possibly getting bigger, possibly spreading undetected to somewhere else . . ."

She jerks her head towards the other end of the village and starts walking. "You want to believe the doctors are on top of it, but there's that nagging doubt in the back of your mind that they've missed something." Pausing, she turns to look at me and raises her eyebrows questioningly.

"Surely it's entirely natural to feel like that?" I say, knowing that if I was in her position, I'd feel it tenfold. "But you have to look around at all the women who've survived breast cancer and tell yourself that you're going to be like them."

"And what about the ones that die?" she says quietly. "What if I'm going to be like them?"

I make a loud tutting noise. "Now I *am* going to tell you off for being so negative. You've headed it off at the pass with the operation, and the chemo is going well. There is absolutely no suggestion from any quarter that you're not going to beat this."

"You're right." She closes her eyes for a few seconds and takes a deep breath. "Come on, Olivia, snap out of it and put on your happy face. It's Christmas." She opens her eyes and puts on a deliberately fake grin.

I roll my eyes heavenward. "Oh, very convincing. Come on, let's head back, it's bloody freezing."

As we approach the stile, she stops in her tracks and raises a forefinger in the air to catch my attention. "I know what will cheer me up!"

"What?" I pause, one leg hooked over the stile.

"An update on your love life. That's always good for a laugh."

"Gee, thanks," I say flatly. "Actually, mere mention of it is likely to send us both running for the Prozac."

"That bad, huh?" She follows me over the stile and we start to walk back to the house.

"If bad means nonexistent, then yes. Mind you, I've been so busy with my new job that it's probably a good thing not to be distracted by matters of the heart."

Olivia looks doubtful but doesn't contradict me. "Have you heard any more from Simon?"

I shake my head. "Nah. I sent him the e-mail I told you about . . . you know, saying that I didn't think things were going to work between us . . . and he replied with something huffy along the lines of 'Oh well, your decision,' and I haven't heard from him since."

"Were you hoping to?"

I think about the question for a moment. "No, not really. Even though I found him very attractive, I knew by the end of our last date that it wasn't going anywhere. The old me would have carried on seeing him, just enjoying the sex . . ."

Olivia laughs. "There's a lot to be said for that, you know . . ."

I wrinkle my nose. "There's less than you'd think. For me, anyway. I've changed quite a lot in recent months."

"Anything to do with my Big C?"

"Very much so." I nod. "It's taught me that life's too short to fart about being halfhearted about your relationship and your job."

"So, sex aside, what was so bad about him?" asks Olivia, stopping briefly to readjust her trouser leg.

"There wasn't anything *bad* as such, there just wasn't much to him beyond having a laugh. There wasn't any depth."

Olivia frowns at me. "Aren't you expecting a little too much so early on? You'd only just started seeing each other."

I laugh. "Yes, that did sound a bit wanky, didn't it? What I mean is that our conversation didn't flow easily, not about serious stuff anyway, and I don't think that's something that develops with time. It's either there at the outset or it isn't."

Olivia shrugs. "Well, you know best what you feel. So are you back on the dating circuit again?" She reaches our parents' gate and pushes it open.

"Nope. I deleted my ad after that, and haven't had the urge to browse." I follow her down the driveway and we both linger by the door, removing our boots. "Funnily enough, there is one bloke who'd seen my ad back in the beginning and finally got round to e-mailing me last month. We've struck up quite a friendly dialogue, strictly through the computer though."

Olivia lifts her left leg for me to help tug off her Wellington, and I duly oblige.

"Do you know what he looks like?"

I nod. "Yes, he sent a photo over a couple of weeks ago. He's quite pleasant-looking, nothing exceptional. But he seems really nice and down to earth. We chat about all sorts of things and seem to have a lot in common. He's called Seb," I add as an afterthought. "It's funny, but although I haven't met him, I've told him so much about my life, about you, about Matthew and Emily and so on . . . I suppose the anonymity almost makes it easier."

She lifts her other leg. "So *are* you going to meet up?"

I shrug. "He hasn't suggested it and neither have I. To be honest, I'm happy to leave things as they are, particularly as I'm so busy with my job."

I go to push open the front door, but Olivia places a hand on my forearm to stall me. "I know you've got heaps going on in your life, what with your new job and everything that's been going on with me," she says quietly. "But don't lose sight of the bigger picture."

"What do you mean?" I frown.

"Your job doesn't keep you warm at night." It's one of her favorite phrases.

"Yeah, yeah." I sigh, raising my eyes heavenward. "And the graveyards are full of people who thought they were indispensable to their companies."

"And no one ever lay on their deathbed and said 'I wish I'd worked harder.'" She laughs. "You may well scoff at the clichés, madam, but they're all true."

"And your point is?" It's absolutely freezing now and I'm anxious to get inside.

"That you're thirty-four and have only a limited amount of time if you want to meet the right man and have children, which I know you do. Keep searching." She lets out a long sigh. "I like my job, but it meant fuck all when I found out I was ill. It was having Michael and the kids that meant everything."

I slap a gloved hand against my open mouth. "Oooh, I'm telling Mum you said 'fuck,'" I tease, stepping into the house.

"Don't care," she replies in a singsong voice, following me into the hallway. "Fuckety, fuckety, fuck fuck!"

Thirty Four

It's midnight and all's hell!" bellows Richard, throwing his
arms around me as the chimes of Big Ben resound around
Tab's packed living room. "Happy New Queer, sweetie!"

"Ditto." I smile, then think to myself, Let's hope the next 365
days are more cheerful than the last lot. I step to one side to embrace Lars just as the familiar strains of "Auld Lang Syne" boom
out of the CD player. "Oh no," I groan, instinctively crossing my
arms in readiness. Richard grabs one of my hands, and a man I
don't know but recognize as one of Will's rugby friends grabs the
other. They both start pumping my arms in time to the music. Automatically mouthing the words, I'm smiling broadly as an in-
stinctive reaction to all the beaming expressions in the circle
around me. There are plenty of faces I don't know, but it feels
good to be celebrating with all the old ones, anyway.

It's Tab and Will's party, so naturally they're here, and you already know about Richard and Lars. Then there's Madeleine over
there, flirting outrageously with one of the rugby players, and
Ben's here, too, having persuaded Anne and Ralph to keep an eye
on things at Sunshine House for the night.

And most importantly of all . . . well, to me anyway . . . there's Olivia and Michael, looking the happiest and most relaxed I've seen them in a long time. She's due for another session of chemo next week, but in the meantime, she's determined to see in the New Year in a positive frame of mind.

You know those fantastical dreams you sometimes have? Where, maybe you're singing a pitch-perfect song in front of the Albert Hall to rapturous applause, then suddenly it all goes badly wrong and your face and voice distort, the audience looking on in abject horror?

Well, there's Kara and Dan across the room, ruining my other-wise idyllic New Year moment with their irritating mugs—hers smug, his sheepish. They have been putting on a nauseating display of togetherness for most of the night, their mouths clamped to-gether like a mollusk to a rock. Take your pick as to which is which.

I gave Kara a rigid, half smile across the room earlier in the evening, but other than that, I haven't exchanged a word with ei-ther of them and don't intend to.

"Auld Lang Syne" comes to a thankful end and I reclaim my arms to pick up my glass of wine from the coffee table. At least, I *think* it's mine, but I'm past caring, having sunk several glasses al-ready.

"Happy New Year!" I feel a hand on my back and swivel round to see Olivia's smiling face. She looks fabulous in a stunning, over-the-top red wig, but I can tell by the shadows under her eyes that she's tiring fast.

"Happy New Year to you too!" I gather her in my arms and squeeze tightly, burying my face in her neck. "This one's going to be *so* much better than the last."

"God help us all if it turns out to be worse." She laughs, rais-ing her eyes heavenwards.

Michael appears at her side, brandishing a fresh glass of champagne. "Here you go. Just this one," he says, passing it to her. "Then it's back to soft drinks, I'm afraid."

"Yes, doctor." Olivia grins, doing a mock salute.

Michael turns to me and plants a kiss on the top of my head. "Happy New Year." He jerks his head towards Olivia. "I'm taking her home in a minute. She mustn't overdo it."

"Spoilsport." Olivia pushes out her bottom lip, but it's easy to see she'll be grateful to get home and rest. She takes a small sip of the champagne, then places it on the coffee table with a finality that suggests she won't be picking it up again. "Come on then, let's hit the road. I'll just go and say thanks to Tabitha and Will."

Michael and I watch her walk through into the kitchen, then turn back to face each other.

"I think you might have to keep a watchful eye on her tomorrow," I say quietly. "New Year's Day can have a funny effect on people. You either feel upbeat and determined to alter the things about your life you don't like, or it all feels out of your control and you feel crashingly depressed at the thought of more of the same."

Michael nods. "I always keep a watchful eye on her anyway, but I know what you mean. I shall be extra vigilant tomorrow and make sure she's kept occupied. Come round if you like."

"Thanks. I may well do that."

Olivia reappears at our side, her coat thrown over one arm. "Ready?"

Michael nods. "We might see you tomorrow then?"

"I'll let you know in the morning." I smile. "Depends on the hangover. Ciao." I hold my glass up to toast them, then wander through to the kitchen where, to paraphrase the old song, people always end up at parties. Closest to the booze, I suppose.

"Hello, stranger." Ben is standing just inside the door talking to a man, who, judging by what resemble two small cauliflowers either side of his head, is from the rugby club. The thought idly crosses my mind that he might be the one Will saw Ben embracing.

"Hello, Happy New Year!" I clink my glass against both of theirs. Ben's friend waves at someone across the other side of the room and wanders off in that direction.

"Was it something I said?" I say to his retreating back. "Or . . ." I sniff theatrically into my left armpit.

Ben smiles. "He's a bit henpecked. I suspect his wife saw you hone into view and clicked her fingers for him to move away."

I grin and shrug. "Oh well, it's nice to know I could actually be *seen* as a threat, I suppose."

"Well, you do look lovely."

"Thanks." I look down at my outfit of plain, black sleeveless top, pencil skirt, and black kitten heels. "We aim to please."

He reaches across to the counter nearby and picks up a bottle of wine, refilling my glass. "So how have you been? We haven't spoken in a while."

"Er . . ." I place my finger on my chin in mock thought. "Actually, it's only been a couple of weeks and that's probably because we've both been rather sidetracked by Christmas."

"Probably." He nods in agreement. "Good one?"

"Not bad. We all went to Mum and Dad's, which was nice. You?"

"Same. Except Mum and Dad came to Sunshine House as I was on duty. There was only one family staying there, so it was quiet but pleasant." He shrugs. "And how's Olivia? I saw her earlier and she looked as if she was having a good time."

"She's getting there." I cross my fingers and hold them up in front of his face. "One day at a time."

"Good, glad to hear it." He takes a swig from his can of lager. "And the new job still going well?"

"*Love* it!" I nod enthusiastically and drink more wine.

"I still can't believe you walked out of the old one in a row over little old us." He places a hand on his chest and smiles.

"It was a long time coming." More wine. "Sunshine House was just the catalyst," I slur.

"So, Olivia improving, job great . . . life's looking up, eh? And what about the love life then?" he adds casually.

I turn down the corners of my mouth. "Nonexistent."

He looks surprised. "No more Internet dates?"

"Nah, gave that up as a bad job. I *was* seeing someone briefly, but it didn't work out."

"Oh? Why?"

One side of my nose scrunches up. "It just didn't feel right." The excess of wine is now making my head spin. "We had great sex though."

I notice Ben's expression harden slightly.

"Oh, sorry," I add hastily. "I forgot you don't like talking about sex."

Now he looks faintly perplexed. "I never said that. From what I can remember . . . and my memory is slightly hazy . . . I merely said that sex is just *part* of a happy marriage and people get too hung up on it."

I look at him wordlessly for a few moments, absorbing what he's said and feeling this overwhelming, alcohol-fueled compulsion to dare to tread where others have failed.

"Ben?"

"I love a girl who can remember my name." He grins.

"Are you gay?"

The smile evaporates. Oh dear. "Pardon?" His cheeks have flushed slightly, but I'm not sure whether it's embarrassment or a reaction to the heat in the overcrowded room.

"Are you gay?" I repeat, looking over my shoulder to check no one's listening. "It's all right, I won't tell anyone if you are."

His features have hardened again. "Well, thank you very much. I'm so glad I can rely on your discretion." His voice has hardened, too.

Having jumped into this conversational abyss with both feet, I do what I always do when I feel awkward. I overcompensate and witter on before the other person has had a chance to elaborate.

"It's just that Will said . . . you know, Will . . ." I point across the room to where he's guffawing loudly with two of his friends.

"Yes, Jess, *he* introduced *us*, remember?" Ben interjects, slicing across my waffle. "*What* did he say? I'm all ears."

If sober, at this point I would have picked up on his hostility and backed away from the subject, coming up with some explanatory twaddle about Will simply mentioning that Ben seemed more sensitive than most men. But, having drunk a skip full of various white wines, I plow on regardless.

"He said that he'd seen you embracing one of the other rugby players at the club recently."

"I see." His tone is icy and he's looking across the room towards an oblivious Will. "What did he see *exactly*?"

I frown, trying to remember. "Um, not sure, but I think he thought you were kissing."

Ben's pupils seem to have dilated to pinprick proportions and there's a small twitch throbbing away in his right cheek. He looks furious, but says absolutely nothing.

"It's just that as I told you all about Olivia," I burble, filling the awkward void, "I wanted you to know that if you have a big secret

it would help to share, then I'm your woman." I finish my procla-
mation with what I hope is a reassuring grin.

"I see." A tone of granite.

"It's nothing to be ashamed of, you know," I continue, only the
top of my head visible now in the giant hole I'm digging for myself.
"It's just that I like you and really want us to be friends, and you
said you hadn't had a girlfriend or a relationship in a long time, so
I thought perhaps . . ."

But he doesn't seem to be listening, clearly distracted by
something happening over my left shoulder. He suddenly manages a rigid smile.

"Hi, Tab, great party," he says over my head.

I turn round to find Tab standing immediately behind me, a
look of determined intent on her face. She places a hand in the
crook of my arm.

"Thanks, Ben." She smiles. "I hope I don't seem rude, but do
you mind if I drag Jess away for a few minutes? There's something
I need to discuss with her."

Ben makes a theatrical gesture with his hand. "Be my guest.
Jess and I can catch up later."

Before I can reply, Tab is leading me out into the hallway, gesturing for me to sit on the bottom step of the staircase. She lowers
herself next to me, her face flush with excitement.

"It's very early days, but I'm absolutely bursting to tell someone other than Will . . ." She pauses, studying my face for any
kind of reaction. Thanks to the aforementioned surfeit of alcohol,
I merely look gormless. "I think I might be pregnant!" she adds.

"Ohmigod! That's fantastic!" I leap to my feet and start jumping up and down, then realize I may be giving the game away and
instantly sit back down again. I grab her hand and squeeze it instead. "How far gone?"

She peers round the edge of the stairs to check no one is lurking in the hallway. "As I said, it's very early days. Only about six weeks, so anything could go wrong at this stage."

"Of *course* it won't go wrong," I whisper reassuringly. "God, I'm so *excited* for you! What a great start to the new year." I hug her. "I'll bet Will is chuffed to bits."

"Like a dog with two dicks." She grins. "He's absolutely dying to stand on a chair and tell everyone here, but I have strictly forbidden it until I'm past the vital first three months."

"So, this is as a result of the IVF?"

She nods. "Yep. To be honest, when we went for a follow-up the other day, I had resigned myself to the fact that I wasn't pregnant, so when they said I was it took a while to sink in." Her eyes are shining at the memory. "I had to stop Will doing handsprings down the corridor."

We both hear footsteps coming down the hallway and stop talking instantly. A couple I don't know appear at the foot of the stairs, their coats on.

"We're off now, Tabitha." The woman smiles. "Thanks for a great party."

Tab stands up and kisses her on both cheeks. "Thanks for coming. And we must have that lunch soon."

Whilst they're talking, I stand up and whisper in Tab's ear that I'm off to the loo. When I reemerge, she's still at the bottom of the stairs, saying good-bye to a couple of Will's rugby friends. Squeezing past, I head back towards the kitchen.

The party has now thinned out substantially, with people standing in small pockets around the outside, a large gap in the middle of the room.

Ben has his back to me, talking to Madeleine and the rugby player she has been glued to the side of all night. Poor lamb, those rugby scrums will be nothing compared to the sexual Olympics he'll be put through when she gets him home.

In an uncharacteristic display of public affection, Richard and Lars are snogging in the corner near the CD player, now blaring out a medley of '70s disco hits. But no one's dancing.

Sighing, I pour myself a glass of water and start to think about heading home. I'm drunker than I've been in ages, but underneath the fog I recall my conversation with Ben with mortification. It's definitely time to call it a night. Tab has offered me her spare room, but if I can persuade Richard to take a slight detour, I might hitch a lift in his pre-booked cab.

"Hello, stranger."

I swivel round to find myself face-to-face with Kara, just walking through from the living room. Dan is a few paces behind and joins her at my side.

"We were just talking about you in there," she says, jerking her head towards the door. "Interesting . . . very interesting indeed."

My head is pounding now, the New Year hangover already settling in for a long stay and not a painkiller in sight. "Really?" is all I can muster.

"Yes." Her heavily made-up eyes are hooded with evil intent. "Dan was just telling me about your little tête-à-tête in the pub."

"What?" I'm genuinely baffled, assuming she can't be talking about *that* night as it was such a long time ago.

"Oh, come on, Jess, don't play Little Miss Innocent," she hisses under her breath. "The night you were supposed to be getting answers for me, remember? He's just told me *everything* that happened."

I glance at Dan, but he's staring at the floor, scraping his boot back and forth across a mock marble tile. The urge to shout "taxi!" and run down the corridor is overwhelming.

"Kara." I sigh wearily. "I have absolutely no idea what you're talking about."

She shifts her weight from one foot to the other, then places her hands on her hips in an aggressive stance. "Then let me refresh your memory. You had too much to drink and came on to *my* boyfriend when you were supposed to be helping to get us back together."

"Sorry?" I say incredulously.

"You just couldn't bear it, could you?" she says shrilly. "That whilst you were grubbing around the Internet and shagging married men, I was enjoying a normal, happy relationship with a man who adored me. You just *had* to try and spoil it."

I laugh hollowly. "You *are* joking?" It suddenly strikes me that the music has stopped and the room has fallen into deathly silence.

"No, I'm deadly serious." Her tone is venomous.

I stand there mute for a few seconds, looking from one to the other. Dan has lifted his head now, but is still looking anywhere but at me.

"Dan?" I try to catch his eye. "Is this true? Is that what you said?"

He glances at me uncomfortably for a nanosecond, then looks away again. "Yep. I felt she had to know," he says into the distance.

And suddenly—flashback. I feel another pivotal moment taking hold, just like the one that finally sent me over the edge in Janice's office. Another gross injustice, not only in front of an audience, but this time in front of my friends. I feel the same surge of energy overtake me, rippling through my body at a five-alarm rate despite my champagne haze.

"You absolute, Grade A, duplicitous *wanker!*" I shout, looking at him, then turning back to Kara. "*He* came on to *me*, not the other way round."

Kara shakes her head slowly as if I'm a hopeless cause. "Pathetic. Quite, quite pathetic."

I take one step away from her, turning my back in irritation, then swivelling round again. "No, Kara, I'll tell you what's *pathetic*. You and him." I jerk my head from one to the other. "He came on to me and yes, we kissed, long and hard if you must know. But then I came to my senses and left. Alone." I glance to the other side of the room to see Richard, his jaw practically hitting the floor with what he is witnessing.

Turning back, I point at Dan. "Prior to that, he had spent the entire evening telling me what . . . and I quote . . . a fucking *cow* you were, and how you were pestering him to get married and how it had made him realize that he didn't love you."

I pause for breath. Kara is rooted to the spot, ashen faced with anger, whilst Dan is shaking his head at her, imploring her not to believe a word I'm saying.

"He also said you were constantly nagging him to get a proper job, something in the City if I remember rightly . . ."

Kara's facial expression doesn't change, but I notice a fleeting bolt of panic flash into her eyes.

"That's true, isn't it?" I demand. "And how would I know that if snake-boy here hadn't told me? I'm telling the *truth*, Kara, I have absolutely no reason to lie."

I stop and stare at her defiantly. One couple in the corner are valiantly pretending not to listen to this *Jerry Springer Show* unfolding before their eyes, but despite their low conversation, I know they're listening. Everyone else in the room is blatantly absorbing every word.

Kara takes a deep breath. "On the contrary, Jess, you have *every* reason to lie." The harsh shrieking has now been replaced by a wounded tone. "You've always been jealous of me. Jealous of my confidence and my looks, jealous of my relationships, and particularly this one. Yet I have always overlooked all that and strived to be a good friend to you, regardless. And this is how you repay me."

I feel another surge of anger rolling through me. "Brilliant.

Just *brilliant. Me* jealous of *you*?" I scoff. "I don't think so . . . you're bitter, twisted, humorless, . . ." I hold up a finger for each adjective, ". . . desperately insecure, duplicitous, bitchy, and, quite frankly, just a little bit dull. Which all adds up to you being one giant pain in the arse."

I take a couple of steps to the right and reach for the back of the chair, where I've hooked my handbag, preparing to leave.

"And you know what else? You and I have been friends . . . whatever that means . . . for years and years now, and only the other day I was thinking '*why*?' I've never really liked you, yet for some reason I always put up with all your shit, hanging on in there in the vague hope that, one day, you might show *some* appreciation for my loyalty . . . that it might all turn out to be worthwhile in the end. But you never did. You just carried on browbeating me, ridiculing me whenever you got the chance . . . treading all over your little people-pleasing friend. Even that Internet ad was designed solely to try and humiliate me, to hammer home the suggestion that I couldn't meet anyone the *normal* way. You were mortified when you thought I'd met someone nice, then nakedly thrilled when he turned out to be married . . ."

I let out a long sigh and hook my handbag over my arm. "You're just a hard-faced old cow, Kara, plain and simple. Dan had that right. Our friendship is a false, abusive one and I want no further part in it. If I ever see you again, it will be too soon."

I stop speaking and turn to the rest of the room. "Apologies you had to hear all that," I say to no one in particular. "But it had to be said."

"On the contrary, hear fucking hear!" It's Richard, leaning against the kitchen sink. "Never darken my Dior again!" he adds, looking over at Kara, who's still eyeballing me defiantly.

Suddenly, Tab appears between us. "Kara, I think you and Dan had better leave," she says quietly.

I place a hand on her shoulder. "No, Tab, don't worry. I'm leaving now anyway. Sorry about all that, I hope it didn't ruin your party." I walk out of the kitchen door into the hallway, turning round for one last remark.

"Kara, you and Dan really should get married, you know. I can't think of a couple more deserving of each other."

I smile thinly at them, scan the room, and turn on my heel heading for the front door. My final image from the party is of Ben standing alone in a corner, a look of terrible sadness on his face.

Thirty Five

Oooh, St. Charles Place with a hotel, that's $750, please!" I hold my hand out towards Michael.

"Aunty Jess?"

"Yes, my darling Emily?"

"Why do you *always* win at Monopoly?"

"Because I always buy up the cheap properties and build on them as soon as I can," I say pompously. "Daddy may well scoff at my tactic, but it works every time . . . whilst he's still struggling to buy even *one* house for his ostentatious Boardwalk and Park Place."

Michael pokes his tongue out at me, whilst Matthew, sitting to my right, simply looks puzzled.

"Ostin . . . ostin-stay-shuss," he struggles, "is that anything to do with Austin Powers?"

Olivia and I share a small smile. "No, darling," I reply. "It means pretentious . . . you know, showing off."

Counting the money Michael has handed to me, I place it on top of my vast pile of cash and ruffle Emily's hair. "I think I've won, don't you?"

Olivia looks at her watch. "Yes, come on, I need the table cleared for lunch anyway. Jess wins . . . *again*."

"The winner!" Hands raised aloft, I do a victory lap of the kitchen before running down the hallway to the living room, two delighted children squealing in my wake.

We fall into a bundle on the sofa, my arm round each of them. "Right! What film shall we watch?"

"What she means is, what film will *you two* watch while she falls asleep," says Michael, flopping into the armchair opposite.

One hour's time and one lunch later, I'm back at the kitchen table, my top pants button undone to accommodate my bloated stomach. "That was great, thanks." I hold up my glass of lemonade in a toast. "Here's to Olivia, and Happy New Year one and all."

"To my beautiful, charming, delightful wife," says Michael, leaning across and kissing her on the cheek.

Olivia raises her eyes heavenward. "Yes, you *can* go and watch the rugby," she laughs. "Creep!"

Michael needs no second bidding and hastily grabs his glass of lager. "I'll watch it in the bedroom so the kids can finish watching their film downstairs," he says. "See you later."

"Coffee?" Olivia looks at me inquiringly.

"I'll make it." I force myself to stand up and walk over to the kettle. "You've done quite enough for one day. How are you feeling?"

"Great, actually." She smiles. "I'm not usually a big fan of New Year's, but I feel very optimistic about this one."

"Good." I smile. "That's what I like to hear."

"I enjoyed Tab's party," she adds, flicking through an old copy of *OK* magazine. "Did we miss anything by leaving so soon after midnight?"

I widen my eyes, suddenly realizing she doesn't know about

the showdown with Kara. "Yes, you missed your sister's finest moment. Let me make the coffee and I'll fill you in."

*I*t's 6 p.m. and pitch black by the time I arrive back at my flat, exhausted but extremely mellow after a contented afternoon spent gossiping with Olivia at her kitchen table.

Having deliberately left my mobile phone at home to escape intrusive calls from the outside world, I rummage in the bottom of the fruit bowl to retrieve it. Six missed calls, three new messages.

"Richard will be one, Tab will be another," I say out loud. Sure enough, I'm right. The third is from Madeleine, with the distinct sound of a man's voice in the background and lots of giggling on her part. All are ringing for a postmortem on the gunfight at the OK Kara Corral.

Knowing Richard will be at home with his mobile switched off, I deliberately choose to call the latter and leave a message. I need to be in the right, energetic mood for a high-octane conversation with him, and I'm not.

Fake gas fire on full blast, telly on mute, and legs curled under me on the sofa, I pick up the hands-free phone and punch in Tab's home number.

"Hi there, it's me. I'm just calling to say that I know we've been friends for ages, but you really get on my tits and I don't want to clap eyes on you ever again."

Tab bursts out laughing on the other end. "I never liked you either," she retorts.

"Sorry about that." My voice is serious now. "I hope it didn't screw up your party."

"On the contrary, it rejuvenated it," she enthuses. "It was

starting to wind down until the you and Kara moment, then after you'd gone it was really buzzy again with everyone talking about what had happened."

"What about Kara? Did she spontaneously combust into a small, steaming blob on the kitchen floor?"

"Not far off. After you'd walked out, she stood there motionless for about another minute, just staring at the ground. Then Dan tapped her on the arm and asked if she was OK, and she turned on him with all guns blazing."

"Really?" I say delightedly. I'm relishing the thought.

"Yes, she said . . . or should I say spat . . . something like 'I don't know who to *fucking* believe,' then marched out of the kitchen with him in hot pursuit behind her."

"And?"

"And then we heard the front door slam and they had both gone."

I purse my lips. "Bloody hell, I'll bet he's having a really shit New Year's Day."

Tab laughs. "You bet. Mind you, sounds like he deserves it if what you were saying was true."

"Of *course* it was true," I snap, annoyed she might even contemplate the thought that I'd made it all up. "You don't seriously think I'd invent something like that, do you?"

"No, no, not at all," she replies hastily. "I just thought you might have exaggerated slightly . . . you know, just to wind her up."

"Nope. It was pretty much verbatim what happened. He's such a slimeball. I couldn't believe it when she came to your birthday dinner and said they were back together."

"Well, as you said last night, they deserve each other. Did you enjoy the party otherwise?"

"I had a lovely time, thanks. And it was nice to catch up with Ben. I haven't seen him for ages." I feel slightly nauseous as I remember what was said.

"Yes, I saw you talking to him. Is he OK?"

I pause for a moment, mulling over whether to tell Tab the full, unexpurgated version of our conversation. I decide she's trustworthy enough. "Don't tell Will, but I asked Ben outright if he was gay."

She audibly gasps. "And what did he say?"

"Well, that's just it. He didn't."

"He must have done or said *something*," she says incredulously. "That's a pretty big question to have been asked."

"I know, but just as I had asked it, you came over and interrupted us. Do you remember? It was when you came to tell me about the pregnancy."

Tab groans. "What bloody great timing on my part. Didn't you speak to him again later?"

"No, I didn't get the chance. When I went back into the kitchen he was talking to someone else, then the whole Kara business happened and I left."

She's silent for a moment, then takes a deep breath. "You should call him tonight."

I shudder at the thought. "I can't, Tab, I feel so hideously awkward now for having mentioned it. I could kick myself, I really could. He's such a nice man, and I feel I've ruined our friendship by pushing such a sensitive subject on him in such an appallingly insensitive manner." I sigh and shift slightly, stretching my aching legs out in front of me. "It feels like it does the day after you've gotten really drunk and ended up shagging an old friend. You know, when you feel the whole axis of your relationship has shifted and will never be the same again."

"Shall I ring him and see if he mentions it?" says Tab.

"No, absolutely not," I splutter. "You wouldn't call him out of the blue at the best of times, and New Year's Day would seem *really* suspicious. He'd know I'd put you up to it." I let out a long, slow breath. "No, I think I'll use the coward's way out and e-mail him."

"Well, let me know what happens." She clears her throat. "Look, gotta go, Will has cooked dinner and, as it's a once-in-a-year occurrence, I'd better look appreciative and savor it. I'll call you tomorrow, OK?"

After she's put the phone down, I sit there for a few minutes, pondering what to do about Ben. I decide that an e-mail still is the best option. It offers a distance that's easier to cope with, and he can read it several times without pressure before deciding how to respond. Deep down, I'm also afraid of what a direct phone conversation might yield. I don't think I could bear it if he was ice cold or overtly hostile, though he certainly has every right to be. Along those lines, he might just delete my e-mail altogether. But at least I'll know I've tried.

Lifting my laptop onto my knees, I switch it on and wince slightly, the bright screen hurting my eyes. There are a few new e-mails, but a quick scan reveals that none of them are from Ben.

However, there is one from my new cyberbuddy, Seb Northam, dated today.

Dear Jess,

Happy New Year!!! I vaguely remember you saying you were going to a party, so hope you enjoyed it.

I also went to a party at a friend's house, but can't really remember much as I drank myself stupid, made a complete spectacle of myself doing a solo rendition of "Oops upside your head," and am deeply regretting it this morning. My mouth feels like the inside of a parrot cage.

I didn't get up until midday, and have just made myself a Cup-O-Soup and a mushroom toast topper. What a glamorous life, eh?

Do you realize it's now been just over two months since we started writing to each other? We've exchanged photographs and lots of very personal information—not least your feelings about your sister's breast cancer—and I feel we have got to know each other pretty well.

So all that remains is to actually meet! I have refrained from suggesting it before because I sensed that, maybe, with so much going on in your life, you weren't ready to do so.

But as we stand on the threshold of another new year, my hangover has numbed me enough to pluck up the courage to say that I would dearly like to actually clap eyes on you in the flesh.

No pressure, just two cyberfriends seeing if their relationship has a chance of crossing into the real world.

So I'm going to take a leap of faith here and book us a table for lunch on Saturday. Let's make it 1 p.m. at Rawnsley's restaurant on Walton Street, SW1. If you turn up, fantastic. If you don't, then at least I'll know for sure that you're not interested in extending this relationship beyond the occasional e-mail, which I've enjoyed very much, by the way, don't get me wrong.

This may all sound very Sunday afternoon movie, but hey, wouldn't life be dull without a little bit of old-fashioned romance?

Yours,
Seb xx

I stare at the screen blankly for a few moments, absorbing what he's written. Over the past few weeks, we have indeed shared many hopes and thoughts that, normally, it would take me longer to impart to an actual boyfriend.

The reason for this, I muse, is twofold. With a new boyfriend you're trying to impress, you always present a rather false, permanently jolly side of yourself in the early stages, anxious not to show weakness until you both know each other a little better. Seb's not a boyfriend, so I've felt no reservations in sharing my every little up and down over my new job and, most of all, Olivia.

Secondly, as anyone familiar with e-mail knows, the barrier of the computer between you is almost like passing on information through a third party. It makes you more succinct in what you want to say, flirtier, and a hell of a lot braver. There are no immediate reactions to deal with, no facial expressions that suggest hurt, disappointment, or pity, no interruptions or contradictions, just a self-indulgent, unhindered flow. Consequently, it can be very cathartic, a form of cyber therapy.

The burning question is, would finally meeting him spoil it all? Would it burst the comforting bubble we have been happily conversing in for so long?

I'm not so sure, but as it's only Wednesday, I've got three days to think about it. Right now, I push it to the back of my mind, wanting to concentrate on my e-mail to Ben.

Dear Ben.

No, too formal. Delete.

Yo there.

Yo? Have I *completely* lost my marbles? I sound like a children's TV presenter. All that's missing is a thumbs-up sign.

Hi there.

That's better. Friendly and casual, that's the style I want.

It's New Year's Day and I'm suffering from quite a hangover. But then, you'd know that because you had to suffer the drunken creature that led up to it!

I haven't drunk so much since . . . ooh . . . last week, and my New Year resolution is to cut right back on the alcohol and lead a blameless life of abstemiousness. Well, for at least a month anyway.

Anyway, enough of my wittering. I wish I could say that I was so drunk last night that I don't remember a word that passed between us. But sadly I do, and I'm mortified that I could have been so insensitive to ask what I did in such circumstances. Hardly the right time or the place, was it?

So I want to apologize profusely for doing so, and say that your private life is absolutely none of my business and I should never have intruded. My only defense is that, because I confided in you so early about Olivia, I suppose I felt our friendship was closer and more confessional than it actually was from your point of view. I overstepped the mark and I'm sorry.

For what it's worth, I couldn't care two hoots whether you're straight, gay, bisexual, trisexual (!), or totally asexual. All I care about is that you've been a very good friend to me and I hate the thought that, instead of waiting for you to tell me yourself, I may have hurt you by being so intrusive.

So can we just forget that conversation ever happened? Please? I want to press rewind and go back to how we were—a friendship with no pressure, just good mates who are there for each other in times of crisis.

Groveling apologies again, and I hope you can see your way to forgive me.

Jess x

I reread it a couple of times, then click on "send" before I can change my mind. I just hope it does the trick. Sighing, I close the lid of my laptop and lean back against the sofa, my thoughts full of how different my life is just one year on.

Last New Year's Day, there was no Ben, Kara and I were friends (at least of a sort), and I was still working at *Good Morning Britain* and hating every minute of it. I was single but—in the absence of an Internet ad—still following the traditional route of trawling wine bars and parties. And most poignantly of all, Olivia didn't have cancer.

I wonder, not without some trepidation, what twists and turns my life will have taken another year from now.

Thirty Six

The wind shoots noisily down my bedroom chimney, jolting the grate and waking me with a start.

Disoriented, I sit bolt upright and take a few seconds to realize that the world hasn't ended and I'm not late for work. It's 10 a.m. Saturday morning and I sink gratefully back onto my pillow, fantasizing about having a housekeeper who would now bring me a refreshing cup of tea. Or an obliging boyfriend who would do the same, perhaps?

For the first time in ages, I find myself lamenting the lack of a serious relationship in my life, and not just because I'm too lazy to get off my backside and make my own tea. No, even thinking back to the days of the hapless Nathan, there was something reassuring about waking up on a wet weekend morning and having someone to cuddle up to or even just slop around the house with. Company on tap if you wanted it, a long, solitary bath with a good book if you didn't.

As a singleton, there isn't that choice. Sure, I could hit the phone and invite myself to someone's house, but sometimes that feels like piggybacking on their lives rather than simply living my own.

Sighing, I haul myself out of bed and pad through into the kitchen to make that much-needed cup of tea. Waiting for the kettle to boil, I unplug my laptop from its charger and switch it on.

There are four new e-mails, all work related, and my heart sinks. It's now been three days since I e-mailed Ben to apologize about my behavior on New Year's Eve, and the silence has been deafening. Like staring at a phone you want desperately to ring, I have been obsessively checking my in-box at least once an hour, silently willing there to be a reply from him.

But nothing. I can only assume I have offended him so greatly that he's either going to make me suffer for several more days, or he's simply decided to do what I have finally done with Kara and cut me out of his life altogether. Let's face it, who needs friends like drunken old me?

Scrolling down, I double click on Seb Northam's e-mail from earlier in the week, the one suggesting lunch today. What harm can it do, I muse, as I stand up and cross to the kettle.

After all, we've been cyberchatting for a couple of months now and he seems personable and funny, not to mention passably pleasant looking in his photo. Not an oil painting, but then again, not a seaside postcard either.

And if I'm honest, Olivia's little Christmas Day speech about life's priorities has been playing on my mind. Yes, thirty-four is still young in so many ways, but if, as I do, you want to get married and have children, then time is of the essence. Particularly if you want to do things the traditional way of meeting someone, giving it a couple of years to make sure you're right for each other, getting married, *then* trying for a baby. By my calculation, even if I met someone right now, my ovaries would be approaching 104 by the time I got round to needing them.

Nope, there's nothing else for it. I've got to get back out there and date. Starting now.

Rawnsley's is a traditional English restaurant with stalwarts such as braised beef and Guinness pie or fish and chips on the menu. Both are scrawled on the "specials" blackboard outside, along with beef stew and dumplings.

I loiter outside for a few seconds, taking deep breaths and trying to calm myself. God knows why I feel so nervous when I have unabashedly turned up for so many dates with complete strangers and not felt in the slightest bit jittery. Perhaps it's the fact that Seb and I have already revealed so much, despite never having clapped eyes on each other. Ducking into a doorway at one side of the entrance, I take out my pocket mirror and check my hair and makeup one last time. The latter is "au naturel," in other words, equally as much as any other kind of makeup, just less obvious. I hope.

After a good hour of deliberation and frustration at home, I have opted for a black polo neck sweater, cream trousers, and black ankle boots, with a cream parka jacket on top. The look can best be described as that ubiquitous oxymoron "smart casual." Right. Here I go. The restaurant is dark, very dark. Great for hiding any blemishes, but less obliging for an attractive first impression, given that you have to squint alarmingly to be able to see anyone.

There are only two tables currently occupied, and both of them already have three people en suite. So, unless I have unwittingly agreed to a group date, I'm the first here.

I contemplate leaving and walking round the block a couple of times, but I don't think my hair could cope. Besides, being first puts me in poll position to scrutinize him as soon as he comes squinting through the door.

"Madam, how may I help you?" A hand-wringing, obsequious waiter hones into view, dipping his entire body below mine as if I'm the King of Siam.

"I'm meeting a Mr. Northam here for lunch," I reply.

"Ah yes, he's here."

"He is?" I peer into the gloom, wondering how I could have overlooked a solitary diner.

"Yes, he's out the back."

Out the back? Bloody hell, I think, if he can't get a table in the main part of a virtually deserted restaurant he must have a *really* imposing presence. What have I gotten myself into?

"Let me take your coat and I'll take you through," says the waiter, gesturing to a small door at the rear of the room.

Following him, I start to panic slightly about the decision to come, and seriously contemplate doing an about turn and escaping. I now wish I'd suggested coffee in a brightly lit, crowded café, rather than agreeing to lunch in this gloomy, half-empty place. If I decide after five minutes he's not my type, it's going to be incredibly difficult to curtail an intimate lunch in an isolated back room.

Before I can make a decision, the waiter is tapping on the door. "Hello, sir? Your guest is here."

He tentatively pushes the door open, and I peer in over his shoulder. It's a small, dimly lit room with just one table for two laid out in the center. Seb is sitting in the nearest chair, his back to the door.

"I'll leave you now, madam." The waiter smiles, standing aside for me to walk in. He closes the door behind me, and I stand there motionless for a couple of seconds, taking in the surroundings. A small ledge-cum-dado rail around the room is peppered with tealights flickering in the gloom, and in the center of the table a large church candle adds to the slightly eerie ambience. George Michael's "I Can't Make You Love Me" plays softly out of two speakers positioned in the far corners of the ceiling.

"Hello?" I say tentatively, craning my head towards Seb, who still hasn't turned round. The image of *Psycho*'s mother in her rocking chair snaps into my mind.

Taking a couple of steps forward, I walk past the side of his chair and turn to look at him. The blood drains from my face and my nerve endings stand to attention.

"What the fuck are *you* doing here?" I exclaim, feeling my cheeks flush hot with a mixture of confusion and slight anger that some sort of trap has been set without my knowledge. We all know how I hate surprises.

"Ah yes, a typical Jess-style greeting. Lovely to see you too." He smiles sheepishly and gestures to the chair in front of him. "Sit down."

"No thanks." I stay where I am, my hands on my hips. "Ben, what's going on?"

His expression is apologetic. "I'm Seb Northam."

Brow furrowed, I plonk myself into the chair without thinking and turn to face him. "OK, you've lost me."

"I'm Seb Northam," he repeats. "It's an anagram of Ben R. Thomas. My middle name is Robert, by the way . . . I don't think I ever told you that," he adds matter-of-factly.

I blink rapidly, my brain computing what he's just said. "So *you're* the one who's been sending me all those e-mails?"

He nods, giving me a nervous grin.

"*Why?*" I ask. "Why not just e-mail me as yourself?"

"It's a long story." He sighs. "Are you going to share a glass of wine with me and stay and listen to it, or carry on being hostile?"

"I'm not hostile," I reply indignantly.

"Oh no, not at all," he says, arching an eyebrow. "Scowling expression, body turned to one side, arms crossed . . . no, no . . . not hostile at *all*."

I unfold my arms and turn my body round to face him front on, but a faint scowl is still evident, more through continuing confusion than anything else. "Go on then, pour the wine."

He duly does, and hands the glass to me. Holding the stem of his own, he raises it. "Nice to see you."

"Nice to see you too . . . *Seb.*"

"Now, now, you see? There's that hostility again."

"Well, what do you expect?" I splutter, a small dribble of wine escaping from the corner of my mouth. "I send you an apologetic e-mail, you don't even bother replying, then I turn up for a date with some supposed stranger I've been conversing with for a couple of months and find out it's *you*! I don't even like surprise birthday parties, so this is *really* pissing me off."

He waits for me to finish, his mouth set in a firm line. "Well, sorry you're pissed off, Jess, but it was the only way to get through that thick skull of yours."

"Get what through?"

He sighs again, a longer, deeper one this time. "This wasn't how I envisaged this at all. I wanted it to be special." He sweeps his arm towards all the candles and slumps back in his chair with an air of hopelessness.

"*You* did all this?" I say, with a note of surprise. It hasn't struck me before, such was my shock at seeing him.

He looks at me incredulously. "Well, who the hell do you think did it?"

I shrug. "I don't know. I hadn't really thought about it. I suppose I imagined it was for something happening later."

He slaps his hand against his forehead. "Two hours of hard

slog to create a romantic ambience and you think it's for some bloody birthday party or whatever later on. I may as well have booked a table by the toilets in a Happy Eater."

"Sorry." I wince pathetically. The word "romantic" sears itself into the front of my brain, and for the first time I focus on what this might be all about.

He shakes his head slowly, as if I'm a lost cause. "So do you want to hear the long story or not?"

"Go on then," I say, leaning forward on my elbows.

Taking a deep breath, he looks at me apprehensively. "On second thought, fuck the long version . . . The truth is . . . I think I'm falling in love with you."

I stare at him blankly for a couple of beats, my stomach lurching. "You're falling in love with me?" I parrot.

"Yep. Think so." He looks at me expectantly.

"But I thought you . . ." I tail off awkwardly.

"Ah yes, you thought I was gay," he says helpfully. "Don't worry, you can say it."

"So you're not then?"

"Nope. Not one iota, although I *do* have a couple of Judy Garland albums I should probably confess to."

"A dead giveaway," I say. Inside, my heart feels like it's about to break out of my chest at his revelation, but I'm not sure whether it's through panic or excitement. I haven't yet had time to assimilate it properly or form a response, so I decide to gloss over it for now. "Now I feel even *more* stupid for what I said on New Year's Eve."

"Forget it," he says simply. "Considering what you'd been told, I suppose it's understandable you thought that."

"You mean the locker room embrace?" I sip my wine and study his face for a reaction.

He raises his eyes heavenward. "That wasn't what it seemed at all."

"Do you want to talk about it?"

"Not really, as it's very personal to the other person. But I'll tell you anyway, just to clear up any lingering doubt." He bites his lip. "The guy plays for the rugby team. I don't really know him that well, but he knows what I do for a living, so when his younger sister was diagnosed with leukemia recently, he wanted to talk to me about it, to get some advice and insight and be reassured. He approached me after practice one day and we got to talking and, understandably, he became very upset. So I gave him a hug. And that's it." He shrugs and looks straight at me.

Needless to say, I feel like a complete fool, and I could cheerfully throttle the moronic Will, who clearly can't tell the difference between a reassuring hug and a gay kiss. "And how is his sister now?" I ask.

He smiles. "Luckily, she has the most curable form of leukemia, so she's going to be just fine."

"Thank goodness. Let's hope it stays that way." I take a sip of wine and continue to try to stop my mind from reeling, to try to process everything that's being said.

"So . . ." His eyes bore into mine. "What are your thoughts on my little declaration?"

I shrug. "It's no big deal. I quite like Judy Garland too."

"*Jess* . . ." he growls. And I grin, despite myself.

"Sorry, but it's quite a shock. One minute I think you're gay, the next you're telling me you might be falling in love with me. It takes a little time for a girl to digest all that."

He purses his lips, looking doubtful at this explanation. "But you must know whether you feel happy or appalled by the news?"

"Not appalled, that's for sure," I say.

"But not happy either?" He looks disappointed.

"I didn't say that, did I?" I reply softly. "It's just a lot to take in, particularly that Seb Northam business. What was *that* all about?"

He pours the last of the wine bottle into our glasses, and I notice there's another sitting in an ice bucket by his side. The waiters have obviously been told to stay well away until called.

"Well," he says tentatively, "I kind of figured that you might not think of me in *that* way. You know . . . we met through Will, didn't get off to a very good start, and then became friends because of your TV report on Sunshine House. Hardly Romeo and Juliet, is it? And I know how you like to feel an instant *spark* in relationships, because you've told me enough times."

I wonder whether this is the time to interject and point out that I've had a radical change of heart over that particular relationship rule of mine, but decide to save it for later.

"I'm very mistrustful of that whole spark business," he continues, "because it always wears off and leaves a residue of disappointment. To my mind, it's much better to be friends with someone first."

He reaches across the table and grabs hold of my right hand. I feel a tingle that surprises me. "You see, I already *know* that you can be unerringly stubborn when you think you're right about something, that you occasionally suffer black moods in the mornings, and that, just sometimes, you become totally focused on work to the exclusion of all else. I know *all* that because we've been friends first.

"We've already learned the worst about each other and can go forward with no surprises, whereas normally, you discover the worst things about your partner *after* falling in love and it sometimes erodes what you have."

He lets go of my hand and leans back on his chair, stretching his left leg out to one side and cupping his hands behind his head.

"But none of those worst things matter because I also happen to know you are one of the kindest, most loyal people I have ever met, someone who can appear to have a hard shell to those that don't know her, but who *I* know to have an endearingly soft center."

"Just call me M&M," I quip, trying to ignore the fact that my insides are fluttering with apprehension.

"Anyway." He sighs, moving his arms in front of him again and leaning forwards on the table. "Because of your penchant for dating total strangers rather than mates, I felt the only way to woo you, if you like, was to start from scratch by pretending to be someone else . . . voilà, Seb Northam. I tweaked a couple of facts about him so you wouldn't suspect, but otherwise he's intrinsically me."

I nod my head slowly, smiling slightly to show I'm not cross. "And the photo?"

He laughs. "Ah yes, the photo. It's my brother James, taken at his birthday party a couple of years ago. I figured we look similar-ish, but not enough for you to figure out the truth."

"It certainly worked," I concede. "I didn't suspect a thing."

His face turns serious again. "Jess, you have no idea how hard it was for me to be developing these feelings for you, all the while listening to you talking about all the dates you were going on. It was so frustrating."

"So why didn't you just ask me out?"

He looks derisive and clicks his fingers. "Oh yeah, just like that. Easier said than done, particularly as questions like that have a habit of ruining good friendships. I *was* close to it at one point, but then Will casually mentioned that you had the hots for some bloke you'd met through the Internet, and I thought I was going to be sick with jealousy."

"Ah, yes." I nod sagely. "Simon R.I.P." I make the crucifix sign across my chest. "Sadly, he didn't live up to the hype."

"Glad to know the voodoo doll worked then." Ben grins, run-

ning a hand through his hair. "Anyway, I had earmarked New
Year's Eve as the time I was going to sink my own weight in booze,
confess to the Seb thing, and finally pluck up the courage to try
and ravish you, but . . ."

"But I accused you of being gay," I interrupt with a sheepish
smile.

"Precisely. Silly cow." He raises his eyes heavenward to show
the insult is meant affectionately. "So that's why I came up with
the idea for this lunch."

Grabbing the second bottle of wine, he pours us two generous
glasses. I can feel the alcohol relaxing me now, stripping away the
earlier tension caused by this little surprise. The combination of
candlelight and a windowless room is disorientating, and it could
easily be nighttime, but a quick glance at my watch shows it to be
1:30 p.m.

"So are we going to eat?" I inquire, waving my glass at him.
"Because if I have much more of this on an empty stomach, you
might have to carry me out of here on a stretcher."

Smiling warmly, he's clearly relieved that I'm showing no
signs of a quick exit. "Sure. Shall I just order a couple of plates of
stew and stodgy dumplings to line the stomach?"

"I'm on the Fatkins diet, so that sounds perfect," I say, maintaining eye contact as he stands up.

After he's disappeared through the door into the restaurant, I
take a deep breath and try to take stock of what's been said so far.
Most crucially of all, I try to nail down exactly what I feel about it,
as I know that whatever I say today will probably make or break our
relationship, be it as friends or lovers.

It's true I have never thought about Ben in a sexual way, but
that could easily be explained away by the fact that, right from the
outset, Tab alluded that he might be gay. On the plus side, I felt
bereft when I thought I might have upset him with my insensitive

blethering on New Year's Eve. But was that simply because I value his friendship or because, subconsciously, my feelings ran a lot deeper? And if they don't now, could they?

Whoops, no time to dwell on all that. He's back.

"Two plates of stodge on its way." He grins, settling back into his chair.

"Excellent."

We sit there, smiling at each other, for what seems like an eternity. Both clearly wondering where the conversation goes from here, neither knowing quite how to restart it.

He clears his throat. "So why did you come on a date with Seb Northam?"

"Pardon?"

"What was it about him that made you decide to turn up today?" he elaborates.

I shrug. "Dunno really. He seemed very nice, and I figured that as I was single it wouldn't do any harm to at least have lunch with him and see what he's like in person."

"That's it?" He raises his eyebrows. "You weren't blown away by his witticisms, drawn in by his overpoweringly attractive personality?"

I laugh. "Oh yes, that too of course."

"Glad to hear it."

My expression turns serious. "And something Olivia said made me come along as well."

"Oh?" He leans forward slightly.

"She said that having a good relationship and kids was what life was all about . . . that work doesn't keep you warm at night." I stare down at the table, absentmindedly picking at a fleck on the cloth. "She also pointed out that I'm thirty-four and time is running out if I want to have a chance of finding the right person before my ovaries shrivel to the size of raisins."

Now, let's just pause a moment here. Can you *imagine* repeating what I've just said on most first dates? The man would leave skid marks.

But Ben stays firmly in his seat, not even a flicker of panic on his face. Quite the contrary, in fact. He looks absorbed.

"So you thought Seb might have a chance of fulfilling that criteria?"

I purse my lips. "Maybe. Maybe not. But I thought I'd never know if I didn't at least give it a try."

"And what about Ben R. Thomas?" he asks softly. "Can you see yourself achieving it with him?"

"Who knows?" I smile enigmatically. "We'll just have to wait and see."

Thirty Seven

*I*t's May 3, and I'm thirty-five today. All together now, aaaaarrrgh!

Actually, I'm just being overly dramatic, as ever. I feel absolutely fine about it, particularly given the year I've had. Truth be known, I'm just glad to have reached this milestone in one piece.

Last year, if you remember, was the "surprise" party that Olivia tipped me off about, with Kara's even more hateful surprise present at the end of it. Little did I know then that it would set me on a journey to run the full gamut of single—well, mostly anyway—men and their dating foibles.

So, this year, I have headed any planned surprises off at the pass and organized a little party myself at a cheap and cheerful Italian restaurant just a few hundred yards from my house.

On the promise of a set menu for twelve heavy drinkers, the staff have agreed to section off the rear of the room for my exclusive use, and Tab and I have been here for the past couple of hours decorating it with brightly colored table confetti, candles, and various shaped balloons bearing the words "Happy 30th." Just my little joke.

"Ta dah! That looks fantastic!" Tab stands back to admire her handiwork, a garish "Happy Birthday" banner stretched from one corner of the room to the patch of ceiling just above the table. "I think we're just about done."

I rush over to grab the corner of the stepladder as she starts to climb down. "You shouldn't be on that bloody thing in your condition," I chastise, patting her bulging stomach as her feet hit terra firma.

She waves a dismissive hand at me. "Nonsense, I'm fine. I'm in the blooming stage. You know, where you want to nest all the time. I spend my life up stepladders at home, putting right all those irritating things that Will and I have been ignoring for months." She holds her arm up and bends it at the elbow. "Strong as an ox, that's me."

I smile. "Funny isn't it? Despite your bit of trouble conceiving, you now seem to be having the least problematic pregnancy of all time."

"I know, and thank the Lord for it. I don't think I could have coped with morning sickness *and* the ghastly Janice."

"Ah yes, how is the miserable old witch?"

"The same. Testing laughing gas on a daily basis, having us all in stitches. She's a real card." Tab squints at a small, stained clock on the far wall. "What time is it?"

I look at my watch. "Eight on the dot. Someone should arrive in a minute, probably Richard and Lars, as they're always so punctual."

Sure enough, barely have the words left my mouth than Richard bursts in through the door of the restaurant, a vision in tight, black PVC jeans and a T-shirt bearing the charming slogan "Do I *look* like a fucking people person?" I wince at the thought of my mother's expression when she sees it.

"I take it The Ivy was fully booked?" he says, casting a derisive eye over the interior.

"Fuck off." I smile sweetly. "Where's Lars?"

"Just unloading your present out of the Pickfords van. He's right behind me."

Right on cue, Lars ambles in, carrying a large parcel beautifully wrapped in silver paper.

"Happy birthday." He grins and hands it over.

"Thanks, honey." I kiss him on both cheeks. "I'll open it later. Glass of bubbly?"

I can ill afford it, but I have spent roughly $500 on providing champagne and wine, with everyone else agreeing to fork out for their meal.

Leaving Tab to ensure that Richard and Lars are furnished with drinks, I walk through to the kitchens to have one last chat with the chef. As he's Italian and barely speaks any English, this involves much hand-waving, miming of various culinary tasks such as tomato chopping, and lots of smiling in the hope that he'll do me proud with a delicious birthday meal.

By the time I reemerge fifteen minutes later, most of my guests have arrived and are gratefully slurping their way down their first glass of champagne.

"Darling, you look divine!" Mum sweeps down on me, her double pearls clacking together. "Happy birthday! But you're not thirty . . ." She waves her hand towards the balloons.

"It's a *joke*, Mum." I smile thinly. "Where's Dad?"

"He's sitting down in that corner, talking to Michael. I don't know what about, but I'd hazard a guess at rugby." She glances over her shoulder. "But never mind them, doesn't Olivia look *fantastic*."

I follow her eye line to where Olivia is chatting animatedly to

Madeleine. She does indeed look sensational in a black gossamer sleeveless cocktail dress and dainty diamante encrusted sandals with kitten heels.

Her hair is now growing back nicely, cut into a short, urchin style that frames her face beautifully and makes her eyes look huge. She can still look gaunt in a certain light, but she's starting to fill out again in all the right places, her appetite having returned to normal.

After finishing the last of her chemotherapy, she had a month's respite before moving on to the less debilitating radio-therapy. Now that's over, she's deemed to be in remission and the game of watching and waiting has begun. Just occasionally, she still gets a little panicky about the cancer coming back, particularly when she reads similar stories in the newspapers.

But for the most part, she's getting on with her life and trying to be as normal as possible for the children. Matthew and Emily's packed memory boxes are tucked away in a dark corner of the attic, and that's where I hope they'll stay.

"Hey you." I sidle up to Olivia and plant a kiss on her right cheek, still cold from the outside air. "You look amazing."

"Doesn't she?" Madeleine leans across to give me a kiss. "I was just saying exactly that, and I *love* the hair. I'd keep it like that."

Olivia smiles. "I must say, it's so much easier to look after, but Matthew says that mummies should always have long hair, so on that basis, I'm growing it back to shoulder length."

I turn to face Madeleine. "You look . . . um . . . different," I falter.

Given that this is the woman with a penchant for bustiers and "pussy pelmets," as Richard so fetchingly describes short skirts, Madeleine has undergone something of a transformation this evening. She's wearing tailored black trousers, a beige cashmere top, and black suede loafers with a little metal bar across the front. Her hair is sleekly combed into a ponytail.

She looks slightly sheepish. "I know it's not exactly my style, but Marty loves me to dress like this," she whispers conspiratorially, glancing across the room to where he's talking to Will.

Marty is the rugby player she met at Tab and Will's New Year's Eve party, the one whose face she snogged off most of the evening, then dragged home afterwards. But, unusually for Madeleine, who generally sees one night as a long-term commitment, they have been dating ever since. Even more surprisingly, she has remained faithful.

"The same man for five months and now you're changing the way you look to please him?" I tease. "My God, it must be love!"

Her face flushes slightly. "I'm not sure about that, but I do know I have no need to look elsewhere. He's *fantastic* in bed . . . such stamina! He can go for hours."

Olivia lets out a low groan. "God, I can't think of anything worse than someone grinding away for days on end. I much prefer quickies." She grins.

They both look at me, as if my view will be the deciding factor.

"Oh . . . um . . ." I stumble. "I suppose I like a little bit of both really."

"What are you three whispering about?" Michael has appeared.

"I was just telling them we like quickies," says Olivia.

"As opposed to what?" he quips, ruffling her hair.

"When's dinner?" It's Dad, rubbing his hands together in glee at the thought of impending nosh.

I look at my watch and see it's 8:30. "Good point." I clap my hands together loudly, trying to get everyone's attention above the hum of noise. "Grub up, everyone!"

I ignore my mother's look of horror at the sight of one of her daughters using such a vulgar expression to announce dinner. No doubt she'd like to see me tinkling a solid silver gong.

It's clear where I'm expected to sit, as Tab has attached two helium-filled birthday balloons to the back of the chair. Moving into position, I notice everyone else is standing around, waiting for me to direct them to seats.

I pat the chair to my left. "Olivia, you come here, please, then Tab there . . ." I point to the chair directly opposite me. "Everyone else, sit where you like . . . except for here." I jerk my head to the empty chair on my right.

I'll bet you're chomping at the bit to know who that's for, aren't you? OK, maybe not *quite* that excited, but you'd like to know, right?

Hang on. A blast of cold air hits the side of my legs as the restaurant door opens and the final guest marches in breathless.

Handing his coat to a lurking waiter, he holds an arm aloft in general greeting to everyone assembled, then walks round to the empty chair by my side.

"Sorry I'm a bit late. It took me longer than I thought to get here." He bends down and plants a tender, lingering kiss on my lips. "You look absolutely beautiful."

I beam with pleasure. "Thank you, darling."

A chorus of greetings and welcomes resounds from my other guests: "Hello, Ben!" "Good to see you, mate!"

So there you have it. The man who has a special, reserved place at my side is Ben. Ben R. Thomas, to be precise.

I hope that, after accompanying me along the rocky road to dating enlightenment, you're pleased that it's him. Because I know I am.

Finally, after days, months, *years* wasted on the unsuitable, I have a straightforward, delightful man with a sense of humor, the heart of a gentle giant, and the right priorities in life. A man who works selflessly to help others, yet still finds the time and the energy to be a wonderfully considerate boyfriend to me. And best of all, my family adore him.

True, it took me a while to realize what had been staring me in the face for some time, but then again, we didn't get off to a great start the first time we met and I *did* think he was gay. So that's my excuse.

Anyway, it's all immaterial now because we're so blissfully happy. Richard would say nauseatingly, and has done so on several occasions.

In case you're wondering what happened during the rest of our surprise candelit lunch . . . in between the main course and dessert, it dawned on me that Ben had gone to the trouble of creating Seb Northam in order to woo me in the way he thought I wanted to be wooed; he'd put up with my ridiculousness about thinking he was gay (and forgiven me, apparently); he'd taken the trouble to book a private room at a restaurant and decorate it with candles; *and* he'd been brave enough to say outright that he might be falling in love with me.

All I had done was turn up, and it was high time I made an effort too.

So I threw caution to the wind, walked round the table, sat on his knee, and sliced through the sexual tension by grabbing the back of his neck and snogging his face off. To my wonderful astonishment, I felt the sparks fly—and from that moment on, it was smooth sailing. High on white wine and happiness, we charted a course back to my flat and fell into bed, where we stayed until the following morning, wrapped in each other's arms. And as you ask, yes, the sex was bloody great.

The past five months with Ben has taught me a lifetime of lessons, one being that sex doesn't *always* have to be mind blowing. Sometimes it can be soft and slow, sometimes frenetic, and sometimes just downright quick, perfunctory, and lazy. He's absolutely right when he says it's an important part of a relationship, but not the be-all and end-all.

I realize now that, in the past, I mistook strife for passion. If a relationship was a constant melee of ups and downs, I thought that meant it was exciting. In retrospect it wasn't, it just meant the person dishing out the problems was a Grade A pain in the arse.

I have also learned that just because you don't feel that "pow" at the start, doesn't mean that it won't develop at a later date. It may only have been four months, but I already know that I love Ben deeply, at a level to which I have never even come close before.

We already knew so much about each other, and since we've been dating we have learned much, much more. But the familiarity hasn't bred contempt, only a sense of comfort that comes from knowing you're with someone who cares for and supports you.

And so, dear reader, you might be wondering . . . do I regret all those wasted hours of going on Internet dates?

Not a bit of it.

OK, so I finally met the man of my dreams the traditional way—through a friend of a friend in a wine bar. But in a bizarre way, it was still the anonymity of the Internet and his alter ego that gave Ben the courage to set up our first date. In the end, the all-important first steps of our fledgling romance were carried out via the twenty-first-century form of epistolary courtship—e-mail. Jane Austen, eat your heart out.

Leaning slightly to my right, I reach over and grab Ben's hand, giving it a gentle squeeze. He gives me a loving smile, then scrapes back his chair to stand up, kissing my forehead as he rises.

"Ssssh, everyone." He taps a teaspoon against his champagne glass. "A toast . . ." He holds the glass out in front of him. ". . . to Jess on her thirty-fifth birthday."

"Happy birthday," they chorus, all holding their glasses aloft before taking a sip. Or a hearty swig in Madeleine's case, much to Marty's obvious disapproval.

Ben remains standing.

"I just want to say a few words about the birthday girl," he continues, "because I know how much she means to us all."

The room falls completely silent, everyone concentrating on what he's about to say.

"It's safe to say it's been quite a tough year for Jess, first and foremost because of what's happened with Olivia." He pauses and looks at my sister for reassurance that it's all right to mention it. She responds with an assenting smile.

"Of *course* Olivia's trauma was the greatest of all, but I know that her illness affected Jess more than she ever let on. But she chose to confide in me, a virtual stranger.

"In a way, that was how we got to know each other and became such great friends. So Olivia . . ." He raises his glass in her direction, "as tough as it's been, thank you for that. And I must say it's fantastic to see you sitting here tonight, looking absolutely stunning. Long may it continue."

Everyone breaks into spontaneous applause and Olivia flushes bright red with a mixture of embarrassment and delight. Ben continues.

"I also know that Olivia's illness changed Jess irrevocably and made her look at life from a completely different perspective, namely that our time on this planet is too precious to waste doing things we don't want to do.

"So it was good-bye to *Good Morning Britain* . . ." A cheer goes up. ". . . and good-bye to Kara, who I never met but I understand wasn't particularly pleasant . . ."

"Darling, she made Leona Helmsley look like Goldilocks," drawls Richard.

Ben smiles, then his face turns slightly serious again. "And, thankfully, it was 'hello' to me. We've been together for four months now, but I suppose because we were friends first, it seems like a lot longer."

"A bloody life sentence, I should imagine," Richard chips in again, giving me a theatrical wink.

"Do you *ever* have an unexpressed thought?" I poke my tongue out playfully at him, then turn my face back up towards Ben.

"So," he continues, licking his lips as if slightly nervous. "I know we're all here to celebrate Jess's birthday, but there's something else I'd like to throw into the mix if I may . . . particularly as everyone who means something special to her is right here in this room . . ."

He pauses for a moment and fumbles in the left pocket of his jacket, pushing the chair to one side with his right hand. Dropping onto one knee, his left hand comes into view holding a small black box which he flips open. Inside is an exquisite, antique diamond ring.

"Jess . . ." He looks up at me, naked apprehension in his eyes. "Will you marry me?"

My mouth suddenly feels dry, as though my tongue is three times its normal size. The surface of my skin morphs into one giant goose bump, and an involuntary shiver zigzags its way down my spine. I had absolutely no idea this was coming.

Over the years, there are countless times I have thought about the moment when a man would ask me to marry him . . . how I would respond in a mature and considered way, appearing pleased but maintaining great dignity.

Oh, fuck it.

"Yes, yes, yes!" I shriek, leaping up and wrapping my arms round his neck. "Just you try and stop me!"

Bowled over by the euphoria of the moment, I bury my face in his neck and inhale his familiar smell that has become like a drug to me. I'm vaguely aware of the room erupting into whoops and cheers behind me.

Eventually pulling away, I look into Ben's face, now free of the previous tension. He's grinning broadly, his eyes tearing slightly.

Olivia and my mother are both sobbing loudly, clinging onto each other with unbridled delight that "Jess the fickle" has finally landed herself a decent, loyal man rather than a feckless, out-of-work musician who would be the new Sting if only he could get out of bed in the mornings.

"Congratulations, love, I'm thrilled for you." Dad appears by my side, his arms extended.

I fall into them. "Thanks, Dad. What a surprise, eh?"

He shakes his head. "Not for me. Ben rang me first to ask if I minded. It was our little secret."

I widen my eyes at him. "And did Mum know?"

"Are you kidding?" he scoffs. "Radio Helen? I don't think so."

After a couple more minutes of congratulations from all quarters, the restaurant owner gestures that he's ready to bring out the starter courses and everyone heads back to their seats.

As the buzz of general conversation fills the room, Olivia squeezes my leg and smiles warmly. "This is the best get-well present I could ever ask for," she says quietly. "I feel as happy as I did on the day Michael and I got engaged."

"Well, I just hope that our marriage ends up being as successful as yours," I reply.

"Oh, it will." She nods slowly. "You've got a good man there."

"Yes, I think so too." I beam. "And to think I so nearly didn't realize it."

Ben reappears at my side, pressing the "end" button on his phone. "I've just called Mum and Dad," he says, "and they send their congratulations. So do Anne and Ralph."

He stoops down and gives me a lingering kiss before tapping his champagne glass against mine. "Here's to the future Mrs. Thomas."

"And here's to the future Mr. Monroe." I beam. "It's been a peculiar journey, this one. But I've found you at last."

Jane Moore is the author of the international best-selling novels *Fourplay* and *The Ex Files* and a columnist for Britain's bestselling newspaper *The Sun*. A multi-media personality with extensive radio and television experience, she writes regularly for *The Sunday Times* (London) and formerly cohosted the acclaimed British version of *The View* (*Loose Women*). She lives in London.